A THIMBLEFUL OF HONOR

THE MACPHERSON SERIES

Linda Lee Graham

Repository Press, LLC

Repository Press, LLC
PO Box 7198
Cave Creek, Arizona 85327

A Thimbleful of Honor/ Linda Lee Graham. -- 1st ed

ISBN978-0-9864170-1-6

www.lindaleegraham.com

Publisher's Note: A THIMBLEFUL OF HONOR is a work of fiction. Names, characters, places, and incidents are a product of the author's imagination. Locales and public names are sometimes used for atmospheric purposes. Any resemblance to actual people, living or dead, or to businesses, companies, events, institutions, or locales is completely coincidental.

Cover Design by Jennifer Quinlan of Historical Editorial

Copyedit by Jennifer Quinlan of Historical Editorial

In memory of you, son, who grasped the meaning of honor.
We will love you beyond our last breath.

In 1745, Charles Edward Stuart, son of the exiled Stuart claimant to the throne of Great Britain, launched a third and final attempt to restore the Stuart court.

Following a clandestine landing on Scotland's coast, Charles's army gathered soldiers on its march south. Some, ardent supporters of the Jacobite cause, joined his army willingly. Others, either staunch supporters of the current Hanoverian court or apolitical, did not.

Yet willing or not, all who joined were named traitors.

Summer 1745, Badenoch, Scotland

Three years. *Three*, when it was inconceivable George would leave Scotland for one.

Surely, Wylie had misunderstood. Gnawing the inside of his cheek, he prodded a frog with the toe of his boot until it found shelter in a clumping of reeds, then turned toward George.

"Three years is a hellish long time, George."

George ignored him. Resting on his haunches, he sorted the stones piled on the riverbank, handling them one by one, rubbing surfaces and testing weights.

"George?"

"I heard ye."

"Well then?"

"It's no more than it was yesterday or the day before, Wylie."

Scowling, Wylie swatted at a swarm of midges. Uncle Henry's plan to send his son George to university on the Continent trounced Wylie's own. Now, George wouldn't see Wylie and Miriam wed, nor would George himself wed until after he returned. Their sons would not share a childhood, cousins of the same age.

Had George and Uncle Henry reckoned on any one of those things?

"Here," George said, holding out a stone. "Try this."

Having wagered sixpence that Wylie could best Lachlan Shaw at skimming stones, it now seemed George planned drilling Wylie until he believed it himself.

Either that, or George hoped to distract Wylie from Uncle Henry's madcap scheme.

"Forty splashes, aye?" George added, his hand still extended.

Forty? Wylie blinked, looking askance at his cousin. "Criminy. Ye said I was to best Lachie's twenty." Wylie's finest skim had bounced fifty times, but he'd replicated it only twice. Trying for a third? Uncertain, he grimaced.

"Aye, well. If ye aim to settle . . . " George shrugged, a corner of his mouth quirking downwards. "It's only I told the lads ye had Lachie's skill twice over, ken?"

Hell yes, he did. Likely more than twice over. Snorting, he took the stone from George and turned it, hefting its weight.

Solid.

Rubbing his chin, he scanned their surroundings for anything that might mar the river's ripple-free surface. The rain had stopped, as had the breeze. Behind him, the ferry crossing remained deserted, and the ferryboat banked.

A corner of his mouth inched up. On a day this fine, perhaps anything was possible. He turned and eyed George.

"I reckon a lad with your brains could finish university in two years if he put his mind to it," Wylie said, lifting a brow in challenge. "Eighty splashes says ye'll try."

George opened and closed his mouth, as if aping a minnow, then barked short a laugh. "Ye make eighty, cousin, and I'll try finishing in one."

Wylie grinned. "Ye're on." Before George could retract, Wylie shed his boots and stockings and waded shin-high into the frigid water, anchoring his feet in slime. Setting the stone between his thumb and index finger, he curled his fingers beneath it and stretched his arm high—then crouched, pivoted, and sent the stone sailing.

It hit straight and true, landing on its leading edge before it again took flight.

"Nice," George said, nodding his approval with lips pursed, his tone sage and scholarly.

Wylie didn't respond. His jaw ground tight, he locked his gaze on the stone. Skim after skim after skim, he willed it to rise.

George trotted down the bank, reciting the number of splashes. By the time he'd counted seventy, he'd taken to dancing about like an eijit, whooping and hollering.

Holding his breath, Wylie stayed planted.

It just might make it.

CHAPTER 1

May 1770, Badenoch, Scotland

ODD HE COULD share his ship with scores of men for months on end and feel no urge for privacy. Three weeks alone with his sons, and Wylie Macpherson craved it. Hopping from the farmer's cart before its wheels stopped rolling, Wylie eyed the nearest hill, intent on stealing a few moments alone.

"We are here, Papa?" Dougal asked, climbing down after him. "At Grandpapa's?"

"Soon."

Will followed his brother down, his gaze sweeping their surroundings. Tensing, Wylie waited for the lad's assessment, for on the heels of winter even *he* thought Badenoch desolate and dreary. Still, he didn't care to hear it from a sixteen-year-old with too many opinions as it was.

Mercifully, Will remained silent. Wylie exchanged a few words with the farmer and watched the cart clatter off, then turned to his sons. "Stay here."

Without awaiting a reply, he scaled the nearby hill at a trot, the worn soles of his boots skidding over loose gravel. At the summit he stopped, his breathing labored, and stared at the scene below. It was much like other pastoral scenes—mountains and valley binding a serpentine river.

Yet it *wasn't* another, and if his mind had doubted, his heart did not.

Recognition filled him, crippling in its certainty, and for an instant he couldn't move. He knew every bend and tributary of that stretch of river—every hidey-hole that might shelter a trout and every pool that might harbor a salmon.

A lifetime ago, he'd considered it his. Glencorach, the estate he once called home, lay on its opposite side.

A stiff breeze kicked the thickets lining the riverbed just then, sending a whiff of damp clay and memories to mingle with the reek of burning peat and the lowing of restless cattle. A trickle of unease, slick and foul, toyed with his innards. He bit the inside of his cheeks until they hurt, blocking the memories before they garnered strength.

Something wasn't right. How could nothing have changed?

Retreat.

Shifting his feet, he stayed put.

Why would it have changed? A quarter of a century meant little to the Highlands.

Had he expected to find the countryside populated with a string of new garrisons? Each armed with a sentry of redcoats marching guard over its parapets, firelocks primed and glinting in the afternoon sun, prepared to sound the alarm that traitor Wylie Macpherson had dared return?

Aye, well . . . maybe.

You're not that important, lad.

Undeterred by logic, his unease grew, squirming now, and the fingers of his right hand twitched, instinctively reaching for the hilt of a sword that wasn't there.

He closed his eyes and took measured breaths, willing all emotion flat. It was the scent of those damned cattle rousing memories. Nothing more. He carried a pardon now; the past was dead.

Slowly the unease died, and he sensed his sons' presence. Removing his hat, he swiped his sleeve across his forehead and hooked his thumb over his belt. Hoping something besides himself had claimed their interest, Wylie sucked in a breath and turned. Both boys stood staring at him.

Will, his eldest, had sprouted to Wylie's height this last year, but that was where all resemblance ended. Will's face was smooth, sculptured angles, his complexion porcelain-like, and his hair, a sleek raven-black, rarely fell loose of its ribbon. Dapper, Will was, in both his dress and his grooming. Wylie would not name him fastidious—yet—but there was no denying the lad kept everything in check, including his dignity.

On the other hand, Dougal, according to Wylie's father, was the image of Wylie at age seven. He rarely stilled. Even now he hopped from foot to foot, pushing aside a tangle of red curls with one hand and tugging at his jacket with his other, reminding Wylie he'd forgotten to get the blasted thing altered while in London.

"*Qu'est que c'est?*" Will asked.

What is it? Everything. A lifetime's worth. Yet nothing he cared

2

to discuss.

"Papa?" Will said, his tone insistent.

Wylie ran a hand over his hair, gathering loose strands, and resettled his hat. Stooping, he retrieved his pack and slung it over his shoulder. "English, Will." They'd left France behind. Speaking French here attracted unwanted attention.

Will turned, muttering, "*Oui, Papa, à votre guise.*"

Wylie's mouth thinned. As he wished? That would be a first. While Dougal still believed the tides rose and fell on Wylie's command, Will, sixteen and shrewd as Socrates, knew better.

Clenching his teeth, Wylie stayed silent and started down the hill alone, his gaze trained at his feet. If he didn't rise to the bait, Will couldn't poke. Besides, an hour or two more, and both boys would be in the competent hands of Wylie's father.

And—if he kept his gaze trained at his feet—he just might convince himself this was an anonymous hill in an anonymous country.

Glancing over his shoulder, he checked his sons' progress. Will was nowhere in sight. Dougal, his gaze locked on the loose maze of stones, hopped two short steps to Wylie's one. Wylie slowed.

If he'd awaited his father in London as they'd arranged, he'd not be headed down this hill. Even now he could turn back and send word to his father requesting they rendezvous in Crieff.

No, not Crieff. Edinburgh.

No, not Edinburgh. London. In London, as they'd planned.

Turn back.

He jerked his head, again denying retreat. He'd come this far; he'd continue. Within twenty-four hours he'd be climbing this same hill and heading south. Alone.

"We must cross that river as well?" Dougal asked, drawing aside him, his breath coming in pants.

"Aye, but there's a ferry yonder." Hoisting Dougal on his shoulders so he could see, Wylie pointed out the wooden shack-like ferryhouses on each bank and the ferry itself, a low, flat barge resting atop gravel on the opposite side. Cattle milled on both banks.

"I see cows, Papa. And the ferryman."

"Mm-hmm." A stocky fellow with barrel-shaped arms stood aside the barge with his pole in hand, deep in conversation with a couple of drovers. Wylie hoped they weren't Cragdurcas drovers.

If either his cousin George or Uncle Henry were in the ferryhouse . . .

Cease. If those were Cragdurcas cattle, neither George nor Henry would handle their sale. Uncle Henry's factor would be in that ferryhouse, not the Cragdurcas Macphersons themselves. The only family he'd encounter on this brief foray into Scotland would be his father—a Glencorach Macpherson.

Setting Dougal down, Wylie tousled his mass of curls. "Where's your hat, lad?"

"It's too small."

Pursing his lips, Wylie blew out a long breath. "Right." Moments passed before he ventured asking, "Is your brother coming?"

Will drew aside them then, startling Wylie. The boy had inherited his late mother's grace as well as her features.

"I am here," Will said.

English. Praise be—a concession from the lad.

"See that pass north of the ferry landing, Will? It leads to Glencorach House."

Will nodded, seemed to hesitate, then asked, "Why did Grandpapa not meet us in London?"

Wylie's father had lobbied ceaselessly for Wylie's pardon and had planned meeting Wylie in London to witness the fruition of his labors and collect his grandsons. Yet he hadn't, and Wylie had grown impatient awaiting him. "I'm not certain."

"He expects our visit here?"

Visit. Grunting, Wylie looked down, ostensibly watching his steps, and hoped Will hadn't noticed the heat crawling up his neck. Will may suspect Wylie planned leaving him and his brother with their grandfather.

Wylie hadn't found the right time to tell them.

His mouth quirked at the lie. There would *never* be a right time to tell them such a thing. Once Wylie settled in America, they'd follow, but he doubted that would count for much.

Not when weighed against today's abandonment.

CHAPTER 2

SEATED AT A rough wooden table inside the ferryhouse, Anna Macrae slid her finger down a document, tallying its numbers a third time. Certainty was a must on Cragdurcas transactions; Henry Macpherson's account was vital to her father's factoring business.

The light dimmed, and the document grayed. Looking up, she noted the Macguires, the two drovers who'd shared her table a moment earlier, now stood at the room's only window. Angus Macguire had heft enough to block the little light it offered; adding his younger brother Sammy as a shade made her wish she'd brought a candle.

Firming her lips, she looked back at the document, squinting.

"Anna," one of the men called. "Did ye hear what I said?"

She hadn't. "Mm-hmm."

Henry Macpherson would lose a substantial profit selling these cows winter-lean. Why throw good money after bad? Surely he knew his grandson's gambling was habitual. Everyone knew.

Let it rest. It's not your concern.

Family was family, and Henry Macpherson went to great lengths for his. Besides, she wasn't privy to Henry's plans for these proceeds. The timing of this sale, following days after his grandson's arrival, might be coincidental.

"It's nearly ready, Mr. Macguire," she said, starting her tally again. Her musings, coupled with the tenor of the men's voices—raised in an animated dispute about who knew what—had distracted her.

She couldn't afford the occasional miscalculation as could her father—or any other factor in Scotland. It didn't signify the drovers could scarcely arrive at five when adding two plus three; they'd not let an error pass. The busiest busybodies in Badenoch, they'd tell everyone in the district of her mistake. Within a fortnight no one would trust the woman who dared masquerade as a factor.

It wasn't a secret she aided her father. She had for years. When his eyes troubled him, she'd check his calculations. When his rheumatism troubled him, she'd pen his documents. She'd even composed a few, as there were now times he struggled moving the words from his mind to his voice or his pen.

Until today, however, she'd not replaced him in public.

The recent death of his longtime friend, William Macpherson, had rendered her father befuddled more often than not, and this morning was one of those times. Fortunately the drovers hadn't fussed upon seeing her, for she hadn't an alternative.

Each night she prayed her father's condition was temporary. Each day she acknowledged with a trickle more acceptance that it might not be so. Once others knew of his decline, a proper factor—one who was not a woman—would be solicited forthwith. What then?

She'd cope, one way or another. If she must marry Mr. Montgomery to make ends meet, then so be it.

"That's not what I asked ye, lass," Mcguire said.

Arriving at the same figure, Anna dipped her quill and signed, ignoring the drover.

A. Macrae, Glendally.

Anna or Alan. Who would know but a handful of drovers who didn't give a whit? Sprinkling the signature with sand, she looked up and said, "It's ready to sign, Mr. Macguire."

"That's him, I tell ye," Angus said. Abandoning his window post, he lumbered across the dirt floor toward Anna. A tall man, Angus tended to walk as if climbing a slope, perhaps due to the countless hills he climbed driving cattle to and fro. Snatching the quill with a leathery hand, he scrawled his mark without reading a word.

"Hmmph. Ye might be right," Sammy said, addressing his brother. "Anna, ye knew Wylie Macpherson in '45, aye? Back when he was a boy?"

Her head shot up, and her hand jerked, knocking aside the inkwell. *Wylie?*

To her, Wylie had seemed a man even then. A reckless, impulsive, glorious young man of fifteen.

"Of course she knew him, you sot," Angus said.

"She was old enough, I reckon. I hear tell his pardon done come through. Hadn't thought I'd live to see that. Lad's been on the run o'er twenty some years."

6

A sooty, metallic scent yanked Anna from her reverie. Her heart drumming a rapid staccato, she righted the inkwell and blotted the spill with her last scrap of paper. Wylie couldn't be here; he was in London. Miriam had posted that letter only yesterday.

"I'll wager it was Henry Macpherson's money what bought it," Angus said, contributing his wisdom on the matter of Wylie's pardon. "Ol' William couldn't have managed it."

Anna's jaw set. Oh yes, he could, and he had.

"Some folks got themselves a whole nother set of laws. Ye ken John Eddy's boy?" Sammy asked. "Ye didn't see him up and running. He stayed put and took his punishment. Downright honorable. Man's kin ought to have honor."

Fool. Her nose twitching at the odor, Anna waved the document, drying what remained of the spill, and held her tongue. John Eddy had suffered no less heartbreak than Wylie's father had all these years. If John had had the resources to get his boy out of Scotland, he'd have done so in a heartbeat.

"Honor? You eijit. Eddy's boy didn't stay put; he just got caught afore he ran. Last I heard, he's *still* rotting in that Edinburgh prison." Angus spat his contempt, then snatched his cup and downed its remainder. "Nay. Wylie'd been my son, I'd have had him run same as ol' William. Lads that age don't know one fork in the road from another. Him and George didn't join them Jacobites without a heap of persuading."

Angus banged the cup down, and Anna's inkwell bounced. Scowling, she wiped it clean and capped it.

"Takes a hard man to send his son to the gallows," he added. "Even a king ought not ask that of a man."

"Don't stop Himself from asking," Sammy muttered.

"Heard Wylie married himself a French lass. Got two boys half-frog." Angus walked to the window and cocked his head. "That one's got two."

Wylie *did* have two sons. Anna crossed the room, avoiding the clumps of spittle littering the dirt floor. Holding her breath, she looked outside. There was only one man on this side of the river. He wasn't facing her, but she supposed he could be Wylie; his height seemed right. His hair, tied in a ribbon at the base of his hat, was a lighter shade than she remembered, but perhaps the glossy dark red had faded. It had been nearly twenty-five years since she'd seen him last. People changed.

Lord, she had. She'd been only eight when he'd run.

"Well, Anna?" Angus asked.

Feeling faint, she released the breath she'd been holding. "Aye. I knew him."

"Is that him?"

The man outside turned and walked toward the ferryhouse, his stride long, sure, and somehow familiar. Her heart bounced, and a surge of warmth swirled and filled the space beneath it. She closed her eyes, reveling in its comfort.

He's come home.

Her eyes snapped open. Why though? He should be awaiting his father in London.

Pressing fingers to her lips, she stifled a cry of dismay. The letter.

He hadn't received that letter.

He didn't know.

CHAPTER 3

"AYE, 'TIS WYLIE," Anna said. "Scat, the both of you, and hold that ferry. Don't either of ye address him. Not a word, hear? He doesn't know about his father." At their blank stares she added, "He's Laird of Glencorach now, and it's best he not hear it from you lot."

Willy-nilly, Anna stuffed her satchel, thrust the ink-stained note into Angus Macguire's hands, and exited the ferryhouse.

When Wylie first looked Anna's way, his expression seemed one of such melancholy that for a moment she thought he *had* learned of his father's passing. Then she drew nearer and saw she'd been mistaken. His expression wasn't melancholy; it was empty.

"Welcome home, Wylie," she said, coming to stand before him.

The river's rush and rumble sounded almost a frantic roar of a sudden, jumbling her thoughts, and she couldn't say more. Unaccountably tongue-tied, she could only stare.

Blessed Mother, why did God allow men to age as well as this one had?

He'd done well for himself; that much was clear. The Macraes were by no means wealthy, but Anna knew fine cloth when she saw it. Hugging broad shoulders, his coat just hinted at loose, and his breeches, hanging from narrow hips down long legs to buckle smartly below his knees, just hinted at snug.

Fine and expertly tailored. William hadn't exaggerated accounts of his son's success.

Wrinkling his brow, Wylie's gaze narrowed as if he were trying to place her. His eyes had tiny lines beneath them now, lines that curved and creased while he studied her. But they were still a warm chocolate shade, and they still fired a certainty deep inside her: Wylie Macpherson offered sanctuary from all the world's ills.

Or so it once seemed to a fanciful young girl.

And, apparently, to a now aging woman with an untoward urge to throw herself into a near-stranger's arms.

Yet he wasn't a near-stranger, was he? William, finding a willing ear in Anna, had shared every step of his son's life over the last twenty-five years.

"Anna," Wylie said finally, his brow clearing. He frowned, as if still uncertain, then his expression abruptly changed. "Little Anna Macrae." With an open grin, he grabbed her arms with two hands and hoisted her up, swirling her a turn as he had when she was a girl. She caught faint whiffs of coffee and a campfire's smoke, underlain by a heady male scent.

"You've grown some, lass," he said, setting her down. He placed a hand at the small of his back in what she hoped was mock pain.

Her senses still swirling, she crossed her arms, clutching the heat his hands had left, and forced a laugh. "Aye, it happens. Look at yourself, groaning at the weight of a wee lass. Why, the Wylie I remember could heft a horse and not break a sweat."

From the corner of her eye, she noted the Macguires slink from the ferryhouse, their gazes locked on Wylie. Then, from behind Wylie, two boys approached, the older of the two with more of a glare than a stare. His sons, presumably.

Heavens, but every young lass in the parish would be in a blather by morning. The eldest was . . . well, even with that glare, the lad was beautiful. And the youngest was his father all over again.

Taking Wylie's elbow, she nudged him to face the lads. "Your sons, then, aye?"

"Aye. Will," he said, indicating the boy with the powerful glare, "and Dougal."

"Welcome, lads. I'm Anna Macrae. It's pleased I am to be meeting ye both."

The boys nodded, saying nothing.

"I'd hoped to intercept my father on his way south, Anna, and save him the journey," Wylie said. "I asked at the coach stations, but no one had seen him. He hasn't left yet, I trust?"

She hesitated, uncertain how to answer.

"Anna? Has he left?"

Wylie's uncle should be the one to inform Wylie of William's death, not her. Could it wait?

Nay.

She placed her hand on Wylie's forearm, ignoring the

10

possibility of Will's seeming disapproval. "Wylie, I—that is, Miriam meant to post—"

"Miriam? Is she well?"

Hearing something near longing in his tone, she frowned. All these years, and he still cared for that woman? She darted a glance Will's way, but both boys had wandered toward the drovers, who now sat propped against the ferryhouse, playing dice.

"Aye. Wylie, your uncle wrote ye, but it seems the letter was misplaced."

He gestured toward the cows. "My uncle's cattle, aye?" he asked, changing the subject. "Is Alan inside, then?"

"Father? Nay. I handled the exchange."

"You?" Wylie lifted a brow. "Things have changed."

"Not so much. It's only Father was ill this morning."

"Hmmph. I expect Henry couldn't wait," Wylie said, his expression sardonic.

It seemed William had been right. Wylie still harbored ill will. "Nay, it's not that." She crushed a fold of her cloak in her fist. Telling him on a public ferry path that he'd lost his father seemed so wrong.

Would waiting until they'd neared Glencorach be less heartless?

As if he expected bad news, Wylie's mouth set in a grim line, and he briefly closed his eyes before regarding her steadily. "You best tell me what was in the letter."

She released her grip on the cloak and inhaled a fortifying breath. "It's your father. He passed away a fortnight ago."

Seeming to shrink before her eyes, Wylie stepped back, his shoulders crumbling. His mouth fell open and he stared at her, his eyes filling.

"He didn't suffer," she assured him, her own eyes wet. "It was his heart." Still he stared at her, his chin now trembling, and she wished she could take him in her arms. But between the watching drovers and his sons, she dare not. "He had every intention of meeting ye in London. But it was sudden."

"I see. It . . . it's a comfort to know that." His voice broke, and he looked toward the southerly path. Sucking in a breath, he exhaled it in a long sigh.

"My father and I will do everything we can helping ye settle in, Wylie," she said in a low voice. "Things are a bit of a jumble, but nothing ye and Father cannot sort."

His head whipped toward her, his eyes narrowing. "Settle in? I've no intent to settle in. Alan will manage."

She blanched. "What?" Did he mean to imply he wouldn't continue to Glencorach? "Surely ye plan . . . What are ye saying?"

"I needn't go on. Father had a buyer. He'll occupy sooner rather than later."

Lord, did he mean to leave from here? "There's been an offer, 'tis true, but there are matters that must be handled first. And ye'll want to see your family before you sail off."

"You've just told me I've no family aside from my boys."

No family? Her jaw dropped. If William heard Wylie say that, he'd surely spring from his grave. What of the Cragdurcas Macphersons?

"For cert, ye do, Wylie Macpherson! And lest ye forget, William wanted the boys to live on Glencorach for a time before joining ye."

"With him, Anna," he said slowly, as if she were simpleminded. "Not with the new owner."

Anna almost smiled at the thought of Mr. Montgomery living with Wylie's boys. An aging bachelor who sometimes claimed he wanted children, Mr. Montgomery shied if any were near.

"Of course not. But the sale's not final, and your father told the buyer it'd be a year or more. He had so many plans for his grandsons."

Hoping his grandsons would love Glencorach and that he'd not be forced to sell, William had been certain Will could succeed him, given five years under his wing.

It seemed, however, William hadn't shared that bit of his dream with Wylie.

"But it's not to be, aye?" Wylie's smile was sad. "I'm certain Alan can handle whatever's left to handle. I intend—" He scrubbed a hand over his face, shook his head, and then sighed. "I don't know what I intend, truth be. I'll send your father word from London afore I sail."

Needles pricked her spine, and she stiffened. He truly meant to leave.

If Wylie didn't return, the sale to Montgomery wouldn't proceed now or one year from now—not with that mortgage.

Her father should have told Mr. Montgomery of the mortgage

months ago, well before advising William to consider Montgomery's offer. That mortgage required Henry Macpherson's release, which Henry would not give until he spoke with Wylie.

Mr. Montgomery would not blame Henry. He'd blame her father, and rightly so. A factor should never forget a debt.

It didn't signify that William had also forgotten he'd mortgaged Glencorach for more than its worth.

Anna took measured breaths, slowing her growing panic. "Nay, my father cannot handle what's left to handle. Ye're to return, if only to pay your respects to your father and to help mine. There are decisions to be made, and with your father gone, ye're the one to make them."

William had counted on her and her father. If Wylie walked away, Glencorach would stand discarded until it crumbled. William would never have wanted that.

"Anna, your father is capable—"

"Nay, I'll not hear another word on it. Ye're to return, else I'll know ye a coward with nary a thimbleful of honor."

His eyes narrowed to slits, glittering like shards of muddy ice on a clear November day. He opened his mouth and then clamped it shut, his jaw rigid while a muscle pulsed in his cheek. She nearly took a step back, but then he turned and stalked away, leaving her to gawk after him.

It seemed the new laird was unaccustomed to having his actions questioned.

Dougal came and stood beside her, his gaze locked on his father's back. "Papa is angry?"

Anna placed a hand on Dougal's shoulder, watching Wylie retreat beyond the ferryhouse. Dougal repeated his question, his voice breaking mid-speech. Before she could question the urge, she knelt, forgetting Wylie.

"I had distressing news of your grandfather, Dougal."

"But we are to visit him. Papa said." He stepped back and looked up at someone behind her. "Tell her, Will."

Coming around her to place a hand on his brother's shoulder, Will maneuvered Dougal out of her reach. "What is it?"

She stood. "Your grandfather has passed on. It was unexpected, Will. Lord, the man's deepest regret was not seeing the two of you again. He spoke of ye both so often."

"Who did you say you are?"

Will's tone implied an underlying accusation, as if he questioned not only her motives, but her character. She swallowed a wave of sadness that Wylie's own son should be so mistrusting.

"I'm Anna Macrae of Glendally. Glendally is scarcely a mile west of Glencorach. Alan Macrae is my father. He's factor for a good number in the area, including your father."

Will snorted. "My father has a factor?"

"He does now. Your father is Laird of Glencorach."

"Is he? You are certain of that?"

Puzzled, Anna searched Will's face. "I am," she answered slowly. "Ye've been told of Glencorach, aye?"

Will raised a side of his mouth in something that wasn't close to a smile. "We have been told nothing, Anna Macrae of Glendally. We have heard nothing but whispers."

She cocked a brow, her ire rising. "Well then, William Macpherson of Glencorach. It's a fair thing ye've come. Ye find yourself hankering for the truth, ye'll ken who to ask. Now fetch your father. The ferryman's waiting, and he has matters more important than the likes of us." Wylie *would* continue to Glencorach. She wouldn't believe otherwise.

Will snorted, the sound derisive. "The cattle?"

"Aye. The cattle."

Dougal sidled out from behind his brother and touched her arm. "Will means that maybe Papa is not that laird, for here Papa is a traitor."

What? Her blood fired sizzling hot, and her hands flew to her hips. Of all the rot. Believing the worst of their own father.

"Your father is no traitor."

CHAPTER 4

AN HOUR later, Wylie marched the track toward Glencorach, his teeth gritted and stride long.

This was a mistake and why he'd agreed to it . . . he had to have been addle-witted.

If not, he would be by morning. For if—no, *when* he closed his eyes tonight, he'd find himself back in that dank cellar, shackled to a wall aside his cousin, shivering while cattle brayed incessantly outside. Once that dream unsheathed its claws, he was apt to relive it for days, smelling nothing but mold and feces, scratching at nonexistent vermin and shrinking at each clang of metal.

He hadn't much cared for the experience the first time around. Reliving it . . . wondering if even then . . . or if not then, precisely when . . . *why* . . . his cousin George had plotted his betrayal.

Enough! Wincing, Wylie silenced the obsession before it caught wind and he couldn't. He became aware of the quiet and looked over his shoulder. A half-mile back, Anna and his sons still slogged their way through waterlogged heath.

Bloody hell. His chances of returning to that ferry by nightfall dwindled with each step they dawdled. Anna could skip over that heath if she'd only but try, and the boys would have no choice but to keep pace.

If only he'd left them at the ferry, he'd have settled things with Alan by now and be on the road back.

Hell. If someone had had wits enough to post a damned letter, he'd not even be here.

He gnawed at his lower lip, then spat. Nay. If he had waited in London as planned, he'd have received that letter.

If, if, if.

At length he reached higher ground. Dodging fresh dung, he veered north until he reached the drove road traversing the lower folds of the Monadhliath Mountains. His anger cooling, he stopped muttering and saved his breath for the climb.

There was still the uncanny sensation that not a day had passed since he'd last seen this countryside. Aside from a thicker belt of trees lining the river, the moorland was utterly familiar. He half expected to see his father around the next bend, navigating the rock-studded track with his walking stick and his dog.

Perhaps it was a blessing Father had ended his days in his beloved hills.

Behind him came the grind of shifting gravel. He turned and saw Anna, still bundled in a cloak, her hair tidily hidden by her cap. He'd not have recognized her at the ferry if there hadn't been something familiarly uncomfortable in the way she looked at him.

Her eyes, an unusual shade of moss green, had studied him a bit longer than was polite, conveying an odd sense that she sought—and found—something others hadn't known to look for.

But if that were true, if she could read beyond his expression, she'd have placed miles between him and herself.

"I fear Will's taken a dislike to me," she said, coming beside him.

"You're speaking to me, then?" he asked. What a hellcat she'd become. The top of her head barely reached his chin, and she actually thought she might order him about.

His mouth bent in a mocking smile. Right. And who was walking where?

"Ye're the one who stalked off, Wylie, not I."

True enough, but of the two of them, he'd kept a civil tongue. He chose not to comment. He owed her a great deal; she'd filled the place of a daughter when Father had none.

He slowed his steps to match hers.

"Will can be a trial. It's naught to do with you, Anna, but with me. He's often charming, or so I've heard from the lassies." He adjusted his pack and searched for the words. "You're certain my father didn't suffer?"

"He suffered for years; I'll not tell ye false. But at the end? No more than he had been."

She'd know. The Macraes had been staunch friends for as long as Wylie could remember, and his father's letters indicated Anna was in and out of his house on a daily basis, aiding him with one task or another, perhaps even penning his letters.

"Were you the one writing his letters? From time to time they've not been in his hand."

"Aye. He wrote so many—to you, the commissioners, his

16

friends in London—his fingers pained him."

A spasm pulsed at his rib cage. Wylie envisioned his father hunched forward at his desk. Day after day, writing letter after letter, pleading for the life of his only, albeit misguided, son.

Wylie's blood had been decreed attainted following the '45 Rising—tainted and corrupted by treason. Without a pardon he could not inherit Glencorach, nor could his descendants.

He'd accepted the decree. His father hadn't.

The spasm expanded, squeezing his heart up his throat, and he couldn't speak. He'd robbed his father of a life surrounded by family. And for what? Wylie had never been a passionate supporter of Charles Stuart.

Christ, what a misspent life he'd led.

"Wylie Macpherson, if ye be thinking what I think ye're thinking, ye're to stop at once," Anna said. "None of it was your fault. It'd grieve him to think ye thought it was. He never blamed you. He and Henry blamed themselves for the whole of it. If they'd paid heed to the Pretender's son and his whereabouts, they'd never have allowed ye to drive those cattle to Crieff."

She made no mention of blaming George, he noted. If he were assigning blame, he'd assign a hefty portion to his cousin as well as himself.

He grunted. "Nothing would have dissuaded us from making that drive, Anna." Their fathers had promised they might do so the year prior, dangling it like a carrot before a mare once they'd earned it. They'd hoped for the tryst at Falkirk. Their fathers compromised with the Crieff Tryst, a smaller cattle fair at little more than half the distance.

"Mayhap. Even so, William could list twenty reasons why he was to blame. I believe he held on as long as he did because obtaining the pardon was the one gift he could give that had merit. He managed it at long last."

Surely not. Surely Father had known the gift of his unwavering support held far more merit than the fickle support of King George.

And if he hadn't?

Wylie kicked a loose rock, sending it flying.

"Wylie? Did ye mean to pass it by?"

Pausing, Wylie took stock of their surroundings. Behind them, five stones rose from the ground. Two stood tall, three tilted at an odd angle. Four others lay amidst the heather, one intact, three in pieces. Together, the stones formed a lopsided circle of untold age. Whatever lofty function they served in the past, they now marked the lane to Glencorach House and had for nearly a century.

The house lay a quarter-mile west, behind a line of birch trees. He regarded the lane, an odd warmth filling him, and his vision blurred. For an instant he was fifteen again, leaving home as a man for the first time and headed for the Crieff Tryst with George. They'd paused here and looked back.

"Stop your gawking, Wylie. If our beasts aren't at the ferry first, we'll be hours behind. Glencorach will be here when we return."

"Ye don't think it might seem different, George?"

"Nay. It's us who'll be different."

Canny lad, his cousin.

Anna laid a hand on his arm, returning him to the present. Avoiding her eyes, he looked over his shoulder, affirming the boys still followed, then back at the lane.

He dreaded walking into that house. How could he atone for all that had happened?

"I thought we'd go on to Glendally," he said at length, turning back to her. "I'll settle things with your father, and then the boys and I will return to London."

She studied him, her lips parted and eyes soft. "Ye ought to have a look around first. If ye'd like, ye and the boys could join us for a meal afterwards. Ye'll likely not sup otherwise. Martha's at her brother's today."

He shifted from foot to foot, eyeing his boots. "Martha stayed?" Martha had been his father's servant for as long as he could remember.

"Aye, she hopes to stay until things settle. Remember, the sale's not been finalized. Ye have choices, should ye wish to proceed otherwise."

Ignoring her reference to choices, he looked again toward his sons.

"Would ye like me to take them to Glendally?" Anna said, seeming to guess his thoughts. "Ye can fetch them at supper."

Thanks be. His eyes filled, and he bobbed his head. "I'd be grateful if you would," he said, then started down the lane before she responded.

He imagined the three of them watching him and the back of

his neck burned. Dougal, his eyes squinting and mouth slightly agape, Will, his jaw clenched square in angry judgment, and Anna—well, he no longer knew Anna well enough to guess her expression.

The rock-strewn lane was wagon-width wide. Once Wylie passed the tree line, the lane split in two. One path went left to the barn, the other led toward two low stone walls joined by a dilapidated gate. He walked toward the gate.

Glencorach House wasn't a grand manor. Made of stone, it rose two stories without wings. His father purchased it in 1730, promising Wylie's mother they'd add on as their family grew. He'd abandoned those plans when Wylie's mother and sister, Eliza, died three years later.

Wylie climbed the stone steps to the door, noting the third step still sloped at a precarious angle. The previous owner had claimed the step confused the fairies and kept them out of the house. Father deemed the man too lazy to fix it, but Mother, believing the story, decreed the step must stay.

Father hadn't called for its repair after her passing. Maybe he'd believed the fairy story.

He ought to be at this front door now. He'd open it laughing, calling for Martha to come and meet his grandsons whilst at the same time warning Will and Dougal not to trip over that "blasted third step."

Dougal would grin and ask how the step came to be tilted. Will would remain silent, wondering why no one had torn the steps out and rebuilt them.

The ache in Wylie's chest swelled and rose, demanding release. He willed it down. Anna had granted him one last time alone with his father—he aimed to take it.

Opening one door of the double-door entry, he entered, his nose twitching at scents hauntingly familiar. Old leather, old wood, old rugs.

Home.

CHAPTER 5

ANNA SLIPPED through Glencorach's rear doorway early the next morning. Martha, standing at her work table, turned to greet her.

"D'ye ken what's lying about in my parlor, Anna Macrae?"

"Ye mean 'who'?"

"Don't sass me, lass." The gray-haired woman shuffled toward Anna, her eyes brimming with unshed tears and her mouth stretched in a sad smile. "The young master's come home. After all these years, he's come home. And Master William . . . " Embracing Anna with flour-coated arms, Martha burst into tears.

Anna's own eyes filled. "I know, I know," she said softly, patting Martha's back. Wylie arriving mere weeks after William's death seemed bitterly unfair. "God decides the rhythm of things. It's not for us to question, aye?"

Though question she did. William had lived *only* for Wylie these last years. Oughtn't he have had the chance to see his son on Glencorach soil once more?

Her breath caught on a sob. God was more than generous with tears. Why not time?

"His list . . . the things he planned . . . his grandlads . . . " Martha stuttered, voicing her grief.

Swiping her sleeve over her cheeks, Anna stepped back and gave Martha's shoulders a stern shake. "Some of that list was your own creation, Martha McAlistar. Lest ye forget, those lads will be looking to fill their bellies, and ye're known to set a fine table. William would've wanted ye to manage without him, aye?" She pressed her handkerchief into Martha's hand.

"His grandlads? They're here?"

"They will be. For now, they're sleeping at Glendally." Unless they lay awake, bewildered at their father's abandonment. She doubted it, though. She had the odd certainty they took it in stride.

"Ooch, why didna ye say so at once, then?" Martha blew her nose and waved Anna toward the hall. "Ye go on now, lass. I've things to do, and weeping's no' one of them."

"Is he awake, then?"

Martha shook her head. "No' I last saw." She pantomimed the lifting of a cup.

Anna grimaced. Her lips pressed tight, she left the kitchen. If he wasn't awake, he soon would be. He'd two sons in his care, and he'd deserted them without so much as a by-your-leave.

Wylie lay on the hearthrug, his knees drawn up and arms crossing his middle as if he were cold. She reached over him to place a peat brick on the smoldering fire. He didn't stir, though each breath out rustled his hair. Kneeling, she watched the strands, bronze laced with silver, rise and fall.

A ragged scar, hidden the day before by his hat, ran from behind his left ear to his left temple, a memento of the '45 Rising. He'd been wounded in a minor skirmish fought several miles west, and in earlier years she'd thanked God for the unknown redcoat who'd dealt the blow. Coming days before the rebels' defeat at Culloden, the injury, though grievous, had allowed Wylie's family the chance to rescue him. Within forty-eight hours, Wylie was safely aboard a ship bound for France.

He hadn't washed, and his face, carrying the dust of travel, was tracked with trails from his eyes to his chin, as if he'd been crying. Then she noted his arms weren't crossed against the chill as she first thought. They instead clutched a frame to his heart, one she recognized. It held the sketch she'd drawn many years ago, the one of Wylie and William.

Oh, Wylie.

Dropping to her rump, she put her fist to her mouth.

That sketch was one of her best. Eight years old and besotted, infatuation had guided her hand. Wylie, thankfully, had been ignorant of her adulation, being besotted himself with Miriam Grant. But when William first looked at the drawing, he'd turned and regarded Anna for a long moment. She knew then that he'd guessed her feelings for Wylie.

But he'd never teased her for it, not once.

As years passed, she'd thought it possible William took comfort in knowing she shared his love for his son.

She swallowed. Her chances at seeing Wylie like this again— unguarded and unmasked—were incalculably few. Instead of waking him, she studied him, absorbing the changes time had wrought until she was certain her pencil could commit them to parchment.

Did you know how very much your father missed you, Wylie? He never lost hope. He began each day with thoughts of you and your new family, spent each afternoon composing yet another letter—either to you or the powers that controlled your fate—and ended each night on his knees in prayer for your well-being.

Tears wet Anna's cheeks and her breath caught on a sob while she stared at Wylie. Draping her arms over her knees, she hugged them close and rocked, caught in grief's stranglehold.

If she could do nothing else, she could show Will and Dougal the homeland their grandfather had loved.

The home their own father had loved before he'd been exiled.

CHAPTER 6

SETTING HER chores aside for the balance of the morning, Anna guided Wylie's sons on a tour of his estate, determined to show them the Wylie she remembered. The ground he'd trod as a boy, the friends and tenants who'd loved him.

Traitor, her arse. The mere thought caused her teeth to grit, and now they ached with it.

It was a bonnie day to be out. Dougal walked backward through a field of heather, facing her, and Will walked beside him, carrying Anna's basket and steadying Dougal each time he stumbled. She glanced toward the path to Glencorach.

Still empty.

Why had she thought he would come?

A corner of her mouth quirked in irritation. She hadn't. She'd hoped. But it was midday now, and if Wylie were coming, he'd have joined them by now. Martha knew where to find them.

"He will not come, Miss Macrae," Will said.

So Will knew she watched for his father. "Why not?"

He lifted a shoulder and batted at a swarm of midges, sending a whiff of whisky her way. "He will not have the time."

The whisky, no doubt, was courtesy of Robert Moy, Glencorach's principal tenant and tacksman. Without explanation, Moy had snatched Will away within seconds of their introduction. "Well, then, shall we return by way of the river?"

Both lads nodded.

They'd visited Moy after visiting Baile Dùil, the nearby township. If it hadn't been impolitic, Anna would have skipped Moy's altogether, as the man vexed her past reason. Each day of the last fourteen, he'd been at Glendally, pummeling her father regarding Wylie's intentions.

Mother Mary, as if her father knew Wylie's intentions. Wylie himself didn't know—how should his factor?

In truth, though, *all* the tenants wanted to know Wylie's intentions. Mr. Moy, as Wylie's tacksman, was merely the most boorish of the bunch.

"We may fish the river?" Dougal asked, tearing her from her thoughts. All morning he'd scarcely paused for breath in his chatter.

"Not this time. Perhaps ye can persuade your da to take ye in a day or two." She looked at Will, wondering if she could venture a question. Until now, he'd been silent all morning. But drink may have loosened his tongue.

"Will, did Mr. Moy show you his property?"

Will nodded.

"His still?" she probed. Moy's "visiting still," the one he kept in a secluded glen aside the burn, served as a gathering place for local residents and every ne'er-do-well in the district.

Again, Will nodded.

"Was anyone else there?"

"Some," Will answered, now turning his back to her.

Immediately she envisioned armed, unwashed men with beards to their bellies and a Black Watch-like past that included cattle-reiving, pillaging, and extortion. She drew in her lower lip, worrying it.

Should she have been more vigilant?

"People here like Papa, Miss Macrae," Dougal said.

Her chin shot up, the ne'er-do-wells forgotten. Lordy-be, and why wouldn't they?

"Well, I should say so!" Many of the tenants had dropped their work and wandered home upon hearing the new laird's sons were out and about. If they were disappointed at not seeing Wylie, they'd kept it to themselves and regaled the boys with tales of their father as a child.

Wylie had been a parish favorite. Even the loyalists amongst them had forgiven his rebel actions.

Coerced actions.

A butterfly dallied near, and Dougal jumped after it, cupping his hands in the air to trap it. Thankfully he missed. "Then why were we . . . " Scrunching one side of his face, he appeared to struggle for the right word in English.

They were polite young men. Sometimes English didn't come easily, yet they'd not resorted to French all morning. She opened her mouth to say, "residing in France," but Will spoke first.

"Living in exile?" he offered.

24

She arched a brow. Must he phrase it as if there was cause for shame?

"The government made a mistake in judgment, Dougal, so your father thought it best to keep his family in France. We all make mistakes. Even important men. Wouldn't ye agree, Will?"

"Some of us more than others," Will said, appearing not the least repentant.

She bit her tongue before asking in which camp he fancied himself a member.

They climbed a small slope, and a tower came into sight. A crumbling ruin, the peel tower stood on a rocky embankment and rose high above the river.

"We're nearing the peel tower. Turn around, Dougal," she said, raising a hand and twirling a finger. "Ye keep at it, ye'll likely tumble off the cliff and into the river. What will I tell your da then?"

"You will tell him I tumbled off a cliff and into a river."

She rolled her eyes. The boy shared his father's wit as well as his features.

"What is a peel tower?" he asked, complying with her request.

"I expect ye'd be calling it a lookout or mayhap a castle tower. This one's nigh on three hundred years old. An antiquity. Some say it was home to six generations of lairds."

"What did the lairds look out for?"

She flapped a hand. "Cattle-lifters, marauding clans, and the like." They drew aside the stone tower, and she took Dougal's elbow and held it while they peered inside. "The Highlands were once a wild and dangerous place."

The tower's ground floor, paved with dirt, was divided into two rooms. A stone staircase climbed the south wall of the room on the right. "Ye see the stairs are crumbling?" she said, pointing. "Ye're not to climb them. These days this tower's only to mark the boundary between Glencorach and Cragdurcas."

"Were those stones we saw yesterday an antiquity?" Dougal asked.

"The ones standing in a circle at Glencorach? Aye. Some say they mark an ancient temple, though best not let the reverend hear ye repeat it."

Will gave a small snort and walked inside, crossing to a window opening. She followed with Dougal.

"This is the river we crossed yesterday?" Dougal asked. Tiptoeing, he peered out the window at the river below.

She nodded. "Your father passed many an hour thrashing this stretch when he was a boy."

"You were with him?" Dougal asked.

"As often as he'd allow it." She laughed, remembering. "For cert, it was often. I carried food."

"Did you fish?"

"Nay. I'd watch." And sketch. If anyone knew the number of sketches of Wylie Macpherson she kept stashed in her trunk, they'd know her for the fool she was.

Dougal tugged on her skirt. "What is Cragdurc?"

"Cragdurcas? Why, your grandfather's brother, George-Henry Macpherson, owns Cragdurcas. Ye've no doubt heard your father speak of his Uncle Henry."

Both boys shook their heads, and Anna stifled the impulse to do likewise.

Why had Wylie told them nothing of his life in Scotland? Did his background shame him now that he'd traveled the world?

"We have an Uncle Alec," Dougal said.

That surprised her. She hadn't known Wylie's wife had a brother. "Oh?"

Dougal nodded. "Mama said he is not our true uncle, but Papa's partner and our friend. Mostly he is Will's and not mine. Will writes him letters."

William had mentioned an Alistair Dunlap from time to time; perhaps this Alec and he were one and the same. She left the tower, and the boys followed.

"Who is George?" Will asked, settling on a stump a short distance away.

"George is kin. He's your father's cousin."

"And you. Who are you?" Will asked, as if he found her previous answer unsatisfactory.

"Will, no," Dougal said, seemingly taking issue with his brother's tone.

"Not kin, Will, but a friend."

"Friend."

Will could teach the reverend a lesson or two; he'd managed to make a word reek of sin. She might have laughed if not for Dougal's scowl.

"Do Will and I have cousins here?" Dougal asked, turning from his brother.

Cousins galore, if one considered the second through tenth. Unable to keep them straight, Anna never belabored labels beyond first. "Your father had no siblings, so ye have no cousins."

"We have girl cousins in France. One is—" He broke mid-sentence, staring at something behind her.

CHAPTER 7

ANNA WHIRLED, expecting to see Wylie.

Instead, George Macpherson limped toward them. She smiled, pleased. "Bless me, George Macpherson. What are you at, you scoundrel, sneaking up on a soul like that?"

George was still a handsome man, though his years showed more than they ought. His thick brown hair had faded and receded to a thinning gray crown—a loss she attributed to both emotional and physical pain.

"Bless you indeed, Anna," George answered. "Few would accuse a one-legged cripple of sneaking anywhere." He bent and kissed her cheek. "I heard ye've seen him," he whispered. "When may we speak?"

Her heart ached at his urgency.

William had warned them of the wall surrounding Wylie. A wall built of bitterness, one reason could not breach. Neither she nor George would believe him, not of the Wylie they knew. After yesterday, however, Anna did not think the possibility farfetched.

George straightened, studying her. Slowly the light in his eyes died, as if he guessed her thoughts.

Attempting a smile, she reached for his hand and squeezed it. "Tonight. Walk me home from kirk."

Dougal came from behind her. "What happened to your leg, sir? Why are you a cripple?"

The smile George turned on Dougal seemed effortless. "My leg, ye ask? Why an Indian in South Carolina thought I'd do better without it."

"In America?" Dougal's eyes widened and Will left his perch to join him. "Did you fight for it? Surely you did, sir? With swords and pistols and knives?"

"Oh aye, I most certainly did. However, I think that story is best left to another day." Placing a finger on his chin, he stepped back and studied the boys. "Now tell me, are you two Wylie Macpherson's boys?"

They nodded in tandem.

"I thought so." He removed his hat with a flourish and bowed. "George Macpherson, at your service." Glancing at Anna with raised brows, he added, "Your first cousin once removed."

Anna sniffed at the mild reproach. George set such store by his genealogy. In truth, they were all related; one had only to look back. "George, meet Dougal and Will."

"Pleased to make your acquaintances. Dougal, in truth I'd have known you in a crowd for Wylie's son, but Will . . . Pardon my boldness lad, but I'll hazard a guess you favor your mother. A striking woman, no doubt."

No doubt, indeed. In the past, nothing had turned Wylie's head faster than a beautiful lass.

Though with Renalda, Wylie may have looked past the surface. William had had nothing but praise for his daughter-in-law.

"She was," Will said.

"I was very sorry to learn she'd passed," George said.

Anna studied Will, picturing a feminine cast to his flawless, symmetrical features, and her fingers twitched for a pencil. Capturing those vivid blue eyes without paints would be a challenge, but given his starkly contrasting inky-black hair, she might succeed.

"Mr. Macpherson, do we have more cousins?"

"Call me Cousin George, Dougal. And aye, my son Jay is your second cousin."

Anna took George's arm. "As long as ye're here, George, sit with us a spell and eat."

"My thanks, Anna. I hoped ye might ask."

She sat and pulled bannocks and a jug of ale from her basket, slightly embarrassed at the simple meal.

Dougal reached for a bannock without hesitation. "Cousin George, when will you tell us of the Indian?"

"Hmm. Let us say in six days. Will you still be here in six days?"

Anna looked at Dougal. Would he hazard a guess? Wylie hadn't spoken two words to either boy since learning his father's death. After spending the morning with them, she wasn't certain that was unusual.

Dougal looked at Will. Will shrugged and picked up a bannock, turning it a time or two before venturing a bite.

Undeterred, Dougal said, "If not, Cousin George, you must

29

promise to tell us before we leave."

"If I must, Dougal, then I shall."

"Tell us a different story now."

"Aye, George," Anna said. She loved George's voice. Melodious and deep, it had long ago earned him the spot of favored storyteller at community *cèilidhs*. "Tell the story of Janie and Ian. In English, if ye please," she added, doubting Wylie had taught his boys Gaelic.

"Ah, an interesting choice," George said, nodding. "I say that lads, because their story took place at this very tower." Lowering himself to the ground, he leaned back against a tree. The boys followed suit. "Ian Macpherson it is, then."

"He is our cousin too?"

"He's surely one of your ancestors, Dougal. But this story takes place over a century ago, so ye'll not be meeting him in this life." George adjusted his position, settling in, and Anna closed her basket and clasped her hands, anticipating the distraction.

"Now, our young Ian was his father's pride and joy. As such, he didn't want for a thing. His father owned the largest estate in Badenoch, ye see, and he could afford to give the lad all he might need. He hired the best nursemaids and, when the time came, the best governess he could find. It may sound a paltry thing, but it was no small feat in those barbarous times. The affording of it was the least of it. Enticing a learned lady to the Highlands, now that was nigh impossible. But he managed, and there was a big to-do over this governess."

"She was pretty?" Dougal asked.

Anna smiled. A heroine must be easy on the eyes.

"Nay, lad, she was fearsome looking, for the laird believed bonnie lassies courted trouble. But trouble lay ahead, for this governess had a young niece—a motherless young niece named Janie. The governess implored the laird, begging he welcome Janie into the family fold. The laird, though anxious not to lose the governess for whom he'd searched high and low, was reluctant."

Dougal sat up straighter, frowning. "But she was a motherless niece, Cousin George. Her father could care for her, *oui*?"

For an instant, George knit his brows, as if perplexed. Then his posture straightened and he lit up from within, as if he'd spied an old friend. He looked at Anna. Grinning, Anna raised a shoulder. The lad was his father's child.

"Did I say motherless?" George asked, his smile broad. "My apologies, Dougal. I stand corrected. And I must say, only your father has dared so before now."

Dougal grinned, as if delighted at the comparison, and Anna's smile softened. George rarely told a story precisely the same way, and often he peppered his tales with vague inconsistencies. She suspected he did the latter out of habit, one he'd developed on Wylie's account. Wylie had relished picking George's stories apart; it had been a game between them.

"Now, where was I? Ah, the problem of our *orphaned* young niece. Now, ye might ask why the laird was reluctant to shelter her. Well, our good laird, he was no fool. He knew that his Ian and this Janie would become boon companions. They were of the same age, ken. He feared that as time moved on, their attachment might assume a, shall we say, a warmer character. That would never do."

"Why? She was fearsome looking as well?"

"Nay, Dougal. She was a child of reduced circumstances, something much worse."

Dougal looked at Will.

"*Appauvri,*" Will murmured.

"Aye, Will, impoverished. Still, the laird had a generous heart. He set his reservations aside and took the lassie in."

"He was right, was he not, Cousin George? Ian and Janie become warm companions?" Dougal asked, bobbing up and down on his knees.

"Ye ken the story, then, lad?"

Lips pressed tight, Dougal jerked his head from side to side. Again Anna grinned. George loved such an audience.

"Well, as Dougal's guessed, Ian fell in love with wee Janie. He knew he must conceal it from his father, for from the day of Ian's birth, the laird had planned an alliance with the Macdonalds. His father would not welcome news of a penniless orphan bewitching his son.

"Ian was torn. He loved his father, but he couldn't bear severing ties with Janie. Janie suggested they meet in this very tower. It was not so ruined then, and it was private. Add to that, it lay beside the river. Ian could wet a line at some point in their tryst and string up a meal for his father. When accounting for his hours, the lad could claim he'd been fishing."

Will barked short a laugh, and Anna looked toward him,

31

astonished. He sat with his elbow resting on his knee and his chin cupped in his palm, watching George with nary a trace of the apathy he'd displayed for the last twenty-four hours.

George chuckled. "I wouldn't try it, lad. Your da is keen to that subterfuge."

Will's only answer was a lopsided grin. His father's grin. Anna's heart tripped. She blinked and gave her head a small shake. This was the "charming" Will Wylie had referenced. Thankfully she wasn't fifteen and susceptible.

"What happened next, Cousin George?" Dougal asked, again fidgeting on his knees.

"Well, Ian and Janie met so for months. Then one day a horrific storm caught them unawares. There was thunder and lightning and a torrential rain fell from the heavens. Within minutes they heard a great roaring. The river was in spate.

"Ian paced the tower, fearing his father would be frantic. Countless times the man had warned him to stay clear of the river in a storm. Countless times he'd told Ian stories of lads caught unawares and swept off their feet when the rising river roared past."

"Could Ian swim?" Dougal asked. "Papa taught me to swim."

"Did he, then? Ye're a fortunate lad, more fortunate than our Ian," George said.

"He was afraid?"

"Of his father, aye. If Ian didn't return soon, his father would come looking. But he couldn't return with Janie, nor could he leave her. In his worry, he scarcely noticed when his cousin Matthew sought shelter in the tower. As for Matthew, he was astonished to find Ian and Janie together."

Matthew? Anna frowned. There was no cousin Matthew in Ian and Janie's story. A suspicion took root, and Anna tried catching George's eye. He ignored her.

Was George telling a story of himself and Wylie, with Janie as Miriam?

"Because Janie was poor?" Dougal asked.

"Nay, Dougal. Because Matthew believed Janie fancied him."

"You said she'd promised herself to Ian."

"Ah," George said, wagging a finger and grinning. "Not this time, lad. Ye must listen closely, for I said only that Ian fell in love with Janie. Our Janie was a canny lass and knew she must marry.

But she also knew how Ian's father might view such an alliance. She thought it prudent to have another lad waiting."

Dougal grimaced and then nodded.

George paused, shifting his position as if pained, and reached for the ale. After a long swallow, he said, "Well, as you might imagine, Matthew accused Ian of the worst sort of treachery, and Ian, once he realized Matthew fancied Janie, accused Matthew of the same. They drew their dirks and circled one another. Janie ran from Ian to Matthew and back, imploring them to stop. She wept and she screamed, vowing she'd throw herself into the river before allowing them to harm one another."

Anna's mind raced, wondering at George's point. He and Wylie had never fought over Miriam, not to Anna's knowledge. Anna distinctly recalled believing George didn't care for Miriam.

Until he married her, that is.

"Why did Janie care? She tricked them," Dougal asked.

"She was a duplicitous lass, aye, but not a cruel one. When they paid her no heed, she ran into the storm, hoping they'd sheathe their dirks and run after her. And so they did, but the rain fell in gray sheets, darkening the day. They couldn't see past their hands, and there was no way to know where she'd gone. Ian chose north and Matthew south."

"Which one found her, Cousin George?"

"Neither. A farmer downriver found her body the next morning."

Anna had it wrong, then. For Miriam, of course, was alive and well. Perhaps George, sensing Dougal's interest in family connections, merely embellished his story with a cousin.

Dougal's eyes grew wide. "Someone killed her?"

George lifted his hands, palms upright. "Mayhap. Or mayhap she slipped in the mud and the river carried her off. Or mayhap she jumped from one of the cliffs as she'd vowed. In cases such as this, conjecture is useless. Things are often not as they seem."

"Then it will be a secret forever, Cousin George? For they have all died."

"The truth may come out with time, Dougal. Janie haunts this river, and folks say she's eager to tell her story to those brave enough to seek it."

"How will she know?" Dougal asked.

"Ye must prove it to her. Ye must shelter in the tower for three moonless nights in August, and a storm must rage two of the three. On the third night—if and only if the river's in spate—ye'll hear her weeping and wailing. The sound will draw ye to where she perished.

"Stand toe to toe with a wisp of her spirit, and she'll tell ye her story."

Dougal paled and Anna stifled a chuckle, noting even Will now leaned forward. Swallowing, Dougal asked, "Have *you* followed her weeping?"

"Me?" George pointed at his chest, shaking his head. "Nay, lad. It takes a brave man to stand toe to toe with Janie."

"But you wrestled an Indian, Cousin George!"

"I'd rather battle six Indians than confront a weeping lassie."

Dougal frowned, then asked, "What did Matthew and Ian do then?"

"Oh well, that." George heaved a long-lingering sigh and shook his head. "That's the saddest thing, ken. Matthew and Ian were bitter enemies for the rest of their lives."

Will grunted, his expression skeptical.

George looked at him, a smile playing about the corner of his mouth. "Must I stand corrected again?"

"*Non.* It is only I had envisioned a different ending."

My word. All morning long Will had scarcely uttered a word in her presence. Minutes with George, and he uttered full sentences.

George leaned forward, his gaze intent on Will. "Tell me, lad, for my stories grow stale. I may add your ending to my repertory."

"Is it not odd that neither Ian nor Matthew blamed Janie? Or deduced the facts between them? For if neither of them brought her harm, it is apparent she harmed herself through foolishness."

George gave a small start and then slapped his thigh. "By God, Will." He fell back against the tree, laughing. "By God . . . my thoughts exactly."

Anna frowned. She may have been right in her suspicion. The story wasn't precisely the same, of course, but there were similarities.

She sympathized with George's resolve to explain his actions in person. His guilt at testifying against Wylie was an enormous burden, one he'd carried for many years. But even if Wylie listened, he may not forgive.

And if he didn't?

Well then, George would lose even hope.

Yet was George hinting at more than his testimony? Had Wylie once intended marrying Miriam?

Her mouth thinned. Nay, for if so, George surely would have known, and he'd not have married her himself.

"It lacks the flair of your ghost and storm," Will said, jarring Anna from her thoughts.

"Of course. And it falls rather flat in the retelling," George said, nodding. "I know, I used it once. Still, knowing I'm not alone in my appraisal pleases me." He took another swallow of ale and reached for the cork.

"George?" Anna said, still uncertain at George's motivation in changing the story.

"Hmm?" Preoccupied topping the bottle, George didn't look at her.

She waited until he did, then held his gaze. "Tell me, for it has slipped my mind. What is the name of that story?" From the corner of her eye, she glimpsed Will's glance slide from George to her.

George didn't blink. "Has it, then? Why, it's called 'The Betrayal That Wasn't.'"

A heavy weight pressed against her chest. So the story *was* about George's testimony.

George had made peace with the loss of his leg. The loss of hope?

She feared he'd not recover.

CHAPTER 8

WYLIE SAT perched on the window seat, his head throbbing, and studied his father's chair through a shaft of afternoon sunlight.

A different chair, yet as tattered as the last, and there was still a dark spot on the stone floor beside it, marking the place a dog had lain. Closing his eyes, Wylie envisioned his reception if Rusty had lived to greet him. Eighty pounds of canine slamming him against the wall for a tongue-lapping.

Father never did hold with disciplining his hound. His son, yes.

Will had begged for a dog. Wylie, despite Rennie's pestering, hadn't allowed it.

A dog was one more thing to grieve when gone.

His gaze shifting from the chair, Wylie absorbed the memories one by one, forgoing the urge to sink to the floor and bury his head in his hands.

The unrelenting tick of the mantel clock, marking time's passage.

The waxy scent of the cake Martha used to polish the tables. Tables, he noted, still leveled with a bit of bark under the odd leg here and there. The one nearest held a bannock, placed there by Martha after her attempts at luring him to the table proved fruitless.

And again, his father's chair.

Swallowing, Wylie sucked in a breath, grabbed the bannock, and crossed the room. At the armchair, he touched the worn leather and found it cool, another testament to absence. He set aside the bannock and retrieved the framed sketch he'd held earlier, now propped on the mantel. Slowly, as if to give his father's spirit time to vacate, Wylie sank into the chair.

The sketch was of him and his father standing beside the river. His head bent, Wylie tied tackle to his line. His father stood with creel in hand, his gaze locked on Wylie.

Anna had drawn it the spring of 1745, shortly before he'd left home. He'd just turned fifteen, and he and his father had spent the day fishing. As usual, Anna tagged along with her sketchbook. So earnest she'd been, selecting her spot, sharpening her charcoal, and smoothing flat her paper.

Our creels will be full, lass, afore ye draw your first line.

But it's to be special, Wylie.

He'd felt an ogre when her eyes brimmed with tears at his teasing. Especially once he'd seen the sketch.

It *was* special. His brows near meeting, Wylie studied it anew, picking out details. It was better than good—it was remarkable given her age at the time. The likeness to his father was uncanny. Wylie traced the outline of his father's face, holding his finger a hair's breadth above the parchment, careful not to smudge the charcoal. Many artists might have captured the prominent nose and ready smile. Not so many could have captured the love and pride in his father's eyes as he regarded the son at his side.

Would one year more have been too much to grant?

A quiver started in his gut, gathering strength the longer he stared, and the frame trembled in his hands. He set it aside before he dropped it.

This wasn't how things were to happen.

Father's last letters had been filled with plans for the boys. Anticipation leapt from his pages, and Wylie couldn't help but smile when he read them. For the first time in a long time, Wylie had added more than grief to the man's day.

Had the thought of one day leaving Glencorach been that final burden, the one Father's heart couldn't withstand? He'd seemed eager at the prospect of joining Wylie in America.

If Wylie had any heart, he'd have guessed that for a bold front.

What a bloody, selfish bastard he'd become. Father belonged here. Resting his chin on his fist, he eyed the room dispassionately.

It was remarkable this place still stood given half the family had marched with the Jacobites. The king's army had torched many homes for less. Had Father been shunned by his neighbors when the soldiers marched through? He'd never said as much. But he'd not indicated he needed funds either, and it was apparent he had.

There was an air of shabbiness about the parlor that Wylie did not recall. The window coverings were patched, as was the cushion atop the window seat. The throw rug was worn through in spots, and the glass beside the decanter was chipped.

He'd noted the same outside. Fences in need of mending, half-dead trees in need of pruning.

But not all was shabby, and it seemed someone still minded the things that brought comfort. A fire was laid and the cubby hole beside it was piled with peat. A stack of books, his father's pipe, and a decanter filled to the brim lay on the table aside him.

Vases scattered the room, carrying sprigs of dark blue flowers. He suspected they'd been filled by someone other than Martha. There had never been flowers on these tables when he was a boy. Though these were near wilting, he found them vaguely comforting.

Rennie had kept their home filled with flowers in summer. He'd never seen the sense in it until she was gone.

Without her, there'd been no flowers, no visible sign someone cared. The house seemed less a home.

He picked up the pipe and ran his finger over its well-worn stem. He could have helped. He may have been barred from returning, but his boys weren't. They might have spent summers aiding their grandfather, if Wylie had thought to send them.

He could help now for that matter and step into his father's shoes. It was truly all his father had wanted.

Should he?

Only yesterday, the possibility of a new beginning seemed a reality. A beginning far from Scotland and far from France. Doors stood open with this pardon, doors that had been barred for years.

He had connections in East Florida. Traders and merchants, some of whom he counted as friends. Land grants were generous, opportunities existed, and the colony's governor was a Scot from the Highlands. Wylie would be on familiar ground.

It was the first dream to quicken his blood in years.

Should a man with children take risks if he has no wife to share in their care?

Should a man willfully ignore something his father had fought to keep?

He rested his elbow on the chair's arm, propped his chin on his fist, and stared at the dust motes floating in the sunlight.

William Macpherson, Laird of Glencorach.

What do I do now, Father?

Tenants looked up to their laird.

I can't do this.

They relied on their laird to see them through bad times.

I can't.

To lead, a man must be sure of his own path. Could Wylie claim so?

His head swung from side to side. Not here, not in Badenoch.

He couldn't stay. He hadn't the heart or the will. He couldn't even manage two boys properly.

Anna was wrong. There were no choices. His only option was to put things in order and then sell. He'd see to the necessary repairs, he'd pay the outstanding debts, and he'd sign whatever document Alan Macrae put before him—but he'd be aboard the *Eliza* by week's end.

Will and Dougal would sail with him. He'd make shift. Somehow. He may not be the father his own had been, but he wasn't completely inept. They could do worse.

Slouching farther into the armchair, he eyed the bannock through slitted eyes. His belly ought to hold more than the whisky. Picking it up, he took a bite.

Pain shot from his teeth to his ears, and he rubbed his jaw, wincing. When had he last eaten?

He sprang upright, wondering the same of his sons.

No. Martha said they were still with the Macraes. Anna would see them fed.

Collapsing back, he pressed a thumb and finger to his temple and waited out the throbbing.

You have two boys to tend, Wylie Macpherson, and you best start tending.

His conscience of late had assumed Rennie's voice. Either that or she'd taken up haunting. Regardless, he'd squandered enough of the day contemplating a pair of shabby window coverings. Grunting, he heaved himself up and crossed to the hall.

The room opposite the parlor was his father's study, home of Glencorach's account books. The door at the far end of the hall led to Martha's kitchen quarters. The staircase, an unpretentious wooden affair, consumed nearly half the hall's space. Holding tight to the stair rail, Wylie negotiated the stairs a step at a time.

There were two rooms at the landing; he entered the one to the right, the one once his. The jug at the basin was empty, and aside from the washstand and bed, so was the room. Turning, he spied his bag across the hall, just over the threshold of his father's bedchamber.

Martha seemed under the impression he planned filling his father's boots.

As if that were possible.

Leave the bag or lug it back?

His head hammering, he swayed a fraction. Too much to reckon. He crossed the hall. Turning a blind eye to his father's personal items, he poured water into the basin and washed. He should have been at the Macraes some twenty hours past.

The sooner he met with Alan, the sooner he could leave Scotland.

CHAPTER 9

FROM DOORSTEP to doorstep, Glendally was a thirty minute walk by way of the drove road and ten by way of a well-worn path through the heath. Tilting his face to the sun, Wylie took the path.

Cutting through Glendally's back yard, he bypassed a goat pen, the shed where Mrs. Macrae once stored gardening whatnots, the ramshackle barn for their pony, and a garden in various stages of planting. A low stone cottage, surrounded by flowers, roofed with sod and thatched with heather, backed up to a dwindling store of peat.

Alan Macrae, principal tacksman to Wylie's uncle, leased Glendally from the Cragdurcas Macphersons. Alan's subrents, coupled with his factoring fees, provided the Macraes an adequate living, and Alan could have afforded more substantial lodging. But the man had a healthy abhorrence of debt and lived well within his means.

Wylie rounded the cottage and knocked at the front door. It opened immediately, and he stood face-to-face with a woman who carried a cloak over her arm, as if she were on her way out. Caught off guard, Wylie stared at her, his fist hovering midair. *Anna?*

Her hair, capped the day before, cascaded down her back in a thick red mane that reached past her waist. She'd tied a portion of it back, and loose strands wisped about her face, sparking off those startling green eyes.

Fetching enough, but it was her figure that had him staring.

Criminy. He'd thought *Eliza*'s masthead had curves.

"What is it, Wylie?" she asked. "Was it a butler ye expected?"

He blinked. No, but it seemed he'd expected her cloak had hid the body of a child.

He'd handled her at the ferry. Cloak and cap aside, he should have noted she'd become a woman.

"Of course not," he said, recovering his wits. Stepping inside, he closed the door behind him. "You look different than you did yesterday. It took me aback."

She arched a dark red brow and sniffed. "If ye've come to fetch Will and Dougal, they're carting water from the stream."

"Why haven't you married?" he asked before thinking.

Her eyes widened, snapping fire. "I suppose I haven't time to care for more men."

He cringed, reminded she'd cared for his father in his stead. "Please know I'm forever in your debt. For all you did for my father, and now for my boys. I apologize for my thoughtless question."

Still . . . were the lads in Badenoch all blind?

Her mouth thinned. "Nay, Wylie. It's I who apologize." She gave her head a hard shake, setting loose a curl. She pulled at it, then released it, sending it spiraling up the side of her face.

He fisted his hands, repressing an impulse to touch.

"I never meant to imply William was a burden. He was never that. He was dear to me, and I'd not have had it any other way. As for your boys, we've enjoyed their company, especially Father."

Truly? Fancy that.

Not questioning his good fortune, he stayed silent a beat, half hoping she'd extend another supper invitation. She didn't.

Behind her, the box bed's curtains were pulled open, and Dougal's and Will's bags rested at the foot of the neat and tidy bed. His gaze drifted to the small fire smoldering in the hearth against the far wall, canopied by a hanging chimney. No pots hung from the chimney chains.

His mouth tightened. Hopefully his boys hadn't eaten more than the Macraes could spare.

"I'm certain Will and Dougal enjoyed your father's company as well," he said, looking back at her. "I know I always did. Is he here? I'd like to settle those matters you mentioned."

"Now? I'm expected at kirk."

"Is he expected at kirk as well, then?"

She hesitated, then shook her head. "Nay, but he prefers I sit in on his meetings." She looked over her shoulder and past the box bed, again giving the curl a tug. "I take notes."

What the devil? Did she want him to meet with her father or not? He clasped his hands behind his back and studied her. "You insisted I come, Anna."

"Ye can surely wait until morning."

"I plan leaving tomorrow. Besides, I'm here now." He held her gaze until she reddened and then scowled.

Her chin resolute, she shoved past him. "Father is in his office."

Why was she the one peeved? She *had* insisted, hadn't she?

He turned and watched her exit, her long hair swinging with each sway of her hips. Deep within him something stirred. Something half-forgotten and unexpected.

Something unwelcome.

Don't even think about it, lad.

He pulled the door shut, scowling. Since when did women attend church meetings with their hair uncovered?

The Macraes' home was small, but boasted four windows and two hearths—which was four windows and one hearth more than most tenant cottages. The common area, comprising two-thirds of the home, held a hearth at one end and the box bed at another. To the left of the entry and past that bed was a small bedchamber and L-shaped office. It was there Wylie sat an hour later, knowing no more of his accounts than when he'd entered.

"The rents?" Alan asked. "My apologies, Wylie. The rents . . ." A portly man, Alan had frizzy red hair several shades lighter than his daughter's, and it seemed he still had difficulty taming it. His brows, always prominent, now hooded eyes more gray than green, as if years of squinting at documents had molded them in place.

"I know that ledger is here, lad."

Wylie steepled his fingers. A lone candle flickered in a battered tin holder, casting a meager circle of light over the paper-strewn desk. While Alan rifled a third stack of ledgers, Wylie looked around. The office appeared to now double as the widowed factor's bedchamber, for a raised platform, topped with heather-stuffed linen, rested in the corner beside the hearth.

"Bloody hell, no, that's not it. If Anna were here . . . "

At this rate, Wylie would be here another hour. Leaning forward, he placed a hand on the stack, gaining Alan's attention.

"No apologies necessary, Alan; I've come without notice. Can you tell me if the rents are current? We'll look at the detail in the morning, when Anna is here to find the ledger." If they met early enough, he could still make tomorrow's coach.

Seeming relieved, Alan stopped searching. "Fourteen of them are behind."

Wylie raised his head, disbelieving. "Fourteen?" How had

Father managed? "Are you certain, Alan?"

Alan met his gaze and blinked, suddenly seeming unsure. He shut his eyes and extended a hand. "Wait. Let me think." Finally he opened his eyes and shook his head with an apologetic grimace. "Nay, six are behind. It's fourteen who are current."

Right then, that wasn't a disaster. But hell, what was wrong with Alan?

"They've made payment arrangements, I assume?"

"Where was it ye said ye've been, lad? We've not seen ye in years."

Wylie stifled a groan. *Not again.* "In France, Alan. Tell me, do you have arrangements with those delinquent?"

"In France, ye say? Your father certainly missed ye."

"Aye, I know."

"We all did." The factor studied him, as if he were waiting.

Wylie was at a loss. The Alan he remembered could recite the yield of six estates for six years running. He and George had loved coming here. George, because Alan filled their heads with facts, and Wylie, because Mrs. Macrae filled their bellies with warm stews.

"I was sorry to learn of Mrs. Macrae's passing," Wylie said, belatedly regretting he hadn't had the decency five years past to send a condolence letter. He hadn't even said as much to Anna.

"I miss her every day. And now, my dearest friend, William. Ye've suffered your own losses, so ye know."

Unwilling to sit through Alan's commiserations yet again, Wylie merely nodded. "Well, then. The tenants who aren't paying, do we know why?"

"Aye. They've lost sons to war and emigration and haven't the hands to work their fields. They pay when they can."

Fair enough. He nodded, pleased Alan now seemed himself. "Do you know the man planning to buy Glencorach?"

"Oh aye, that would be Anna's Archie. Archibald Montgomery."

His heart skipped a beat. Straightening in his chair, Wylie narrowed his eyes at Alan. *Anna's* Archie?

God's teeth. He'd let his guard down and greeted her as a friend. Was this why she'd shamed him into staying, then? The quicker the sale proceeded, the quicker she'd become Lady of Glencorach?

Nay. That title was a meaningless courtesy. It meant nothing to Anna; she was far too sensible.

Right?

Biting the inside of his lower lip, he filled his lungs with air. *Eijit*. He understood little of women and even less of the one Anna had become. She may aspire to a title, meaningless or not.

"I don't recall an Archibald Montgomery, Alan. Who are his people?"

Alan, again preoccupied, methodically tore a page from a ledger and didn't answer. Hoping it wasn't one of Glencorach's ledgers, Wylie scratched a brow and ducked his head, hiding his dismay. He'd never get the place sold without a proper set of accounts.

"Alan? This Montgomery, who are his people?"

"He's with the revenue," Alan said. He laid the freed page on a pile of similar loose pages and glanced up. "The local exciseman."

Wylie's jaw dropped. A revenue man. His heart drumming a quick tempo, he stared at Alan while racing through the implications, the ledgers forgotten.

Had his pardon been a well-laid trap by the revenue agents to lure him into Scotland?

Before last week, when Wylie's partner Alec dumped six cases of black-market French brandy on a beach south of Montrose, he and Alec hadn't plied their trade on Scotland's shores.

What a fool Wylie was not to have been suspicious. That customer had come from nowhere.

Oh, for God's sake, stop. He and Alec were moderately successful free-traders, no more. The amount of excise tax they shirked didn't warrant an elaborate entrapment scheme; the timing of the Montrose transaction was mere coincidence.

The idea of a trap was absurd.

Ludicrous, even.

He dragged a hand down his face, wondering if Alec were right and he'd become a suspicious old woman. He gave Alan, who was still speaking, his attention.

"He's been in the district for nigh on five years now," Alan said, his hands now clasped. "Most tolerate him, even Moy. Ye remember Robert Moy, don't ye?"

Oh aye. He remembered Moy well enough. The man leased Glencorach's largest plot of land. He didn't do much farming, but he produced a hell of a good whisky, most of it illegally.

"I remember Moy."

"Well, Moy's had a few runs-in with Montgomery. It's to be

expected given Moy doesn't report half of what he brews, but there's no real animosity between them. Montgomery's anxious to fit in, so he's willing to look the other way from time to time. Tell me, what did ye think of your herd?"

Old woman or not, Wylie would write Alec and bade he cease dealing in Scotland. They didn't need the connection; they had America. If this Montgomery had half his wits about him, he'd be on the alert upon learning Wylie was in the district.

"What's that?" Wylie asked, belatedly realizing Alan awaited a response.

"Your herd. It's a healthy lot this year. Have ye been to the glen to look them over?"

Hell, no. Nor did he intend to.

Cattle summered in the sheltered glens of higher ground, where the grass grew sweeter. At present, nearly all of Glencorach's workers would be lodged at summer shielings, minding the herds.

Having no wish to be reminded of the boy they recalled, Wylie planned being aboard his ship before they returned.

"Nay, though that reminds me. Why is my uncle selling cattle in May?"

"Who says that he is?

Wylie rubbed the back of his neck and looked toward the hall. One minute the man was lucid, the next senile. Only the day before, his daughter handled the sale at the ferry.

"No matter," he said, shaking his head. "Listen, Alan. Are you certain about this Montgomery buying Glencorach?" Alan may have confused him with someone else. "I can't fathom Father would sell to an Englishman. Especially one with the government."

"The English are the ones carrying money. What else could he do?"

"Still. This is Glencorach." And Anna? Surely Alan hadn't meant to imply Anna thought to marry an Englishman.

Alan drew his watch from his waistcoat pocket. He opened and then closed its cover, three, nay four, times in succession. Wylie pressed his fingers to his thumbs one by one, forgoing the urge to snatch it.

"Mr. Montgomery is with the revenue, ken," Alan said, his eyes on the watch.

"Aye, so you've said."

"He wants to meet with ye."

Wylie couldn't breathe for a moment. "What's that?"

"He wants to meet with ye."

"Concerning what?" he asked, carefully keeping his voice even.

Alan looked at him then as if he were the one barmy. "Glencorach, of course."

Wylie stood and paced the room. This meeting had gone on long enough. He needed air. "How binding is Father's agreement with this man, and what matters require settling?"

"Negotiations have deteriorated." Pocketing the watch, Alan seemed again to summon his habitual acumen. "Delinquencies are only part of your trouble. The thing is, Glencorach carries a mortgage. Therein lies the hitch. It's more than the price Montgomery is willing to pay."

Rounding on Alan, Wylie shook his head. Alan confused Glencorach with another estate. "Nay. Father never mortgaged Glencorach."

"Will ye sit, lad?" Alan asked, appearing discomfited.

"Father did not mortgage Glencorach."

"It was a long time ago."

"He'd have told me, Alan. We were in constant contact."

"He—"

"Nay, Alan. You're mistaken. He'd have told me."

"I'm sure he would have. But we'd forgotten it existed."

"Forgotten?" Wylie dropped into the chair and regarded the factor. "Forgive me, but it's unlikely one could forget a mortgage. Payments are expected, aye?"

Again Alan reached for his watch.

A trickle of unease waltzed round Wylie's chest. What if Alan was correct about the note's existence but mistaken on its timing? If it were a very recent note, Wylie wouldn't know of it, nor would payments have begun.

Had his pardon been so costly that his father financed it?

"What is the date of this mortgage, Alan?"

"It was signed in 1746."

His bowels churning, Wylie shut his eyes and pressed fingers to his temples. 1746.

Not the pardon, then. Likely payment for his flight to France.

Filling his lungs with air, he looked at Alan. "Why?"

"Once ye were attainted, your father was desperate to protect the estate. He planned for your return, ken? If he were to die before ye were pardoned, he feared the government would confiscate your home."

Until this pardon, Wylie could not inherit Glencorach, nor could his sons.

Alan continued when Wylie remained silent. "Ye must remember that at the time, Wylie, we all thought you wanted Glencorach. So we drew up the mortgage note."

True enough. From the time he could walk he'd tagged after his father, eagerly learning all he could of the land and its inhabitants. Following in his father's footsteps had been his dream. Tending Glencorach and its families ... marrying and raising his own family ...

It had been within reach. All of it. Until that winter. Could Wylie truly walk away?

Yes.

"Fair enough," Wylie said. "But now we know I don't want it."

"It's not that simple."

"You've said the mortgage is a fabrication. Tear the note in two."

"Ye misunderstand, lad. Your uncle holds the mortgage."

"So?"

"He claims he'll settle it with ye and ye alone."

Of course he did, the wily old bastard. Propping an elbow on the desk, Wylie rested his chin on his fist. "Why is that, Alan?" he asked wearily.

"I expect he wants something. He wasn't happy William planned selling."

Devil take it, this could have been handled years ago. Once Father knew Wylie didn't want the estate, he could have had his brother mark the debt paid.

Wylie slumped back in his seat and shook his head, disgusted.

"Like I said, Wylie, we'd forgotten the note existed. So much time had passed."

But a mortgage? Christ's sake, how could they have forgotten? He stood again and paced, his hands fisted.

"Why didn't *you* remember, Alan? You're his damned factor."

Alan flinched. "I know," he whispered. He looked toward the hall, blinking repeatedly as if to ward back tears. "God help me, Wylie, it seems I can't ... Forgive me, son, but my memory doesn't serve the way it once did."

Wylie's shame was instant. Dropping into the chair, he reached across the desk and squeezed Alan's hand. "I apologize. It's not your fault. I know that. It's my own."

If not for his father, he'd turn his back on this and leave tonight. But he couldn't leave matters in limbo.

The note was a sham. He'd simply demand Uncle Henry mark it satisfied in full.

His mouth twitched. Easier said than done. Uncle Henry must know he was back, yet he hadn't visited Glencorach, as Wylie had half dreaded he would.

As if he'd followed Wylie's thoughts, Alan said, "I visited Cragdurcas this morning. I hoped we might all meet here, at Glendally, and resolve this. Henry refused."

Bloody hell. Uncle Henry intended him to go crawling, hat in hand, to Cragdurcas.

CHAPTER 10

IT WAS NEARING twilight when Anna entered Wylie's kitchen two days later, her basket filled with flowers. The room was clean, quiet, and dim, indicating Martha had retired. Lighting a candle, Anna retrieved vases from the cupboard and set about refilling them.

She'd thought she'd see Wylie on her doorstep the day prior, armed with questions concerning her father's state of mind. As one day passed into the next, she'd become concerned.

If he was out and about visiting old acquaintances, fine. If he was sprawled in his chair before a cold hearth, she might not hold her tongue. Self-pity was a dangerous indulgence few could afford.

Wrapping her arms about the vases, she picked up the candle and headed toward the parlor.

"Ah, the answer to the flower mystery," said the new laird, sprawled in his chair before a cold hearth, glass in hand and decanter nearing empty. His chin and cheeks were finely shaded with a days-old beard.

Her jaw set in disappointment.

He rose and took the candle. "I wondered who rustled about in my kitchen."

"And ye didn't care to discover the interloper? I might have robbed ye blind."

Making no comment, he collapsed back into his chair and propped his feet on a stool.

"Why are ye sitting alone in the dark?"

"Seems my sons have found better company."

"They're at Glendally. Father's teaching them card games." Given his mental decline, her father rarely played other than the simplest of games these days. The boys' frequent visits, however, had sparked a rebound, and she'd left him teaching them the finer points of whist.

Setting the vases down, she stepped to the window to draw the coverings, then paused when she glimpsed Wylie's reflection. The wavering candlelight did odd things to his profile, somehow unmasking the years and the hardness they'd bestowed.

She hardly dared think it, yet something in the set of his jaw hinted at uncertainty. Nay, not that.

Need.

Her heart pulsed in recognition, filling her chest with a sudden ache.

His turned his head toward her then, bringing his gaze to meet hers in their reflection. He held it, and suddenly she couldn't swallow. Something within her flickered, blossoming with each tick of the mantel clock.

Abruptly he averted his eyes and grunted. "I recall playing with your father. I hope he's teaching them to fight as well."

Foolish chit. Her jaw set, she jerked the coverings closed and returned to her vases. "Father never cheats."

"I know that. It's the ones Alan fleeces who doubt."

"One shouldn't wager what one cannot lose," she answered primly, her fingers busy tidying blooms. Two stems bent in her haste and she slowed, inhaling one calming breath, then another. "Ye're welcome to join them. Father could use a fourth and your sons, their father."

"Fatherhood. Yet another task I've failed."

"I didn't say that."

"You didn't have to." He looped one ankle over the other and slouched farther into his chair. "Anna, is . . . I mean to say, your father . . ."

Squaring her shoulders, she ignored him, her gaze fixed on the flowers. She'd not confirm her father's failings with this man, nor would she answer the questions bound to follow.

"No matter," he said finally, apparently reconsidering. "It's nothing."

Thanks be. She adjusted one last stem and then crossed the room. Striking flint, she knelt, holding the tinder to the peat until it caught. "I know ye're grieving, Wylie. But ye've matters to consider. It's best ye start, aye?"

Sipping his drink, he grunted.

"Father told ye of the mortgage. I thought ye'd visit Cragdurcas."

"How do you know I haven't?"

She'd have heard from George if he had. George was a

tinderbox, pinning all his hopes on an opportunity to speak with Wylie.

Some looked to God for absolution. George looked to Wylie.

Brushing his feet from the stool, she sat and faced him, ignoring the flutter in her chest at his closeness. Wylie had always filled more space than he should. Even now, even though she was an adult, his presence crowded and surrounded hers.

"Have ye?"

"I intended to." He gave her a small smile. "It seems I am a coward."

Never.

While she struggled for the right words, she played for time and fingered the plaid he'd draped across his knees, thinking it familiar. Her brows drawn, she flipped up a corner, examining its weave.

"You remember it, then," he said softly.

She looked up at him. "It cannot be the same one."

"Oh, aye. It can, and it is."

The plaid was one of her first, and she'd given it to him.

It had meant something to him. Why? "Ye kept it?"

"Aye."

She shook her head, astonished. "After all this time." She could scarcely credit it. All the places he'd been, all the years that had passed, and he'd kept it. It's a wonder it hadn't come apart; her workmanship was questionable. "Surely ye can afford better?"

He chuckled. "If ever I get to feeling sorry for myself, I'll bring it out. Just so I'll recall the day a wee lass half my age crossed rebel lines carrying a plaid and a satchel of food for her kinfolk. Surely I have the will of that one wee lass."

Her heart stilled a moment, then tripped in its hurry to recover. Truly?

Wylie Macpherson—the same lad who'd once filled the daydreams of every lassie from lochs Laggan to Insh—had thought twice of her, the dowdy and willful Anna Macrae?

Fancy that.

Her chin rose an inch, and she smiled, glad she'd considered her words and held her tongue. It seemed her handiwork said them for her.

"I'm not half your age." She ran her hand over the weave, recalling the hours her mother had spent at her side, assisting her.

Wylie didn't respond. She looked up and found him studying her, his brown eyes intent beneath long, dark lashes.

"Nay," he said with infinite slowness. "But you were at the time and recalling that is a useful distraction. One that's stopping me from moving your hand from atop this plaid to beneath it."

The words slammed into her, unexpected and unsettling. She yanked her hand away and rose to step back, but the stool fell to one side and she lost her balance. In an instant, he was on his feet. He caught her by the elbows, steadying her.

"Forgive me, Anna."

His touch burned through her gown, stirring sensations long buried. She was no innocent lass half his age. She was a grown woman who'd loved and been loved. A woman capable of anticipating both his reaction and hers if she *did* run her palms up his thighs.

A woman capable of reveling in that anticipation.

One who now thought of nothing but the warm aching throb filling her core.

Try, Anna. Think of needlework . . . count stitches . . . something.

"Say something, will you, lass? I spoke out of turn. Look at me."

He towered over her, and the heady scent of whisky and male clouded her senses. Seconds ticked out on the mantel clock.

Stiffening, she locked her gaze on his chest, mentally tallying the pendulum swings. When she was sure of her voice, she said, "Release me, please."

Immediately he complied. Then, his hands held high and palms facing out, he sat.

She took a steadying breath, banking the ache of need. It was herself she didn't trust, not him. She was no temptress, even on her best days.

"Will you stay?" he asked. His gaze darted to the rise and fall of her chest and then quickly away. "Don't go. We'll talk, aye?"

Talk? She'd come only to learn his intentions regarding Glencorach. If he offered conversation, who was she to quibble? With effort, she slowed her breathing.

"May we talk of something ye may not wish to speak of?" She had a hundred questions of that long-ago winter.

"Possibly," he answered, his gaze narrowing.

"Will ye explain why ye stayed with the Jacobites?"

His mouth thinned, and he turned his head toward the fire.

"You're right. I don't wish to speak of it."

"I'll leave ye to your contemplations, then."

He turned and held her gaze, seemingly assessing her resolve. "It's to be a trade, is it?" he asked, brow raised. "Your companionship for my soul?"

"Pssht, ye do go on. It's a question, no more."

He shook his head in seeming defeat and held out his empty glass. Resuming her seat, she reached for the decanter, pleased her hand was steady. "Ye're drinking this faster than the lads can make it."

"Is it Glencorach whisky, then?"

"Aye, and ye've not much on hand. Your father reasoned it would be less for the exciseman if he kept his stock low."

Wylie straightened in his chair, seeming suddenly intent. "Does he come around often then, the excise?"

"Often enough." Archibald Montgomery visited Glendally several times weekly. Father and William had teased her repeatedly that it was not in the line of duty. "There's a good many stills in the area."

Wylie raised a brow. "You're certain his reason for visiting is the stills?"

She sniffed. "Ye've been talking to my father." Scooting the stool back, she folded her hands in her lap. "Mr. Montgomery is a friend of ours, no more."

When he didn't annoy her, which was rare.

"Hmmph," he said, the noise skeptical. He put the glass to his nose, then held it to the light, swirling the liquid. "It's very good. Did Father think of selling it?"

She forced a puff of air from her nose. "Not without a license. William wouldn't have crossed the road in front of a redcoat if he thought it would harm your chance of a pardon. Now, will ye tell me what happened that winter? From the beginning? I've tried and I've tried. But I've yet to understand why ye stayed on with the rebels."

He stared at the whisky so long she thought he'd forgotten she was there. She waited silently, watching his expression become increasingly remote.

"George and I had been in Crieff nearly a week before they nabbed us," he said finally. "It had been one fine adventure up until then. Have you been?" he asked, looking up at her.

"To Crieff? Not during the Tryst."

"It's a sight. Hills black with cattle and streets thick with drovers. All we'd anticipated and so much more. The competition, even, was fiercer than we'd expected. But George negotiated top price for our cattle; I'll give him that." He shook his head slowly at the memory. "Soon as George assumed his king's English, those brokers took notice. He had them forgetting he was a backward lout from the Highlands." He paused, quirking a corner of his mouth. "A talent that served him well, no doubt, when he wrangled his life for mine."

Oh Lord, let's not travel that road tonight. That was between him and George. "Had ye made plans to return home?"

He nodded. "We'd sold all our cattle, paid off the drovers, and planned returning after one last night of revelry. We'd heard the rumors by then: the clans were rising for Prince Charlie. But we'd paid them no heed. Only a month or two before, our fathers claimed the rebels attacking Ruthven were no more than a cluster of barmy malcontents. Who were we to question?"

They'd all smelled the smoke from the rebels' torches at Ruthven Barracks that day, yet not a one of them considered it would foretell another rising. Even outnumbered, the army subdued those rebels with few casualties.

In hindsight . . . well, hindsight invariably told a different story.

"But surely ye'd have heard of the Jacobite victory in Prestonpans?" It was all anyone could speak of once the news reached the parish.

"Aye, but again . . ." He briefly shut his eyes and shook his head. "Hell, we were fifteen, Anna. We'd waited years for our chance to man a drive to market. Prestonpans was days south; we weren't of a mind to turn tail because of it." He looked at the fire, his fingers tightening round his glass, and she noted he now wore his father's ring.

"I expect we grew careless, and our judgment suffered. It was the Camerons who collared us. They were traveling to Edinburgh to join the prince. If they'd ridden through Crieff even one day later, we'd have missed them. Do you ever think on such things? How in one minute, something you hadn't anticipated might change your life past all knowing?"

"Nay. Dwelling on such things changes nothing."

"Practical Anna."

She knit her brows, unsure if he meant to criticize. "They took you to Edinburgh?" she prompted.

"Not at once." Still staring at the fire, he said nothing more for a moment and then gave his head a quick shake, as if to discard a thought.

"Were ye bound, Wiley?"

"Hmm?" He looked back and blinked upon seeing her. "Bound? I suppose you could name it that." Running a hand up his forearm, he shifted in his seat and swallowed, the lump in his throat working visibly. "But not in Edinburgh."

"Did ye try to escape then?"

He sighed, shaking his head. "Edinburgh was crawling with Jacobites. It seemed as if the whole town was in full Highland dress, wearing white cockades and bonnets atop their heads. They marched from one street to the next, complete with pipers and drummers. It was splendorous, truth be," he said, his eyes unseeing as he recalled the memory. "It was as if we'd taken on yet another adventure, atop the one we'd had in Crieff. By that time we weren't certain the prince wouldn't take all of Britain."

Prince indeed. That pretentious pretender had nearly caused Scotland's destruction. "What of the others they pressed into service? Did any try to escape?"

"Some," he said with a small lopsided smile, "The chains the Jacobites clapped about their wrists made the matter less splendorous."

Without thinking, she reached out. Before touching him, she came to her senses and clasped her hands tight. "But not you and George."

"Nay. By then we led drills and it didn't seem right. I know how that sounds now."

She kept silent, not knowing what to say. So often it had seemed Wylie thought with his heart, not his head.

"Most of the lads were crofters with no knowledge of weaponry aside from their pitchforks. The officers knew George and I had drovers' passes to carry our broadswords, so they chose us to train the crofters to use them."

"The farm lads had swords?"

"Aye, the Jacobites salvaged arms from the fallen English at Prestonpans. We drilled from dawn to dusk. It kept us warm during the day and too weary at night to care for things that once mattered. It changed us, Anna. We became one, a unit, if you will."

His gaze pinned her, his tone beseeching. "By the time we marched into England, the lads would do anything I asked of them. They gave me their best. I could do no less than give them mine. That's the only explanation I can offer. I couldn't run and leave them behind."

The intervening years vanished, and she glimpsed the fifteen-year-old lad he'd once been. Her heart clenched. Suddenly she understood. "You were their leader," she said softly.

"George and I both."

She looked down at her hands, declining to agree. She suspected those boys had deferred to Wylie. It was the same with the lads at home.

It wasn't because he was the laird's son. Nor was it because he was competent and educated. All the same could be said of George.

It was because he was Wylie.

Wylie never asked another to do what he'd not do himself. He could, for cert. She'd seen many a lad jump to do his bidding, proud that over all others, Wylie knew he could see the task finished.

Wylie cared for others and spent time learning their stories. Even at fifteen, when he'd accompanied her father on rent days, he'd let it slip that Paul McDuff had forfeited his last three chickens to pay a doctor to tend his five bairns, and mayhap it'd be best if Alan allowed an extension. Or that Angus Macpherson's wife was expecting yet again, and perhaps in lieu of the goat Angus offered up, Alan might take the whisky Angus kept stashed behind the privy.

Her father had returned from those treks filled with such stories, and she'd listen while he relayed them to William. Both men nearly busted with pride at the retelling.

George, normally succinct, had explained it thus: Wylie inspired loyalty simply by being himself.

Could circumstances truly have robbed him of his essence? Or did that essence merely lay dormant, awaiting the opportunity to reawaken?

He had changed; she sensed that. But to sit in that chair and let events follow an uncharted course when he had the choice to do otherwise?

"Are you even listening, lass?"

No, her thoughts had drifted. "Aye. Ye were telling me of your time in England."

He eyed her with suspicion, then went on. "We spent most of that winter back in Scotland. Our regiment missed the fighting in Stirling and Falkirk by days. I'll admit I was sympathetic to the Jacobite cause by then. On our march through the Lowlands, we'd seen evidence enough to justify a rebellion. King George's army laid a heavy hand upon Scotland. Even our fathers would have attested to that."

True enough. All staunch Hanoverians, their fathers favored the Union. But Scots at heart, they didn't hold with the army's brutality.

"Your uncle and your father searched Falkirk and Stirling for you two," she said. "They were absent for months."

He nodded. "I know. We didn't much want rescuing by then, and eluding them wasn't difficult." He leaned forward a fraction and placed a finger under her chin, lifting it. His gaze met hers, and her breath caught in her lungs. He still had the softest brown eyes, and at this moment they carried what might be affection.

"But you, Anna. You managed it. A wee lass, bearing a blanket, food, and news, and somehow you crept into an armed rebel camp and found us. You were eight years old! When I'm not in awe, I shudder thinking what might have happened. I still don't know how you did it."

Perhaps it was admiration she glimpsed, not affection.

Truth be, Anna shuddered herself when recalling it. But George's mother had been on her deathbed, bereft of all family, and people whispered that Wylie and George camped nearby. So in the midst of a blizzard, Anna wrangled one of the farm lads, Mowart, to show her the way.

They'd plowed a path through snow drifts well over her head, numbing her hands and feet past all feeling. Mowart kept no more than three feet ahead, but because of the blizzard, she'd struggled to keep him in sight.

She could easily have perished beneath one of those drifts. She hadn't been afraid of dying; at the time it'd seemed the more peaceful of options. She'd been terrified at the possibility they'd find her still alive beneath the snow. Her mother's wrath would have known no bounds.

If she closed her eyes, she could still feel the stinging slap of her hair, heavy with ice, hitting her cheeks with each step of that two mile trek.

Worse was the stinging shame of the temptation to keep the plaid for herself and turn back.

She'd never known a cold such as that, not before or since. It had been a foolhardy expedition at best.

"No one paid me much mind; a child is of little consequence," she said. "George had to know his mother was near death, and I wanted to remind you of your promise."

"My promise?"

"When you and George left that September, you promised me you'd be back."

He stared at her so long she feared she'd revealed too much. She pushed his finger from her chin and turned her head. "Ye didn't come home with George." She'd been so sure he would.

"I didn't, and I have no defense. But George couldn't stay, not with the news of his mother. We all helped him desert."

When he fell silent, she prompted, "And then?"

"And then my memories are something of a blur. We fought one skirmish and then the next. We never marched as far as Culloden, or rather, I never did. I don't remember how it happened, but in April I woke aboard a vessel bound for France. I was wrapped in this plaid, and the bandage round my head was clean."

"George was responsible for the bandaging." Wounded, Wylie had been left for dead, but one of the rebel lads had slipped away and sought help. He'd found Anna, and she'd found George.

George had tended the wound. His fingers slippery with blood and his sight blurred by tears, he clumsily stitched it closed while Wylie remained unconscious. When night fell, he slung Wylie over his back and carried him home.

William and Henry Macpherson had prepared for such an eventuality. Within hours, Wylie had been safely aboard a vessel sailing for France.

"Nay, George wouldn't know my position. I think it was one of the lads in the unit. I never knew what became of those lads. I fear they were slaughtered at Culloden."

"It *was* George. He knew your position most times. Remember I accompanied my father on his rounds of the farms. I overheard many things, and I'd pass them on to George. He'd leave food where he thought it might be found."

"You're certain?"

"Of course; I aided him. When a lad came with news ye were wounded, George went and stitched your wound. He carried ye home himself." It was important he know George had never deserted him. She reached for his hand, squeezing it.

His lips twitched, and she had the impression he wouldn't take her at her word. "I don't recall the time clearly."

"George planned to accompany ye to France, but by then your uncle and father were back and they wouldn't allow it. But George did all he could. Did ye think it odd to wake and find yourself wearing new boots?" She hoped one of the crew hadn't stolen them; they'd been well paid to look after Wylie. "Ye were wearing boots when ye woke, aye?"

His nod seemed hesitant.

She leaned forward and brushed the hair from his forehead. His hair was still thick, even at his temples, where strands of silver outnumbered those of reddish-brown. The wound had healed, though not in the clean white line it might have. She traced it with a finger.

"Ye were fevered, Wylie. Perhaps that's why ye can't recall."

He wrapped his fingers around her wrist and held her in place when she would have backed away.

"Perhaps," he agreed, holding her gaze.

Her mouth went dry. Swallowing, she wet her lips.

He was drinking. He still carried a torch for his cousin's wife. He had children. Sons who might return at any moment.

All should signify. None did. None but the tingling awareness trickling down to her belly.

"Christ, but you're tempting," he said softly.

She swayed forward a fraction, and his gaze strayed to her mouth. For an instant she thought he meant to kiss her.

Fool.

Within days, he'd return to France or the sea or wherever he intended to flee. If he meant to kiss her, it was to pass time before his escape.

He swore beneath his breath, the oath in Gaelic. Then he closed the distance between them and touched her mouth with his own. It seemed a fleeting touch, so insubstantial that if her heartbeat hadn't clamored otherwise, she wasn't certain she could name it a kiss.

But it was. Fleeting or not, it was a kiss. And a glorious one at that.

He deepened the touch then, his mouth moving on hers, and her lips parted. The tip of his tongue traced between them, and a wave of sensation exploded within her, rupturing all rational thought.

A dizzying reel unlike any she'd danced before. His mouth a fiddle, driving the pace. Urging—nay, demanding—a response.

Dropping her wrist, he clasped her waist and pulled her close. What remained of her wits spun off, abandoning her, and she curled her fingers into his shoulders.

Steel-hard shoulders, unyielding.

Unshaven cheeks rasped over hers. Her pulse pounded in her ears.

She lifted her arms and curled them around his neck, crushing her body against his.

Without warning, he pulled his mouth from hers. She blinked, then opened her eyes to see him staring at her, his expression guarded.

Her arms fell to her sides.

Her head still spun. The tips of her fingers and toes still tingled. Had he felt nothing?

His hands dropped from her waist.

Nothing. He'd kissed her mindless and felt nothing.

Humiliation shrank her insides.

Then, mustering her dignity, she straightened before he guessed her turmoil.

"George . . ." Lord, what was it she had been saying? Dignity be damned. Her insides were tied in a cottar's knot. George what? His . . . his wound. Aye, George had stitched his wound. "George thought to hide ye here afterward," she said. "Here at Glencorach. He—"

"Anna, I didn't mean to . . ."

Don't you dare tell me you didn't mean to. You think I don't know you regret it?

"George didn't think the wound would heal—"

"Enough, lass. I—"

"He didn't think the wound would heal without proper care," she said quickly, her words tumbling over his. "But your father

61

insisted ye leave for France at once, so they hid ye in a wagon and drove ye to the coast."

She had the sinking feeling she'd already said all that. He'd think her a simpleton. Her ardor chilled, and she felt the fool.

Wylie sighed, his mouth twisted in resignation. He fell back against the chair. "No matter. It's likely for the best," he said, his voice flat. He sipped his whisky and studied the fire, seemingly signaling an end to his confidences.

Best that his father insisted on France? Or best that he'd not prolonged that kiss?

Both, surely. The silence lengthened and she adjusted her posture into its familiar bearing.

Prim and unyielding.

Her armor in place, she said, "Wylie?"

He slanted his eyes toward her and lifted a brow, waiting.

"What now? Ye can't continue to drink the days away."

He shut his eyes a moment, then grimaced and looked away. He set his glass on the table. "It's a temporary indulgence only," he said at length.

He could indulge himself at night and attend to his responsibilities by day, couldn't he?

"The tenants have asked after ye. Will ye visit them soon?" Preferably before they resumed pestering her father.

Twirling the ring on his finger, he kept his gaze on the fire. "I think not. My future's not here."

"And where is it ye think it is?" she asked, knowing she overstepped. He was a laird; she was a factor's daughter. Questioning him was not her place.

"America."

Her forehead creased, and she blinked. "America?"

"Aye. I can start over in America." He turned and faced her. "With this pardon, I can begin again."

She went rigid. Begin again, her arse. She'd heard that story, right before her Burt sailed with the promise to set up a prosperous household for the two of them. He perished crossing the Atlantic, before setting one boot back on American soil. And for what? Everything they could have wanted was right here.

She'd never taken another beau.

"I've news for ye, Wylie Macpherson," she said. "We begin again each morning, each one of us, as soon as we wake. There's nothing magic about it. With God's grace, it's a gift of our own making." Rising, she swatted soot from her gown. "Ye want to begin again, try rising on the morrow with a clear head."

He stood, frowning, and she backed out of his reach.

"We'll speak again after ye visit your uncle."

"God's teeth, you're angry?" He looked both mystified and irritated. "Why?"

"I'm not." She shut her eyes and gave her head a shake. "I suppose I am. But not at you." Before he could respond, she left the room, adding, "My father will wonder what's become of me. I must go." Now, before the tears came.

There were three males at home who knew where she'd been. Each would wonder if she entered with red-rimmed eyes and a dripping nose. She took the long way back, needing the time to recover.

Wylie had every right to be mystified. She had no claim on him. His plans, whether they be for America, China, or Africa, merited no more than a cursory interest.

Wylie was not Burt. He was not in her future, and she was not in his.

Nonetheless, she cared for him—had *always* cared for him. And minutes ago he'd made her feel things she'd forgotten she could. Things she hadn't realized she missed. Suddenly *desperately* missed.

Was there any harm in indulging? He'd been somewhat inclined himself—he'd said she was tempting.

Harm? Good Lord, had she forgotten the all-encompassing devastation following Burt's ill-fated journey to America? It had crippled her for nearly a year.

Measure that against one night of pleasure?

Desire was fleeting. Grief was not.

But it may not be one night. It may be two, even three. And she was older now. Surely with foreknowledge, things could be different. Yes, Wylie's interest was passing, and yes, he planned leaving soon. But forearmed with that knowledge, she could shield her heart. Bask in his interest while he was here and emerge unscathed when he left.

No! Don't be a fool, Anna Macrae.

Groaning, she dug her fingernails into her palms and turned up the lane to Glendally. Within minutes the cottage came into view, bathed in moonlight. Warm, welcoming and safe. She stood on the front path, gazing at it until her heartbeat slowed. A lone rabbit took flight, and her flowers shivered in its wake.

She couldn't trust herself. If she didn't find a distraction for the balance of Wylie's visit, she'd do something foolish. A sensible distraction, one that wouldn't turn her insides out.

Mr. Montgomery.

Cold doused her, and her shoulders hunched. Grabbing the corner of her apron, she blotted her eyes, straightened her shoulders, and strode down the path.

Aye, Mr. Montgomery would serve.

CHAPTER 11

THE NEXT morning, for the third time in two days, Wylie set out for Cragdurcas. His first two attempts had resulted in retreat at the boundary. This morning he would cover the distance.

At the drove road, he paused. Though faster, the river path was isolated. If he instead crossed open fields, others would note his progress and guess his destination. If nothing else, pride would carry him over that damned boundary, and if it didn't, well, he could hear the tongues wag.

Wylie Macpherson, the traitor who'd run, couldn't stand toe to toe with his own uncle.

"Like hell," he muttered. He started across the closest field, his steps crunching on frost-covered heather.

It wasn't that he *couldn't* stand toe to toe with Uncle Henry, it was that he didn't care to. The man had a knack for making him feel two feet tall whenever he misstepped, and Wylie had yet to atone for his biggest misstep—dragging his cousin into the Rising.

For without Wylie's influence, George, being perfect, would have come straight home from Crieff, before causing his father a moment of worry.

Uncle Henry no doubt envisioned it such.

Normally, his uncle would be right. But for whatever reason, George had been the first to toss taunts at the Camerons that long-ago afternoon. He'd been drinking—but Wylie hadn't forced the whisky down his throat with a funnel.

George had also been the one who'd deliberately undersold their last lot of cattle, knowing full well that it would cut the market price and infuriate the Camerons, who stood in line behind them. Not only that, George had cast slurs on the largest of the Camerons' tacksmen—a cocky buffoon for cert, but a buffoon with a score of armed men standing at his heels.

Of course if George hadn't, Wylie would have, for a bitter rivalry existed between the two clans.

Still, it had been George who'd started the whole of it.

Did Uncle Henry know that?

Wylie gave his head a shake, his mouth twisting in a self-deprecating smirk. Christ, was he fourteen or forty?

Why the hell had he come home in the first place?

"Ye're to return, Wylie, else I'll know you a coward with nary a thimbleful of honor."

Right. Anna.

What did the gossips say of wee Anna Macrae and the revenue man? Were Montgomery's intentions honorable? Or, at any rate, more honorable than his own?

He hoped no one had spotted her leaving Glencorach last night. Speculation would spread faster than a flame on thatch, and he'd hate it if it were directed toward her—especially if it reached her suitor's ears. Assuming Montgomery *was* a suitor.

Damned fool if he wasn't.

That kiss hadn't been an impulse. He'd experienced an unexpected urge to embrace her from the moment she'd bustled in, filled with purpose and skirts swishing.

Once she'd plopped down on the stool in front of him, the itch gathered wind. For nearly an hour he'd watched firelight dance over her features until finally concluding, why not? She'd either bolt or she'd stay. If she'd bolted, *c'est la vie.* If she stayed, it was only a kiss.

He hadn't reckoned on being wrong.

Her mouth sparked a flame that had ripped through him, much like lightning striking a foremast and sizzling its way to the deck. Only the deck hadn't been his toes.

Thankfully she'd bolted, for he wasn't certain he'd have left it at a kiss. As it was, he couldn't shake the memory for the life of him. He'd tossed and turned most of the night until he finally gave up the effort and rose.

Why had he kissed her? He'd leave soon; why complicate things?

He snorted. God help him if he found *that* puzzling. If a comely lass couldn't rouse his interest, he should sell his ship and idle his remaining days in a rocker.

Suddenly the Macphersons' front stoop loomed before him, and he stopped short, surprised. Then he grinned. Anna had been a fine distraction; he'd actually traveled the distance.

He stood, studying the fading varnish on his uncle's massive front doors, and his grin faded. Getting here now seemed the easy part. Biting the inside of his cheeks, he shifted his weight from one foot to the other and considered his options.

Release the latch and walk right in, same as he'd done in years past.

Turn on his heel and head back to Glencorach. Try this again tomorrow.

"... *else I'll know you a coward with nary a thimbleful of honor.*"

Right then. Third option. Raising his fist, he knocked, then stepped back and waited.

The door opened immediately, as if someone had been waiting, and Uncle Henry stood before him. Wylie's heart skipped a beat, and he blinked at Henry's resemblance to Wylie's father.

Though heavier than his brother, Uncle Henry had the same prominent beak-like nose, heavy brows, and dark brown eyes. They differed in that Henry habitually wore his hair tucked beneath a wig, as if he were perennially expecting callers.

"Wylie!" Uncle Henry boomed.

Wylie cringed. He'd timed his arrival to catch his uncle alone, while others still slept. A bellow like Uncle's would wake the entire household.

He stood silent while the man studied him, dropping his gaze when Henry's dark eyes filled.

Bloody hell, did he plan to feign a fond kinship? After holding Glencorach hostage to a sham loan?

"Good morning, Uncle Henry. I've come on a matter of business."

"By God, lad, it's been far too long." Clasping Wylie's arm, Henry pulled him over the threshold and tugged him close.

Wylie stood rock-still in the unwanted embrace, mystified by his sudden urge to return it.

This hadn't been the scenario he'd envisioned.

His stomach clenched. Had Father been right? Did Uncle Henry hold him blameless for George fighting with the Jacobites?

No. Not possible.

Henry held Glencorach hostage.

Besides, if so, then George had testified against Wylie on his own accord, without prodding from his father.

Christ, he couldn't think straight. He pulled back, disentangling himself. "Shall we meet in your study?"

"Nonsense. Ye'll eat with us."

Bile rose, burning his throat, and panic seized him. Us? No, he would not. For he was suddenly certain "us" meant George, Miriam, and their son.

Wylie had envisioned George and Miriam happily and remotely ensconced in Edinburgh. He'd even entertained the notion of visiting when passing through the week prior. Show George he could let bygones be bygones.

Truth be, however, Wylie had no intention of letting those particular bygones be bygone.

If George and Miriam lived at Cragdurcas, then a meeting may be unavoidable. But not today. Such a meeting required forethought and unassailable defenses.

He wasn't prepared. He hadn't slept or eaten. His thoughts were in a constant muddle. Just seeing Uncle Henry spun his world on its axis.

Encounter George as well, atop everything else? He shook his head.

"Nay, Uncle. This is business. I have only a few moments—"

"Ye've kept me waiting for days, lad. Ye'll stay."

"I've no wish to interrupt your meal. Besides, I've eaten," he lied.

Henry placed a hand on the small of Wylie's back. "Ye'll join us, lad, or we'll not speak of what ye've come to speak of," he said softly, his voice laced with steel.

Cunning bastard. Wylie's mouth twisted. He wasn't sure how, but he'd lay odds Uncle Henry had planned this. Perhaps he'd set one of his ghillies to tracking Wylie.

In which case Henry would know of Wylie's humiliating retreats the days before.

Gritting his teeth, he allowed his uncle to steer him forward.

Unlike his brother, Uncle Henry had followed through on plans to add space to his home. While the center portion of Cragdurcas Manor followed the same floor plan as Glencorach House, Uncle Henry had replaced the simple staircase with a curved one of varnished pine. Wainscoting lined the walls. The parlor on his left, widened by the addition of a north wing, allowed room for a gleaming Jamaican mahogany table and set of chairs.

A quick glance at that table determined "us" included only

George and Miriam. Approaching quickly, Wylie dropped into a vacant chair at the nearest end. "Don't get up," he said, fixing his gaze on the ancestral portrait hanging directly opposite. He hadn't the stomach for another embrace. Let them attribute his bad manners to the French influence.

George, who had inched up, sat. After a brief silence, he spoke. "Hello, Wylie. Welcome home."

Wylie momentarily averted his gaze from the portrait and acknowledged his cousin. "George," he said, nodding curtly.

Criminy, George had aged—and far more than the years allowed. Did he himself look that old?

A thinning crown of silver had replaced George's dark brown mop of hair. And his face . . . those lines about his mouth and eyes seemed etched by something other than laughter.

Odd. He'd always counted on George's humor to lift his own brooding moods, and George had never failed him. Laughter had lined his face at age fifteen.

Eijit. He's failed you in every way that counts.

Besides, he'd observed George for less than a second following a twenty-five-year absence. Add to that, the room's lighting was poor. There were no easterly windows, and Uncle apparently hoarded candles.

Misfortune etched no lines on that man's face. He had all a man could want. The promise of a prosperous estate, a living father who doted on him, a son . . . and a beautiful wife.

Whom Wylie must acknowledge before he could take a proper breath. Swallowing, he turned toward her.

She stared at him, her gray eyes glistening and unblinking, and the half-forgotten longing surged, filling him.

Miriam.

Every bit as lovely as when he'd seen her last. Her hair, pinned to one side, was still a gleaming chestnut brown and lay over her shoulder in the manner of a maiden. Her complexion was a flawless ivory—more so than he remembered, as if the blood had drained from her face.

Didn't she know he'd returned? Surely she did. By now, the entire parish knew.

He tore his gaze from hers. He'd been mad to come here.

"Mrs. Macpherson," he said, trying for the coldest tone he could summon. He bowed his head.

"Wylie," she answered softly.

His gut clinched, and he nearly winced. She had a way of saying his name that could do that. It was as if her voice caressed, not addressed. He'd never forgotten it. He studied his place setting and fingered the silver, turning it over and over.

"Eat something, Wylie," his uncle said from the other end of the table, breaking her spell.

A servant hovered near with the breakfast tray. Clasping his hands in his lap, Wylie nodded. Within seconds his plate was filled with toasted bannocks and a heaping helping of salmon.

"I wasn't certain when you'd come, Wylie, so I proceeded with William's service. We could plan another memorial, if you'd like."

Wylie kept his eyes on his plate. "That's unnecessary, Uncle. I've visited his grave and paid my respects." He'd felt Father's calming presence at the site and planned to visit it again before leaving. He didn't require the spectacle of a memorial. "I appreciate you handling the details of the service."

"Of course."

Aside from the clink of tableware, the room was uncomfortably quiet. Silently, Wylie cursed his uncle and stabbed the fish with his fork. Not one of them had wanted this encounter.

"I noticed your cattle at the ferry, Uncle," he said at length, filling the silence. "Anna said you had a buyer."

"Aye," Uncle Henry said, pulling apart a bannock. "Let's save talk of business for another day, lad. We've a lady present."

Surely he didn't mean to postpone *all* business.

"You've seen Anna?" Miriam asked, an edge to her voice, as if peeved by that. "Before you visited Cragdurcas?"

"Aye. She was at the crossing when my sons and I arrived."

"You have a fine set of sons, Wylie," George said.

In a flash of heat, Wylie's blood rushed to his head. He nearly leapt across the table and grabbed his cousin by the throat. When had George met Will and Dougal?

Anna.

Damn her to hell and back. His cousin could charm the stripes off a Monadhliath wildcat. Wylie didn't want him within ten meters of his sons. Surely Anna knew that.

His lips twitching against an unreasoned response, Wylie instead forced a nod, knowing the gesture discourteous.

"We have a fine son as well, George," Miriam said, seemingly admonishing her husband. "Did you know, Wylie?"

Did he know? Did he know she'd borne his cousin a son whilst Wylie thought she anxiously awaited his own return from France, stitching samplers to quiet her worry over his safety?

Good God Almighty. She'd truly asked him that.

He blew out a breath and squared the salmon on his plate with painstaking precision. "Yes, my father wrote me. I trust he's well. He must be in his twenties now?"

Miriam smoothed the linen in her lap and smiled. "Twenty-four and a major in the army. My father purchased him a commission some years ago."

"You must be proud," he said, reminded of her wealthy connections. A Grant from Strathspey, Miriam had come to the parish that long-ago summer to companion a widowed aunt. Accustomed to the finer things in life, she'd made no secret of her disdain for Badenoch.

If memory served, Wylie's attachment to the region was the one thing she'd taken issue with. Undoubtedly there'd been more, or she'd not have married his cousin in lieu of following him to France.

"Yes, exceedingly proud," she said. "He'll be down shortly, and you can meet him."

"Another time, perhaps," Wylie said, less than eager for the encounter. "I must get back soon. Will and Dougal are expecting me." Another lie. When the boys returned after Anna's departure last night, he'd told Will that he'd be gone most of this morning.

Miriam pinned a wayward lock and patted it smooth. "We don't see Jay often. All of his associates are in London so he rarely comes home. I suppose that's my fault. I insisted he attend school there. It's a fair distance, true, but Edinburgh's schools..." She shuddered.

"I'm certain you missed him," Wylie said, for lack of a better answer. He and George had attended an Edinburgh school, and they managed well enough. George, of course, had done more than just manage, and his father had planned sending him to Germany— to attend the university all proper Hanoverians aspired to send their sons.

Homage to King George and the House of Hanover and all that.

Those plans had fallen by the wayside once George fought with the Jacobites, paying homage to Bonnie Prince Charlie and the

House of Stuart instead.

With an elegant white hand, Miriam gestured a servant to refill her ale. "Oh no, Wylie," she said, after taking a sip. "I didn't have a chance to miss him. I joined him. Surely you remember my father keeps property in London? I was there whenever Jay was in term. George and his father discouraged it, but I believe a boy needs his mother. Wouldn't you agree?"

Hell no. Without forethought, he looked at George, who was looking at him. For an instant George wore a faint smile, and it was as if they were fifteen again, making sport of the lads whose hovering mothers escorted them to school. The bolt of feeling accompanying their shared thought took Wylie unawares, and he quickly dropped his gaze.

Shaken, he struggled forming a coherent reply to Miriam's question. "That was fortunate for you, ma'am," he answered finally. "Rennie also preferred Will and Dougal close."

"Rennie?"

"Wylie's wife, Renalda, Miriam," George said, shoving food about his plate with his fork. "We were sorry to learn of her passing, Wylie."

"Oh. Yes, of course. It must be very hard on your boys, Wylie," Miriam said, reaching to caress his hand. "A mother's love and support is so important. I daresay it's the one thing a young man can count on in troubling times."

Wylie drew back, the salmon settling uneasily in his belly. Her action *was* a caress. Not a consoling pat nor a perfunctory touch, but a lingering caress—with her husband in view.

"Thank you for the kind thoughts," he said, suddenly more eager to escape. He looked toward the door and saw a young man pass through.

He froze, his chest tight. *No.*

It was one thing to know Miriam had borne George a son. It was something else altogether to come face-to-face with that son. Wylie didn't think he could breathe.

"Jay," Miriam said, her delight apparent. She patted the empty chair beside her. "Come join us. Meet your cousin Wylie."

His chin held high, Wylie stood.

Dissipated was the first word that sprang to mind. Like his grandfather, Jay wore a wig. Jay's, however, appeared slapped on haphazardly. Strands of unkempt hair poked from beneath it.

He bore no resemblance to the Macphersons. Somehow that made matters easier. Releasing the breath he'd been holding, Wylie greeted the lad.

"At your service, sir," Jay responded formally, bowing his head. Then, moving to the vacant chair between his mother and grandfather, he slumped into its seat.

Wylie resumed his own seat slowly. He studied Jay, curiosity overtaking discomfort. There truly was no trace of George in Jay's features. Sharing Miriam's wide-set gray eyes and full mouth, Jay was clearly his mother's son.

The same mother who now piled the lad's plate with food. Wylie caught himself before raising his brows.

"Another late night, I see," Uncle Henry muttered, his mouth quirked in a grimace.

"Yes, sir." Jay answered, his gaze trained on his plate.

"I trust ye've no plans on attending that recital, lad. I expect ye to return to London this afternoon and take care of matters."

"No, sir. I don't plan attending that recital. I plan to return to London."

"No! Surely not today, Jay," Miriam said. "We agreed you'd speak with . . . " She glanced at Wylie and her voice trailed off, as if she thought better of what she'd meant to say.

Good. Someone recalled families weren't to air their grievances before guests.

"Do some hard thinking on that journey, lad," Uncle Henry said, not taking Miriam's cue. "Plenty of officers on half-pay don't stay abed past noon. Talk to your cousin Wylie, here. He's no stranger to adverse conditions, yet he's managed to prosper."

Wylie looked askance at his uncle. Unbelievable. The man looked to *him* for support with a wayward offspring?

He'd thought he'd been dizzy walking into this room.

And where had George's thoughts wandered? He'd scarcely acknowledged his son.

Wylie conceded his perception might be off, especially as he refused to look directly at his cousin, but it seemed to him that George was overly preoccupied studying Wylie. As if he found Wylie's reaction to Jay, the living proof of his betrayal, far more interesting than Jay himself.

As if he took no pleasure turning the knife without witnessing the pain.

Wylie tore a piece from his bannock and stuffed it in his mouth, affecting disinterest. He'd not give George the satisfaction.

"The family has an invitation to Bloomhall later today, Wylie," George said quietly. "We won't attend, but perhaps you'd like to take your boys."

So he was wrong. No knife. He reached for his ale.

"I shouldn't think Wylie wants to visit the Bloomfields, George," Miriam said. "I daresay he doesn't care for that type of music."

How would she have any idea what he did or didn't want to do? Wylie had the urge to accept, just to be contrary, but in truth, she was right; he did not want to go. Though he knew the name, he'd never spent time with the Bloomfields.

"Thank you, but no," Wylie answered. "I have other plans." This first step, now behind him, filled him with purpose. Following this meal, he'd speak with Uncle Henry. By midday, he'd hand Alan the canceled note.

Miriam beamed at him, then turned and patted Jay's hand, as if to keep him awake. "Do tell us of your travels, Wylie," she said. "I've heard you've been nearly everywhere. Jay's anxious to hear of your adventures."

What the devil? His brow raised a fraction. Did she think he'd been on an extended tour of the Continent all these years? "Perhaps later, Mrs. Macpherson. Uncle, may we meet now? There's an urgent matter I'd like to discuss."

"Of course, lad. Not now, but first thing tomorrow. I'll come to Glencorach."

His temper rose and his jaw hardened, but Wylie knew better than to argue. The set of his uncle's shoulders was unmistakable.

A clock in the hall struck the hour. He finished his ale in one long swallow and stood. "Very well. Forgive my abrupt departure, but I've stayed longer than anticipated. Good day," he said, inclining his head.

Tossing his linen atop the table, he added, "Uncle, I look forward to seeing you at daybreak."

CHAPTER 12

WYLIE'S RESENTMENT flared with each step home. Uncle Henry had planned that debacle.

There had been no letter informing him of his father's death. Instead, Uncle Henry had used silence as bait, knowing full well Wylie's concern would eventually draw him home. Then that mortgage, surely a fabrication, had reeled him to Cragdurcas.

And he had gone, fool that he was.

Glencorach House came into view and Wylie halted, studying it. It wasn't as grand as Cragdurcas. Surely not up to snuff for Uncle Henry. But it could be. It had possibilities.

Perhaps George, fancying a property of his own, had put Henry up to the scheme.

His lips hardening in a tight line, Wylie continued walking. For George to sit so coolly, a mere three seats from Wylie, and calmly plot while his father dangled Wylie's inheritance . . .

The gate at the side yard, hanging lopsided with one hinge broken, stuck fast when Wylie tried opening it. He took a step back, aimed the heel of his boot, and kicked. The gate broke free of its last hinge and flew before clattering to the stone walk.

When the devil would it be enough? First his life, now his estate? He kicked the gate again, adding a string of unmerited curses.

"Papa?"

Startled, Wylie wheeled at the sound of his son's voice. Dougal stood alone on the front walk, his eyes wide.

"I didn't see you, Dougal." As a rule, he kept his temper in front of the boys. It made it easier to counsel they keep theirs.

"You are angry."

"Not at you."

"May I visit Anna and Mr. Macrae?"

"Have Will take you to the river instead." He no longer wanted his sons at Glendally. The Macraes were complicit in his uncle's schemes.

What Wylie ought to do was leave tonight and have Alan Macrae earn his keep. Mortgages—if indeed there was a mortgage—were a factor's business. If Alan couldn't manage it, then so be it. Glencorach could slide into bankruptcy and his cousin could have it for a song.

"Will is sleeping. May I help you fix the gate?"

He opened his mouth to refuse, then shut it when he saw Will exit the front door. "I asked you to look after Dougal."

"What happened to the gate?" Will asked, ignoring the rebuke.

"Papa broke it and said his sailor words. I am to help fix it," Dougal said, seeming eager at the prospect. "You will take us to fish the river after, Papa?"

"Papa will not have time, Dougal."

"I'll thank you not to answer for me, Will." Wylie picked up the gate and fingered the broken hinge. The wood beneath it had rotted. He had some carpentry skills, though he never relished using them. Perhaps he *should* fish the river.

"We could visit Mr. Moy on our way," Dougal said, seizing on his hesitation. "We met him yesterday. He gave Will whisky."

Will cuffed his brother's shoulder, knocking him forward a step. "What is a tacksman, Papa? Mr. Moy says he is one."

Wylie stifled an unexpected urge to grin, familiar with Will's diversionary tactic. The boy needn't have bothered. No harm came of a dram now and again, even to a lad of fifteen. It hadn't harmed him.

On second thought, maybe it had. He and George had had several drams the night they'd been collared.

"He holds the longest lease on our land. Most of our farms are subleased through him."

"He is a man of importance?"

"Aye." At times Moy had seemed to fancy himself the laird.

Yet he wasn't. Wylie now was.

Wylie's anger receded as he thought of the tenants. With his father gone, their situation was as uncertain as his own. The difference was that they were powerless. Wylie wasn't.

Was there any sense in leaving before hearing his uncle out?

It's possible he'd read the situation wrong. He'd been anxious, his thoughts in a muddle; he may have drawn the wrong conclusions. It wouldn't be the first time.

Perhaps Henry wanted the same thing Wylie's father had

ceased asking—for Wylie to forgive George's betrayal.

George had never stopped writing. Every few months, when the growing pile of letters became too big to ignore, Wylie would return them. Tempted as he'd been to fling them into the ocean, he wanted no doubt to exist that each remained unopened.

If Uncle Henry did indeed want Wylie to forgive and forget, Wylie would explain it was impossible. Some wrongs were too grievous to right. If he kept a tight rein on his temper while explaining, his uncle would see reason, just as his own father had.

If the mortgage existed, there was every possibility Wylie might hand Alan a note marked "paid full and final" by tomorrow afternoon.

And if that were so, today was his last opportunity to walk his land. Still examining the gate, he said, "Perhaps we will visit Mr. Moy and see how things have changed over the years."

"Cousin George could inform us of changes," Dougal said.

Wylie dropped the gate and whirled toward Dougal, his temper hot again. *God's teeth.* He didn't require his cousin's help in running this estate. "Did *he* tell you that, then?"

"No, Papa." Dougal shook his head, backing up a step. "But he has lived here always."

Wylie knew more of this land than George Macpherson ever would. Wylie had planned tending it; George planned leaving it.

He paused, the memory overtaking him before he could parry it with another, and a pang of adolescent ache poked at him. George truly *had* planned leaving Badenoch—for university and whatever came after.

Wylie learned of it late that final summer, in 1745, and the knowledge had devastated him. Yet it hadn't signified. Within weeks, both of their lives had spun past all knowing.

Wylie grunted, and a corner of his mouth twitched. So cocksure he'd been as a lad, so certain he held the reins to the future.

Something to recall when dealing with Will.

"George may have lived here always," Wylie said, answering Dougal, "but I prefer seeing for myself."

Moy's place wasn't far. Wylie, his sons behind him, quickly found the narrow track that led there and followed it west.

"Wylie!"

Wylie paused and turned toward the sound, placing a hand on his brow to shade his eyes. A man, short in stature and slight in frame, stood in a field, his elbow propped on a hoe. He raised a hand, waving.

"Mr. Moy's son, Papa," Dougal said.

So he was. Bobby was Robert Moy's youngest, and they'd been friends when boys. Wylie crossed the field. "Bobby. It's been a while. A farmer now, are ye?"

"Aye, well. I'm not one for starving, ken?"

"Aye, I do that," Wylie said, recalling the fetid waste that had kept him alive that first year in France. The contents of his belly churned, and he swallowed.

Bobby didn't look all that far from starving as it was, but then the Moys were a scrappy lot. Fierce as hell though, and good men to have at one's side. In years past, a young man in Bobby's position would have sought glory on the battlefield. In peacetime, Bobby had few choices. Bemoan fate or feed himself and his family.

Quickly, Wylie searched his memory, racing through twenty years of his father's letters. Bobby had married outside the district . . . Madeline? No, Matilda. Matilda and three boys.

"I hear you've married a bonnie lass from up near Inverness. Matilda, aye? And you've three braw lads to show for it?"

Nodding, Bobby grinned. "Aye and another on its way," he said, his pride evident. He pointed in the direction of the township. "And I've a small herd of my own as well as a goat."

"You're doing well, then. Will I meet Matilda?" he asked.

"She'll be in the glen with the bairns through July. Ye've fine lads, yourself, Wylie. Anna brought them by." Bobby shifted, suddenly seeming discomfited. "I ken well it's not my place to ask, but the thing is, well, ye'll be staying, aye?"

The question caught Wylie off guard, and he shrank at the worry behind it. He may have disclaimed responsibility for Glencorach and its tenants, but for now, the responsibility was his and his alone.

For all he knew, Moy's lease may soon expire.

What were Montgomery's plans for these tenants? Did he plan extensions or evictions?

"Some things need settling." Confessing he'd soon be on a ship bound for Florida would do little to ease Bobby's worry.

Besides, Father must have thought Montgomery a fair and reasonable man. He'd not have proposed handing him his estate otherwise. Montgomery would extend the leases.

Bobby's shoulders dropped, and his mouth twitched as if he wanted to probe. Instead, he said, "We all grieve your father, Wylie."

Silent, Wylie nodded. His own grief too raw, he'd not share memories in the midst of an open field.

Bobby, seeming to understand, canted his head in the direction of his own father's house. "He'll know ye're coming." Turning, he went back to his field.

Watching him go, Wylie frowned, tempted to call him back. Surely he could offer *some* reassurance, no matter how slight.

"Who will know we are coming, Papa?" Dougal asked.

Shaking his head, Wylie turned. He couldn't reassure Bobby of a damned thing. Which was why he shouldn't be wandering these fields. He should be at Glencorach, mending the damned gate. He was here to settle the estate and pass it on, no more.

"Mr. Moy," Wylie said. Moy's own tenants served as lookouts as well as farmers. The arrangement allowed him time to conceal his illegal stills if a threat approached.

Moy hadn't thought Wylie a threat twenty years prior. But now?

"Let's go," he said, suddenly curious. The gate could wait.

Moy's thatched cottage wasn't in the township. Tucked in the lower folds of the Monadhliaths, it sat in a secluded glen beside a burn. Behind the cottage, the burn narrowed and darkened. Granite, tufted with heather at its base and juniper at its peaks, towered over each of the stream's banks, nearly meeting in the middle.

The situation, a perfect cover for Moy's illicit activities, resembled a tunnel. In the past, the shadowy passage concealed several working stills and an underground cache of jugs.

Wylie found Robert Moy standing at the side of his cottage, deep in conversation with three men. Two of the three were strangers to Wylie. The third was a man he'd just met.

I'll be damned. Jay Macpherson.

Wylie paused in the yard, keeping a respectful distance while straining to hear something of their topic. But nothing, not even the timbre of voices, pierced the stream's roar.

Waving a welcoming hand, Moy concluded his conversation and crossed the yard to greet Wylie and his boys.

Wylie studied the group Moy left behind. Both strangers wore broadswords; one also carried a pistol. Those were the visible weapons; who knew what they concealed beneath clothing.

If Wylie had to guess, they were from outside the local clans. Broken men, perhaps, outside all clans. He didn't believe them drovers. Their bearing was too wary.

Perhaps they were reivers. If not, then men hired to retrieve stolen cattle from reivers.

Moy drew near, and Wylie shifted his attention. Like Bobby, Moy was wiry and short in stature. Unlike Bobby, his dark eyes constantly darted this way and that.

"Glencorach," Moy said, addressing Wylie. "It's been a long time." He acknowledged Will and Dougal with a nod.

Wylie blinked at Moy's use of his father's title, then responded, "Aye, Mr. Moy." After exchanging a few pleasantries and acknowledging Moy's condolences, Wylie indicated the armed men and asked, "Those two friends of yours?"

Moy shook his head. "Hell, no."

Then Jay's? Jay seemed to know enough of them to be uneasy. His shifting posture brought to mind a hare caught between a fox and a hound, as if he couldn't decide which way to flee.

The odd thing was, Jay's gaze kept shifting toward Wylie, as if *he* were one of the predators.

"They come for the whisky," Moy said. "Come on inside and sit a spell. The missus has a pot on the fire."

Wylie's lips quirked. Moy didn't trust him.

Fair enough. The man hadn't seen him for decades—he was right to be cautious. Still, Wylie would lose sight of Jay if he went inside, and he was curious about the lad's connection with the others. "Could we talk over a few matters first?"

"Oh, aye," Moy said, a shrewd glint lighting his eyes. He canted his head toward the cottage. "Go on in, Will. Take Dougal. Mrs. Moy expects ye."

Did she, then? How . . . snug. Anna had been thorough in acclimating his boys.

Why did that irritate him?

Because acclimating them was his duty, and he'd shrugged it.

And what of it? Many of these families had lost a brother,

father, son or husband in that war. Was he to blame if he couldn't face those surviving, knowing full well their men would be alive if they hadn't followed their lairds' sons?

Will caught Wylie's eye, a question in his. Wylie nodded his consent. Placing a hand on his brother's shoulder, Will started toward the cottage. When they reached it, he cuffed Dougal's shoulder and pushed him over the threshold. Before following, he went to Jay, exchanged a few words, then stooped and pet the dog at Jay's feet.

Hell, Jay too? Anna had indeed been busy.

"Ye'll have talked with Will, then, aye?" Moy said.

Wylie waited until Will turned toward the cottage before he looked back at Moy. "What's that?"

"Ye'll have talked with Will? The lad thought we might come to some arrangement."

A kernel of dread took root in Wylie's chest. *Devil take it, Will. What did you tell him?*

Moy made it his business to know something of everyone. How he managed it, Wylie hadn't a clue. But he had no doubt Moy knew he dealt in smuggled goods.

Given Moy's occupation, he'd be quick to perceive an opportunity. Perhaps he'd tested the waters with Will. And Will, with a nose for profit as keen as Wylie's partner, Alec, may have responded in kind.

With effort, Wylie kept his face impassive and let instinct drive his answer. "Now's not the time, Mr. Moy." Moy was capable of molding a situation to his advantage. Until Wylie spoke with Will, Wylie couldn't be certain who had said what.

"He seems a sharp sort, your lad Will," Moy said, apparently judging now *was* the time.

"Oh, aye, he is that."

Will, after apprenticing for years in his mother's family shop, had turned an eye toward Wylie's business once Rennie passed. It was a risky business at best, and Wylie wasn't keen to take the lad on. Recognizing Will's competence, his partner Alec was.

"Lad says ye might lend me a hand with the distribution side of my endeavor."

So there it was, then, and the ink barely dry on his pardon. Wylie blew out a breath, irritated. "Did he, then?"

"Aye. He said ye had a profitable market for whisky." Moy held his gaze, intent.

Damn you, Will. You've not a clue what you've done.

"I'm not certain it's wise, Mr. Moy. I'm likely under some scrutiny."

"It'd be worth your while."

With an exciseman nosing round the district? He doubted it. "What's Jay Macpherson doing here?" he asked, changing the subject.

"Same as the others," Moy answered. As they watched, Jay tucked something inside his coat.

"How well does he know those men?"

Moy shrugged, his eyes darting to the side. "The lad's a customer. I expect he's met them from time to time."

"Hmmph." It wouldn't hurt George to keep a closer eye on his son. "Tell me about the excise," he said, feigning interest in Moy's endeavor. He had his own reason for wanting to know more of Montgomery, and Moy was an excellent source.

"He's easily enough handled, once ye know what he's about."

Wylie's gaze narrowed. Complacency was dangerous. "Which is?"

"Montgomery's one of those who feels he's less than enough. So long as ye make him feel he's worth reckoning with, ye'll have no trouble. I heard Customs didn't want him. Transferred him to Excise. Seems he's a'feared of the sea."

Wylie's mouth flattened. Anyone with half a brain carried fear of the sea. No man with a quarter of a brain would admit it. "Does he come by often?"

"More often than warranted. He's had his eye on the Macrae gal for some time now."

So it was true. An unexpected niggle of irritation flared. "Is he in your pocket?" Wylie asked, ignoring the sensation.

If the man was corrupt, he had no business courting Anna.

"Nay." Moy grinned, adding, "Not that he knows. Once in a while, the lads and I get careless, ken. Intentional like. Give the cove a chance to make a seizure."

A sideways bribe. Revenue men were permitted to keep a portion of the seizures they made. Occasionally a smuggler might intentionally allow goods to fall into an officer's hands. It accomplished the objective—the exciseman eased off, his pockets padded—and it implicated neither party in a bribe.

"He's satisfied, then?"

Moy raised a side of his mouth in a sardonic grin. Scratching his chin, he shook his head. "Can't claim that. Montgomery misses the clues more oft than not. But what more can I do? Deliver whisky to his doorstep?" Moy shrugged. "I offer the cove coin, he's liable to clamp chains on my wrists."

Wylie grunted, trusting Moy's appraisal. Moy hadn't survived all these years by misjudging the opposition. Still, in Wylie's experience, excisemen didn't miss opportunities to make a quick seizure. Nor, he thought, did Anna tolerate fools.

Something didn't fit.

Either that or, as Alec had become fond of claiming, Wylie was losing his nerve.

Easy enough for Alec to judge. He didn't have two sons in his sole care; he could afford to be reckless.

"I ken what ye're thinking, Glencorach. But in truth, Montgomery's slow to catch on. There's no risk coming from that quarter. Think on it, aye?"

He'd think about it long enough to write Alec and tell him to lay off Will. As for Will, he'd find a different approach; Will paid less heed to Wylie's dictates than he did a buzzing fly. "I'd like to help you Mr. Moy, but I must pass. I'm leaving shortly."

A side of Moy's mouth fell, and he stepped back. "If that's the way of it, there are matters we must discuss at once." He jerked his head toward the group. "I best be seeing those gentlemen off. Wait, aye?"

"Of course."

Jay strode toward Wylie, passing Moy without speaking. He seemed at ease now, and the dog, a collie, trotted beside him.

"Cousin Wylie," Jay said. "It's good to see you again."

"Hello, Jay." The hours since breakfast had been kind to the young man. He no longer looked ill. "Were those friends of yours?"

An odd expression passed over Jay, as if mention of the men made him uneasy. Then he shook his head. "No."

Wylie thought of pressing, but discarded the impulse. It wasn't his place, and he had enough on his hands with his own sons. "Are you headed for London?"

"London?" Jay seemed surprised at the question and shook his head.

Perhaps the lad dozed through that portion of this morning's conversation. "My mistake."

"I'm off for Inverness later today."

"You live in Inverness?" Wylie asked, curious.

"No, but an opportunity arose there that I can't afford to ignore. When I return, I hope we might speak of Glencorach."

Wylie stiffened. "Oh?" What possible interest could George Macpherson's son have in Wylie's estate?

"I won't be gone long," Jay said agreeably, seeming unfazed at the edge in Wylie's tone. "I hope to speak with you before Mother does. I've asked her not to speak to you at all, but she's rather headstrong."

Wylie's brows knit at the mention of Miriam. She'd never shown an interest in Glencorach. Perhaps she simply hoped to speak with him alone and had fabricated a business-like reason.

Would he welcome the opportunity? He frowned. Hell if he knew.

Jay bent, stroking the dog's head. "This is Molly. She was one of Uncle William's dogs. We were headed to Glencorach. I thought you might keep her while you're here. The drovers left her at the shielings with the women, and she wouldn't stay."

Miriam forgotten, Wylie bit his bottom lip. Why hadn't he thought to ask who cared for his father's dogs? "Um, I . . . "

"I know you're leaving, sir," Jay hastened to add. "But I thought while you were here, Molly could spend time at Glencorach before returning to Grandfather's kennel. I think she misses Uncle William. Will said he would take care of her."

Wylie regarded Jay for a moment, taking note of his earnestness. Then he knelt and extended a hand. The collie stepped forward and sniffed, studying Wylie with soft brown eyes.

I'm a poor substitute for him, Molly. But Will might suit.

"Thank you, Jay. That was thoughtful." And something the lad's father would have done, before he'd turned treacherous. "I expect we can keep her for a day or two." He stood and searched for a trace of George in Jay's answering smile, but found none.

Drawing a thin rope from his pocket, Jay looped it over the dog's head and handed the end to Wylie. "You won't need this once she sees her home." Taking a step back, he stretched out a palm. "Stay, Molly." The dog whined twice, then sat and thumped her tail on the dirt. Jay walked away.

The men turned from Moy at the same time. One of them took a path leading west into the hills. The other headed into the canyon. With a scowl and a head shake aimed toward Wylie, Moy followed. Wylie took it to mean their own conversation would be postponed. He watched Jay, curious as to which party he'd follow. Surprisingly, Jay followed neither and instead walked the trail to Cragdurcas.

Wylie looked down at the dog, who now gazed up at him.

"Do you fancy a task, Molly?" The dog's eyes brightened, and she balanced her weight from one front paw to the other, alert and seemingly awaiting orders. "Well enough, then. You've met your quarry. You're to tear down the lad's defenses, if only for an hour."

Once Will had hung on Wylie's every word. Given an hour, Wylie could surely set the lad straight. Under no circumstances would Wylie ply his trade in the Highlands.

He ran his fingers over his neck, imagining the chafing hangman's noose.

CHAPTER 13

"IT'S LOVELY, isn't it, Miss Macrae?" Archibald Montgomery reined in the carriage horse and indicated the vista with a flap of his hand. Bloomhall, the seat of Englishman Arthur Bloomfield, towered in the meadow below, its image mirrored in the adjacent loch. "If I don't look too far afield, I fancy I'm far from this dreadful place and back in England."

Be cordial, Anna. Many men speak without thinking.

Built for display rather than defense, Bloomhall wasn't the least bit grim. And unlike the estates she was accustomed to, formal gardens surrounded the Georgian manor—gardens with no eye toward function. Anna turned to Montgomery, her smile pleasant.

"It *is* lovely, sir." They were in Scotland after all.

Mr. Montgomery was a decade older than her and several inches shorter. His physique was slight, more so than her own, and she feared he'd falter if tasked with carrying a full pail of milk from the barn. He wasn't altogether unattractive, however. He had large owl-like brown eyes which often softened in what she imagined was affection, a set of rosebud lips she envied, and a ruddy, unmarked complexion.

Returning her smile, he fumbled beneath the seat and pulled forth a bottle of ale. Uncorking it, he took a long draw. After an audible swallow, he extended the bottle. "I'm so pleased you changed your mind and came. You'll enjoy it, I assure you."

She wasn't as certain. For people of her station, the acceptable entry into such an estate was through the service entry. But if nothing else, she was curious; Bloomhall's gatherings were notorious.

Most nearby Englishmen were military officers living a frugal rural life on half-pay. Mr. Bloomfield of Bloomhall was the exception. As rich as Croesus, he owned sugar plantations in Jamaica and Barbados. Her mother had always claimed an excess of money led to idleness, and idleness, in turn, led to debauchery. She'd warned Anna repeatedly to keep clear of Bloomhall.

Her mother needn't have worried. This was Anna's first and only invitation to the estate, and the occasion promised no debauchery. Mr. Montgomery, primly protective of her virtue, had promised her father they'd depart promptly at six, immediately following the afternoon's music.

Not that she minded. She hadn't time for debauchery.

Declining the ale, Anna murmured a polite response—the same she'd given his prior assurances. "I'm certain I shall. I've not had the opportunity to visit before."

Raising his chin a notch, Montgomery squared his shoulders, as if pleased he could enrich her domain. "I've been often, though this will be the first time this season. Mr. Bloomfield returned only last week."

The horse swung its head, straining to reach a bit of foliage, and the carriage rocked. The ale bottle tipped and spilled. While Mr. Montgomery scrambled out of its reach, Anna grabbed the bottle and swiped the spill before it wet her gown.

"D'ye have the cork, sir?" she asked, extending a wet palm.

His face pink, he fumbled for it in his waistcoat and then in his jacket, not meeting her gaze. Forgoing a sigh, Anna raised the bottle and took several long swallows. It was a good quality ale, somewhat stronger than the watered ale she was accustomed to. Perhaps she should finish it.

At length Mr. Montgomery located the cork. After capping and stowing the bottle, he snapped the reins. The carriage lurched, and Anna fell back against the seat. They began a swaying descent down the rutted track, and she gripped the handrail, intent on not colliding with Montgomery. God forbid he think her forward, or worse, take the contact as an invitation.

One day she might welcome his touch. Today was not that day.

At the bottom of the hill, two servants, both dressed much finer than herself, hurried across a gravel drive toward them. One took the reins, and the other helped her descend. To his credit, he didn't blink at her well-worn gray frock.

Montgomery rounded the carriage to stand at her side.

"Mr. Bloomfield suggests his early guests enjoy the gardens," the footman said. "Shall I lead the way, sir?"

Montgomery's mouth thinned and a muscle pulsed in his cheek, as if he were pained their host wasn't standing by, awaiting them. Anna intervened, before his pettiness colored the afternoon gray.

"I should like nothing more. Could we, Mr. Montgomery?"

Montgomery blinked twice before answering, his eyes softening instantly when she smiled. "Oh. Well then, yes. Yes, indeed."

He raised his elbow, and she placed her hand on his arm, relieved he hadn't snapped at the footman. They followed the man up the stone steps and inside.

Anna did her best not to gawk once inside. Bypassing a mahogany staircase that flowed to the second floor, the servant led them down a massive, portrait-lined hall toward a set of glazed terrace doors, then out onto a wide stone terrace.

"Oh my," she said softly, sucking in a breath. Flowers, all in manicured beds free of weeds, blanketed a lawn that sloped toward the loch. The beds were separated by paths of the same width, giving the garden a boxy, orderly appearance.

Envisioning the effort it required to create and maintain, Anna shook her head slowly, astonished.

She hastened down the steps and onto a path, still gripping Montgomery's arm. "'Tis very orderly, aye? I fear Mr. Bloomfield's garden shames mine."

"I haven't had the pleasure of seeing yours."

She laughed. "Oh, ye have, for cert. It surrounds the cottage."

His face reddened to the line of his wig.

Lord, she'd embarrassed him. "Ye'll not be the first to mistake it, Mr. Montgomery." Given the orderliness of most aspects of her life, she took pleasure in her garden growing wild. Besides, she scarcely had time to manicure her appearance, much less a garden's.

He coughed into his fist and changed the subject. "I'm astonished you've lived here all your life and have never been to Bloomhall."

She doubted he was astonished in the slightest, as they'd covered the topic several times this afternoon. It seemed she hadn't shown a proper appreciation for his connections. "Truly? Well, tis unlikely a factor's daughter would be receiving such a grand invitation. So I'm delighted ye've requested my company. I'd have not had the chance to see these gardens otherwise."

"I know you'll equally enjoy the music." His tone turned eager. "I believe the musicians will play Handel's Water Music. I heard it performed at the gardens in London several years ago. Handel wrote it for the king, you know. Did I ever tell you my father attended the river party where it was first—"

Oh please, not again. "Ye did," Anna interrupted. One would think his father had received a personal engraved invitation from King George himself, when from all accounts half of London had attended that river party.

"Oh."

He looked so crestfallen that Anna regretted her bad manners. Shamed, she hastened to fill the silence. "Are today's musicians from London?"

"I believe so. Mr. Bloomfield's daughter is one of them, and she's up from London."

"Ye're speaking of Sarah?" Anna paused to admire an unfamiliar flower. An unusual shade of orange, it would set off her bluebells to perfection.

He blinked, seeming surprised. "Yes, I believe her Christian name is Sarah. You know her?"

Anna shook her head. "Only of her. She and Miriam Macpherson were once close." Sarah resided at Bloomhall often when she was younger, the last time being during the '45 Rising. Sarah and Miriam, both fifteen and beautiful, had quickly become friends. Given the intoxicating lack of a mother's supervision and the constant presence of redcoats visiting Bloomhall, it wasn't long before the girls set tongues to wagging. There'd been talk of Sarah marrying one of those visiting soldiers.

"Truly? Miriam of the Cragdurcas Macphersons?" Montgomery asked. "I suppose the Macphersons were invited today, then. Do you think they'll come?"

Anna gritted her teeth. Of course they were invited. Aside from Bloomfield, Henry Macpherson was the largest landholder in a twenty-mile radius. The squire had invited the Macphersons, William included, to his home many times over the years. They didn't often accept.

But would they come today?

Henry wouldn't. He still mourned the loss of his brother. Jay and Miriam, perhaps, though Anna wasn't certain Miriam and Sarah were still friends. In any event, she doubted George would come. He rarely accompanied his wife. Anna suspected Miriam preferred it that way.

"I don't know," Anna answered. Her gaze slid past him toward the terrace, and she noted others stepping outside. While they were still alone, she knelt, quickly snipped the orange bloom between her thumb and forefinger and palmed it. The gardener would never miss it, and the seeds might germinate.

"If they do come, they'll bring the cousin with them, won't they?" Montgomery asked, oblivious to her petty larceny. "I'm anxious to meet him. Tell me, has your father spoken to him about Glencorach?"

"Aye, he has."

He helped her rise, frowning, and they continued walking. "I do wish he'd keep me informed."

For mercy's sake, Wylie had been here mere days. There was nothing her father could relate.

"I believe Father merely reacquainted Mr. Macpherson with general estate matters." Slanting away, she slipped the bloom into her reticule.

"Be that as it may, I hoped for some certainty by now. I assume you've spoken with the man. What did you think? Does he appear to have repented?"

Anna's cheeks heated at the thought of last night.

Nonsense, she chided herself. Just because she couldn't shake the thought of that kiss didn't mean Montgomery shared her obsession. He knew nothing of it.

"Repented for what?"

He stopped in his tracks and turned wearing a glare, apparently appalled at her ignorance. "He rebelled against the king, Miss Macrae."

Oh. That. She rocked back a step and bit her lip, stifling a self-deprecating smile. "I'm certain he's repented for that, Mr. Montgomery. Besides, the king has pardoned him."

Montgomery sniffed, seeming skeptical. "I've written to London about him."

She gaped at him, momentarily speechless, and her heart rate quickened in alarm. Mr. Montgomery wouldn't be the first revenue officer who advanced his career providing intelligence on the Scots. But Lord, that rebellion was twenty-five years in the past. What could he possibly write?

Had she put Wylie at risk by encouraging him to return?

"I am a king's officer, Miss Macrae," he said, seeming to sense her astonishment.

"But . . . why would you do that?"

He placed a hand at the small of her back and guided her toward the loch, a discreet distance from other guests. "I have a moral duty to know the affairs of those residing in my district. Tell me, what has he been doing?"

Doing? Living his life, as they all had been. "How do you mean, sir?" she asked, confused.

"Has the Stuart court provided his support?"

What rubbish. She stopped walking and stared at him, wondering if he'd gone daft. The Stuart court had no call to support Wylie. "Of course not."

"Then how has he lived? Was his father sending him money all these years?" He rubbed his chin, suddenly appearing thoughtful. "I suppose that would explain the estate's condition."

Her jaw set hard, and she turned from him. As if Wylie would take money from William. And aside from the fact that it involved trading, she wasn't entirely certain what it was that Wylie did. William had been uncharacteristically cagey at the subject of his son's livelihood.

A rhythmic, repetitive whoosh sounded overhead, and she looked up. An osprey sailed toward the loch, its legs extended and its talons curved in a matched set of blades. Without warning it plunged feet first into the calm, black water, disappearing in a wide-spread splash. When it resurfaced, it clutched a squirming trout whose size rivaled its own.

For a moment it seemed as if the fish might win the struggle and drag the osprey back under. Soon, however, the osprey garnered strength and took flight. Airborne, its prize firmly entrapped, it shook and shivered above her, water streaming from its plumage.

Droplets hit her face, and she shuddered, wrapping her arms around her middle. Were the droplets from the raptor? Or from its helpless prey?

The osprey's quarry had been outmatched. As would Wylie, she feared, if the government took an interest in him once more.

"Miss Macrae, are you listening? As an officer of the king, I should know if Glencorach has been used to provide a rebel's support."

She wished he'd stop referring to Wylie as a rebel. She swiped a thumb over her cheek and faced him. She'd not hand an "officer of the king" a weapon if she could help it. The Scots were outmatched as it was.

"It's my understanding he married a prominent merchant's daughter," she said, purposefully ambiguous. Not knowing Wylie, Mr. Montgomery may conclude Wylie lived off his wife's largesse.

"Ah," Montgomery said with a sagely nod. "Well then, do you think he'll cause trouble while he's here?"

"I do not." She wasn't certain what trouble Wylie *could* cause, even if he were of a mind to. In fact, Mr. Montgomery seemed the one intent on causing—or even manufacturing—trouble. Perhaps to further his career, perhaps to lower the asking price of Glencorach.

He sniffed. "I suppose time will tell."

She nodded absently, grateful he seemed to have set aside his suspicions. She'd come here to forget her obsession with Wylie, not to dwell on it.

"Tell me. What did you think of the man?"

Mother Mary. *So* many questions. Did he intend to court her or not?

Was she wrong to expect Montgomery to sit beside her on a lakeside bench? Wrong to think that they might listen to Spring's song while the sun warmed their shoulders? She hadn't been courted in years. She swallowed a sigh. "Perhaps you should speak with my father." A bell sounded across the garden, summoning guests inside.

"You told me you were childhood friends," he said, shaking his head in apparent exasperation.

Her heart sank as her confidence fled. She'd always known Mr. Montgomery sought a marriage of convenience. Yet she thought he might care for her, if only a smidge. That he might *want* to court her, if given the chance.

It ought not to matter, but it did. It had been heartening to believe someone fancied a life spent by her side. She blinked several times, her eyes moist. It had been a mistake to come. She'd know no one inside. She didn't belong here; her gown was decades from *any* current fashion, and she'd left hours of chores unanswered.

Her shoulders dropping, she ignored his probing and asked, "Have you heard Mr. Bloomfield's daughter play?"

"I . . . I haven't had the pleasure," Montgomery said, seeming flustered by the switch in subject. He looked toward the house. "I imagine the hall is filling. Shall we find a seat?"

Nodding, she placed a hand on his arm, scarcely noticing the garden as they retraced their steps.

A servant met them at the terrace and directed them through a northerly door and into a large red-papered ballroom. Anna's nose twitched at the smell of cold, damp neglect. Chandeliers hung the length of the room, heavy with unlit candles and crystal drops that shimmered each time the door to the outside opened and shut. Wood fires smoldered in three cavernous hearths but did little to warm the shadowy room.

Rows of chairs were the only furnishings. She and Mr. Montgomery took seats in the back, silent while the room filled. Idly, Anna counted the chandeliers' candles until she noticed a plainly dressed woman in the second row rise and wave her way.

Why, Mary Tanner. Or rather, Mary Macpherson; she'd wed Ewan Macpherson of Inverness, a banker, some five years back. Anna visited the couple on her market treks. She smiled, returning the gesture.

Mary's husband, Ewan, tugged on his wife's arm, and Mary bent and whispered something in his ear. With a wide grin, Ewan swiveled and waved. Mouthing the word "after," Mary sat.

Alice Brock was here as well. And Sybil Ferguson. And goodness, so was Sybil's sister, Sarah Ferguson. All wearing nothing more elaborate than their Sunday best. Her humor restored, Anna settled into her seat while Mr. Montgomery chatted companionably with the man sitting beside him.

At the far end of the room, a servant set out music stands and lit the accompanying candles. Four dark-haired men, their coats, neckcloths and breeches all black, strode into the room, one carrying a violin, three carrying wind instruments. A tall woman dressed in white accompanied them. Fair-haired, with a thin face and high forehead, the woman was assuredly Sarah, for she carried a violin.

Anna had assumed the afternoon promised a simple string quartet, something she saw rarely enough. The prospect of wind instruments was a treat. She shifted in her seat for a better view and studied Sarah. She looked older than Anna had expected.

Years older than Miriam, in any event.

Mercy, Anna herself looked older than Miriam, so that was hardly surprising. Miriam had perfected an artifice with her cosmetics; she had little else to occupy her time. Wylie would find her unchanged.

It had always mystified her that Wylie hadn't the wits to see past Miriam's appearance. He wasn't a dolt. Quite the opposite. Yet he'd somehow missed the fact that Miriam had cared no more for him than she had for five others.

She'd asked her mother her opinion at the time. Laughing, her mother told her it took some men longer to see truths than others—but in the end, each invariably did.

Invariably? Anna wondered. Miriam had once bewitched the sense right out of Wylie. She may easily do so again.

Enough!

She was here to enjoy an afternoon with a man who may soon be her husband—not to fret over the reluctant laird. Why should she care if Wylie took up with Miriam once more?

Other than to be sad for George, of course.

Mr. Montgomery was right. She might hurry that sale. Now that Wylie was back, Henry would forgive that note, and with her help, other matters could be quickly handled. Her lips firming, she nodded. She'd speak to her father tomorrow.

Just then two gentleman carrying large brass horns walked in. Anna's eyes widened, her mouth forming an O of surprise. She'd never heard horns played. Dressed in long black coats and gold-striped waistcoats, the gentlemen took seats beside the other musicians and adjusted their music stands.

She turned to Mr. Montgomery, who smiled broadly, seeming just as delighted.

Facing forward, she grinned. Perhaps with a bit more effort, she might come to like this man.

The first chords sounded. She closed her eyes, allowing the melody to nudge aside any lingering worries.

Life would return to normal. Perhaps even now, Wylie and the lads stood aboard the afternoon ferry.

EARLY THE next morning, Wylie stood at his father's washstand and shaved by candlelight, his gaze alternating between his flickering image and the dimly lit road outside the window. If Uncle Henry came at dawn, he'd find Wylie waiting.

Misjudging the curve of his chin, Wylie nicked his neck and muttered a curse. He reached for a cloth and held it against the cut for a moment, then dipped it into the frigid wash water and pressed it over his face, hoping the cold might clear his muddled thoughts.

One of the few memories he had of his mother was at this window. She'd often wake him early so that they might watch the sun inch over the peak of Cairn Toul. On days like today, when the snow-covered summit reflected a soft yellow and the sky a steel blue, she'd pull him close and whisper, "This will be a good day, Wylie."

It *would* be a good day. It must.

Uncle Henry would come as promised. Their business could be complete by noon, and his business with Alan immediately thereafter. He'd take the afternoon ferry and be aboard the *Eliza* by month's end.

Grace, one of Martha's nieces, stood at the foot of the stairs when Wylie descended an hour later. "Your uncle waits in the parlor, sir."

"Thank you. Bring some tea or something. Martha will know."

Bobbing her head, the girl scurried down the hall. Wylie entered the parlor and found his uncle seated in his father's armchair.

Claiming the master's chair. One point to Henry.

"Good morning, lad." Grabbing the cane by his side, Henry rose and hobbled two steps toward Wylie.

"Are you ailing, Uncle Henry?" Placing one hand on his uncle's shoulder, Wylie steered him back to the chair.

"Comes and goes, lad," Henry said, lowering himself inch by inch into the chair. "My health is failing. It won't be long before I join your father."

Two points. Wylie grimaced, already exasperated. Scheming old buzzard had been fine the day prior. Did he truly plan to play this card?

"It grieves me to hear that, Uncle."

"Hmmph. Some say ye haven't a care for your family."

Wylie's head came up sharply. *The hell you say.* He bit his tongue until it pained him and said nothing.

Unlike some he could name, he'd *never* betrayed this family. Not once.

Grace returned with a tray of refreshments, so quickly that it seemed Martha had prepared ahead. She set it down, and his uncle waved her away.

Another man might have bristled at Henry's proprietary air. Wylie ignored it. He hoped to rid himself of Glencorach, not claim it.

Besides, the "family" comment rankled. When had he *ever* turned his back on his family? He hadn't climbed aboard that ship to France. Wounded and unconscious, he'd been transported, abandoned, and then exiled.

Not a day passed since that he hadn't worried over his father.

"Let's get to it, shall we?" Henry said, seeming oblivious to Wylie's simmering anger. "I believe we have the matter of a mortgage to settle."

Startled, Wylie tempered his thoughts. He'd half expected his uncle might sidestep the topic for a bit, if only to remind Wylie who had the upper hand.

Clasping his hands behind his back, Wylie gave a curt nod. "We do, and I'll come right to the point. I'd like you to mark the mortgage paid-in-full so that the sale may proceed."

"Hmmph. I haven't seen a pence in payment. Will ye have me perjure myself, then?" Taking a scone, Henry settled back into the armchair. "Sit, will ye, lad?"

Pence in payment, his arse. Dragging a hand across the back of his neck, Wylie blew out a breath, resigned. So there *would* be a battle.

He moved the tea tray to the parlor table and replaced it with the decanter and two cups. Then he picked up a tableside chair, positioned it directly in front of his uncle, and sat.

"It was my impression that the note was not valid," Wylie said, keeping his voice even. Leaning forward, he poured a small measure of whisky into each cup, passed one to his uncle, and sprawled back in his chair with the other.

"It's a sham through and through, lad," Henry said, nodding either his agreement or his thanks for the dram. "I falsified a financial document with the full intent to defraud our government. A crime it was, make no mistake. But it's happy I was to do it, for the sake of my nephew's future."

Wylie nearly smiled, impressed in spite of himself. Trust the old man to spin a tale whilst keeping to the truth. Uncle Henry wouldn't have wanted Glencorach to land in the government's hands any more than Wylie's father would have. "Aye, well. I appreciate your foresight, Uncle, I do. But my future lies elsewhere, so I'm hoping we can come to an agreement."

"What is it ye propose, lad?"

Wasn't that obvious? "I propose we tear up all copies of the note as if it never existed."

"Do ye, now? How many copies do ye suppose that is?"

He hadn't actually considered how many and was unsure why it mattered. Humoring the man, he took a guess. "Three. As it was a sham from the start, I can't see Alan troubling to make more than a copy for you, Father, and himself."

"Aye, there'll be those." Henry popped the last bit of scone into his mouth and then sipped his whisky, brushing crumbs from his jacket. "Then there will be the copy for the Commission for Forfeited Estates. See here, lad. I'm famished. Bring that tray back, will ye?"

The commission? Lost in thought, Wylie retrieved the tea tray and set it on the hearth.

Father hadn't written of the commission. Not once.

Swift vengeance had come on the heels of the '45 Rising. Tasked with seizing rebels' estates, the government's men scoured the Highlands. Macpherson of Cluny's home had been seized, and that was only miles off.

Cluny, however, had been chieftain. Wylie had been a mere fifteen-year-old lad, one of no consequence and certainly no property. Why had *he* warranted a commissioner's attention?

He cleared his throat, hoping his voice wouldn't sound faint.

"The commission?"

"Aye, the commissioners turned this district upside down in '47. One of them knew ye for William's only heir. Alan gave him a copy of the note so he'd know Glencorach was not worth the attention. And then, of course, there will be the court copy," his uncle added, turning from Wylie while he chose another scone. "Alan recommended I file a creditor's claim with the court, ken, so I'd be protected from any other claimants. There'll be a record of that."

Good God, why?

"But why, Uncle Henry? Why go to the trouble? Father was alive and well. He carried no suspicion on his account, and there was no reason to believe I'd inherit. For all the government knew, I was dead."

Scone in hand, Henry straightened. "Ye think the army didna ken where it was ye were, ye're a damned fool. William got word within weeks of your signing on with that French privateer." Henry shook his head, as if resigned to his nephew's foolhardiness. "Thank God ye had the sense to sail with one plundering the Spanish and not the English."

The army didn't know half as much as it thought it did, then. At his captain's orders, Wylie had boarded each and every ship captured. Many of the privateer's victims had flown Britain's colors.

It was true that once he captained his own ship, he didn't accept commissions to harass the British. But that wasn't due to any lingering regard for his mother country. It was merely because the rewards were small. The Spanish, not the British, habitually carried small fortunes. Besides, he'd known George was aboard Britain's ships from time to time. He'd not raise a sword against his treacherous cousin, no matter the circumstances.

Some in this family retained a shred of loyalty.

He sipped his whisky, letting it linger on his tongue until it burned, and waited a beat before answering.

"Aye, well, the fact remains that my father was alive and well. I didn't stand to inherit, so the trouble seems unwarranted."

"Perhaps ye're not the best judge of what was warranted, given your absence."

Christ's sake, so now it was *his* fault he'd been absent?

"Uncle—"

"I don't want to hear it, Wylie. That escapade of yours and George's had far reaching consequences, and it was your father and I left dealing with those consequences. Everything we did, including your cousin's testimony, we did because we thought it for the best."

Wylie's fist tightened around his glass, his pulse pounding at the mention of George's testimony, and he swallowed back a wave of nausea.

Keep at this, Uncle, and you can keep your note. Glencorach be damned.

Is that so, Wylie Macpherson? And what of our boys?

He blinked. *Criminy, Rennie. Rest in peace, will you?*

He may not always know the lads' whereabouts, but he hadn't forgotten them.

Swallowing, Wylie kept quiet until his pulse slowed. He'd not be baited into losing his temper, nor would he be coerced into dropping the matter, if indeed that was what Henry intended.

"What is it you suggest then, Uncle?" he asked in a measured tone.

"I have a proposition."

Of course he did. Wylie remained silent, waiting. It best not require that he sit and chat with his snake of a cousin.

"I'll not tear the note up as if it were never valid. But I'm prepared to mark it paid in exchange for services rendered. And make no mistake, lad, I intend to collect."

Services?

Wylie took a deep breath and released it slowly. "Rendered by me, I expect?"

"Aye."

"Should I assume you have the service in mind?"

"Aye, I've several. The most urgent is the schoolmaster. The position came vacant last month."

What the devil? Wylie fell back in his chair, certain he'd misheard.

"You want *me* to be a schoolmaster?"

"Don't play the idiot. We need to fill the position and negotiate the salary. We are the only landowners left in this parish, and the kirk session has put us on notice. I haven't the inclination to do it on my own. I expect ye to attend to your responsibilities as heritor."

Wylie almost laughed, the notion ludicrous. Wylie Macpherson, last in his class, choosing a schoolmaster. Was this a farce? "I haven't any notion of a schoolmaster's qualifications," he said, watching his uncle closely.

"Ye propose to leave me with the duty alone?"

It was a small parish, and there were few landowners. However, Wylie recalled there being three, not two. "Angus Gordon of Balcor is a heritor, aye? Surely he—"

"Balcor hasn't resided in the Highlands since he married that Sassenach wench in '62."

"His factor, then."

"His factor claims he hasn't the authority. Don't think your father and I didn't try. Balcor will cover his share of the expense. He has to date, at any rate." Henry shrugged. "Face it, lad. The parish holds only two heritors of consequence. Macpherson of Cragdurcas and Macpherson of Glencorach. How will it look to the elders if ye abandon your responsibilities so soon after your pardon?"

If this was a farce, he had to hand the man credit. He seemed to have considered all implications.

It would cause talk if Wylie ignored the elders. As a rule, the elders comprising the kirk session were chosen from the most close-minded, sanctimonious men in the parish. Still, what did he care? The elders could grumble until they choked on their bile; he'd not be here to hear it.

"It's not I mind helping you, Uncle. But again, I know nothing of choosing a schoolmaster." He wasn't prevaricating. He truly knew nothing—Rennie had dealt with their sons' schooling. It seemed an important task, however, and interviewing candidates could take weeks. Then, no matter who they chose, the elders would find fault and the parishioners would quibble. That was the way of things.

Henry reached for the decanter and refilled his cup. "It grieves me to hear ye say that, as I know nothing of it either. Old Reynolds was schoolmaster for fifty years, and this is the first time since I've been a heritor that the position's been vacant."

"Reynolds? You're replacing him?" Reynolds was schoolmaster in the years he and George attended the parish school. He was a decent enough sort. "Why would you do that?"

"He's dead," Henry said, looking at him as if he were daft. "The man was over eighty."

Wylie blinked. Dead?

He'd liked Reynolds; they'd become friends once their student-teacher relationship had ended. Wylie wouldn't have minded passing a few pleasant hours with him over a dram while here.

Cease. You haven't thought of Reynolds in years. Don't get maudlin now.

"But that's neither here nor there, Wylie. The kirk session allowed us an extension due to William's passing, but they stipulated the matter must be resolved within the fortnight. As I understand it, there are three candidates to choose from. I fear the salary will be higher than four pounds a year. Reynolds was a bargain. These young ones won't be so obliging."

"Uncle, I'll wager Mr. Montgomery will interview in our stead. Let's get the details of this sale resolved so that he might."

"Are ye listening, lad? Damn your tongue, ye're as stubborn as a mule. We've already had one extension, I'll not ask for another. Besides, Montgomery is an outsider. I'll not let an outsider make a decision like this for the parish, and neither would your father. The new schoolmaster might well serve another fifty years."

Devil take it, then ask George. "Surely your son can aid you, or even—"

"George isn't interested. Hasn't been for years. And don't dare mention that popinjay or ye'll feel this cane on your backside. If that boy doesn't succumb to the pox soon, I'll be surprised."

"Popinjay?"

"Miriam's son."

His brow furrowed. That was odd. Jay seemed a decent enough sort. His uncle, however, had never been one to form unreasoned judgments. And with family, Henry was known to make allowances.

He was sitting here talking to him, wasn't he? The traitor-turned-privateer black sheep of the family.

"Oh, aye," Wylie said. "Your grandson."

Henry snorted, though he didn't elaborate. Propping his leg upon the footstool, he took another sip from his cup and settled back. "Now, the first interview is this afternoon at four. The sooner we decide, the sooner it's behind us."

This afternoon? "Today?"

"Aye."

Well then. Uncle Henry hadn't fabricated the matter after all.

"Very well. I'll accompany you." Today was acceptable. Today he could do. And since neither he nor his uncle knew enough to assess this man's qualifications over another's, they may as well choose him. "You'll take care of my matter immediately thereafter."

"One thing at a time, lad. The minister was at my door yesterday about repairs to the manse, and it wasn't the first time. He likens living in the manse to living in a barn. He has a list he'll discuss with us."

If it's not one thing, lad, ye'll find it's another. Ye'll also find ye'd have it no other way.

Maybe at one time, Father, but no longer. It cost too much to care, and the price was never paid in coin.

"Repairs are something Mr. Montgomery can handle. Clear the note and the manse will be his first order of business."

"Glencorach will be paying its fair share, for cert. But I'll not be trusting a Sassenach to pay up later when I've got a Scot here and now."

Wylie closed his eyes briefly, summoning patience. "Very well, if we can table the matter today. Is that all?"

"Nay. A number of women have put some concerns before the kirk session. The women know we're coming, so I'm certain they'll want to speak with us this afternoon. Meet me at three, and we'll walk over together."

God's teeth. A number of women? Women's concerns could range from inherited rights to an abandoned pew to fingering a philanderer for adultery. Wylie had no patience for petty concerns. It may have been easier if his uncle *had* insisted he sit down with George.

Wylie stood, signaling an end to the conversation. "This afternoon, then."

Henry stood as well. Ignoring Wylie's dismissal, he turned a slow circle, surveying the room, his expression now one of sorrow. Intent and focused, he looked as if he were sweeping in memories, storing them for the last time.

They'd been close, his father and uncle. Closer than most brothers in Wylie's ken. Perhaps it wasn't so hard to believe, as Alan claimed, that they'd forgotten the mortgage.

"Lord, but I miss him, Wylie."

Wylie nodded, a lump fast filling his throat. "I know."

"Ye weren't raised with a sibling, so I'll wager ye don't. William was the only one left with whom I could share stories of our childhood . . . memories of our parents. Now there's no one to correct me if I embellish the size of that stag I bagged in '35. No one to remind me if the scent our mother carried was bergamot or lemon." He lowered his head, as if to hide his trembling lip. "No doubt it seems of little importance, and I expect ye're right. But some days I convince myself it was bergamot, and the next day I curse myself a fool, for of course Mother smelled of lemon." He looked at Wylie, his eyes glistening with unshed tears. "Now that I have no one to ask, the question has become one of utmost importance." Shaking his head, he hobbled from the room, muttering, "Such a waste. Such a blasted, god-awful waste."

Hauling in an unsteady breath, Wylie stared after him, his heart hammering an erratic beat. Damn the man, he required no lectures on loss.

Perhaps he'd not made peace with all that had happened, but he'd learned to live with it, as had his father. Uncle Henry though . . .

It was clear Henry hoped to resurrect the nephew he remembered, and that he planned to plumb Wylie's depths without mercy until his soul slurped free. Henry had the line, he had the hook, and he had the bait.

Henry had not, however, reckoned on two things.

One, Wylie's distaste for the bait.

Two, when Wylie first learned that he must abandon his home, his heritage, and his father . . . that he'd been cast aside by his family, his friends, and his country . . .

His soul had been shattered, its pieces scattered.

CHAPTER 15

ANNA LINGERED in bed the morning after her outing and considered the tasks awaiting her. Fetching fuel, reviewing accounts with her father, meetings at the kirk, meal preparations with Mrs. Baxter—none inspired her to rise. Instead, she stared unseeing at the bed's ceiling and passed a finger over her lips.

When was the last time a man looked at her and saw a woman?

She couldn't count Wylie Macpherson. Wylie was at a crossroads, and she served a distraction while he puzzled his destination.

Nor, it now seemed, could she count Mr. Montgomery.

How had that happened? She'd had suitors besides Burt. Several, in fact. When had that changed?

Why had that changed?

She gritted her teeth. Mother Mary, she hadn't time to waste good daylight in self-pity. Casting her blanket aside, she rose and propped open the window's shutter for light. She reached for her gown and then paused. Behind it hung another everyday gown, one she'd worn during Burt's courtship. Its dark fabric had worn a bit thin, and it fit a tad too snug about her bosom. But its trim was a flattering shade of moss green that Burt once claimed matched her eyes.

Should she have stopped caring if men found her attractive?

On impulse she chose the older gown and slipped it on. Then she combed the tangles from her hair and pulled a long-disused box of ribbons from her trunk. Taking care not to wake her father, she carried it to the common room, propped open another shutter, and riffled the box, searching for the ribbon that matched the trim. Once she found it, she tied it around her hair, wishing she owned a looking glass.

Did it matter? She was still Anna Macrae, and she was still on the wrong side of thirty.

And Anna Macrae best saddle her pony and ride to the peat bank now if she hoped to speak with her father before noon.

She donned her cloak and grabbed her sketch pad and pencils. Sadie Macpherson would be at the peat bank this morning. A skilled seamstress, Sadie had offered her services repeatedly in exchange for Anna sketching her family. Anna could use a new gown, and it was past time to take the woman up on her offer.

The community peat bank was a patch of low ground a mile or so northeast. Most of the year the meadow was deserted, a boggy marsh not worth the trouble to cross. In early spring, however, during the dry season, it teemed with people. Working the bog was a task as essential as spring planting; the fuel gathered must last a full year.

Anna heard the children before she saw them, and her pony's ears flickered. Leaving the high ground, the pony picked its way down a rocky path flanked by tiny white flowers to a meadow piled with drying peat.

The smaller children darted between the peat stacks, calling to one another in a game of hide-and-seek, and mothers shouted scoldings each time their play threatened to topple a hard-earned pile.

Anna dismounted, tangled her reins in an outcrop of heather, and untied the small stool she carried. One of the McPhee boys came and greeted her. After asking him to fill her creels with peat, she retrieved her pad and pencil and surveyed the women, returning smiles and nods. Catching sight of Sadie, she called out and waved.

A small, kerchiefed woman with a round pink face looked up and smiled. She stacked the peat brick she held atop a tent-shaped pile, swiped her hands over her apron, and hurried toward Anna.

"Don't tell me ye've brought your pad at long last," Sadie said, frowning. "The bairns be at the shielings with their auntie."

"'Tis always the way of it." Anna circled the woman. Staging the mountain behind her would offer the best contrast. "I can begin with ye, aye?"

"Here?" Raising hands blackened with peat to her begrimed cap, Sadie drew her brows tight and grimaced, pinching her round face into a mask of horror. "Nay!"

Anna bit back a smile. Who was she to quibble with vanity? "Och, ye're right. I must catch ye at your needlework, with the glow of the fire behind ye and a cradle at your feet."

Sadie dropped her hands, and her mouth curved in a smile. "Aye, that sounds nice, it does. But will ye start on my Mike now ye're here?"

"Aye." Picking up her stool, she followed Sadie to the cutting bank.

A trench, as wide as it was deep, cut through a long length of bog, exposing a bank of rich black earth. The men had been working it on and off for three weeks, and the face of the bank was now over six feet deep.

Mike Macpherson, a braw, dark-haired man in his mid-thirties, stood at the bottom of the trench, cutting cubes from the bank with his peat iron. His brother Archie, another braw lad two years Mike's junior, worked beside him, hoisting each cut cube to the ground above. Both men had discarded their shirts, and their chests and arms, baked brown, glistened with perspiration.

Anna grinned. She'd enjoy this task.

"Mike!" Sadie called. "Anna is here to sketch ye. Mind ye not disgrace me, aye?"

Mike Macpherson glanced up, his weathered face scrunched in an expression of disbelief. He studied his wife, as if gauging her intent. Finally he shook his head and raised a side of his mouth, seeming resigned. Sadie blew him a kiss and walked away.

"Best get my good side, lass," he called up to Anna.

"Ye've nothing but good sides, Mike," she called back. Archie said something to Mike she couldn't hear, and they ribbed each other a bit, flexing their muscles and laughing before they returned to their work and ignored her.

Checking the sun's position, Anna placed her stool accordingly and opened her pad. She studied Mike, her pencil moving as she did. Capturing both motion and strength in her lines, the work consumed her, and she scarcely noticed when someone rode up behind her. Only when a pony snorted, spraying a dribble of blow over the back of her neck, did she turn and see George.

"George Macpherson," she said, her tone less than kind.

"Nice work, Anna."

"It was before ye got it wet." She pressed her sleeve over the page.

George grinned, touching his hat in greeting. "Ye ought not mind, given it doesn't resemble Mike."

Frowning, she looked back at the sketch and slammed the pad

shut, her face burning. George was right. The man's face looked remarkably like Wylie's.

"Inbreeding," she muttered. "Ye Macphersons all look alike."

George laughed and dismounted, landing on his good leg. "Why are ye here? Someone would have delivered peat if ye're low."

As payment in kind, Glendally's tenants supplied the Macraes with peat. The service was one of many their leases required, but requesting delivery of Glendally's annual supply before it was due seemed unfair.

"Anna?" George said, suspicion in his tone. "Ye didn't ask, did ye?"

"It's not their fault we're low, George. We've had unexpected visitors. Besides, I had business with Sadie, so coming here was no bother." She stood and picked up her stool. Between this draft and her memory, she could complete a proper sketch later. "I ought to return though; I lost track of time. Why are *ye* here?"

"Tommy Tanner came down from the shielings early this morning. He said some men rode through yesterday afternoon, men nobody recognized. I thought I'd best ride up and take a look."

"The cattle, then? Are they all accounted for?"

George shook his head and looked toward the mountains, his brow creased. "He thinks five are missing from Glencorach's herd."

"Five?" If someone were lifting cattle, they'd steal more than five. Five cows were hardly worth the effort. "Tommy's certain they hadn't wandered off?"

"Nay, he's not. I expect he's only nervous. He's heard Wylie's back, and he wants all in order."

She looked at his pony, noting for the first time that he'd strapped on a rifle. "If it's Glencorach's cattle gone missing, should ye be the one going after them?"

George didn't answer and looked at the ground. With his cane, he scattered a few rocks. "He's come to Cragdurcas, ken. I came to tell ye, but ye'd gone to Bloomhall."

She knew at once he meant Wylie. She reached for his elbow, gripping it. "George! Why didn't ye say so at once?"

"We exchanged few words. He arrived at breakfast, stayed through the meal, and then left." George shrugged. "He wouldn't even look at me, Anna. I don't know what I'd hoped for, but it wasn't that. Did ye know he plans to leave within days?"

She nodded, biting back words of consolation she herself wouldn't believe. It seemed unlikely Wylie would grant George the time of day. Releasing his elbow, she asked, "Does your father know of the missing cattle?"

"He wasn't home when Tanner arrived."

That was neither here nor there. She dreaded Wylie finding out second-hand that some of his assets were missing, especially after the matter of the mortgage.

Did George plan to tell him?

"I'll tell him," George said, as if reading her thoughts. "Once I see that they've not wandered off. Wait while I speak with the men, and I'll see you home."

She nodded. After speaking with Sadie, she walked to her pony, tucked her pad away, and mounted. One of the lads hoisted her creels, now laden with peat, onto her saddle hooks. The pony sidestepped, resisting the added weight, and the boy whispered a few calming words before securing her stool.

George returned and mounted with the aid of his own stool. Pulling it up with its attached rope, he secured it to his saddle.

She thought of the women at the shielings, alone and vulnerable, distanced from their men. "Did the women see those men?" she asked.

"Aye. Seems the men were civil, though not forthcoming about their business." He canted his head toward the path, indicating she should climb first.

On the way back, George peppered her with questions of Bloomhall and the squire's guests—more, she suspected, as a diversion than from curiosity. When they reached Glendally, he followed the long path to the rear yard, steering his pony clear of her flowers.

"Let me know what ye find, aye?" she said, dismounting.

George didn't answer. Instead he stared at the disintegrating thatch covering her home.

"Ye've enough on your mind, George Macpherson, without worrying over the Macraes. Father will take care of it."

George shook his head. "So ye've said. He hasn't though, has he? And ye're setting a dangerous precedent by not calling for the repairs yourself. If ye hope to assume this lease, Anna, ye'll have to prove to my father ye'll assume authority."

George seemed to think she could become tacksman on Cragdurcas, once her father passed on. A woman tacksman wasn't unheard of—in the next parish, Janet Macintosh held a tack in her own right. But Anna wasn't Janet.

Rather than debate it, she sidestepped it. George was a dear friend and worried over her future; she'd not treat his concern lightly. "I'll speak with my father again."

George's mouth opened, then closed, as if he thought the better of what he meant to say. At length he said, "Before I go, I'll stack your peat."

"Nay." She held up a hand, stopping him before he dismounted. "I'll do it. Ye see to the cattle."

He shifted in his seat, his saddle creaking. Finally he nodded, turned his pony toward the hills, and rode off. Only once he was out of sight did Anna glance back at the roof. She worried as well; the rains would come soon.

Shaking her head, she turned and emptied the creels, stacking the bricks in the spot where, God willing, a thousand more would rest next week. Once finished, she rinsed her hands at the pump and went inside.

Mrs. Baxter, a trim, flaxen-haired young woman, turned from the kitchen fire and greeted Anna, her smile bright.

"Good morning, Mrs. Baxter," Anna said. "I've brought fuel."

"I wondered where ye'd gone off."

"I stayed longer than I intended. Is my father awake?" When Anna and her father lost their cook to influenza late last winter, Mrs. Baxter, one of their tenants and newly widowed, had asked if she might fill the position. In Anna's eyes, she was heaven sent. With more energy than her predecessor, she'd become indispensable.

"Aye, and he's asked after ye."

"He was asleep when I returned last night.

"He wasn't himself, miss. He sat staring out his window for the longest time. After tea, he crawled into bed. I hope ye don't mind that I left while he slept."

"Of course not." Her father's judgment hadn't deteriorated so that she feared leaving him alone. Not yet anyway. Mrs. Baxter set a bowl of hot porridge on the table and poured a cup of milk. Anna sat, her stomach rumbling.

"So Glencorach's lads didn't come by, then?"

"No ma'am, not while I was here. Shall I start a pot of tea for your da?"

She nodded, her mouth full. It was just as well the boys hadn't come. It would make their leaving easier to bear.

A short time later, Anna stood with a tea tray outside her father's room.

"There ye are, Anna. Come in." Rising, he cleared a spot on his desk for the tray. "I'm anxious to hear of your afternoon with Archie."

She crossed the room, not at all anxious to discuss it. "Mrs. Baxter thought ye were feeling poorly last night."

"Weary, not poorly. Tell me, did you enjoy Bloomhall?"

Somewhat. She nodded and poured tea into two cups. "The musicians were talented. I wish ye'd joined us."

He chuckled. "I'm thinking Archie did not. He's waited a long time to step out with ye."

Yes, she'd once thought so. "Aye, well perhaps. He's not so patient regarding Glencorach, however."

"Glencorach?" His brow creased. "Lass, surely ye didn't spoil—"

"He raised the subject, Father, not I," Anna interjected. "And he was quite adamant in pursuing it." The matter still rankled, irrational or not. "Do ye think we could go over that account this morning? He's asked for a list of matters yet to handle and hopes to discuss it with ye tonight at supper."

Her father studied her, his expression thoughtful. If it turned from thoughtful to pitying she might run from the room in tears. Yesterday, she'd glimpsed an unwanted spinster within. She couldn't bear it if her father saw that same stranger when he looked at her.

At length he nodded. "Aye, I expect we could. Young Wylie is anxious as well."

True enough. Especially as "young" Wylie was getting no younger and eager to be on his way. She sat facing him. "Shall we start with the rents?"

"Aye, we always do." He pulled a ledger book from the shelf behind and set it between them.

He'd pulled the correct one. Thank you, Lord, for small mercies. She thumbed through its pages. "Ye'll agree Mr. Moy's the one who is behind?"

"Nay. Ye must recall the whisky."

She looked up and stared at him. "What whisky?"

He held her gaze, seeming puzzled, and something akin to worry furrowed his brow. Not for the first time, she imagined thoughts tumbling round in his head, each jostling another for its proper slot, until hopefully they fell into an order that made sense. Sometimes they didn't. Now though, it seemed they had, for he blinked, his brow clearing.

"Of course. I'd forgotten. William asked that I not say anything. Moy's paid his arrears in whisky. He made an arrangement with William."

Truly? "Why would William agree to that?"

"It's all Mr. Moy could offer."

Fiddlesticks. He had grain he could offer. He chose to make whisky with it instead.

"Thirty barrels, I'm guessing it'd be by now," her father added.

She swallowed, an ache of dread rising. Thirty? Good God, surely not.

"What is it, Anna?"

"Mr. Montgomery . . . What of Mr. Montgomery?"

"Ah." He gave her a lopsided smile and nodded. "Therein lies the problem. William was keen to help Moy, but not once did he think the arrangement would last this long." He shook his head. "For cert, he didn't think he'd sell Glencorach to the revenue."

"So . . ." She struggled finding her voice, for certainly, if Mr. Moy hadn't the coin to pay his rent, he hadn't the coin to pay his excise tax.

It would be hard to argue Glencorach kept thirty barrels on hand for personal use. Without excise stamps, Mr. Montgomery could—and likely would—seize those barrels.

Years of rent . . . gone.

The reason behind Moy's persistence regarding Wylie's intentions was suddenly clear. "So Mr. Moy has transferred his tax problem to the Macphersons."

Her father avoided her gaze and reached for his tea. Running his finger around the cup's rim, he studied its contents. "Aye."

"Do we know for a fact Mr. Moy has set Glencorach's share aside?"

Her father nodded. "William was kind, but not a fool. It's in

111

Glencorach's cellar."

Her brow creased. She'd helped Martha take stock of things after William's death. The cellar shelves were nearing empty. "Are ye certain, Father?"

"Of course, I'm certain. William and I took count in February."

Then where was it?

Blessed Mother, what would Wylie think when he learned the Macraes couldn't account for his rent, nor, if George were correct, his cattle? Incompetence at best, especially on the heels of learning they'd forgotten a mortgage.

Fraud? Would he consider it fraud?

Maybe William drank it.

"William wasn't drinking his rent, was he?" *Could* someone consume thirty barrels in three months?

Her father rolled his eyes toward the ceiling, playfully beseeching help from above. He used to do that with her mother. She couldn't find it in her to smile.

"William was not drinking his rent."

"But it's not in the cellar. Martha and I tidied the shelves the week before last."

He drew his brows together, frowning. "Ye tidied the second cellar as well, then?"

Relief rushed through her, and she exhaled a long breath. She hadn't thought of that cellar in years. Its entrance concealed behind a shelf filled with ale barrels and preserves, she hadn't *seen* it in years.

"Oh, thanks be." She gave her father a smile. "I worried it'd walked off, ken, seeing as it was unattended. I'd forgotten that cellar. Well, then, we can't let Mr. Montgomery be thinking he'll collect this sum from Mr. Moy, right?" she asked, pointing at the ledger.

"What?" Rubbing his chin, he examined the sheet. "Where do you . . ." He paled.

Frowning, she leaned forward to see what had alarmed him. "What is it?"

He ran a finger down a column. "Look at the credits, Anna. I didn't record the payments made in kind. But Moy owes nothing."

Oh no. She hadn't known to check. He'd kept the arrangement from her. "Ye couldn't have missed recording all that, Father. It's here somewhere, I'm certain." She pulled a pile of loose papers forward and shuffled through them.

Her father rocked back in his seat, covering his face with his hands. "How could I miss something so simple yet so important? I shouldn't do this any longer, Anna, not with my memory failing. I just can't—"

"Here!" She waved the sheet she'd found like a flag, commanding his attention. She'd seen it before yet hadn't known its purpose. "Perhaps you thought it easier to keep them separate."

He shook his head in seeming disbelief. "I was so certain I'd remember," he said softly, as if to himself.

"Ye did; ye knew something was missing. Ye needn't worry; it's all here. We'll adjust the ledger."

"You don't understand, lass. I think I told Wylie ... I can't remember what I told him," he said, shaking his head.

Anna bit her lip and worried it. She'd known better than to let Wylie in here without her, yet she'd allowed it.

What *had* her father told Wylie?

"We'll sort it." If necessary, she'd pass off whatever it was as an error she'd made or an oversight due to William's passing. She stretched out a hand and clasped his. "Ye mustn't take it to heart."

"But I must. If others begin questioning my work, there's no use. All of this." He waved a hand before letting it thump on the desktop. "It's no use."

"That's enough of that talk." She handed him the sheet. "Here, ye begin by recording the credits next to Moy's rent. I'll check your postings, and ye'll check my tallies. Come now, Father. Nothing is as bad as it first appears."

He drew in a deep breath and released it, then nodded. "All right." He reached for his quill, pausing before he dipped it in ink. "What about the next time, the time I can't even recall what it is I must repair?"

Such as their roof? The thought came unbidden, and she pushed it aside. "We'll cross that bridge when we come to it. Don't borrow trouble."

He smiled, albeit weakly. "Your mother used to say that. Lord, but I miss her."

"As do I. But don't think of joining her. I'll not have it."

"It will get worse, Anna. What will we do?" he asked.

Her father had taught her to read and cipher sums. From his fireside chair, he'd told her stories of fairies and dragons. Then, when the dragons invaded her dreams, he'd carried her from her bed to the front room and rocked her before the soft red glow of the fire, telling her stories of fearless and powerful princesses.

How many miles had he traveled to fetch a doctor each time her forehead was warm? How many lads had he terrified upon learning they'd made her cry?

He'd spent a lifetime slaying her dragons. Her turn had come to slay his.

"We'll get by, Father." And they would; she could set this straight within minutes, before seeing to her chores. "Would ye like to accompany me to my meeting this afternoon? We'll return before Mr. Montgomery arrives for supper."

"With the ladies?" He shuddered, his face assuming a mask of horror. "In spite of appearances, I haven't lost *all* my sense. I thank ye, but no. Besides, look out the window."

She did as he asked, smiling when she saw Dougal hop-scotching his way through the backyard and Will ambling behind.

"Ye go on about your business, lass. Wylie's boys will keep me company."

"It won't take us but a minute to—"

"I'll work on this later, Anna," he said, his tone one that brooked no argument. "Archie will have his list tonight."

"Very well." She stood slowly, reluctant to leave the task unfinished, and went to welcome the boys.

Dougal brushed past her when she opened the front door; Will lingered on the threshold.

"Papa gave us a dog and took us fishing, Miss Macrae," Dougal said. "His uncle visits now, and we may not disturb them."

A dog? Did he mean to stay? Warmth spread through her and she smiled, feeling better than she had all morning. Perhaps something might come of the attraction between them. "He gave you a dog?"

"*Oui.* Her name is Molly."

Hope plummeted. That was William's dog, the collie who'd decided herding cattle didn't suit.

Fool. Her hopes must rest on Wylie's departure, not on his staying. That man could break her heart without knowing he held it.

"That's a fine name. I once had a doll named Molly."

"Papa caught three salmon." He spread his arms wide to

114

indicate their size. "Will almost caught one, but he must first learn the proper way."

She glanced Will's way and saw that he studied her.

Her heart climbed to her throat. It was the same speculative look he'd given her when she'd returned from Glencorach the night before last.

"Three's a . . . a fine catch," she said, her voice hitching as she tore her gaze from his. So what if Will guessed her feelings for his father? Wylie was an attractive man; surely she wasn't the only woman who noticed.

"We gave two back to the river," Dougal said, squirming as he tugged at the hem of his coat. "Miss Martha cooked one. We ate it for supper and for breakfast. She said we will have it for dinner this afternoon and maybe again for supper. What will you have for supper?"

She laughed. Perhaps they could trade suppers; her father no longer fished. "I'm not certain. But if Martha's not expecting ye, ye're welcome to return." Though why they'd want to was beyond her. It would likely be broth and bannocks, as it'd been four nights running.

"Could Papa come?"

Three words and her pulse picked up speed as if she were a schoolgirl in braids. She flushed, again feeling Will's scrutiny. "If he'd like, he's welcome."

"I will tell Mr. Macrae about the fish," Dougal said, turning and running toward her father's room.

"Miss Macrae?" Will said, speaking for the first time.

She turned to him, wary. "Aye?"

"I wonder if you meant what you said at the ferry."

Surprised, she asked, "Might ye be a wee more specific?" As a rule, she meant what she said. On the other hand, she'd said a great many things that morning.

"You said if I wanted to know the truth of things, I should come to you."

Oh Lord, *that*. Her temper had prompted that. "Aye."

"Papa and Cousin George. It is not as it should be. Why?"

The porridge she'd eaten roiled, and she placed a soothing hand on her belly. Why had she made such a rash promise?

"A long story that is, Will." And one Wylie would not thank her for telling, especially since he'd not seen fit to tell Will himself.

Blue eyes held hers for a long moment. Then he said, "Cousin George. He is the G. Macpherson of the letters?"

Anna might feign ignorance. Pretend she hadn't seen the beribboned stacks of returned and unopened letters lining George's library shelves. George practiced self-flagellation as surely as any repenting zealot, his whip the ribbon he chose to tie each new stack.

She'd not pretend; she'd like to see it end. Besides, Will was extraordinarily perceptive.

She nodded. Will dropped his gaze and followed his brother.

Chagrined, she watched him go.

Of all the questions he might have asked, why had he chosen the most difficult to answer?

Why hadn't he questioned Wylie's politics or why she claimed his father wasn't a traitor? Why hadn't he asked why some in the district had fought with Prince Charlie and some hadn't? Or questioned his father's pardon?

Instead, with uncanny accuracy, Will targeted the thing she believed most responsible for changing his father.

According to William, Wylie refused to listen to the reasons George did what he did, choosing instead to nurse his anger and misguided grudge.

Will, it seemed, chose to understand, and for whatever reason, thought to ask her for an explanation. She'd promised the lad the truth over idle gossip. It wasn't as if he wouldn't hear the story from Robert Moy or one of Moy's cronies.

She hurried to her father's room before she wavered. Both boys stood at his side, examining the bottled ship he'd pulled from the shelf. "Will?"

Will looked toward her.

"We'll speak of the matter later, aye? This afternoon."

He regarded her a moment, then nodded. "*Oui*. Papa expects us soon, but we will return."

She didn't know the complete story. But what she did know, she would share.

CHAPTER 16

LATER THAT same morning, Wylie carried a ledger to Glencorach's tool shed. Propping the door open, he peered inside, wrinkling his nose at the damp, metallic odor. Two ploughs and a small cart blocked his entry. He set aside the ledger and dragged them to the yard. Studying them, he rubbed his thumb over his lower lip.

Each minute his uncle toyed with him, the longer this equipment sat idle and the less the estate was worth.

Instead of inventorying, perhaps he should visit Anna and inquire into the whereabouts of his field hands.

No, he should finish this task and ask Martha that question. Dallying with Anna Macrae was the *last* thing he should do.

Muttering a curse, he entered the shed, ducking to avoid the baskets and creels hanging from the rafters. He turned a slow pivot on the clay floor. He'd need a lantern to count the small implements crowding the shelves on the far wall, but he could make headway by tallying the spades, shovels, and tackle lining the walls near the door. He walked out, retrieved his ledger, and spotted Dougal walking toward him.

"You're back. Is Will?"

Dougal nodded. "It is time to eat; you will come?"

"Aye."

"Papa, Mr. Macrae showed us a ship in a bottle. The masts were not like *Eliza*'s."

Wylie grinned, recalling the hours he'd spent studying that same ship when he was a boy. "Designs change over time, Dougal. He built that ship many years ago."

"Will you show me how they have changed? You could make me drawings like Miss Macrae's."

Few could make drawings like Miss Macrae. "Maybe later." He closed the shed door and followed Dougal across the yard, pausing at the pump to rinse his hands. "Listen, Dougal, after we eat, I want you to take the dog out so that I may speak with Will alone."

Dougal nodded, seeming unsurprised at the request. "You will speak with him of the girl, *oui?* She has too much of his time."

Girl? Wylie's mouth flattened. He'd planned to speak to Will of Robert Moy. He knew nothing of a girl. "What girl?" he asked, turning from the pump to see Dougal enter the house. Grimacing, Wylie followed.

The parlor side table, hinged on both ends, was now fully extended so that it would comfortably accommodate six people. Will sat at its middle and Grace hovered nearby, adjusting the tableware.

Wylie dropped into the chair at the head of the table. He fingered the table linen, recognizing it as one he'd sent his father from Portugal. It looked as if this were its first use.

Dougal plopped into a chair beside his brother. "Miss Macrae said we may come to her house for supper tonight. May we? You too, Papa."

Wylie looked up at Dougal, the linen forgotten. If Anna herself had asked him to come, he surely wanted to go. He hadn't seen her since her abrupt departure the night before last and was uncertain they were still friends.

"Did Miss Macrae require an answer?"

Dougal shrugged and Will turned to him, his gaze seeming almost speculative.

"On second thought, it's likely I'll still be with my uncle; we're to meet later today," Wylie said before Will read too much into nothing. "You two may go."

"We could come with you instead?" Dougal asked.

"No."

Martha entered carrying a plate filled with bannocks. "Grace is learning the table, sir. I hope ye willna mind." Setting the plate before him, she added, "Robert Moy stopped by earlier while ye were visiting your father's grave."

Following Henry's visit, Wylie had sought a few moments respite at his father's gravesite. "Oh? Did he say why?"

"He's anxious to speak with ye."

Wylie couldn't afford to ignore him. More than six generations of Moys had occupied that land, giving Robert Moy *duthchas.* In the eyes of many Highlanders, those rights by heritage trumped Wylie's right by law. If Moy were of a mind to make trouble for a new laird, Montgomery would be well advised to back off acquiring Glencorach.

"If he comes again, tell him I'll be round later today, once I finish at the kirk. Martha, where are my father's ghillies and laborers?"

"Your uncle gave them work, sir. They'll return once ye settle in." She set a hand on his shoulder and squeezed.

Each time Martha called him "sir," it gave him pause. He didn't bother explaining yet again that he'd no plans to "settle in."

"Will we still be here in four days?" Dougal asked once the women left the room.

Hell, he hoped not. Pulling the plate close, he grabbed two bannocks he didn't want and then shoved it toward the boys. "Why?"

"Cousin George promised to tell us a story after six days. It has been two days."

George. Figures. "Hmmph." He tore a piece from the bannock and stuffed it in his mouth, forgoing a more explicit response.

"It will be a good story, Papa," Dougal said, his tone eager. "About his leg."

He scowled and swallowed, forcing the bannock down. "His leg?"

"The one the Indian in America took."

Wylie frowned, thinking. Will regarded him, his brows raised in something akin to mock surprise. Suddenly, Wylie remembered. George had suffered a terrible wound in America; he'd lost his leg because of it. Wylie's face grew hot, and he dropped his gaze to his hands.

He'd known of the injury, but he'd buried the knowledge, refusing to waste one moment of sympathy on George Macpherson. Then, when George remained seated yesterday... well, the knowledge hadn't resurfaced.

He'd forgotten. It was as simple as that, and he refused to feel shame.

He bit the inside of his cheek, keeping his eyes cast down. Shame was not so easily set aside.

What was the matter with him? How *could* he have forgotten George sustained such an injury? It more than explained the drawn look about his cousin.

He tore his bannock into tiny pieces, still refusing to look up. "Right," he said finally. "Well, I doubt we'll be here that long."

Grace reentered, carrying a plate filled with salmon, turnips, and kale. Once she served Wylie, she moved to Will. Wylie glanced up, at once alert. Grace was the only girl near. Had Dougal meant her?

Something in her manner seemed to change when she approached Will. Nothing overt, it was more that she lingered when reaching over the lad, her breast nearly brushing the side of Will's head.

Wylie studied Grace as if seeing her for the first time. She was older than Will—maybe by as much as five years. A comely lass, one with blazing red hair lining the edge of her cap, a full red mouth, and a sweet expression.

Deceptively sweet from Wylie's perspective, though he doubted Will would agree. Full figured, her breasts nearly spilled from her gown when she bent, and it seemed to Wylie that she tarried to be certain Will noticed.

And notice he did. When she set down her serving plate, Will shifted his right hand a fraction so that it grazed her left while she dumped spoonfuls on his plate.

Abruptly, as if sensing his father's scrutiny, Will darted a quick glance Wylie's way. Wylie frowned. A faint pink stained the lad's cheeks, and he dropped his hand to his lap. Seeming startled, Grace moved on to serve Dougal.

Wylie's blood pulsed hot, his mouth drawn tight. Damn it all to hell. They had been here how long—four or five days? *Days*, and the lad was of a mind to dally with Martha's niece?

This was *exactly* why he'd planned to leave the boys with his father. He didn't have the time, the will, or the knowledge to raise them.

Alec, refusing to see the gravity of his situation, had suggested months ago that Wylie remarry if he were so worried. Wylie dismissed the suggestion out of hand. Alec knew as well as he did that Will would run roughshod over a stepmother. Add to that, Wylie would be saddled with a wife he didn't want.

As would Will if he continued to drop his breeches for every willing lassie.

Rennie claimed it was Wylie's duty to tell Will where he might dally and where he might not. Wylie had found it curious that she'd thought there was an appropriate place for a lad as young as Will had been to "dally" at all, but he'd kept his mouth shut and attributed it to her being French.

He recalled the last time Rennie had pestered him on the subject. It was over two years ago, and she'd met his ship at the wharves after a ten-month absence.

"I'm not ignoring you, Rennie." Wylie stowed his logbook and took a last glance around the cabin before buckling his pack. "I spoke with Will the last time you asked. The lad nodded at everything I said. How was I to know he'd not heed one word?"

"Oh, for God's sake, Wylie. Don't you know him at all?"

The sharpness of her reply caught him by surprise. He turned to look at her and saw what he hadn't noticed moments before. There were deep lines etched between her dark brows and around the corners of her mouth. Lines not there the year before.

Had she been ill?

He knew better than to ask. She invariably interpreted talk of her health as a deliberate reminder of her age. She was ten years his senior, and it'd bothered her far more than it'd ever bothered him.

"Tell me what I should say, then, lass," he said softly. "Tell me the words and I'll say them." He walked toward her and she backed away, her palm extended.

"If I knew the words, Wylie, I'd say them myself. I want you to take him to sea with you. I've tired of talking til my breath gives out."

His features scrunched. Take Will? "You can't be serious, Rennie. Look at those lads." He canted his head toward the porthole, through which they could glimpse his crew on the dock. He'd paid them their wages fifteen minutes ago. Five minutes ashore and they were bargaining terms with the whores.

She placed her hands on her hips. "You've claimed time and time again that that's not the way of it for *all* seamen."

Wylie reddened. Of course he had; what else was he to say? "Why hasn't the lad found work?" he asked. Will had clerked in his grandfather's shop until the old man passed away last year. The new management—Rennie's sister—hadn't cared to keep Will on. Rennie contended her sister didn't want Will looking over her shoulder while she pocketed more than her share of profits. Wylie tended to agree.

"He *was* working, Wylie. For Mr. Savonne, Alicia's father."

Wylie's cheeks puffed as he blew out a breath. Savonne, the unhappy innkeeper with the unhappy daughter, Alicia, the root cause of Rennie's tirade.

"She's not with child, is she?" He propped a hip on his desk and extended his arms. Rennie came willingly, surprising him. For the first time, he realized how thin she'd become. He could count her ribs with his fingertips. He tightened his grasp, placing his cheek on her head and breathing her in. He'd missed her.

"No," she said, sounding suddenly weary. She rested her head on his shoulder. "But mark me, soon there *will* be a child. Girls flock to the lad." She lifted her head and looked at him. "What did your father say to keep you chaste?"

"He didn't. The kirk took care of the matter."

She pulled away, smiling for the first time that morning. "Oh? Tell me."

He shook his head. He rarely spoke of his childhood.

"Please?" she took his hands in hers and slanted her head in a ghost of the saucy manner that had once caught his eye. "I'll make it worth your while, sailor."

That morning had been his first inkling she was ill. He'd told her the story to keep her smiling and been glad he had. Not because she made it worth his while, though she had, but because she doubled over in laughter. Not just the once, but each time she'd recalled it in the terrible months following.

"Papa? Why are you smiling?" Dougal asked, returning him to the present.

"I was thinking of your mother," he said, still lost in thought.

Merde. Had he said that aloud? Both boys stared at him, openmouthed.

Will spoke first, his voice soft, almost tentative. "Will you tell us?"

Hell no.

Well . . . maybe . . . maybe parts. He could modify it some.

Hell, why not? He might accomplish more than one task with the retelling.

He shrugged. "I was recalling the time I told her of Lachlan Shaw and the repentance stool. It tickled her."

Grace dropped her serving spoon, splattering Dougal with bits of turnips. Flushing from her bosom to her hairline, she fussed over the boy a moment, then hurried from the room.

It seemed the kirk still resorted to that stool, then. He'd wondered.

Will, after glancing after Grace, turned to Wylie. "Who is Lachlan?"

"He was a friend." A good friend, one who'd written Wylie sporadically over the years.

While Wylie hadn't returned Lachie's letters, he'd never read or acknowledged them either, an action that now struck him as childish. At the time, it'd been an attempt to keep his past at bay.

"What did he do that tickled Mama?" Dougal asked.

"Well, Lachlan was older than I was; he had just turned twenty." In truth, Lachie and Wylie had both been fourteen at the time—a fact Wylie thought might hinder rather than aid his case. "He fancied Mary Carr, and they'd planned to marry once Lachlan saved money to set up their household." He paused, choosing his words. "But they rushed things a bit."

Both boys regarded him with puzzled expressions.

"You mean hurried, Papa?" Dougal said. "Where? To their new house?"

Wylie sucked in a breath, heat creeping up his neck. "Nay. I mean to say they consummated their relationship before marrying."

Will made a sound in his throat that turned into a series of coughs. He leaned toward his brother and whispered a few words in French.

Wylie cringed at Will's explicitness. Hell, his brother was only eight. But Dougal's puzzled expression cleared instantly. He whispered back, something about a Bridgette and how Will had not tickled Mama when—

At that point, Will twisted Dougal's arm behind his back, effectively ending Dougal's chatter. Dougal grunted and tried biting him. When that didn't work, he pummeled Will with his feet.

Wylie knew the story of Rennie walking in on Will swiving Bridgette—the cobbler's daughter and the lass *before* Alicia—on Rennie's kitchen table. Rennie's temper had flared ginger-hot over that escapade, and Wylie had taken the brunt of it.

Why, he hadn't a clue; he'd been in Kingston when it happened.

"Shall I continue?" Wylie asked, arching a brow.

Will released Dougal and nodded. "*Oui.*"

"Well, as it happened, Mary's uncle was one of the kirk session elders. A session is a church council," he said, clarifying before the boys asked. Rennie had raised them in the Catholic Church. "Her uncle was among the first to notice Mary was carrying—*enceinte.* He reported her to the other elders, and they called Mary to appear before the session."

"She was in trouble?" Dougal asked. When Wylie nodded, Dougal shoved a spoonful of kale into his mouth, chewed once or twice, then mumbled, "What for?"

"Fornication is a sin. You lads understand that, aye?"

They bobbed their heads in unison, though Will's nod was a bit short.

"Why did her uncle not call your friend?" Dougal asked.

Wylie forked a bit of the salmon, then pushed his plate away. Angst filled his belly these days, leaving little room for much else. "Her uncle didn't know who the father was. Mary wouldn't say. That was the elders' question. Or rather, one of their questions."

"Why was it their concern?" Will asked, his eyes turning a frosty blue. He leaned back in his chair, seeming to have also lost interest in the meal.

Wylie reached for his cup and found it empty. Stretching a hand down the table, he grabbed the ale jug. "Neither Mary or her mother could support a bairn, and the uncle knew it well," he said, refilling his cup and Will's. "Without help, the kirk would be tasked with supporting the child."

"Did she tell on Lachlan?" Dougal asked.

"Aye, she did. Unless she fled the parish, she hadn't a choice. Many knew of her and Lachlan. If she didn't give witness, their friends would be compelled to give it."

He and George had pledged Lachie their silence, but Lachie, not intending Mary to suffer the consequences alone, had urged Mary to confess. Wylie had been thankful he'd done so. It was one thing to pledge silence, quite another to lie to the elders. Wylie hadn't been sure he could follow through with the pledge if he'd been called before the session.

Dougal set his elbow on the table and rested his chin on his palm. He regarded Wylie with a frown. "You said Mama was tickled. This is not a funny story."

"Lachlan would surely agree with you there, Dougal. The kirk's censure is not a laughing matter. For three Sundays, he and Mary took turns standing on a stool before the congregation, while the minister chastised them."

Will paled. "*Jesu.*"

"Aye. Public humiliation's an effective deterrent." Especially when it targeted one of your mates.

"Could they not confess the sin privately?" Will asked.

"'Tis but one difference between the Catholics and Protestants. And don't be asking that question of the minister."

"Why not?" Dougal asked. "We must know where to confess. Mama said."

"We'll cross that bridge when we come to it."

Dougal's jaw set, his eyes stormy. The lad set great store on pleasing Rennie, even now.

"Dougal, we won't be here long enough for it to matter," Wylie said.

"You said you did not know how long we would be here."

"Well then, if we are still here on Sunday, I will ask if there is a priest near."

And if he asked the wrong person, he'd likely receive a visit from one of Fort William's officers by Monday. Catholicism and Jacobitism were synonymous in the government's eyes.

"Your mother never laughed at Lachlan, Dougal," Wylie added. "She laughed at the thought of the stool. We often find foreign customs amusing, aye?"

Given a distance of twenty-some years, Wylie had shared Rennie's amusement. But at the time, Lachie's censure had made a chilling impression. Because of it, Wylie hadn't had carnal knowledge of a woman until he was twenty, and that was in an anonymous Caracas brothel, well outside the kirk's reach.

That was what had tickled Rennie above all else, that he'd been a virgin until twenty. A sharp ache and pensive smile accompanied the memory. He still missed her.

Dougal pursed his lips and nodded, seeming satisfied at last. "I will take Molly out now, Papa." Rising, he ran from the room with Molly at his heels, the front door slamming after them.

Will rose to follow. "A word, Will," Wylie said, pointing at Will's empty chair.

Will regarded him warily. Slowly, he sat. "I know what you will

125

say, Papa."

"Indulge me, aye?"

"You need not say it, and you need not worry."

Wylie ignored him. "This is a small parish, Will. Everyone knows one another's affairs. They will know of yours before long. Grace is an innocent young girl, the niece of a longtime family friend. You can't—"

"*Non*, Papa. She is not an innocent."

Wylie grimaced. That must be the Renwick side of the family talking. It sure as hell wasn't the Macphersons. "Will, don't disparage the lassie."

"I mean no disrespect, but she is not an innocent. She is a widow. Her husband died in an accident last year, on the wharves in Glasgow."

Wylie cleared his throat. "I'm not sure that's relevant." He paused a moment and thought. "Nay, it's not. Fornication is a sin, and I suspect it's a greater sin if you don't care for the lass."

"I did not say I did not care for her."

"You care enough to father her child?"

"There will be no child."

Criminy. The lad wasn't an eijit. "Don't be daft. There may very well be a child."

Will shook his head. "*Non*. If I lay with her—and I do not admit to such—there will be no stool at your church. She is barren."

Wylie stared at his son. "How could you possibly know that?"

Will shrugged. "She was married four years without children.

Wylie opened his mouth and then shut it. He wasn't sure that was a logical conclusion to draw, nor was he prepared to debate it. Besides, it sidestepped the question of honor.

Honor was what signified. Honor, if not morality, ought to govern Will's decisions.

Squaring his shoulders, Wylie looked at his son. "Will, I don't care if she's innocent, barren, or married to the minister. I care that you treat her with respect. And that precludes laying with her without a thought for her future. Do you understand, lad?"

Will's eyes widened a fraction. "*Oui*, Papa. I had not thought of it in that manner."

That came too easy. Suspicion caused his own eyes to narrow. Did Will think to patronize him?

"Truly, Papa, I had not. If it worries you, I shall cease."

"Cease what, exactly? I'd like to be clear on the matter."

"Spending time with Grace. I do not wish to worry you or to give her expectations."

Wylie studied him, trying to gauge his sincerity. It was inconceivable to him that Will hadn't thought past his own pleasure. His own father had drummed in respect for others from the time Wylie had toddled.

The possibility his son hadn't considered the consequences of his actions disturbed Wylie. The possibility that he had—and then ignored them—shocked him.

Will had acquiesced, however, and Wylie best leave it at that.

"You may believe me, Papa. We will not be here long. It will not be a problem."

Wylie snorted and shook his head, acknowledging the futility of furthering the discussion. He was curious, however, to know at what point abstinence *did* become a problem for a sixteen-year-old. It had only recently become a problem for him, and it'd been nigh on two years.

"Right then, I'll accept you at your word." Wylie pulled out his pocket watch and opened it, wondering if he had time to discuss Moy.

"Papa, before you go, we should discuss Miss Macrae, as she is the one who is innocent. She arrived at her home after midnight the night before. She was here, yes? Alone with you?"

Wylie's jaw dropped, and seconds passed before he clamped it shut. Christ, how had Rennie managed this lad?

At length he spoke. "What exactly are you implying, Will?"

"I imply nothing. I am certain she left with her honor intact."

"Of course she did," he said, flipping his watch closed, his jaw tight.

Why was Will so certain? It hadn't been easy to let her walk out the door.

"Others, Papa, they will not be certain. As you say, this is a small parish, and you are a man without a wife. A man not so old as to be harmless."

Right then. This talk was going nowhere but sideways. And it had been after ten when she'd left, not midnight.

Will simply employed a diversion.

But if it *had* been after midnight when Anna returned, who had she been with?

He slid his plate toward the center of the table. "I'll not discuss Miss Macrae with you, Will."

Will didn't even wince at Wylie's tone. "You must consider people will talk, Papa, and the revenue man will hear. You will give him cause to take notice of you. I believe that unwise."

Reeling from the absurdity of Will's lecture, it took Wylie a moment to make the connection to Anna's purported suitor, Montgomery. He seized the opportunity to change the subject.

"I agree. Any contact with the revenue is unwise, which brings me to another matter. Mr. Moy told me he approached you about selling his whisky."

Will nodded. "He did. It will be profitable, Papa. I have calculated our expenses, and you will negotiate Mr. Moy's share down. You do that well."

Wylie snorted. At least the lad thought he excelled at *something*. "This is your grandfather's home. Surely you understand it's out of the question." While his father had never probed at the details of Wylie's occupation, Wylie was certain he'd have disapproved if he had. He'd not insult the man by running an operation from his cherished home.

"It is because it is Grandpapa's home that we must do it. There is no risk, Papa. Mr. Moy explained."

Wylie blinked several times. Maybe he was wrong, maybe the lad *was* an eijit. "There is *always* risk, Will. It's foolish to think otherwise. And make no mistake, your grandfather would not condone it."

"I know you must meet your uncle, and you are hurried. I will show you numbers in your account books and explain more when—"

"Will, I said no."

Molly barked outside, the sound raucous and at odds with their conversation.

"When you return, Papa, I will explain more. You will agree the risk is small and necessary." Will stood and walked to the door, then turned. "Thank you for allowing the dog and thank you for speaking of Mama. It is good to remember her." Without awaiting an answer, Will walked out.

His pulse pounding in his ears, Wylie stayed seated, staring after him. *You choose now to be quiet, Rennie?*

The turnips he'd eaten started a slow climb up his throat, and he swallowed, forcing them back.

CHAPTER 17

IT WAS raining when Anna left Glendally that afternoon. She bundled the edges of her cloak in her fist, cast an assessing glance at the low-lying clouds, and hurried toward the drove road. Spring succumbed to winter in the space of a heartbeat in the Highlands, and it paid to be aware. Within minutes she came upon a ploughman who stood staring at the sky, one hand propped on his plough and the other on his hip. When he saw her, he waved.

"What do ye think, Johnny?" she called.

"A teaser, lass. It'll be o'er in an hour."

Waving, she walked on. As she neared the road, a movement to the south caught her eye, and she turned toward it. A man crossed the field in her direction, his gait familiar and his hand raised in greeting.

Wylie Macpherson. He moved with an assurance impossible to mistake.

She paused where the lane intersected the road and waited, smiling. It was no hardship. She could spend hours watching him and often had. It was one benefit of carrying a sketchbook.

"Good day, Anna," he said when he came abreast.

She regarded him, noting he'd exchanged his own hat for his father's bonnet. It suited him. The dark circles beneath his eyes did not. "Are ye unwell?"

He raised a brow. "Is that what passes for a greeting in the Highlands these days?"

She flushed. "Good day, Wylie. I trust ye're well."

He nodded, and the rain pooling on the bonnet streamed to his shoulders. "I hoped I'd encounter you. You'll be going to the kirk this afternoon?"

"Aye. Do ye need something, then?"

"A shield?" He flashed a grin. "I'm for the kirk as well, but first I'm to fetch my uncle. I don't fancy spending time alone with the man."

"Dougal said ye two had met. Did things go poorly, then?"

"Things went as well as I could expect. Will you join us?"

She wished she could. She'd like to witness Henry's approach in bringing this man to heel. "I can't. I'm visiting the township first. Mary Shaw had a baby boy last night."

"She and Lachie?"

Anna nodded. "This makes ten now. For Mary's sake, I hope it's their last."

"Oh aye. For Lachie's sake as well." He chuckled. "I find it hard to manage two." He leaned toward her, reaching for her basket, and she caught a whiff of something she couldn't place, perhaps his shaving soap. If it was, it wasn't entirely pleasant.

She relinquished the basket, and he looped it over his right arm and offered her his left. After a quick glance about for his boys, she took it and they started walking.

Why did he think he couldn't manage his sons? Dougal and Will were good lads; certainly a part of that was due to Wylie. She looked up to say so and saw he regarded her with the oddest expression. His whole bearing had stiffened.

"What is it?"

"Have I placed you in a compromising position?"

She gave him a blank look.

"You hesitated when taking my arm. Would you rather not be seen with me?"

Her lips parted as she stared at him. What rot. "My hesitation was on your account, not mine. Your boys are still mourning their mother. Ye'll not want them thinking I'm latching on to their father."

"Hmm." He studied her, as if debating whether to believe her. At length his shoulders eased a fraction, and he gave her a small smile. "Latching on, is it? My boys like you."

"They like me because I'm no threat," she said, squeezing his forearm.

"I expect it's a bit more than that." He covered her hand with his, pressing back. "I like you as well, and I'm pleased you've permitted my company."

She stared up at him, searching for the truth behind the words. He looked back unblinkingly.

She could spin many a fanciful future on those words.

Your pony likes you as well, Anna. Don't be a fool.

Easier said than done. She'd always been a fool where Wylie

was concerned, and there seemed little hope for it now. She tore her gaze from his.

"Tell me of your morning," she said.

After a moment's hesitation, he answered, "Very well." He recited a dispassionate summary of a meeting that she doubted so straightforward. Henry Macpherson was a master at getting what he wanted, and Anna suspected he wanted his family reconciled and his nephew installed at Glencorach. She couldn't fault Henry for that, but it did mean he'd not make things easy for Wylie.

"D'ye think he's agreeable, then? He'll release the note?"

"That's my understanding. Once I handle this schoolmaster thing and arrange for the manse repairs."

Schoolmaster thing?

Stopping in her tracks, she turned on him, dropping her hand from his arm. "It's not a 'schoolmaster thing,' Wylie," she said, her tone sharp. "Ye're to hire the best man for the job, aye? There's little enough opportunity for the children here. Most will leave. It's important they be prepared."

His gaze narrowed, and a muscle pulsed in his cheek. Belatedly she recalled he was now laird.

"I spoke out of turn," she said quickly. "Of course ye'll do the proper thing. Ye always did."

He grunted and resumed walking. "Some would differ with you there, Anna, including myself."

She followed, regretting the loss of his touch. She almost took his elbow but lost her nerve before her hand rose an inch. Then, by accident or design, he drifted toward her and the distance between them narrowed. The heat from his body warmed her side from head to toe.

After a moment's silence, he asked, "Do you know where I might find a priest?"

Startled, she looked over at him. "A what?"

"You heard me," he said, his gaze trained ahead. "I told Dougal I would ask."

"He's papist?" No sooner were the words out than she wished she could recall them. They were censorious.

"My sons were raised in France, Anna."

"Of course. I didn't mean . . ." She fingered the edge of her cloak. It'd not bode well for Wylie if others knew his sons were Catholic. "I know of no priests near."

"What of the Macdonalds? Surely they would know."

Until last month, the Macdonalds farmed in the Braes of Laggan. "They've been evicted."

Wylie turned to her, his brows drawn in surprise. "What? Because they're Catholic?"

"Either that or a clan struggle. A Macpherson is taking Macdonald's lease, and he's ousting the tenants," she answered, shrugging. "I'll ask someone on the Gordon estates, and ye might try the Braes of Glenlivet, though I know it's some distance away." There was once a seminary there; perhaps it still existed.

"I don't suppose I could ask the minister?"

Ask the minister where he might find a heather priest? Was he mad? She bit her tongue and swallowed. "I think not, Wylie. He knows ye were out in the '45, ken. That's *all* he knows of ye."

A side of his mouth curled in something akin to scorn. "Aye, well. Dougal finds comfort in speaking with a priest. I expect I need to find one."

She nodded, though she wondered at his hurry. America surely had priests, especially in the once Spanish-held Florida. "D'ye mean to stay on?" she asked, clinging to a kernel of hope.

"No. But it's possible I'll stay through Sunday."

Already she felt stirrings of grief at the upcoming loss—for both her father and herself. She blew out a breath and stayed silent while the track to Baile Dùil came within sight.

At the intersection, Wylie paused, though he still watched the way ahead.

Perhaps since she had the chance, she ought to ask about Will. "Wylie, before ye go, Will has some concerns, and I told him I'd speak with him later today. I'm thinking now it might be best if ye spoke with him instead."

Wylie's brow creased as if he were puzzled. Then he sighed. "I'm sorry for that, Anna. I spoke with him earlier this afternoon."

She frowned. Truly? In that event, then, Wylie seemed unnaturally calm. From what William had told her she expected Wylie would rather pull his teeth out one by one than speak of George and that time.

"Oh," she said simply.

Wylie rubbed a hand up his forearm. "I'm not certain Will heard all I had to say, but I tried. If he'd like your perspective, I've no objection." He gave her a lopsided smile. "I'm not the father my own was. I can use all the help I can get with those boys."

"Ye judge yourself harshly, Wylie. They're fine lads, the both of them."

"I expect that's more to do with their mother than with myself."

She struggled for words. "How often were ye at sea?"

He shrugged. "Most of the time."

"How many days a year were ye at home?" she asked, trying a different tack.

Again he shrugged. "Twenty, perhaps."

She stared at him, openmouthed. "Twenty?"

"Aye. Why?"

"Wylie, ye can't compare yourself to William. He was here whenever ye needed him."

He bristled. "Aye, well, you'll recall I hadn't a trade or an income—"

She raised a hand, stopping him. "I'm not saying ye're to blame, mind. I'm saying ye haven't had the chance to be the father your own father was. That's not to say ye can't. Ye're doing more things right than ye know."

"You think so?"

"I do. Ye've only to spend time with the lads to know that's true."

Without warning, he reached forward and pushed back her hood. "I wanted to see your face," he said by way of explanation. "Besides, the rain stopped."

His fingertips brushed her cheek before he dropped his hand.

Her mouth went dry.

She couldn't help herself; raising a hand, she touched her cheek, fancying it warm from his fingers. She stared up at him.

Anna the artist made note of the slow arch of his brow, the strong curve of his jaw, and the full curve of his mouth.

Anna the woman couldn't drag her gaze from the dark, wet lashes shading soft brown eyes, eyes she imagined locked on her mouth.

Would he dare kiss her here? Would she allow it?

Yes.

"Anna, would you be candid if I asked you something?"

She blinked. Not trusting her voice, she nodded.

"The night you visited. Did I do something to offend you?"

If only so. She could bring it to mind and muster her defenses.

"Nay." Vaguely she became aware he was right about the rain stopping. A cooling breeze had swept the sun clear of mist. Once again the river's rumble, fueled afresh by the shower, filled her ears.

"You've made yourself scarce. I'd hoped to see more of you while I was here."

The absurdity of his statement snapped her out of her reverie. She raised her chin and expelled an unladylike snort. "Wylie Macpherson, that's a fib and ye know it. Ye haven't thought of me in years."

His grin was unabashed. "Maybe not. But I've made up for the lack these last days."

She gaped at him. Mother Mary, what was he thinking, saying such things?

"I enjoy your company, Anna. Dougal says you invited me to supper tonight."

"Aye."

"Should I come?"

"If ye like. Archibald Montgomery will be there."

He looked at her, his gaze speculative. "He knows I'm at Glencorach, does he?"

"Aye, he does."

"Right. Well then, we should meet. Especially if he's wooing you."

It was her turn to bristle. So he thought himself her brother?

He grinned. "I'm laird, ken, at least while here. I have a responsibility to see to the tenants' welfare."

She grimaced, stopping short of another derisive snort. He wasn't *her* laird. "See to your other responsibilities; I do well enough on my own." She wrenched her basket from his grip.

He stepped back, still grinning. "I'd like to speak to your father tomorrow about the accounts. I expect my uncle will release that note later today. What time will be convenient?"

"My father manages his own time. Ask him tonight."

"So you no longer wish to be present?"

She frowned; he had her so befuddled she'd forgotten. "Yes, of course I prefer to be present. But tomorrow I'm taking supplies to the shielings."

"You're leaving?" He raised his head a notch and looked toward the hills. After a second's hesitation, he asked, "Do you mind if I accompany you, then?"

She hadn't yet heard from George. If Glencorach's beasts were indeed missing, Wylie ought not to be the last to learn of it.

"I can go on my own," he said, as if sensing her hesitation. "I'll follow at a distance. No one will suspect we're acquainted."

She rolled her eyes. "Ye're free to accompany me," she said, suddenly weary of worrying. George would have reported to Henry by now, and Henry would surely speak with Wylie this afternoon while they were together. "But know I plan to leave before dawn."

"Well enough. Good day, Anna," he said. "Perhaps I'll see you at the kirk later. If not, then at supper. Give my best to Lachie and Mary. Tell them I thought of them only this afternoon."

Nodding, she turned and started down the lane to the township.

That had to be one of the more foolish things she'd ever agreed to. Most of the parish women were at the shielings for the summer. Isolated, they had little to gossip over save each other. Appearing with Wylie Macpherson at her side would set the parish ablaze with speculation.

She blew a breath through her nose, dismissing the concern.

For a few hours alone with the man, she'd risk that and much more.

CHAPTER 18

WYLIE STOOD ROOTED, watching until Anna was out of sight before walking on. Bypassing the track leading to the ruined peel tower, he soon reached the rows of birch trees lining the drive to Cragdurcas Manor. He stopped and pulled out his pocket watch.

Five minutes to three. Had Uncle Henry planned meeting here or at the house? With the toe of his boot, Wylie dislodged a few stones and then shifted idly from foot to foot, content to wait.

It wasn't an illusion, then, this ease that Anna brought. An hour ago he'd have been tearing up the dirt pacing at the wait, for his morning had been brutal and the afternoon promised no better.

First there'd been Uncle Henry's poking and prodding. Then Dougal's disquieting request for a priest. All followed by the shock of Will's seeming disrespect of women—a stark mark of Wylie's colossal failure as a father. More so because Rennie *had* tried to warn him.

Far worse, however, was the shock of his own callous, cold-blooded indifference, and he couldn't push it aside. It sickened him. Devil take it, his cousin had been maimed.

Maimed.

And he couldn't be bothered to remember?

Who *was* this man he'd become?

He had no defense, and guilt clawed at him.

By the time he'd started for Cragdurcas, his nausea raged. Steps from the standing stones, he'd doubled over and heaved his dinner to the heath. When the spasms stilled, he'd rested his forehead against the nearest stone until its cold, clammy surface halted the world's reeling. When he opened his eyes, he'd spotted Anna Macrae walking the lane from Glendally.

Something remarkable happened then, something he couldn't explain.

His insides stopped roiling.

His sense of dread dissipated.

He didn't know why, but it was as if Anna was his beacon in

this hellish tempest, and instead of dismissing the outlandish notion, he latched on to it. His confidence regained, he'd caught her attention and hurried to greet her.

Even now, cooling his heels on the lane to Cragdurcas, the contentment remained.

He felt no shame over his plans to cling to her for the next two or three days. He meant what he'd said. He'd follow her to the shielings whether she wished it or not; he'd tail her like a hound if he must.

And thoroughly enjoy the view. He grinned, envisioning her hips swaying.

Someone's goat bleated in the near distance, and a horse whinnied in reply. He nudged the stones he'd dislodged into a line, then into two lines. He looked at his watch.

Five minutes *after* three.

Hell. Kicking the stones from the path, he heaved a sigh. He'd meet Henry at the house.

The birch trees sounded their own sigh, their canopy of spring green shivering overhead. He walked the track between them, pausing when he reached the circling oval at the drive's end, and scanned the length of the manor. He'd scarcely paid heed to the sight the day before.

There was no denying it was impressive. The added wings appeared original and well they should. Uncle Henry had paid a fortune to ensure it.

He crossed to the front door, and it opened before he raised a hand to knock.

"Good afternoon, sir," a kilted manservant said, inclining his head. "Your uncle will be with ye shortly. If ye'd care to join the captain and his wife, they are taking tea in the library."

Captain? He must mean George. Hell no, he'd not care to join them.

"Tell my uncle I'll enjoy the grounds while I wait." Without awaiting a response, Wylie trotted down the steps and strode toward the grouping of benches beneath the ash grove fronting the north wing. He sat, resting a booted ankle atop his knee. A breeze freed a scatter of raindrops from the leaves above, and Wylie turned his face upwards and opened his mouth, catching some as they fell.

Shifting in his seat, his fingers tapped an impatient tattoo on the bench. Behind him, voices drifted from an open window. Indistinct at first, their tenor grew heated and the words clear.

"You invariably think the worst of him, George. He could come home covered in medals, and you'd claim he stole them."

"Miriam, ye know that's not true. Why can't ye see ye're killing him with kindness?"

Wylie froze, realizing he eavesdropped on an argument between his cousin and his cousin's wife. He considered moving, but if he stood, they may glimpse the movement and then him, making matters worse. He stayed.

"One of us must be kind! Lord knows you aren't. How can you think such an awful thing of your son?"

"How can ye doubt it? He didn't go to London as he said he would. He promised us he'd pay his debts and start afresh. Yet he's in Fort William. Why, I ask ye?"

Miriam and George spoke of Jay. So Wylie had been correct in thinking the lad planned visiting London. Odd, then, that Jay had told Wylie Inverness.

Wylie chewed on his lower lip, wondering himself why Jay had lied about his destination, both to his family and to Wylie.

"I don't know why, George, but I refuse to think the worst. Perhaps he was summoned to receive new orders."

"Come now, lass. Alexander said he saw him in a card game in the wee hours of morning."

"Alexander couldn't wait to discredit him, could he?"

"He has nothing against the lad. I encountered Alexander by chance. He merely mentioned he'd run into Jay while visiting his brother.

"Playing cards is not a crime."

Wylie expelled a breath at Miriam's tone. It was near a whine, and one she'd used long ago with him. He imagined her pouting, arms crossed beneath her breasts to display an enticing hollow to a distracting advantage. In the past, he'd wondered if she assumed the pose deliberately.

Now, knowing a bit more of women, he'd lay odds that she had.

"It's very much a crime if ye can't cover your losses, Miriam. Father meant it when he said no more. Jay's a fool if he doesn't believe him."

"Your father's a brute."

"Father's been exceedingly generous. It can't continue."

139

Wylie stopped short before nodding, though he agreed.

If what George implied were true, Jay wouldn't be the only soldier on half-pay idling time in gaming halls. Nor would he be the only one with debts too steep to repay. Repeated handouts only prolonged the problem.

"He's troubled, I'll grant that. But Jay didn't do what you're suggesting. I *know* he didn't, George. Without a posting, he's at loose ends. Surely you see that. But it needn't be so. If you cared a wit, you'd help me get him settled, and we wouldn't be having this discussion."

"Miriam, don't—"

A door slammed, and George didn't finish his sentence.

Picturing Miriam seething on the opposite side of that door, her hands fisted and jaw clenched, Wylie grudgingly experienced a small shred of sympathy for George.

It seemed he wasn't alone in worrying over his offspring.

He heard the front door opening and rose, expecting he'd see his uncle. Instead he saw Miriam. She came directly toward him, her expression stormy and her steps long and purposeful.

"Don't pretend you didn't hear that," she said. "I saw you from the window."

He blinked. He hadn't intended to pretend anything. Clasping his hands behind his back, he inclined his head. "Good afternoon, Mrs. Macpherson."

She'd neglected donning a bodice scarf, making her gown more suited to a London society evening than an afternoon Highland tea. His gaze strayed appreciatively to the creamy display of skin above its neckline.

"He infuriates me," she said, pacing to and fro before him.

"Your husband?"

He intended conveying a mild interest only. But he suspected his tone carried a hint of resentment, for she stopped pacing and studied him, a faint pink climbing up her slender neck.

Her lips parted when the pink spread to her cheeks. "Oh my, this is awkward, isn't it?"

Wylie raised his brows. "It needn't be, madam." What was done was done. All he'd like from her was an explanation on *why* she'd done it.

An expression of regret wouldn't come amiss either.

She took his hand, clasping it in hers. "I hope you'll still address me as Miriam. May I still call you Wylie?"

Her hands were warm and soft. He didn't care for the sensation and slid his from her grasp, nodding.

Apparently unaffected by his snub, she took his elbow and led him toward the stone path that circled the manor. "Your uncle won't be out for a bit. One of the ghillies is speaking with him about some problem with the cattle. Let's walk."

Wylie allowed himself to be led, forgoing the temptation to look toward the window to see if George watched.

"Twenty-five years, Wylie. It seems little more than twenty-five hours."

He raised a brow. Perhaps, if it were possible to give birth to a twenty-four year old in the space of hours. "Indeed it might, were you not married and mother to my cousin's son."

She looked away. "Well . . . yes. There is that."

"Mm-hmm."

"I scarcely remember that girl. Do you?" she asked, looking back at him. "Do you find me changed?"

How would he know? They'd spoken little since he'd returned. But of course that wasn't the answer she was after. Scratching his chin, he answered.

"You're still very beautiful. Your husband is a lucky man."

She squeezed his arm and smiled. "Thank you for saying that. I doubt you'll hear him say it."

Wylie was beginning to sense that, and it puzzled him. Reluctantly, he asked the question plaguing him. "How is my cousin?"

She made a disparaging noise in her throat. "He's morose, irritable, and uninteresting."

None of those words had ever fit George. Swallowing, he looked down at her. "His injury still pains him, then?"

Her brow furrowed as if his question puzzled her. "His . . . Oh, that. No. Well, perhaps. I expect it might from time to time."

Criminy. He thought *he'd* been callous.

They neared the corner of the house and with a quick look behind her, Miriam hastened her pace. Wylie glanced over his shoulder but saw no one.

"I'm not happy, Wylie," she said, leading him around the corner.

His heart tripped and then quickened in anticipation of her

141

explanation for marrying George.

"I despise this desolate and dreary countryside."

He swallowed a sigh, having heard those lines often enough. In the past, it'd aroused an urge to give her the world. Now, it sparked irritation. She knew she spoke of his homeland, yet she didn't blink an eye at disparaging it.

His lips firmed. That, of course, no longer bothered him.

She came to a stop and faced him. "Forgive my abruptness, but I fear we may not have another chance to speak."

He didn't like skulking behind a house with another man's wife, sharing confidences. "Miriam, I—"

She held up a hand. "It's about Jay. It's important," she said. "I don't know what I'd do without him. Or for that matter, what he'd do without me. The scrapes that boy gets into . . . He's forever at my doorstep." She shook her head, her smile indulgent. "I'm sure you can imagine, having boys of your own."

Other than to remind her that her "boy" was an officer in the army, Wylie was uncertain how to respond. He opted for silence.

"I don't mind though. Once he marries, he may no longer have need of me. I'll do what I can while I can."

He ran his thumb over his chin, curious. "He's planning to marry?"

She shrugged. "At some point. Doesn't everyone?"

Impatient now, he turned from her. "I should see if Uncle Henry—"

"Wait! Please. The thing is, well, it regards Glencorach."

He tensed and turned back, suddenly recalling Jay saying he wished to speak to him of Glencorach, and his hope that his mother didn't broach the subject first.

"What does?" he asked, his voice carefully neutral.

"Your father told us you didn't plan to return, and we . . . we hoped you might consider keeping the estate in the family."

His gaze narrowed. "Pardon me?" Aside from his boys, George and Uncle Henry were his only family. Henry had mentioned no such thing. "George wishes to keep Glencorach?"

She shook her head. "No, no. Not George. Jay. Don't you see, it's the perfect challenge for a young man, and he'd remain nearby. I'd see him often."

Wylie couldn't resist poking her. "You wish him to remain in a dreary and desolate place?"

She didn't even blink. "Of course it's not my first wish. But London's distractions can be troubling."

"Ah," he answered.

"So do you see?"

"I'm not sure. Are you telling me Jay wants to purchase Glencorach?"

A vivid pink crawled up her neck, and she looked to the side. "Well, he hasn't the means to purchase it."

Wylie stared at her, his brows near meeting. Surely she didn't intend he just hand the lad his estate. He had sons of his own to consider.

"You can't mean I should *give* Glencorach to your son?"

She had the grace to look flustered, though she quickly recovered. "It's not as if you are interested. Jay's a family member. He makes a logical choice, wouldn't you agree?"

No, he didn't. "I intend to sell, Miriam."

"Would you consider keeping it?" She reached for his right hand and clasped it. "Jay could be your estate manager. You might work out an arrangement whereby you receive a small share of the profits."

He stayed silent a moment, at a loss for words. Then he said, "There's a buyer under contract, Miriam."

"Oh, that." She shook her head, dismissing Montgomery as an obstacle. "I'm certain you can handle that little man."

Pulling his hand from hers, he left her side, not waiting to see if she followed. "I don't want to keep my uncle waiting."

Bypassing his late aunt's once coveted and now weathered lawn statuary, the stone squirrels and rabbits chipped and etched gray with the damp, Wylie rounded the house. Miriam kept pace, past the front door and on toward the benches where she'd found him. Politely, he dried one with his jacket sleeve and offered her a seat.

She shook her head. "I don't want to sit." Moving a step closer, she stretched a hand to his bonnet. He stood frozen while she plucked at something that adhered to it, coming away with a damp leaf. Discarding it, she fingered the cuff of his shirt, rubbing the linen between her finger and thumb.

Oddly, her touch repelled him, and he took an awkward step back.

"You've done well for yourself," she said.

"Well enough."

"Where will you go when you leave Scotland, Wylie?"

He cast a sideways glance toward the front door. It remained closed, offering no escape.

"I'm pursuing an opportunity in East Florida with several of my trading partners."

She tilted her head. "East Florida? St. Augustine?"

Wylie nodded, surprised at her reaction. "Aye. You're familiar with it?"

"I should think so. Jamie is governor there."

His chin shot up, and he gave her his full attention. "You know James Grant, then? I wasn't sure if you would."

"He's a distant cousin, but yes, of course. You know he's expected in London soon."

No, Wylie hadn't known. "Why is that?"

"His nephew is very ill and will not last the summer. Jamie will inherit the family's estate."

Wylie frowned. "You mean to say he's resigning as governor?" That would be disappointing. The colony's governor was crucial to his venture's success. He'd hoped the man would be a Scotsman, someone with compatible ideals.

"I don't think so, though I can't say for certain. It's my understanding he'll settle his estate and then return to Florida. Would you like an introduction? I'm going to London soon. I'd love your company."

He stared at her. *Bloody hell.*

He'd thought Rennie had mocked the last ounce of provincialism out of him, but apparently not. Traveling alone with another man's wife, a woman he'd once hoped to marry, was well beyond his ken.

"Your husband . . ." He cleared his throat. "I don't think that's wise, Mrs. Macpherson."

"Why ever not? George wouldn't mind."

Wylie doubted that. Even if George and Miriam were at odds, Miriam was his wife. "My sons and I plan to leave Scotland within days."

"You don't have to take them. They could join you in a fortnight. Henry would be delighted to host them for a time. Don't say no. Think it over. I'd love to introduce you into society; everyone will adore you. And I know Jamie would be ever so helpful."

Wylie heard a door slam behind him, and he briefly shut his eyes. *Merci.*

Miriam stuck out her arm, blocking his escape. "Do think about Jay, Wylie. And consider joining me in London. I could become an asset to you, if you allow it." She tiptoed up and kissed his cheek. "I know I've made mistakes, but none that can't be rectified." With that, she turned and walked away.

His mouth slightly agape, Wylie stayed rooted.

His uncle called out his name. Wylie gave his head a sharp shake and turned toward the door.

"I apologize for the wait, lad." Henry hobbled across the grass toward him, still favoring his cane. A boy of about ten trailed behind.

"It's no matter, Uncle. I had company."

"What did she want?"

"Nothing of consequence. Should we go?"

"I expect it's best if we ride." Turning, he barked an order at the boy behind him, and the boy scampered away.

While they waited, Wylie ventured asking after the whereabouts of Glencorach's stock.

"They're here," Henry said, waving a hand dismissively. "I thought we ought not leave them unattended. Take what ye need."

Wylie studied his uncle, puzzled by his seeming preoccupation. At the very least, he'd expected Henry would remind him that he too held an interest in the animals.

"I shouldn't need more than a horse," Wylie said finally.

The stable lad led two saddled horses toward them. Wylie helped his uncle atop one, then mounted himself. They started down the front drive.

"What time are we expected?"

Henry looked up. "What's that?"

"Is something wrong, Uncle?" Wylie asked, concerned.

Henry shook his head and again lapsed into thought.

Wylie frowned. He preferred the prospect of matching wits with Henry far more than the prospect of watching him age before his eyes.

"Let's discuss this interview, aye?" Wylie said at length, attempting to divert his uncle to the task at hand. "We require a strategy." In the past, Henry had counseled the benefits of strategies.

"A strategy." Henry nodded, his lips pursing. "Good idea, lad."

"Since neither of us is qualified to assess a schoolmaster's qualifications, I propose we hire this man today, as long as we can come to terms."

Henry straightened in his seat, seeming more himself. "Fair enough. Shall we stick to four pounds annually?"

Uncle Henry knew Highland economics better than Wylie, but four seemed a miserly amount.

"Well, no more than five, at any rate," Wylie said, suspecting anyone willing to take four had nowhere else to go. "As for the minister's request, perhaps Will and I may complete his repairs."

"Ye're a fortunate man, having a competent son."

Wylie grunted, unsure if Henry meant to imply George or perhaps Jay was incompetent. George might be a perfidious snake, but he was a competent one.

"Nevertheless, Wylie, there's a fair number of tenants who owe the parish their labor. I suggest we choose among them."

Wylie rubbed a thumb over his forefinger, sensing a delay. The men tended to drag their feet performing service labor. Not only was it unpaid, the number of hours owed was always a matter of contention between the lairds and their tenants. "How many men will it require?"

"Ten, maybe?" Henry's mouth twisted while he thought. "We might use Robert McDobb, Henry Pox, Seamus Moy—"

"Stop," Wylie said, holding up a palm. "Do you know their skills?"

"Nay. We'd have to ask about."

Wylie's mouth thinned as he envisioned his uncle "asking about," traveling from farm to farm armed with a bottle of whisky and a deep well of chatter. It would take weeks.

Reaching the end of the tree-lined drive, they reined their mounts onto the road and headed north. "Let's see what the minister requires before we discuss it further. I haven't much time. But we're agreed about the schoolmaster, aye? Neither of us is qualified to assess his qualifications. Our objective is to come to terms."

He looked at his uncle for confirmation and instead thought he detected a calculating glint in Henry's eye.

Wylie ignored it. "We will hire someone today."

CHAPTER 19

GOATS WANDERED freely along the roadside, searching out sparse patches of green. Henry spoke idly of the farmsteads they passed, each little more than a cluster of drab, unkempt hovels, built of sod and roofed with turf. Here and there, Wylie spied a solitary cottar pushing a plough through his allotted strip of heathery waste.

They were a tough lot, his countrymen.

Relieved his uncle's silence had ended, Wylie listened to Henry with mild interest, adding an obligatory comment when called for. If nothing else, it saved him puzzling over Miriam's invitation to London.

He fell silent when he first glimpsed the churchyard, a knot forming in his chest as they drew nearer and his memories gathered strength.

The yard was an ugly patch of land worn bare by decades of footsteps. The school and the minister's manse sat at opposite corners on its far end, and the kirk, a modest drystone of squat gray walls etched black with moisture, filled the yard's center.

He and Henry rode past the kirk, reined in, and dismounted. Wylie secured the horses and laid a hand on the warm, bristly rump of one, stealing a minute to look about.

The knot at his ribs softened, the decades fading. He'd spent countless hours on this property as a boy. Those in the yard and schoolhouse, surrounded by his friends and under Reynolds's kind supervision, had passed swiftly.

The hours inside the kirk, not so much.

The drystone was a far cry from the stunning cathedrals Wylie had seen in France. Yet he knew its unassuming and unobtrusive appearance for a façade; the kirk pervaded every aspect of its parishioners' lives. He'd cared little for Reverend Pul's and the elders' swift, unforgiving, and—in Wylie's mind—unreasoned judgments. Living up to their unyielding standards had been nigh impossible.

The first time Wylie had been subject to church censure—or rather, the first two times—he'd been seven years old. Passing time before dinner, he'd thrown a length of string, baited with his spit, into the river. Reverend Pul, supposedly praying riverside, had seen him and pulled him home by the ear to tell Wylie's father that he'd fished on the Sabbath. When Wylie protested that untruth, explaining he hadn't "a hope in hell of catching a fish without a hook," the reverend added swearing to his crime.

Given his age, the fine had been small.

The last time had been in this very churchyard, when he and George commiserated privately over Lachie and Mary's predicament. Wylie named the elders a "parcel of eijits." George corrected him, calling them a "parcel of *barmy* eijits." One of the cottars' sons had overheard and reported them to the elders. Quite a coup for the lad, given he and George were sons of lairds.

Now that Wylie thought of it, he'd never paid for that sin. The conversation had occurred one summer Sunday in 1745, shortly before he and George had set off for Crieff.

He wondered if George had been summoned for it when he returned to the parish months later.

For that matter, had George and Miriam been summoned to answer for their bout of prenuptial fornication? Jay had been born shortly after their wedding.

"Ye coming, lad?" Henry called.

Wylie slapped the horse's rump and crossed the yard to the schoolhouse.

The school-room was much as Wylie remembered, bitterly cold and smelling of the damp earth floor that never seemed to dry. An oak desk, a long-ago gift from the heritors, stood at the room's front. Four rows of benches and tables faced it. The potential schoolmaster was nowhere in sight.

Wylie noted the bench nearest the door still carried a rudimentary carving of the Macpherson crest, and he smiled faintly. He'd carved that. He'd been six at the time and it'd taken him weeks. Proud as he'd been, he hadn't dared add his initials. Reynolds had never been certain who'd defaced the bench; the parish was littered with Macphersons.

"Well, where is he?" Wylie asked.

Uncle Henry sat on a bench and stretched his right leg forward.

He shook his head, frowning in apparent disapproval. "Late, I expect. Either that, or he left because *we're* late."

If that were the case, they'd need to track him down. Wylie wanted this task complete by suppertime. He walked to a window and propped an elbow on its sill, watching the yard.

"Where is he staying?" he asked.

"Hmm? What's that, lad?"

"The candidate. Which direction will he be coming from?"

"Oh. Either the widow Robertson's or Tommy Boll's."

So from the north, then. He crossed the room and looked out the other window, toward the road leading north. Someone approached the yard from a distance, but as they neared he realized it was a child. He looked back at his uncle, who had propped his elbow on the table and cheek in his hand, his eyes fluttering open and closed.

Abandoning his lookout post, Wylie started pacing. At length he became aware of a faint odor, one he couldn't identify. It was familiar, but so out of place that he couldn't put a name to it.

"Do you smell that?" he asked, turning back to his uncle.

His uncle sniffed the air, frowning. After a bit, he nodded. "Gin, I'll wager."

It *did* smell like gin. Perhaps Reynolds had ailed in his final years and used gin to ease the pain.

Wylie crossed to the desk, intent on checking the drawers for an open bottle. Rounding it, he stumbled over something and nearly fell face-first before he caught himself. A man lay on the floor below him, his legs stretched out beneath the desk.

"What is it, Wylie?" Henry asked, rising. As he hurried forward, his cane thumped a steady beat on the packed earth.

Wylie didn't answer. The man lay belly down, his mud-covered face turned to one side. His black hair, lank and thinning, was combed neatly back and secured in a ribbon. He hadn't moved when Wylie tripped over him.

"Is he dead?" Henry asked.

Hell, maybe. Wylie knelt and touched his wrist, checking for a pulse. Without warning, the man grumbled and then belched. Startled, Wylie fell on his rump, reeling at the stench of rotting teeth.

"Apparently not." Wylie stood and prodded the man's buttocks with his boot.

The man rolled over, revealing a face thin and pock-marked, with a narrow beak-like nose. The hand on his belly gripped an open flask, and spilled gin wet the front of his waistcoat. Muttering obscenities, he covered his eyes with a forearm.

"You can curse a fair stream in English, so I take it you speak it," Wylie said. "What's your name?"

There was another string of obscenities, and Wylie prodded him again, this time harder. "Your name, man."

"Anderson. Robert Anderson." Frowning, the man dropped his arm and struggled into a sitting position. The flask tumbled to the floor. "Who asks?"

Henry hadn't mentioned the prospect's name. Wylie glanced toward him for confirmation.

Henry nodded slowly, a side of his mouth twisted in disgust. "The men funding your salary," he said, his tone one of authority.

Alert now, Anderson clambered to his feet and swayed forward. Both Henry and Wylie took a step back.

Terms only. No man was without fault.

With a grimace, Wylie extended his hand palm up and wiggled his fingers. "Your letter of introduction, sir."

The man fumbled in his pocket and withdrew a paper blotched with varying shades of brown. Ignoring Wylie's outstretched hand, he handed the letter to Henry. Henry didn't take it. Canting his head, he deferred to Wylie.

Unperturbed at Anderson's slight—he rather wished Uncle Henry *had* taken it—Wylie scanned the document quickly and then dropped it to the desk.

"I see your last place of employment was a print shop in London," Wylie said. "Why did you leave?"

"My employer and I disagreed on a matter of principle."

"And that principle would be?" Wylie asked, arching a brow.

"It's a personal matter, sir."

Snorting, Wylie looked at his uncle, who only shrugged. Wylie's mouth quirked in annoyance. "Could you not find work between here and London, Mr. Anderson?"

"I hoped I might escape the temptations of the city in a pastoral retreat."

Henry harrumphed.

Wylie's lips pressed tight. "I see. And have you, then?"

Anderson raised his head, aiming his black, red-rimmed eyes at

150

Wylie. "Have I what?"

"Have you escaped the temptations of the city?"

"I've only just arrived, sir. I can hardly be expected to answer that."

Wylie blinked. His uncle hitched a hip on a corner of the desk and reached for the letter.

Briefly, Wylie considered sending Mr. Anderson off and waiting for the next candidate. But Anderson *did* speak proper English, presumably one of the parish requirements.

Still . . .

Wylie supposed he'd expected the candidate would recite his scholarly qualifications without prompting. Since that wasn't the case, he should probably ask a question or two. "Have you taught before?"

Anderson pointed at the paper on the desk and Henry slid it back toward Wylie. Wylie ignored it, knowing it referenced no teaching experience.

"If you read that, sir, you'll note the number of universities I've attended, Oxford among them," Anderson said.

Eijit. That was no answer.

Why in the hell wasn't George conducting this interview? George would have had a list of questions two meters long and delved into the applicant's background up to and including what his eighth grandfather thrice removed had thought of book learning. If there was such a thing as an eighth grandfather thrice removed.

Wylie had nothing.

Anderson glanced from Wylie to his uncle as the silence stretched on.

It didn't matter *why* George wasn't doing as he should, only that he wasn't. Once again, Wylie must manage on his own.

Groping for another question, he settled on ciphering—his only strength.

"If I sold you six head of cattle at four pounds six pence each, Mr. Anderson, how much would you owe me?"

The man pursed his lips to one side, as if puzzled, then wobbled back and forth a bit. "I hardly think that's relevant, sir. I have no use for six cows, nor do I intend to take up farming."

Why hadn't he stuck to their strategy and asked only about salary?

Ye're to hire the best man for the job, aye?

Right, then.

He couldn't do it. Nor could he face Anna if he did. Dragging a hand over the back of his neck, he sighed resignedly. "Sir, I regret—"

"Your salary requirement, Mr. Anderson?" Uncle Henry interrupted.

Openmouthed, Wylie turned and stared at his uncle.

"Ten pounds a year."

"Will you take four?" Henry asked.

Anderson frowned and appeared to consider it, then he nodded.

A thread of unease coiled in Wylie's gut. "Uncle Henry—"

Henry waved a dismissive hand. "Done," he said, his voice laced with satisfaction. "Ye'll lodge in the manse once term starts. In the event ye find temptations too tempting, Reverend Dow will be near to steer ye clear."

Anderson paled. "I'm lodged at Mrs. Robertson's, sir. I believe that arrangement will continue to suit."

"As ye wish. Don't expect more compensation because of it. Now, we've consumed enough of my nephew's day. Come back this time tomorrow, and we'll discuss details. I expect it best ye come back sober."

Sniffing audibly, Anderson walked to the door in a slow, practiced gait, his head held high.

Baffled, Wylie shook his head.

Henry's mouth curved. "That was easy enough, aye? Good strategy, lad," he said, nodding approval. "Shall we see to the minister?"

Wylie didn't respond, his gaze narrowing as he watched Henry turn and walk toward the door.

They'd just hired a drunk with no experience to school the parish children. For a man once set on sending his son to one of the finest universities in the world, Henry appeared remarkably indifferent.

CHAPTER 20

KNOWING SHE was late, Anna tugged ineffectually at the kirk's door, a massive wood slab twice her size, then kicked it in frustration and tugged again. It always swelled shut after a rain. Suddenly it broke free, swinging open, and she stumbled into Lori Macphee, one of her closest friends.

"I told Maidie it was ye making that racket," Lori said, her wide smile shrinking her blue eyes. Short and stout, Lori grew rounder with each child she bore. Sadly, only two of her five had survived, and sorrow streaked her red hair silver, making the strands visible at the edge of her cap rather striking. She steadied Anna and then pushed the door shut.

The church was low-ceilinged and sparsely furnished with ramshackle pews placed at odd angles. Anna surveyed the room for others and saw that Maidie Macphee, another close friend, stood at the only window. "Am I too late?"

Lori shook her head. "How was Mary, then?"

"She's doing well enough, though she wishes she were here. Where is the reverend?"

"He'll be along. We think Cragdurcas and Glencorach are still in the schoolhouse."

Maidie Macphee, as tall and thin as Lori was short and stout, turned from the window with a mischievous grin, black curls falling from her cap. Maidie and Lori had married twin brothers. Some teased they ought to have found triplets, and then there would have been a brother to spare for Anna.

"Anna Macrae. We saw ye only yesterday, and ye never said a word." Maidie's brown eyes danced as she came forward and elbowed her sister-in-law. Lori gave a small laugh that bordered on a giggle.

"Word of what?" Anna asked. She loosened the fastenings on her cloak and hooked it on a nearby pew.

"Of Wylie Macpherson, lass!" Maidie said, shaking her head in seeming exasperation. "He was always a braw lad, but my word, to see him now. Johnny Grant said ye were walking with him."

Anna stifled a groan. That was fast, even for Johnny. His wife would be none too pleased he'd abandoned his plough to carry tales.

"Charlie says he's a widower," Lori said, her voice tinged with a meaningful lilt. Her husband Charlie ran the ferry and knew a little something about most everyone.

"Aye, he is." These two would marry her off in a heartbeat—though they preferred the groom was not Archibald Montgomery.

"He says ye've cared for his lads these last few days."

Anna shook her head. "Those lads require little care."

"Hmm," Maidie murmured, lifting her brows.

"Now, don't ye start talk, Maidie Mac," Anna said, narrowing her gaze at her friend.

"If talk's what's required to open your eyes, it's glad I am to be starting it. Ye're not getting any younger, and if that gauger's to be your choice, he's dragging his feet."

Anna rolled her eyes. That "gauger" was Mr. Montgomery, and Maidie cared for him less than most.

Maidie's husband, Eneas, sold whisky to several taverns in Inverness. Twice now, Mr. Montgomery's gauge had measured an output larger than Eneas reported. He'd fined Eneas the second time, a fine three times the duty Eneas would have paid if he'd reported the correct amount to the excise from the start.

Maidie asked Anna to intervene, considering the fine a personal affront, but Eneas had told Anna to ignore it, considering it a cost of doing business.

"I've told ye both that he has no interest in marrying me," Anna said.

Lori elbowed Maidie and winked. "The excise frequents Glendally for Anna's rabbit stew, don't ye know."

Anna grinned. Her stew *was* notoriously inedible. "He frequents Glendally because he has business with my father."

"Aye, well," Maidie said, her skepticism apparent. "He'll not have that reason for long."

Anna looked sharply at Maidie, concerned someone had been telling tales of her father's lapses. "Why do you say that, Maidie?"

"Glencorach will no' be selling his land now his attainder's been lifted. He's those lads to think of, aye?"

Relieved, Anna didn't correct her.

"My niece Annalea met his eldest over at Robert Moy's," Maidie continued. "My word, I thought the lass might expire in the retelling." She placed a hand on her forehead, pantomiming a swoon.

"Oh aye." Anna smiled, having speculated it wouldn't take long for news of Will to spread. "She'll find he's an odd one, though. He keeps to himself."

"That's no' what I heard," Lori said, leaning her rump against a pew. She crossed her arms, settling in for a round of talk. "The lad was at the ferryhouse after midnight last night with Gracie."

After dark, Charlie operated a sort of private tavern in the west ferryhouse. The heritors turned a blind eye.

Maidie sniffed. "She's a fast one, that one." Turning from them, Maidie crossed back to the window.

Anna looked after her, frowning. It was well-known that Grace sought a husband to replace the one she'd lost. That didn't necessarily make her fast. She was, however, five years older than Will, which *was* concerning.

Or it ought to concern Wylie.

"Grace was with Will, ye mean to say?" Anna asked.

"If Will is the lad's Christian name, then aye," Lori said. "Charlie called him Glencorach the Younger."

That would be Will. Anna tugged at a loose curl, worrying it a moment before tucking it back in her cap. "Gracie is one of the hardest workers I know," she said, belatedly defending the girl. Martha doted on her niece. "Do ye know why they were there?"

"Well, I dinna expect it was to cross the river."

"Charlie served them whisky, then?"

Lori nodded. "Gracie didna drink, but the lad sipped a dram. Friendly as can be, according to Charlie. He bought Charlie a dram and invited him to sit and speak with them." Lori laughed. "Like as not, he didna expect an earful. Ye ken how Charlie goes on about that ferry."

Anna did. She'd been caught one too many times listening to Charlie drone on and on about the importance of his job, his ferry schedules and his loads. Feigning an interest was surprisingly kind of Will. She looked over her shoulder at Maidie and saw she stood sentry at the window. With a motion indicating Lori should follow, Anna crossed the room and joined her.

"What are ye looking at, Maidie?"

"Cragdurcas and Glencorach have been in there nigh on forty minutes," Maidie said.

"She's worried they'll hire that sot Anderson," Lori said, joining them.

"And ye're no'?" Maidie answered, an edge to her tone.

"They may have come out, Maidie," Lori said with exaggerated patience. "We may have missed seeing them when we were sorting the candles."

Maidie had aspirations for all six of her children and had taken a strong interest in the selection of schoolmaster. She shook her head, unwilling to be soothed. "If that's so, then where are they?"

"In with the minister, like as not," Anna said. "They've an obligation to speak with Mr. Anderson, Maidie. Ye needn't worry they'll hire him. Now, come sit, will ye? We're here to discuss the sharing of the relief fund. We best get to it."

Thirty minutes later, the kirk's rear door grated open. Each woman raised quick hands to her cap, tidying stray bits of hair, then rose. The Macphersons and Reverend Dow strode in.

Wylie's gaze fell immediately on Anna, his eyes widening before shifting to a point over her shoulder.

Her heart clenched in dismay. Her gown. She'd known it hadn't fit properly, yet she'd worn it anyway. Why hadn't Maidie or Lori said anything? She'd have kept on her cloak. Crossing her arms over her bodice, she greeted Reverend Dow.

The minister was a slight man with fair hair and a habitually kind smile that was absent at the moment. He nodded a stiff and silent greeting, giving her the impression he held his temper in check.

She doubted it was because of her gown; he appeared preoccupied.

Henry, however, was unreservedly pleasant. He greeted each of them in turn, inquiring how their respective families fared. Then he propped himself on a pew, rubbed a hand down his thigh, and said, "Well, ladies, ye'll no doubt be pleased to learn we now have a schoolmaster."

Anna's jaw dropped. She stared at Wylie, then at Henry. "But 'twas Robert Anderson ye were speaking with just now, aye?"

Henry Macpherson pursed his lips and addressed Wylie. "That was the man's name, wasn't it, lad?"

Wylie's head swung round sharply to his uncle. Anna couldn't see Wylie's expression, other than that his jaw appeared more rigid than usual.

Henry shrugged. "Ye don't remember either, then. Well, Miss Macrae could be right." He nodded slowly, seeming more certain. "Aye, she is. Robert Anderson, he was, now that I think about it."

Lori took a half step forward. "Begging your pardon, Cragdurcas, but are ye certain Anderson's qualified?" she asked, her voice faint. "Why, the widow Robertson claims he's been abed with the gin since he's come."

"Now, now, Mrs. Macphee. Did ye pay heed when Mrs. Robertson claimed your Lizzie spelled her cow?" Henry asked, his tone indulgent. "Of course ye didn't. That widow means well enough, but . . ." Henry tapped his head meaningfully.

Anna's brows met. What was Henry about? There was nothing wrong with Mrs. Robertson's mind. That had been a fever talking.

Mrs. Robertson had been abed a week last fall with a fever, and Lori's daughter Lizzie had helped her with chores. While it was true that a cow toppled over and died, Mrs. Robertson knew good and well that Lizzie hadn't cast a spell on it. When she recovered, she'd apologized repeatedly for the accusation—to the Macphees and anyone else who would listen.

Maidie spoke before Lori could answer. "But sir, Mrs. Robertson speaks the truth. Charlie fished Mr. Anderson out of the river not two days past. He fell from the ferry when alighting. Charlie says he could scarcely stand."

As yet, Wylie hadn't said a word. Anna tried catching his eye, but failed. He ignored her, staring fixedly at some spot behind the minister instead.

"Ladies, enough," Henry said, raising his hand. "The elders required a quick decision, and Mr. Anderson met our criteria. It's not open to discussion. We should, however, resolve the repairs to the manse."

Not open for discussion? Maidie and Lori looked dumbfounded. Anna trembled, so angry she couldn't speak. The parish might be stuck with that sot for the next thirty years.

"Miss Macrae?" Henry said. He looked at her, and for an instant, so did Wylie. "Did ye have something to say?"

If she spoke, Anna feared it would lead to sobbing. As it was, she blinked repeatedly, staving off tears. She shook her head and turned it, hoping the men hadn't noticed her lip wobble.

"Well then," Henry said. "My nephew judges three men for three days sufficient to repair the manse. I believe John Fraser, Thomas Macintosh, and Eneas Macphee will be best suited."

Anna felt as if the air had been sucked from the room. Of all the Cragdurcas men he could have tapped for services, he'd once again chosen from amongst Glendally's subtenants. The three he'd named were the same three men who only last week had appealed to their tacksman—her father—that Cragdurcas's requests had become burdensome.

The same three men whose appeals their tacksman had seemingly forgotten.

George was right. Sensing weakness, Henry targeted Glendally's tack.

"Sir, Eneas only just returned from carting your bark to the tanner," Maidie said, raising her chin a notch. "He's weeks behind on cutting your peat. He's not had a moment to spare for our fields."

Good for you, Maidie. Don't let him bully you. Anna chanced another look at Wylie for support. He knew as well as she did that the manse could wait until after the fields were sowed. Wylie's gaze, however, stayed fixed at some point in the distance, as if he wished himself elsewhere.

She gritted her teeth. And who here didn't wish likewise, aside from Henry?

Squaring her shoulders, she swallowed and spoke. "With respect, Cragdurcas, those men are Glendally's tenants. Glendally has scheduled the terms of their service. They've done more—"

"Speaking for your father now, are ye, Miss Macrae?" Henry said, his mouth curved in scorn. "He'll not thank ye for it, I grant." Shaking his head, he turned to Maidie and added, "Mrs. Macphee, if your husband finds his responsibilities burdensome, I suggest he take it up with his tacksman and not hide behind a woman's skirts. In the meantime, I expect him here at first light tomorrow," Henry said. "My nephew hasn't the time to dither about."

That got Wylie's attention. He glanced at his uncle, opened his mouth, then shut it, then opened it once more. "I'll handle this matter, Uncle Henry," he said quietly, startling them all.

"Oh, would ye, sir?" Lori said, placing a hand on Maidie's elbow. "That's so very kind."

Anna looked askance at her friend. Wylie hadn't said *how* he'd handle it. His solution may be more onerous than Henry's.

And though she wasn't certain, it appeared Lori had bobbed a knee in her thanks.

Wylie may now be laird, but he'd taught the three of them to play hop-scotch when they were five. Add to that, he'd just hired a lush to teach the parish children. He merited no bobbing knees.

Wylie turned to her. "Miss Macrae? My uncle and I will see you home."

Henry's gaze darted from Wylie to Anna and then back, his gray eyes sparking with something akin to surprise. If so, he wasn't the only one surprised. Anna had been seeing herself to and from home for thirty years now.

"That's so very kind, sir," Anna said, echoing Lori. If Wylie found her tone mocking, his expression only flickered. "But we have business with the reverend, and I'm not leaving."

"Aye, you are. You've guests for supper, aye? Are you ready, Uncle Henry?"

Her pulse slowed to a snail's pace, and she gripped the pew for balance. Laird or not, Wylie hadn't earned the right to take that proprietary air with her. Not after what he'd just done.

"You and Miss Macrae go on ahead, lad," Henry said. "I think I'll sit a spell with Reverend Dow."

"We'll speak soon, Miss Macrae," Reverend Dow said.

Maidie, knowing Anna well enough to recognize her growing fury, spoke up. "Lori and I must be off as well."

Pivoting, Anna marched down the aisle and wrenched her cloak from the pew hook. She wasn't certain who she was angrier with—Wylie and his uncle for the ill-advised hire, or herself for failing to protect her tenants' rights.

She'd not only let down the Macphees, she'd let down her father.

CHAPTER 21

WYLIE REACHED the door before Anna. He opened it, and she brushed past with arms crossed, shoulders rigid, and head down.

If he had to guess, he'd say she was angry.

"Stay here a moment, will you?" he asked once he'd shut the door behind him. Without waiting for her answer, he rounded the church at a trot and retrieved his horse. When he returned, he saw she was a hundred meters down the road. His mouth pressed tight, he mounted and trotted after her.

"I know you're angry," he said once he reached her.

Quickening her steps, she looked straight ahead. "I prefer walking alone, sir."

Sir? Criminy.

Dismounting, he walked beside her, leading the horse behind. Thankfully, her cloak hid that damned gown. Its fit was so snug it left nothing to the imagination, and his imagination did well enough on its own. He'd been surprised Reverend Dow hadn't called it to her attention.

"I'd like to explain."

"'Tis pointless and unnecessary, sir. The heritors' decisions are not up for discussion."

He grunted. "If you're of a mind to throw words at me, at least make them my own." He'd cringed when Henry had uttered those words, fearing he'd bear the brunt of them.

"Aye, well, I expect the sentiments are your own."

Perhaps. He didn't care to be questioned, he knew that for fact.

"I've no wish to make a laird's decisions, Anna. You know that."

"Oh, aye. I know it well enough. It's only I hadn't expected ye'd sacrifice the future of every child in this parish so that ye might be in America a fortnight earlier."

Oh, for Christ's sake.

He set his jaw, a simmering anger of his own starting to burn. He hadn't been alone in that room. Was Henry Macpherson not to share in the blame?

He lowered his head and fingered the rope he held, tracing its twists and turns before his temper took hold. In the end, he hadn't wanted to retain the man. He'd resigned himself to allowing the process more time. Uncle Henry's motivation in hiring Anderson puzzled him; nonetheless, he felt compelled to defend it. Henry *was* Wylie's senior.

"Anderson is well-spoken and well-educated, Anna. Perhaps the Christian thing to do is give him a chance to redeem himself."

Scowling, she snorted her disgust. "And the two other candidates? They're well-spoken and well-educated. Are they to be denied your Christian charity?"

Suddenly uneasy, he studied her. She'd said that as if the other candidates were standing by. Were they? Or had Henry said only one was near?

He ought to have questioned Henry on the particulars. In any event, he didn't intend to display his ignorance on the point.

"It's done," he said, his tone indicating he'd not discuss it further.

"Aye. Ye can mark it off your task list," she said, quickening her steps.

He gritted his teeth. God's blood, she was intractable.

Days ago, he'd known nothing of this. Now he was accountable for "the future of every child in the parish"?

Where was his credit for diffusing the quarrel over the manse repairs?

Something underlay Henry's demands. Something more than a desire for free labor. Demanding more than his allocated share of servitude was—or had been—unlike Henry. Wylie couldn't put a finger on it, but it made him uneasy, especially as it seemed Henry targeted the Macraes.

But why? Alan Macrae—industrious, competent, and organized—made an ideal tacksman.

Or once had.

The horse stumbled, its lead too tight. Wylie dropped the rein and reached for Anna's elbow, stopping her. "If you want me to say I'm sorry, then I'll say it. I'm sorry."

She kept her gaze locked on the ground. "Unhand me," she said quietly, a hitch in her voice.

He complied at once. Was she crying?

"Anna?" he said, uncertain. "I—"

"I'll see myself home from here, Wylie. I think it best ye dine elsewhere."

He flinched as if she'd hit him. Stung, he stood rooted, looking after her until she was long out of sight.

Anna, his only ally.

CHAPTER 22

AT LENGTH WYLIE picked up the reins and resumed walking, uncertain of his destination. Aside from his berth aboard the *Eliza*, he wasn't sure where he wanted to be.

His chest tight and mind blank, he stalled at Glencorach's drive for several minutes. Then he turned and retraced his steps, following the dictates of a habit long forgotten. Veering east, he started down the track to the peel tower ruin.

His river might bring a measure of peace.

Heath soon replaced farmland. Spotting the stone tower, Wylie's stride lengthened, then slowed.

Someone was there.

With measured steps, he studied the trespasser, gauging the man's size and probable purpose. He stopped short. The intruder wasn't trespassing, nor was he an intruder. The tower marked the boundary lines of Glencorach and Cragdurcas, and his cousin, George Macpherson, clearly sat on the side of Cragdurcas.

Propped against a tree, one hand draped over an upraised knee, George faced the river, his left hand resting protectively atop his cane.

The horse snorted, and George turned and saw Wylie.

"Ye needn't leave, Wylie," he said. "I'll go."

The simmering knot in his belly ignited, filling him with a hot anger. *The hell you say. Condescending, patronizing, traitorous dog.*

Wylie didn't require George's permission to be here. Hell if he'd turn tail and run.

"I had no intention of leaving." Dropping the reins, he closed the distance between them and kicked the cane out of George's reach. "Nor, now, do you." Let the man crawl back on his belly like the treacherous snake he was.

George didn't comment, his full attention claimed by his cane. It had landed on the cliff's edge, and they both watched it totter half-on and half-off until it steadied. Tearing his gaze from the sight, George looked up at Wylie, his eyes assessing.

"You couldn't be bothered to help your father interview a schoolmaster?" Wylie asked. "Thanks to you, Cousin, I've a beehive of women breathing down my neck."

And he'd left Anna crying.

George blinked, realization dawning. At one time Wylie had known his cousin's every expression. Given the hours they'd spent in one another's company, words had often been unnecessary. The fact that Wylie could read him even now—the look of puzzlement followed by faint amusement—was disconcerting. The man before him barely resembled the boy.

"You find it amusing, do you?" Wylie asked.

"I'm not one of the heritors, Wylie. What would ye have had me do?"

"I'd have had you offer your advice when Reynolds passed so that the matter was tabled long before now. Reynolds is two months cold." He paced in front of George, five steps forward and five steps back. "Two months the parish has been without a school."

"Aye." George adjusted his position with seeming difficulty and glanced again at his cane. "I did offer," he said, meeting Wylie's eyes. "When Uncle William passed. But my father assured me that ye, as returning laird, would handle it. Therefore, he didn't require my advice."

So Uncle Henry had lied about George's disinterest.

But Henry had had no way of knowing that Wylie would return. Perhaps George was the liar.

Somehow, though, Wylie was certain he wasn't. George's eyes never strayed farther than his boots when compelled to fib—a dead giveaway to all who knew him. Wylie stopped pacing.

"I'm not here as returning laird," Wylie said.

"So I gathered."

"I'd rather not be here at all."

"Aye, I know," George said with annoying patience. "'Tis fortunate then, that ye'll not be here long."

The irony did not escape Wylie. Of the two of them, George had been the one who'd dreamed of roaming the world. The one who'd planned a life in politics, spent both in and outside the Highlands.

Wylie's only ambition had been becoming a Highland laird.

For the first time, it occurred to Wylie that George felt as trapped as he himself did.

"Uncle Henry claimed you'd no interest in choosing the schoolmaster. That you lost interest years ago," Wylie said, suspicion forming.

"Did he, now? Then I expect ye must choose whom to believe. I'd be happy to help."

"There are two other candidates, aye?" Wylie said, watching his cousin carefully. "Are they nearby?"

George nodded, watching him back.

Wylie closed his eyes and shook his head, feeling utterly defeated.

Well played, Uncle Henry.

He stepped toward the cane, nudging it from the cliff with his boot before he bent and retrieved it. He handed it to George, who accepted it without comment. Kicking it had been churlish, and he'd rather not witness George crawling on his belly, treacherous snake or not.

Choosing a tree beside George, Wylie slid down its bark to the ground, expelling a long breath. He sat on the Cragdurcas side, but he was past caring.

"Did you lose your leg below the knee or above?" he asked.

"Below."

"I've heard the peg leg gives men less bother the shorter it is."

George nodded.

"Do you feel the pain of it still?"

George was silent a moment and then answered, "Aye."

Wylie gave a slow nod, unsurprised. "My first mate lost his leg three years ago in the waters off Africa. He still suffers."

Again, George nodded his response.

Perversely, Wylie now considered the conversation a challenge. He draped an arm over his raised knee and leaned forward. "Yet you're not riding. You're afoot."

"Would you ride?"

Wylie chuckled. "Nay." Riding a pony the quarter mile from Cragdurcas Manor would grant the injury the upper hand. "You owe Dougal the story, I hear. I apologize for his boldness."

"Don't apologize for the lad," George said, quirking a corner of his mouth into something near a smile. "I prefer his reaction over others. I often feel as if I'm invisible."

Wylie blinked. *Invisible?* Christ. George was larger than life in his own mind; how could others mistake it?

Uncertain how to respond, Wylie looked away. With his finger, he drew some lines in the dirt, attempting a crude replica of Glencorach's cattle brand.

"Uncle William spoke of his grandsons often," George said, filling the silence before it grew uncomfortable. "I see he had every right to be proud."

Oddly, Wylie now experienced no urge to throttle George for speaking of Will and Dougal. Instead, he felt a bit of his own pride.

"Aye, well. It's Rennie who deserves the credit, not myself."

George made a scoffing sound in his throat. "Dougal is your very image—inside, I suspect, as well as out. And if half of what Uncle William said is true, Will's more like ye than ye know. There's no denying the credit for that."

Wylie *had* glimpsed certain qualities in Will, qualities his father had insisted Wylie shared. He ran a hand across the back of his neck, uncomfortable at the implied praise. "I don't know about that. The lad outmaneuvers my every thought. And that's *before* I have the time to think one."

George smiled. "That doesn't surprise me. He has every parish lass between the ages of ten and twenty in a flutter."

Where did Will find the time? "Aye, well, in that, we differ greatly. I had only the vaguest notion of what to do with a lass at his age. If I pray at all, it's to pray Will doesn't leave his mark behind."

George looked up sharply, his expression almost angry. Then, with visible effort, he relaxed his features and muttered a nondescript sound.

Wylie thought over his words, wondering at his offense. Concluding it was what he *hadn't* said, he offered, "Jay seems a fine lad. You've reason to be proud yourself." George grimaced, and Wylie belatedly recalled the argument he'd overheard between Miriam and George.

George shook his head in something akin to defeat. "It's not easy, being a father."

George had that right. "It's not." Wylie hesitated a beat before saying what had been on his mind since seeing Jay at Moy's. "We spoke at Robert Moy's the other day, Jay and I."

George straightened and frowned. "Ye say that for a reason. Tell me."

"He was with two men I didn't recognize. Armed men."

"Drovers?"

"I don't think so. No herd in sight, and they were warier than a breeding heifer. Moy claimed the whisky brought them."

"Did Jay travel with them?"

"I'm uncertain; they were there when I arrived. However, Jay left on his own."

"Reivers, ye think?"

"Possibly," Wylie said. "Why do you ask that? Has there been a problem with reivers?"

Looking at his boots, George shook his head.

Hell. Wylie's mouth flattened. Why would George lie about that? "Whose—"

"If it meets with your approval," George said, cutting short Wylie's question, "I'd like to interview the other candidates within the next two or three days."

Wylie's eyes widened at George's deference, his worry over the cattle forgotten. Since when were he and George not equals? Not knowing what to say, he smoothed a hand over the dirt, erasing his sketch and starting another.

"The sooner it's resolved, the better," George said, seeming oblivious to Wylie's discomfort.

"Aye, I agree," Wylie said at length.

"I'd like Anna to sit in."

Wylie's head snapped up, his drawing forgotten. Did George fancy Anna?

"Why?" he asked, watching George carefully.

George shrugged. "The parish will feel they had a hand in the decision. Anna's well informed and knows the mothers' concerns."

Had George noticed the waif who'd shadowed them had transformed into a beautiful young woman? "She's not a mother herself, however."

"Nay, but many of her friends are."

Attempting an indifferent tone, Wylie poised the question for which he'd yet to receive a satisfactory answer. "Why hasn't she married?"

Instantly, George's posture shifted, signaling alertness.

Wylie stifled the impulse to cringe. *Eijit.* Why had he asked George, of all people? George was as canny as Cicero. He'd know.

Know what? There was nothing *to* know.

167

"She was promised to a cousin of Lachie's," George answered, his tone casual. "Burt Stevens."

Wylie bit his lip and traced the brand again, keeping his gaze down. He'd never met Stevens, and to his knowledge, neither had George.

"Before they could marry," George continued, "Stevens left to fight the French in America. He liked what he saw of Virginia and planned making a life there when the war ended."

"Anna agreed to emigrate?" Surprised, Wylie forgot to assume indifference.

"So Lachie claimed. It surprised me as well. Anna's a Highland lassie, if ever there was one."

Even so, she'd planned to follow this Stevens. She'd planned to make her home in America.

"He returned for her while I was still in America," George continued. "I don't know all that transpired, nor does she speak of it, but I do know he never made it back. His ship sank in crossing, and he perished in the Atlantic."

Wylie's mouth quirked in a moment of sympathy. Then, unable to keep his mouth shut, he asked, "She's cared for no one since?"

"Oh, I don't know about that," George said slowly, his eyes narrowed in thought. "I believe she might. Mind, she's not said as much."

"It'd be this Archibald Montgomery, eh?"

George's lips pursed as he considered. "Truth be, I don't know."

"He *is* courting her, aye?"

"Alan seems to think so. Montgomery spends a lot of time at Glendally, but as far as I know, he's made no declaration."

Can't fault a man for not wearing his heart on his sleeve.

"Well, there you have it, then. One more reason to settle Glencorach quickly, so Anna herself might settle."

George regarded him, his forehead furrowed as if the remark puzzled him. Then, raising his brows, he nodded in a seeming parody of sage wisdom. "Aye, there ye have it, then."

If George meant to mock, Wylie ignored it. He hoped for Anna's happiness, and he'd make no apology. His father had relied heavily on her over the years, and she'd lent her support willingly.

Anna should have a husband, and one who stayed near. Wylie might pave the way in making that happen. Glencorach would make neither Anna nor Montgomery wealthy, but their lives would be comfortable. More than comfortable, if one considered Montgomery's wages with the revenue.

He stood and went for his horse, pausing when he recalled the tension in the kirk over the issue of the tenants' labor.

He turned and regarded George. "Is your father forcing Glendally out?" By targeting Glendally's subtenants with demands for more than their allotted days of servitude, it seemed Uncle Henry may be forcing, or attempting to force, a reaction from Alan Macrae. If so, Macrae had to act, and he had to act decisively.

George blinked, then looked toward the river. "Alan isn't the man he once was."

Perhaps. But if he didn't step up to Henry's apparent abuse of forced labor, Glendally tenants would subtly retaliate, ending Alan's effectiveness as tacksman. Wylie shut his eyes briefly and sighed. "So he is, then."

Naïvely, it seemed, he'd thought better of his uncle.

"He's protecting Cragdurcas's future," George said, still eying a point in the distance.

George may believe that, but he was no more comfortable with it than Wylie was.

"Who does he have in mind to assume the tack?" Wylie asked.

George shrugged. "I'd like him to consider Anna."

Wylie's brow knit. "His daughter?"

"Why not?" George said, turning to look at him. "Janet Macintosh assumed her father's tack on Invershie's estate. She's managing well enough, and it's been over thirty years now."

"Janet's got more grit than sand. Anna . . ." Anna was a woman in every sense of the word.

Unease followed his quick dismissal. Anna had been raised at the knee of one of the finest estate managers in the district—she may well hope to assume the lease.

He shook the thought from his head. It was of no consequence to him who assumed the damned tack, and to hell with the politics. He could hire a crew from Inverness to repair the manse and be done with it.

Mount the damned horse and ride away. Now.

"So, George, how will you make things right by Alan?"

"There's not much I can do."

"Speak with Lachie." While Lachlan Shaw farmed Glencorach land, Wylie knew from his father that Lachie acted as unofficial spokesmen for all the area's farmers. He'd step in and mediate.

"I have. He's waiting it out for now." George reached for his cane and stood in one fluid motion, seemingly with little effort. It must have cost him; his knuckles shone white atop the cane. "A word from you might help."

Like hell.

Did they think him a puppet, then? Were they manipulating him even now, hoping he'd rise to Macrae's defense, given his father and Alan's close friendship?

"This has nothing to do with Glencorach, George. I trust the Cragdurcas Macphersons will do right by Alan. As for the schoolmaster, I trust you'll hire someone within the next day or two. Tell your father I want that canceled mortgage on Alan's desk by midday tomorrow. If he doesn't comply, I'll start legal proceedings against him."

He wasn't sure on what grounds, but he'd come up with something.

George said nothing, regarding Wylie as if waiting for some signal.

Wylie hesitated, wondering at an appropriate final farewell. Finally, he concluded there wasn't one.

With one long last look at his cousin, he mounted.

CHAPTER 23

WHEN SHE neared Glendally, Anna spotted Will on his knees in her kitchen garden, spade in hand. Grabbing a corner of her apron, she dried her cheeks, then squared her shoulders and approached him.

He looked up, his blue eyes unblinking as he studied her. If he noticed she'd been crying, he didn't remark upon it.

"Did Mrs. Baxter put ye to work, then?" she asked, attempting a smile. Molly trotted toward her, tail wagging, and Anna obliged her with a halfhearted head scratch.

Turning the square of earth he worked, he shook his head. "You said we would talk when you returned. I waited."

With a sinking sensation, she recalled she'd promised to tell him what she knew of the break between his father and George. She hadn't the heart for that right now. She was so angry with Wylie that she may not speak fairly.

Then she recalled what Wylie had said only hours before. "Your father told me the two of you spoke earlier today."

Will's brow furrowed. "He said that?"

"Aye."

Will shifted his gaze to a point past her shoulder while he thought, then he reddened. "We spoke of another matter," he said finally, jabbing the spade in the earth.

She sighed, resigned. "Very well," she said. "We'll talk once I look in on my father."

"Your father sits with Mrs. Baxter, reading aloud to Dougal," he said quickly.

She gave a faint smile at his persistence. "Well, drat. I thought if I dallied inside long enough, ye'd finish the tilling."

"I will finish." He looked up her, his mouth quirking in a rare smile, one that reminded her of his father.

Then again, everything reminded her of his father. "I'll hold ye to that, mind." Shrugging off her cloak, she draped it over a post. Will's gaze dropped to her bodice and lingered before he blinked and looked away.

Mother Mary, this gown was destined for the quilting bin.

She turned from the lad, settling in a section she'd planted a week ago, one where weeds already outnumbered seedlings, and debated where to begin.

"Miss Macrae," Will said slowly, as if sensing her hesitation. "I do not ask from curiosity. I ask so I will understand. Since we have come, Papa does not sleep. He rarely eats."

She swung back to Will. She'd thought Wylie looked as if he'd been ill.

"He . . . " Will frowned and dragged his finger back and forth across the dirt, repeatedly. "He walks his room. When he tires of that, he walks the rooms below. If Dougal or I are downstairs, he will walk outside and circle the yard. I have lost count of the number of times he has walked toward Grandpapa's grave."

Her jaw dropped and she stared at Will, blinking back sudden tears.

She swallowed. "It grieves me to hear that. I didn't know."

Will lifted a shoulder. "There is no reason you should. Papa keeps many things to himself. Most of what I know of him I have learned from his partner, Alec. Only in the last year have I seen these things myself."

"He was very different growing up, ken," she said softly, fingering a weed she'd pulled. "Ye'll not find a person in the parish who hasn't a kind word to say of your father."

"Do you include Cousin George?"

"Oh, aye," she said. "George thinks the world of your father. They were once inseparable."

"Yet much separates them now."

"'Tis due to the '45 Rebellion, or rather its aftermath."

"You said Papa was not a traitor. Yet he fought against government soldiers."

She nodded. "The Jacobites pressed your father and George into service. They did so with a great many lads."

Will shook his head at that explanation, and a lock of gleaming black hair fell loose of its leather tie. He tucked it behind his ear with an impatient gesture. "*Oui*. But Cousin George was not exiled, nor was he named a traitor, as was Papa. Why?"

She opened her mouth and then closed it. How to explain the unexplainable?

"They were separated that winter, when they learned George's mother was ill," she said finally. "Your father convinced George he must return and helped him escape. It wasn't so difficult by then; the officers trusted them."

"Why didn't Papa leave as well?"

"He led a company of lads younger than himself. He felt he couldn't desert them."

Will exhaled through his nose and shut his eyes briefly. Smiling a thin smile, he shook his head, much as a proud father might upon learning of his offspring's escapades. At length he asked, "Was Papa taken prisoner at that last battle?"

"At Culloden? Nay." She ran a palm over the ground she'd weeded, smoothing it flat. "He was wounded before then and transported to France."

"Alone?"

She nodded. "An escort would have drawn attention. George tried nonetheless to accompany him, but your grandfather and great uncle guarded George as closely as the English guarded the coasts."

"So he stayed. He was then arrested for his part?"

She hesitated, then said, "Henry and William spent much of the winter negotiating pardons for their sons—pardons in exchange for their testimonies."

"Testimony?" Will's brows were near meeting and his blue eyes hard. "Against the men they fought aside?" he asked, his disbelief apparent.

"Aye," she said, suddenly uncertain if she should rise and make an excuse to see to supper before she caused a rift among the next generation of Macphersons.

"They were expected to turn on their fellow soldiers?" he asked again, as if to be certain he understood.

"Their lives were at stake, Will," she answered lamely.

"As traitors, all their lives were at stake, Miss Macrae." He tilled another square foot, his spade moving rapidly. "So Cousin George did as they asked? He named my father a traitor in exchange for his own freedom?"

Will made it sound so cold-blooded, but it hadn't been. Not at the time.

As the son of a small landowner, George hadn't merited a traitor's barbarous execution—a slow death by hanging, drawing, and quartering. On the other hand, he'd not have had the mercy of a quick death and been hanged from a branch in his front yard either. The Crown would have strove to make an example of him.

Still, George had steadfastly resisted his father's and uncle's pressure for weeks—up until the moment he hadn't. Anna had never been certain why.

"It wasn't quite like that, Will."

"Did he or did he not name my father a traitor in exchange for his own freedom?" Will asked again, his spade still while his gaze pinned her.

"'Tis difficult to judge others' actions, especially from a distance of over twenty years."

The look he gave her was one of incredulity. "*Non*. It is not. My father would not have done the same. I know he would not, had the situations been reversed."

"Ye cannot know that, Will," she said. "We all believed Wylie would be pardoned within a year or two, if not within months. Not a one of us was prepared for the government's wrath. Your father was out of harm's way. George was not."

"My father would not have done the same," Will repeated, his lips set in a hard line.

She sighed, unwilling to argue the point. Privately, she agreed with Will, though she thought no less of George for it. "Perhaps. But I believe had the situation been reversed, had George been in France and Wylie in Badenoch, George would have wanted Wylie to testify. George would have urged him to do so."

"*You* cannot know that," Will said.

"Nay, but I believe it. Just as I believe that had the situation been reversed, George would have forgiven your father long before now."

Will's brow furrowed as he considered her words. "*Oui*," he said finally, nodding. "You are right. Many would forgive. So there is more."

She scratched her nose, puzzled. "More?"

"Cousin George betrayed my father in yet another way, or my father *would* have forgiven."

She studied Will. What a stubborn pride he had in his father. Had Wylie any idea of the boy's loyalty?

"I know of nothing else, Will."

"The Cragdurcas Macphersons would inherit Glencorach if my

174

father remained in exile, *oui*?"

Her eyes widened. "Will, you cannot think—"

"People do many things for wealth, Miss Macrae."

She shook her head. "I don't believe it of Henry Macpherson, nor does your father."

Will grunted his skepticism. "My cousin, Jay Macpherson. He was born when?"

"He was born in 1746. October or November, I think." Her brow furrowed. "Why?"

"A year older than I expected." Will nodded slowly. "Perhaps my father could forgive his cousin's desertion for the sake of family, but not for the sake of a woman."

"What do ye mean to say?"

"Count, Miss Macrae. Jay was conceived near the time his father deserted. Presumably Cousin George deserted for his mother's bedside. Instead, he warmed his amour's." He glanced at her, a slight flush tinting his cheeks. "Forgive me, Miss Macrae, for speaking my thoughts aloud. But if it is not a matter of honor or money, then it is often a matter of a woman." Looking away, he attacked the earth with his spade.

She stared at the top of Will's head, bemused. She'd been only eight at the time, and the district had been in an uproar over matters of life and death. George's hasty marriage had been of little note.

"To desert for the sake of a woman, one who was not in danger, would be unforgivable, *oui*?" Will said, quickly turning the next row of black earth. "Many men long for a woman left behind. But to desert for such a reason shows little fortitude, and my father possibly would not forgive."

"Especially if your father thought he loved the same woman," Anna said under her breath. She had wondered if Wylie had known that he and George fancied the same lass. George certainly had.

Will glanced up sharply. "What?"

It was too late to take the words back. "At one time your father had an attachment to Miriam Macpherson."

"Did he bed her?"

"Will," she said, frowning. "You forget yourself. I have no idea."

Ignoring the admonishment, Will shot out another question, "Did my father know of his cousin's own attachment?

175

She shrugged. "They never spoke of it in my hearing."

"Did others know?"

"I don't think so, but I'm not certain."

"It would have been a matter of speculation, Miss Macrae, especially as George and my father were once close. Whom did she favor? George or my father?"

"I haven't the faintest idea. Miriam Macpherson has never taken me into her confidence."

Will calmed then and chewed at a thumbnail, seeming thoughtful. Then he asked, "Has she kept the same maid all these years?"

Anna choked short a laugh. "If so, 'tis not likely ye'd charm the words from her, if that's what ye be thinking. Why, she'd be farther along in years than myself."

And it had been years since a man bothered charming her.

Studying her, Will didn't answer. Then his gaze dropped, sliding over her slowly. She should have thought it insolent but somehow didn't. He managed to convey he saw something others didn't, something so intriguing that he couldn't help himself but look, and she nearly forgot who he was. Then he looked up, flashing a grin.

The spell broken, Anna quirked a side of her mouth and shook her head. "Rogue," she muttered.

He chuckled. "Were other men courting Cousin Miriam?"

Why should that matter? "'Tis likely. She's a very beautiful woman and from a good family, one with many connections."

"She could then be . . ." Will paused, again searching for a word. "Select. There were other young men of means in the district from whom she could select, *oui*?"

"None nearby."

"There is a fort nearby."

"Aye, 'tis true." She hadn't considered the Englishmen and pondered a moment. "English officers were about, I suppose. She'd have seen them at her friend's home."

Will regarded her, raising a brow as if waiting for more.

Anna blew out a breath. "Miriam spent much of her time at Bloomhall, visiting her friend Sarah Bloomfield. You might learn more there." She stood, swiping her hands and shaking her gown free of dirt. "I must go in and help Mrs. Baxter with supper."

"I will finish here," Will said, nodding absently.

She retrieved her cloak and started toward the house. "Miss Macrae?" came Will's voice from behind.

She turned.

"If my father was the one who made you cry, I can assure you he regrets it. He will not say it, but you should know that he does."

Her lips parted, and she swallowed, staring at him until he turned back to his spade.

"He likes you, Miss Macrae."

CHAPTER 24

ONCE HE left the peel tower, Wylie's horse, taking advantage of his distraction, ambled toward Baile Dùil, perhaps attracted by the community's early evening noise.

Wylie pulled up rein at a short dyke wall—several alternating layers of turf and stone—and stared at the settlement behind it. In the winter of '46, six lads from those homes—all six someone's brother and someone's son—had sought out the nearby rebel encampment, eager to fight alongside their lairds' sons. All six had perished inside a fortnight.

While it was true he and George hadn't recruited them, there was no changing the fact that they'd followed George and Wylie and had died because of it.

One had been Mary's brother.

"Wylie."

Wylie hadn't heard that voice in twenty-five years, yet he knew it as well as if he'd heard it that morning. Tearing his gaze from the township, he looked down and saw Lachlan Shaw standing at his side. He dismounted.

"Lachie."

Aside from his eyes, there wasn't much of the boy Wylie remembered. A thick black beard covered most of his face; what was uncovered was weathered and browned. For a moment they stared at one another, assessing changes the years had wrought. Then Lachie chuckled, shaking his head.

"Ye wee bastard; I wasna sure ye'd come."

Wylie's mouth curved in a rueful smile. "Nor was I. It's good to see you, Lachie."

"Ye best come greet Mary. Then we'll speak of why ye're here." Without awaiting an answer, he strode into the township and toward the largest of the structures.

Wylie hesitated, fingering the reins he held. A young lad near Dougal's age bolted from the home Lachie entered and approached. "I'm to be taking your horse, sir."

Lachie was one of Glencorach's lessor tacksmen. It'd be easier dealing with him than with Robert Moy, and he *could* help with the manse repairs. Grimacing, Wylie handed off the reins and entered the township, tailing after the man. He ducked beneath the home's cruck-framed porch and into a fog of burning peat and childhood memories.

The Shaws' home was a series of small, windowless areas. The entry opened into the largest: a dim, smoke-filled, dirt-floored room with a soft glowing open hearth, two spinning wheels, and several three-legged stools. A short wall separated it from the cobbled, empty but still pungent, cattle byre on the left. The back side of a box bed separated it from the sleeping area on the right, and past that sleeping area was a smaller, more private space. It was there that Wylie and Lachie retreated an hour later.

The Shaws' oldest daughter, Agnes, lit the ends of a number of firs and arranged them one by one on a small round tin. When the tin glowed in a meager wreath of light, she left them.

Wylie blinked several times, adjusting his eyesight, then dropped easily onto one of the wooden stools. It creaked, rocking with his weight, and then settled. Draping his arms over his knees, he turned the wooden cup he held round and round and listened to the drone of Mary's spinning wheel and the mewing of the Shaws' newest child.

Whether due to the whisky Lachie had pressed upon him or Mary's unreserved welcome and gracious acceptance of his belated condolences, Wylie's discomfort had eased. The soft screen of drifting smoke only added to his contentment, the peat reek mingling with the fragrance of a simmering rabbit stew he'd been asked to share.

"Where do we stand on the labor owed Glencorach?" Wylie asked without preamble. With his fields empty, he figured he must be due several days, if not more. "I need a few men for three or four days to repair the manse."

Lachie shifted, his grimace barely visible in the low light. "What of Balcor and Cragdurcas?"

"I know nothing of Balcor, but I have the impression Cragdurcas has used more than his service allotment." He watched Lachie carefully. "Would you agree?"

Lachie grunted and nodded. "Eneas Macphee's surely."

That had been Wylie's impression as well. "Why Macphee? Does Glendally want them off his tack?"

"Nay, not as far as I can tell. Glendally . . . well, Glendally's oft away with the fairies."

Wylie's mouth thinned and he took a sip from his cup, declining comment.

"I reckon Cragdurcas thinks Glendally willna notice one way or the other that he's meddling. He knows Glendally's daughter will, though, and Cragdurcas is testing the wee lassie's mettle. Anna and the Macphees are tight."

So George was right. Uncle Henry was taking Anna's measure. "Does Anna know this?"

Lachie lifted a shoulder. "No' sure that she does."

If Alan Macrae allowed Henry to press Alan's tenants unduly, Alan wasn't worth a damn to either his tenants or to Henry, his laird. Alan could lose all—the Glendally tack, his tenants, and his position.

"Is the Glendally tack up for renewal soon?"

"Aye, come next spring." Lachie adjusted his seat. "Macphee's tolerating it, but he canna for long. His family has little enough as it is."

"If not Alan, who does Henry have in mind to assume the tack?"

"Dinna ken." His elbows on his knees, Lachie lowered his head and scratched the back of his neck, the whites of his eyes glinting up at Wylie. "But he's an idle grandson, aye? It's a good holding, Glendally is."

Wylie's brow creased. Jay? Jay was a mere whelp. Glendally was a good tack due to Alan's competent management. It could go to hell in a handcart fast.

As could Glencorach, with its rotting fences, empty fields, and an Englishman who knew nothing of a Highland farm.

He pushed both thoughts aside and looked at Lachie. "Do I have the men or not?"

"Oh aye, ye're due. I can have some men at the manse within the sennight."

That was easy. Wylie pursed his lips, wondering exactly how many hours he was due. He settled in his seat, prepared to bargain.

TIME PASSED easily in Lachie's home, the conversation filled with harvests, cattle prices and, once Wylie and Lachie rejoined the women, gossip of upcoming marriages and births. He'd half hoped talk would turn to Anna Macrae and the revenue man—or better yet to Anna and Lachie's late cousin and their proposed emigration—but it didn't, and Wylie knew better than to ask. Women tended to weave narratives from idle questions.

Reluctant to leave, Wylie stayed until the moon shone high in the sky, and then Lachie, also seeming reluctant to break contact, accompanied him to Glencorach, chatting of anything and everything but George Macpherson and the '45 Rising. They parted amiably, each with the false pledge that they'd meet again soon.

Now, standing in his father's room an hour later, Wylie hoisted his haversack over his shoulder with one hand and picked up the lit candle with the other. He trotted down the staircase, stopping in the parlor and filling his flask with whisky before continuing down the hall and into Martha's domain. A small fire glowed red in the hearth, and Martha sat beside it in a straight-backed chair, her arms crossed over her belly and her head lolling forward, snoring softly. She started awake.

"Sir," she said, her gaze falling on him with a frown. "Ye'll not be leaving?"

"I'm headed for the shielings." He opened a cupboard, searching out her store of bannocks. "Why are you in here?"

"The lads might be hungry after a meal of Mrs. Baxter's."

"That bad, is she?" Wylie said good-naturedly. He'd never tasted a meal of Mrs. Baxter's, who was he to protest? "Tell me, Martha, is Archie Tanner still Glencorach's glenman?"

"Nay, that be Angus Tanner, sir," she said, her gaze following him as he searched. "He makes a good glenman, he does. Ye remember Angus, dinna ye?"

Angus had been toddling last Wylie had seen him. Grunting, he nodded while rifling through cupboards. "Is there anything to eat?"

She rose, lit two more candles, and lumbered toward the pantry, wiping her hands on her apron. Kneeling, she opened a bottom door and pulled out a long-disused butter crock. "Aye, but they be a day stale."

"No matter." He opened the crock, then paused and examined its top, a round, pig-skinned covered piece of wood studded with steel. His father's targe? "Martha, this isn't . . . ?"

"Aye, 'twas your father's own and his father's before him."

Wylie would've burnt the damn shield before demoting it to so ignoble a use. Grunting, he deigned no comment.

"If ye wait 'til morning, I'll have ye some fresh." Martha pulled three bannocks from the crock, seeming reluctant to give him less than her best.

"Truly, it's no matter. Tell the lads where I've gone, will you?"

"That I will, but—"

He broke in, forestalling her concerns. "I won't be more than a day or two. Lachlan Shaw will be stopping by the day after next to gather a few tools, aye? If I'm not here, he has my permission to take what he needs. He'll also see to repairing the front gate and the north fence."

Martha nodded with a trembling chin.

Wylie pulled a letter from his waistcoat pocket and set it on the table. "See Alan Macrae gets this, will you?" The letter instructed Alan to draw up immediate extensions for all Glencorach's current leases. Then, once Wylie judged the state of his herd, he would transfer the place to Montgomery. He expected his uncle would have done as he should by then, and Alan was to have all the papers ready for Wylie's signature.

Her eyes wet, Martha nodded mutely, seeming to recognize the signs of a more permanent leave-taking. On impulse, he bent and kissed her cheek. Then he walked out the door.

Our boys, Wylie . . .

Will be sailing with me, Rennie.

That seemed to please her, for she made no further protest.

Once outside, Wylie went to the stable, saddled the horse, and started toward the back track to the hills. He planned riding as far as the upper reaches of the creek, then resting before continuing to the glen at dawn.

The night was mild and clear, the sky awash in stars. Moonlight glinted off the scattered stones, and the night insects worked in full song, seemingly in concert with the beat of hoof on rock. One by one, he silently addressed each and every hill of the Monadhliaths. Dark purple against a midnight-blue sky, they hailed him, welcoming him home.

He'd be lying if he claimed he hadn't missed these hills with every pore of his being. Trusting his horse to keep to the rock-strewn trail, he shut off conscious thought and allowed their timeless gift of peace to envelop him one last time.

Sometime later he realized his mount had stilled. He swiveled in the saddle, seeking the reason for its indecision, and glimpsed a sliver of light through a nearby cottage window.

Glendally.

Anna. He handled the reins, hesitating.

When she'd rescinded her supper invitation, she'd said nothing of the trek to the glen. There remained a chance she'd await him come dawn. Unlikely, but possible.

If nothing else, he should tell her of his conversation with George. Perhaps knowing he'd handled the matter, she'd grant him some measure of warmth when they next met.

Rather than trod through someone's newly plowed field, he dismounted and secured the reins in a thatch of heath and then followed a narrow path through the heather to her cottage. The rattle of a tin lantern broke through the drone of night insects, and he stilled, his eyes searching its source.

Anna. And she was not alone.

A man, one no taller than herself and slighter by half, walked beside her, carrying the lantern. The low rumble of his voice was clipped, its timbre lacking the music of a Highlander's.

The Englishman, then. Archibald Montgomery. Silently, Wylie stepped well outside the swing of the lantern's light and watched the two pause and face one another, Anna with her back to Wylie.

Wylie shifted so he might discern Montgomery's expression. The lamplight, illuminating from below, cast flickering shadows over the Englishman's face, distorting it into a grotesque skull-like mask. While Wylie watched, he took a step closer to Anna.

His heart pounding in his ears, Wylie put a fist to his chin and scrutinized the man's every expression.

From what Wylie could overhear, their murmured

conversation seemed to be of Montgomery's plans for the morrow. Wylie canted his head to one side, an ear aimed toward the couple, but he could still only discern a few scattered words.

Anna said nothing, though she nodded occasionally, giving Wylie the sense she was either disinterested or distracted. She didn't suffer Wylie's conversation without voicing an observation or opinion.

As Montgomery droned on, Wylie felt a stirring of sympathy for Anna. He considered making his presence known, if only so that Montgomery would leave and he could speak with Anna himself. Then Montgomery set down the lantern and put his hands on her elbows.

Wylie went rigid.

Montgomery stepped forward, and Wylie stopped breathing.

Step back, Anna. Now!

Wylie blinked. Had he said that aloud?

If he had, Anna was so taken with the revenue man that she hadn't heard. She stayed where she was.

Montgomery leaned forward at an awkward angle and placed his mouth on Anna's. For the space of a heartbeat, she seemed not to react. Then she raised her hands to his shoulders, as if welcoming his touch.

A singeing hot tide of anger erupted in Wylie, scalding his insides. It surged swiftly, flooding his being, drowning all rational thought until he shook with the urge to run the man through with his knife. The knife that he somehow now clutched.

He stepped forward to wrench Anna aside, and the cottage door creaked open. Wylie froze midstep, and Alan's voice came from within.

"Anna? I can't seem to find my spectacles."

Jerking free of Montgomery's clutches, Anna turned and called, "Aye, Father," her voice brisk. "It's best I come help ye, then."

Wylie's left hand curled into a fist. *Aye, best you do that, and do it now.*

Montgomery turned and took his leave. Only when darkness swallowed his departing form did Wylie's pulse slow and sanity return. An owl hooted in the distance and his hand fell to his side.

Good God, what had that been about?

The knife fell, clattering on the stones at his feet. Bewildered and shaken, Wylie dropped to the ground, cradling his head in his hands.

He wouldn't have run that man through, would he?

He shook his head. He'd have held back before his blade pierced linen.

But to even consider attacking one of the government's men. Had he gone mad?

Anna was entitled to accept that man's suit. She *should* accept it. If Wylie felt an inkling of the brotherly affection he should, he'd wish her to do so.

So why had he come here on some trumped-up excuse after midnight? Why had he been about to risk his pardon to defend her honor? An honor that hadn't required defending?

Furthermore, and perhaps most worrisome, why had learning Anna had once been agreeable to emigration quickened his blood and hovered unacknowledged at the edge of his thoughts since?

Rising, he sheathed his knife and swallowed past a dry throat. Did he hope she'd go with him?

Bloody hell.

CHAPTER 26

IT WAS WELL after midnight by the time Anna closed the door on Mr. Montgomery—no small thanks to Will Macpherson.

What a surprising lad he was. First, assuring her Wylie hadn't meant to make her cry. Then, at supper, producing a bottle of whisky carrying a proper excise stamp out of nowhere—or like as not out of his father's cellar. And finally, encouraging Mr. Montgomery to tell story after story of his work with the revenue.

The men seemed to have a glorious time. Anna had not.

After consuming the lion's share of the whisky, Mr. Montgomery had asked her outside. He'd summoned sufficient courage to ask her to marry him and worse—to kiss her for the first time.

And she'd stood there and endured it.

She swiped the back of her hand across her mouth. Then she uprighted the empty whisky bottle on a corner of her apron until a drop slid the length of the bottle and dampened it. Setting the bottle aside, she scrubbed her lips with the linen.

She wasn't married yet; she didn't have to endure a darned thing if she didn't want to.

Thinking she heard someone stirring, she swiveled toward the box bed where Will and Dougal slept. Its closed curtain was still, and the boys' breathing was soft and even. She extinguished the lantern and sat at the table in the dim firelight, her head in her hands.

It wasn't as if Montgomery cared for her. She offered him a foothold into the community. As her spouse, he'd be welcomed at any table in the parish.

There is no choice but to marry him. Accept what you cannot change and accept it quickly, before he changes his mind.

She would—but not tonight and not tomorrow.

She made her way soundlessly to the cupboard, retrieving the store of fresh bannocks and the bowl of batter she'd prepared hours before. The bowl was crafted of thick pottery and cool. She stirred the batter with a finger and then sniffed it, closing her eyes and glimpsing a meadow filled with butter-colored flowers. Fresh milk, fresh butter, fresh eggs.

Grabbing the butter crock, she carried her stash to the fire and sat on the hearth. She sank her fingers into the crock, pulled out a dollop of butter, and coated a bannock. Then she dipped it into the batter. After transferring the dripping oatcake to a toasting iron, she held it over the fire, turning it until each side was lightly browned.

She had a dozen such oatcakes. Six she'd leave for the boys and her father. Six she'd take with her for Wylie. She'd resolved to plead that he reconsider the new hiring and softening him with food could only help.

Mother hadn't splurged on this treat often, but when she had, Wylie had somehow always known. Invariably, he'd appeared while the bannocks were still hot.

At dawn the next morning, Anna loaded the pony, filling her creels with foodstuffs for the women and bannocks, cheese, and milk for herself and Wylie.

If Wylie still planned coming.

For the twentieth time in ten minutes, she looked down the empty path. Mrs. Baxter would be here in minutes and question her dawdling. It was time to mount and move on.

Hoof-beats sounded then, and her pulse quickened. She looked again, this time glimpsing a man riding. Quickly she turned to her pony and fussed with the creels. She'd not have him suspect she waited.

"Anna, wait."

Her heart fell. George's voice, not Wylie's. Her forehead dropped onto the pony's bristly flank, and she breathed in the beast's pungent musky odor and gathered her wits. By the time George reached her she could turn to him with a smile.

"Ye're out early this morning," she said, wondering if he had news of the cattle. "I trust all's well?"

"Aye." Dismounting, he walked toward her, his step lopsided and light. "I hoped to see ye before ye left." He steadied himself a moment on his cane. "Wylie and I spoke."

Astonished, her smile widened. "Truly?" She held him at arm's length and surveyed him. "Ye appear not to have lost any more body parts."

"Aye, well. There was a moment or two I worried, but the better part of it was civil," he said, grinning wryly. "It was nothing of note, mind. But still, it was something." He squeezed one of her hands, then dropped it and circled her, seeming unable to keep still. She swiveled to watch him. "He asked for my help with the schoolmaster's hiring. Then we talked of the war a bit, then of you. Ye're to help with it, ken. The hiring. In truth, I thought he might stop by to tell ye."

They spoke of her?

He stopped circling and faced her. "Anna, I've written him weekly for more than twenty years now. He's returned every letter."

"It will be different now, George." How could George say they spoke of her and not offer details?

"It already is. He's acknowledged I still live." George chuckled and embraced her, holding her tight a few moments. When he released her, he looked at her with a broad smile. "When will ye return? We've two men to interview."

"I won't be gone more than a day or two," she said, mustering a weak smile when what she really wanted was to shake him. He was more astute than most; surely he knew she longed to hear what Wylie had said of her. She hesitated, then asked. "Will Wylie interview with us?"

"I don't think so. I believe he plans leaving soon."

Soon? Suddenly she couldn't draw in a proper breath.

So that's why he'd spoken to George. He was settling his accounts, and he meant to leave.

George chose *now* to be astute. He watched her, a look of pity dawning.

"Well, I should . . . be off," she said, wincing when her voice broke. She mounted before George could comment and kicked her pony into motion.

Wylie meant to leave.

And she hadn't merited a farewell.

CHAPTER 27

LEADING HER PONY behind her, Anna picked a path over loose stones and climbed a treeless hill, her breath coming in pants.

These hills were her sanctuary, a place of sacred solitude, yet not. The souls of her ancestors surrounded her here, prompting her to take time while she had it. Time to marvel at the morning's cloud formations, time to examine intricate buds bursting into bloom, and time to feel a butterfly's wings whisper against her palm.

Here she was not a worried daughter, an aging spinster, or an economizing housekeeper who stretched a crock of butter long past its use. Here she was simply Anna.

Her mouth curved in a self-deprecating smile. Where had that economizing housekeeper been six hours earlier, when she'd lavished butter she could ill afford on a generous stash of bannocks for a man she'd never have?

Stop.

Must every thought lead back to Wylie? She wished him well, but it was time to wish him gone. She'd wearied of the angst.

A copse of newly green birch trees lay ahead, tucked in a ravine between two hills and marking the headwaters of the creek and a large pool where she could bathe. She pulled the pony off the trail and down a narrow track toward the trees and steps beyond to a clearing. Bounded by reeds, a pool of water stood in its middle.

Sunlight shimmered off its surface, giving an impression the water was warm. It wasn't. But slabs of rocks surrounded it, baking in the morning sun, and she could sit and warm after she washed.

It was almost as if God had designed the spot for such.

After tethering the pony, she pulled a piece of soap from one of the creels. Before she could dwell on her coming discomfort, she disrobed to her shift, discarded her cap, and walked into the pool, past the reeds to where the water was clear. Anchoring her toes into the soft, slippery slime, she ducked under, teeth chattering.

When she rose, she scrubbed with the soap, as much to warm

herself as to clean, and then knelt again to rinse her hair. By the time she resurfaced, the cold had become bearable.

"Are you mad, lass?" came a man's voice behind her.

Her heart slowed to a chilling pause, and she slapped her arms over her chest in a protective cross. She knew that voice.

Turning, she saw Wylie stood atop one of the rocks. Wearing only his shirt and breeches, his wet hair hung loose to his shoulders.

"How long have ye been spying?"

"Long enough that you should blush. Now finish quickly and get dressed. Dangerous men roam these hills, men who'd not think twice of harming a lassie alone."

She *was* mad not to have been more alert. Only the day before there had been reports of strangers. "I know as much of these hills as yourself, sir," she countered, buckling her knees, immersing to her neck. "And I'm not a member of your crew, so I'll thank ye not to speak to me as if I were."

Crouching on his haunches, he seemed to consider her words before answering. "My apologies, Miss Macrae. As laird, then, I bid you finish quickly, before someone wanders by."

Mother Mary, his arrogance set her teeth on edge. He wasn't *her* laird. "Unlike yourself, the men in these hills have more to do than wander here. Cattle to tend, for one." He was right, yet it nettled her.

"Those men wander after stray beasts. Did that occur to you?"

"What occurs to me is that *ye* are the only man here."

For a moment he stared at her, then a slow, almost bashful grin appeared.

She couldn't resist. She returned the smile. "If ye turn, Wylie, I'll do as ye bid. The water is cold, and I've no wish to linger." Unless he lingered with her.

"First rinse the soap from your hair."

She felt the top of her head, then tossed her soap to the bank. Inhaling another deep breath, she ducked and scrubbed.

He was here. Not on the road to London, but *here*.

Her eyes scrunched shut, she rose swaying, gasping again at the cold. Her heart leapt to her throat when warm hands gripped her arms, steadying her. How had he moved so fast? She opened her eyes.

Stripped to the waist, Wylie stood before her, his brown eyes intense beneath thick dark lashes, his smile gone. "You're lovely," he said without a trace of arrogance.

She met his gaze steadily, waiting.

"I suspected as much." With a finger, he moved a strand of hair from where it'd caught at the corner of her mouth.

Her entire body was on the verge of trembling.

"Did you know I think of you often?"

How could she possibly?

"It's no' often ye're silent, Anna. Are ye frightened of me, then?" he asked, falling into his native brogue. He moved another step closer, and she felt the heat radiating from his chest.

Flashes of fire sparked within her, leaving tingling, curling flames of heat, and he wanted to talk?

"Nay," she whispered, the word so soft she barely heard it herself over the thudding in her chest. She raised a hand and laid it against his cheek. His skin was shaded with new beard, rough against her palm.

He leaned forward and kissed her. A soft kiss, undemanding and almost hesitant, but a kiss that sent shivers stretching to her toes.

A kiss that must not end before it truly started.

She looped her arms around his neck and returned it.

His reaction was instant. One hand on her back and the other on her rump, he pulled her close. Her head swam at the rigid evidence of his response, and a long-forgotten, yet somehow familiar, confidence claimed her. It was as if she were twenty again, immune to all consequences and armed with the certainty that only the present mattered.

Their surroundings faded into sensations. His muscled shoulders hot under her hands, strands of his hair cold over her cheeks, and the unyielding planes of his chest solid against the yielding softness of hers.

This was her world. He was in it. It was enough.

Wylie backed them out of the water, his right hand tangled in her hair, his other still cupping her rump. His mouth never left hers as he sat down on the bank, placing her astride his lap so that she didn't touch the ground. Then he raised his knees to support her, leaving his hands free to roam.

Gasping at his touch, her mouth left his, her head lolling back as she relinquished control. He seized it, kissing the length of her.

neck and back, his breath hot beside her ear, his mouth warm. He smoothed his hands down her arms, her thighs, then her calves, raising gooseflesh over every inch of her body. Sparks flared at his every touch.

His thumbs rubbed hard arcs over the balls of her feet. His mouth found her breast, and his tongue teased circles across its tip, warming her through her wet shift. Her body pulsed, aching with want, and she gripped his shoulders, her nails digging into hard flesh.

When he lifted her shift, sensation displaced even thought.

Wylie stirred when a fly tickled his nose. He swatted it, then brushed a hand over Anna's damp hair, smoothing it flat. Her head rested on his chest, her arm curved around his waist.

I care that you treat her with respect. And that precludes laying with her without a thought for her future.

Hypocrite.

"Ye sigh once more, and ye'll have me thinking ye're sorry," Anna murmured.

Tightening his grip, he raised his head and kissed the top of hers. She smelled of the sage-scented soap she'd used earlier. "I'm thinking I *should* be."

With the tip of her tongue, she caressed his nipple. Her touch rippled through him, curling his toes.

"I'm not," she said, then blew dry the spot she'd just wet.

Before he recovered she ran a hand over his hip and down the length of his thigh. His leg jerked, his response instant.

"I've come to realize, Wylie, that opportunities offered must be seized, lest they not be offered twice."

A profound thought, that, since it led her to trail her fingertips up the inside of his thigh. Groaning, he gritted his teeth and pulled her astride him.

"I'm no' a randy lad of twenty, ken."

Straddling him, she smiled down, her green eyes glittering. "Oh? Do ye mean that as a challenge or a warning?"

He'd meant it as warning, but if she continued down this path, it occurred to him he'd not regret naming it a challenge. If he could speak at all, that is. His breath came in a hiss. *Merde*, but she was tight.

A shaft of sunlight filtered through the beech trees and fell on her. It lit her from within, turning her creamy white skin translucent and glowing. He followed constellations of freckles with his fingertips, over the curve of her breasts and her hips. She gave a shudder of abandon that nearly ended him. Then she stilled his hands with her own.

"Look at me, Wylie," she said softly.

Was she mad? He saw nothing *but* her. "I *am* looking at ye, lass. I've never . . . " He swallowed, unable to find the right words. "So help me God, I'll take this image of ye to my grave."

"Ye have no cause to be sorry, Wylie, and I'll take exception if ye feel regret." Her mouth curved, her smile feline, and she slid her hands down his sides. "If ye look back at this day and judge me unwilling, I'll know I erred in some manner."

God Almighty. Who *was* this woman?

"I find you wanton, willing, and utterly irresistible, Anna Macrae. I'll add merciful if ye continue doing what ye're doing."

Smiling, she leaned forward and kissed him, her hair tenting over his face and obscuring their surroundings.

He surrendered to the sensation. It was impossible to feel remorse. For the first time in decades, his soul neared peace.

It wasn't until hours later, when the sun lay in the west, that she pulled from his arms. He propped himself on an elbow and watched her walk to the water, her steps faltering over the stones. "Careful, lass."

"Ye've turned me into a rag doll," she said, steadying herself on a boulder. "Come join me."

"It's cold."

"It will be colder still in an hour." She knelt in the water, scrubbing quickly, and he caught her wince when she moved her hand between her legs.

He rose and found her clothes, riffling through them for her apron so she had something to dry with. He set them at the water's edge and then joined her, gritting his teeth at the cold.

"Your back's covered with cuts and bruises, Wylie." She cupped a handful of water and poured it slowly over his back.

He grimaced, belatedly recalling he'd spent the day on a bed of pebbles.

"Why didn't ye say something?" she asked.

"I didn't notice, and I'm glad of it. You might have bolted if I'd gone for a plaid." He pulled her into his lap and kissed her. Her tongue met his, and he tasted a bit of himself. He groaned, recalling how that came to be. Tightening his grip, he ran a hand over the side of her breast, then cupped its fullness and teased its tip with his thumb.

"Oh no, ye don't. Ye'll not get me started again," she said, pulling back. "I'll not be able to walk."

"We'll not need to walk."

"An enticing offer, sir. But I must go eventually, or someone will come looking for me."

"Who?" he asked carefully, hoping she'd not answer, 'Archie Montgomery.'

"Mrs. Grant and Mrs. Tanner. I'm to relieve them of their stash of cheese and butter."

His stomach rumbled, and she laughed.

"I starved ye as well as caused your back injury. Come, I have food." She pulled away and walked to the bank, retrieving her apron to dry.

Marry me. His mouth opened and he clamped it shut, biting his tongue before the unwanted words tumbled out.

It was the third time that afternoon that the words had risen unbidden. Thankfully, he'd left them unsaid.

The first two times he attributed to lust. This last time was far more unsettling.

When he was sure of his words, he answered her. "Aye, in a moment." Walking to deeper water, he submerged and swam toward the opposite bank, hoping to clear his thoughts.

He'd resolved months ago not to remarry. Why was he now questioning it?

Because the thought had hovered on the edge of his consciousness for days now, after seeing how often Will and Dougal gravitated to the Macraes. And then yesterday, when George said she'd emigrate, it had poked at his consciousness, demanding acknowledgment.

But George hadn't actually said that. He'd said that when she was five and twenty, she'd *considered* emigrating. Now, at thirty plus, her Highland roots were deeper still.

He rose for a breath and his feet hit shallow ground. He'd reached the opposite bank. Lying on his back, he started across, kicking slowly while watching the clouds.

Forget his sons, forget America. What about the way he felt when he was with her? The utter contentment of feeling her breath on his cheek, the curve of her hip beneath his hand.

When he'd decided he'd not remarry, he hadn't a woman in mind. Would marriage be an obligation if it were to Anna, and not to someone chosen solely for the sake of his sons?

He thought of her constantly. There was no denying he anticipated each time he might encounter her.

He'd been advised often to remarry this past year.

He'd responded each time with a list of the reasons why he shouldn't.

It would be helpful to recall at least one of those reasons, but his mind went blank each time he tried.

So then . . .

No!

This day was not at all what it seemed. He'd let lust cloud his judgment.

It had been too perfect. *She* had been too perfect, too . . . accommodating. By rights, she should still be angry. As far as she knew, nothing had changed since they'd last met. He hadn't told her of his agreement with George, yet she seemed to have forgotten the whole schoolmaster debacle.

What was she playing at?

Nothing, she played at nothing. Hadn't he also forgotten the matter? Once he'd caught sight of her disrobing, it had become the furthest thing from his mind. It wasn't surprising she'd forgotten.

Like hell. She'd been spitting angry when last they'd met. Women didn't forget such things.

Standing, he shook his head, strands of hair slapping his face as he slung water every which way. He walked to shore and retrieved the apron she'd left, not surprised to find a full half of it dry. He muttered a curse. What was she about, seeing to his every comfort?

His mouth set in a frown, he dried and dressed. Then he approached her, eyeing the food she'd spread over a short tattered linen.

Bannocks, and they looked as if they were the mouthwatering type her mother once made. Two types of cheese sat in crocks: one white, one yellow. A short jug of milk glistening with condensation—where had she kept that? And a small sampling of dried fruit.

He tore his gaze away, his stomach rumbling.

"Why aren't you angry with me?" he asked without preamble.

She looked up, her brow wrinkled. "Why should I be?"

"You were angry yesterday."

"Oh," she said, the wrinkles clearing. "That."

"Aye, that."

"Well, I spoke with George. He told me ye asked him to take over the hiring, that ye'd reconsidered Anderson."

She'd been with his sons for supper, he'd seen her kissing Montgomery after midnight, and she'd left Glendally at dawn.

"When did you speak with George?"

She cocked her head, her gaze narrowing. "It seems ye're the one angry. Why?"

"When did you speak with George?" he repeated. "You were wrapped round Montgomery at midnight, and you left Glendally at dawn. Does George make a habit of calling in the wee hours of the night, once his wife and your father are safely abed?"

Her gasp was sharp, and for a moment it seemed she struggled to breathe. Her entire body shook, trembling with either anger or shame. Then she tossed aside the crock of cheese she held and rose. Before he could react, she raised a hand and slapped his face. The blow and its force were so unexpected that he stumbled back.

"I don't know what brought that on, Wylie, but it . . . it was . . . it was hateful. Nay, unforgivable," she said, sputtering the words. "What gives ye the right to say such horrible things? Not only of me, but of George?"

He raised a hand to his cheek. He hadn't planned the words. In truth, he didn't know why he'd said them. He didn't believe she and George were carrying on. He could make a case for it, but he didn't believe it.

He suddenly felt ill. His belly churned, his self-disgust acidic. Yet he couldn't stop his next words. "You haven't answered my question."

"It's filth, and I'll not answer it. George is one of my dearest friends. What ye said is filth."

It *was* filth. Even if he could believe it of George, he could not believe it of Anna.

He raked a hand through his wet hair and opened his mouth, then closed it. He had no explanation to offer.

She began packing her pony, jamming crocks and flasks helter-skelter into its creels, and he realized she intended to leave. She'd forget the perfectness of the afternoon and remember only this. She'd come to think he'd used her, that he'd treated her the whore, that he was as despicable as his words.

He stopped breathing, knowing the twisted trails her memory would traverse. By the end of the day, she'd hate him.

If you let her walk away now, you'll regret it to your dying day.

There was nothing he could say to stop her. He'd dealt a blow to kill, not to wound. He'd succeeded.

He might try the truth.

The truth?

Aye, he might.

He swallowed and took a chance. "It *was* unforgivable, Anna. I said it to anger you. I'm sorry."

She continued tidying as if he weren't present.

"I expect I thought if you were angry enough, you'd turn me down flat when I asked you to marry me." She faltered for an instant, then jammed the last crock into her creel.

He continued before losing his nerve. "I feared I couldn't stop myself from asking." He reached for her, and she all but hissed.

"Don't touch me."

Instantly he dropped his hand. "I didn't mean it, Anna. The unforgivable part, not the part about asking you to marry me. I would have meant that." He sucked in a breath. "I *do* mean that. Will you marry me?"

"Oh, do be quiet, will ye?" she said, yanking the pony's reins loose. "Ye're not making the least bit of sense. And if ye think I expect a proposal of marriage because I lay with ye, ye're more addle-headed than I gave ye credit for."

"I'll not deny my head's addled, but I still want you to marry me."

Ignoring him, she led the beast away, ducking under the low branch of a spindly rowan.

Panic gripped him, and instinct guided his next words. "There was another reason I carried that plaid for decades, Anna. A reason aside from the one I told you."

She stilled.

The words had come from the same place "marry me" had sprung. But they were true. Some part of him had known even

197

then, or he'd have tossed the plaid.

"I'll not lie to you. I didn't know the reason at the time, nor did I know it all those years. But I know it now, and it scares me."

He held his breath, waiting for a response. None came, though she hadn't moved. He plumbed for more words, hoping one might pierce her resistance.

"I couldn't bear the thought of losing one more thing I valued, and for whatever reason, your regard was one of the few things I still valued. The plaid was proof you'd given it freely. Don't walk away from me, Anna. Please."

"How could ye think such a thing of me?" she said softly, her head down.

"You're a beautiful and very desirable woman, Anna. George must have noticed."

"He's *married*, Wylie. I would never . . . *He* would never . . . George stopped by this morning," she said, her back still to him. "He was like a small lad, filled to bursting with news."

He took several steps forward. "News?"

"Ye'd spoken to him. He's waited all these years for a word from ye. He wanted to share it."

He'd consider that later. He couldn't think about George, not now.

He sucked in a breath. "In truth, it's not George who worries me so much as Montgomery. My proposal is sincere, Anna. Will you share my life going forward? Will you marry me?"

Turning to face him, she choked short a laugh, shaking her head. "Let me catch my breath, will ye? Ye've only just named me a whore."

What? "I never said any such thing."

"Ye implied much the same. Within hours of learning I'm not a maiden," she said, her cheeks turning pink.

He'd wondered about that but had been nothing but pleased to find that she wasn't. At the time, he hadn't known he'd propose marriage.

Even so, it mattered not.

"That doesn't matter. It . . . I . . . Devil take it, Anna, I think I'm jealous." The emotion was unfamiliar, but he thought that was it.

"Jealous?"

"I came to Glendally to tell you myself I'd spoken with George. He spoke so highly of you I thought he might fancy you. Then I saw you with Montgomery. When you returned his embrace, it angered me. I nearly came forward and ran the man through."

"Ye're jealous of Archibald Montgomery?" she said, as if he wasn't clear.

"You sound surprised."

Raising a shoulder, she shook her head slowly, seemingly perplexed.

"It stands to reason I'd be jealous of another suitor, aye? May I speak with your father?"

At that, her look of confusion fled. She looked alarmed.

His heart sank. "Montgomery's spoken with him?"

"Not yet, but I agreed last night that he might."

"Is that what you want?"

She didn't answer, instead saying, "Wylie, why were ye there last night?"

"Haven't I've just told you? I came to tell you of my conversation with George. I stopped in the shadows when I saw you with Montgomery."

"Ye called at midnight to tell me ye spoke with George?" she asked, sounding skeptical.

"I saw a light in the window. I didn't want you to stay angry with me."

She sniffed.

"If you'll not answer my proposal, will you still allow me to ride up with you?"

She hesitated a fraction, then nodded.

"Will you feed me first?" His appetite, absent for weeks, had returned with a vengeance.

She gaped at him. "Mother Mary, but ye've a high opinion of your appeal."

He shook his head. "Nay, it's a high opinion I have of your good nature."

She shut her eyes and appeared to grit her teeth. At length she blew out a breath and turned to tether the pony.

"You're a kind woman, Anna Macrae. I thank you." Coming up behind her, he brushed a handful of curls aside and pressed his lips on her neck, experiencing an odd thrill when she shivered, her taste now familiar.

CHAPTER 28

ALONE, ANNA could have covered the balance of the mountain pass in thirty minutes. With Wylie ambling beside her, it seemed it would take twice that. She opened her mouth to comment when a flash of good sense stopped her.

He'd been wounded near here. She'd forgotten. He, apparently, had not. Silent, his demeanor alternated between wary and hesitant.

"Wylie?"

"Hmm?"

"D'ye remember much of that day?"

He winced, seeming to know at once which day she referred to. "Could we speak of something else, Anna?"

"Of course." She filled the silence with light stories of his father and hers, and the friendship they'd enjoyed. Wylie squeezed her shoulder whenever she paused, as if urging her to keep talking.

At length they reached the end of the pass, and the world unfurled.

A glen sprawled before them for miles, blanketed green with sweet summer grass and peppered with black cattle. Not more than ten feet from the track stood a set of three long and low shieling huts, temporary summer shelter for those minding the cattle.

Ten to fifteen women milled about outside the huts. Four had carried their spinning wheels outside and now spun in the late-afternoon sun. Others minded small children while still others prepared the day's last meal. In the distance, herdsmen barked orders to the dogs, who in turn barked translations to the lowing cattle, gathering them close for the coming night.

Anna shrugged from under Wylie's arm. "It's best we not touch before the others."

He scowled. "Because of Montgomery?"

She opened her mouth to answer, then shut it. Archibald Montgomery was but one reason.

His mouth flattened at her reticence. "Well enough, then, but we're only passing through to yonder, aye?" he said, pointing down the vast glen. "We've no need to linger here?"

She frowned. "Did ye think to rest amongst the beasts?" From his expression, she concluded he did. "Ye may do so, but I can't. I've come to see friends and exchange supplies." He looked uncertain, so she added, "It would please me if ye stayed near."

"Near, but at a distance." He looked more perplexed than hurt.

"People will talk, Wylie."

"We plan to marry. Will you not tell your friends, then?"

His offer of marriage had flummoxed her, and she refused to allow herself to believe it. What if passion prompted it? He would feel trapped by tomorrow.

The more people who knew, the more complicated things became when he left her.

"We've not yet agreed to marry. And they're your friends as well as mine."

He stood gazing at the women as if he found them unsettling. "I've agreed. It's you who hasn't."

Had he considered whether he could be happy in the Highlands? She'd marry him in a heartbeat if she thought he could. But she'd seen no evidence of that, and it worried her. He'd grow to resent her each time he felt cornered or threatened.

In any event, now was not the time to discuss it. "It'd please me if ye'd stay near, Wylie," she repeated, hoping against hope that he would.

He blew out a long breath, seeming aggrieved, then nodded.

Hours later, Wylie settled amongst a group of Glencorach herdsmen at the edge of the fire's glow while Anna helped the women with chores, glancing every so often his way. It was difficult to tell, but the set of his shoulders seemed to have loosened.

A slow warmth filled her. He hadn't wanted to stay in camp, yet he'd done so for her.

Their arrival had been awkward. She'd felt it as keenly as she imagined Wylie had. First, there'd been a bustle amongst the women to find the laird a stool, which he refused, and then the pressing of food to tide him until supper, which he'd also refused.

The whisky, though, he hadn't refused, and it flowed freely as the men drifted in and out of the settlement. News of the laird's arrival spread quickly, and they'd all come in from the cattle to pay respect.

"Ye haven't taken your eyes off Glencorach for more than a moment, Anna," a voice said quietly beside her. Anna turned from the pot and saw Eliza, Burt's widowed sister.

"Have others noticed?" she asked. She had no secrets from Eliza; they shared a deep sorrow and remained as close as the sisters-in-law they would have been.

Burt and Eliza's late husband, John, had been close friends. In the same regiment, they'd fought aside one another in America and shared grand plans to emigrate. Promising to send for Anna and Eliza as soon as they were situated, they'd sailed off within months of returning home.

Now all Burt and John shared was a watery grave at the bottom of the Atlantic.

Eliza had been with child at the time that ship sank, and she struggled daily to provide for her son and herself, a struggle that showed in the lines covering her face.

"Oh aye, they've noticed," Eliza said. "Is it true, then, that he's been widowed?"

Anna nodded. "He lost his wife year before last."

"Well then, I'll no' think badly of him for the way he's been watching ye."

Like her other friends, Eliza was eager to see Anna married. "He's ill at ease, Eliza, returning after all this time."

"Aye, and why wouldn't he be, then? He's had a time of it, from what I hear. Is it true he played fiddle as a boy?"

"He did." He'd played it well, if a besotted eight-year-old was any judge. But William had made no mention of him still playing. "I don't think he plays now."

"I've brought John's fiddle along. Sometimes ol' Fergus will sit a spell with my lad and teach him." Ducking into one of the shielings, Eliza returned with a fiddle. Gathering her skirts, she strode purposefully toward Wylie.

It took Anna a moment to realize Eliza's intent. Once she did, she groaned.

Do be kind to her, Wylie, when ye refuse.

The men sitting with Wylie drew aside at Eliza's approach, and Anna caught a glimpse of Wylie's expression. Bewilderment at first, and he leaned back a fraction. Shaking his head, he threw up his hands, palms out as if warding off both Eliza and the fiddle.

Stubborn, Eliza persisted, holding the fiddle with one hand and gesturing with the other. The woman was fearless. Then again, Balcor held her lease, not Glencorach. One of the men refilled Wylie's cup to the brim and seemed to join in Eliza's persuasion.

Soon it seemed all the men added encouragement.

At length Fergus, the best fiddler in Badenoch, joined in the fray. A slight-set man, his long gray hair hung free of a queue, wild about a face scarred by smallpox and battle. After directing a few words at Wylie, Fergus picked up his fiddle and dragged his bow across the strings. Eliza set her instrument at Wylie's feet and returned to stand beside Anna.

Those sitting fireside clapped, their rhythm steady, unrelenting, and persuasive. Wylie picked up the fiddle and stood, dangling it at his side as if he found it offensive. Unsmiling, his gaze found hers, his expression thunderous.

She set aside the iron pot, suddenly nervous. She'd pushed him too far; she should have encouraged him to continue into the glen. "Eliza, I don't think—"

Eliza pinched her. "Sing like ye do with George," she said softly, before turning and busying herself with cleaning utensils. "Quickly now, lass. Before those eijits choose a ballad of Bonnie Prince Charlie. Fergus will play whatever ye choose."

Anna's mind went blank. Then Fergus, a man of her father's generation, struck up a tune and her heart sank.

Fergus, with the wisdom of years, hadn't chosen a song of the Jacobites. Instead, he'd chosen "Moggy Lawder," a ballad of a willful young lass and her tryst with a lad passing through.

With raised brows, Wylie scratched his forehead and shook his head a time or two. Then a corner of his mouth curved in something near a smirk.

Anna narrowed her eyes as his gaze landed on hers. Did he think their time by the swimming hole had shamed her? Holding his gaze, she took up the lyrics. Her voice, soft at first, cracked a time or two before growing strong and true.

I'm wearied with my Maidenhead
While I have it in keeping:
But if thou'lt true and trusty be,
As I am Moggy Lawder,
I then will give it unto thee,

But do not tell my Father.

Wylie stared at her, his mouth now slightly agape. Then he grinned and raised the fiddle to his shoulder. After fingering the bow, he played the last few notes of the verse. Everyone in the clearing cheered, the prospect of two fiddles over one signaling a cause for rejoicing. Wylie exchanged a glance with Fergus, and Fergus nodded, quickening the pace.

Thank you, Lord.

Joy, mingled with relief, filled Anna. Still singing, she walked toward the fire. Eliza followed, her son in hand, and the two circled in time with the ballad. Other women and children locked elbows and joined them.

Before Fergus started the next song, one of the young herdsmen, his tone as melodious as George's, joined Anna in singing.

Gamely, Wylie played three songs. When the sun slipped behind a mountain, he passed the fiddle to another and strode toward Anna. She quieted mid-verse, her eyes locked on his.

He bent forward and spoke in her ear, the touch of his lips spreading fire and gooseflesh commingled. "I'll return come morning."

Her jaw slackened, and she went cold. She snatched at his hand, no longer caring who saw. *Don't go, not alone.* "Will ye dance with me, sir?"

A sad smile played about his mouth, and he shook his head. "It's been too long; I fear I'll stumble. Wait for me tomorrow, aye?"

"Wylie, don't go."

"I can't stay, Anna. I . . . I can't. I'll come for you tomorrow."

The note of anguish chafed her heart. Mute, she nodded.

He left her side and strode toward his pack.

He hadn't asked for her company.

She would love him as long as she breathed air. But if their shared heritage troubled him so, could she marry him?

Eliza came and stood beside her. "It was a step forward, Anna. Staying as long as he did."

She wasn't certain that was true and hearing it made her feel no less alone. Swiping a fist over her eyes, she turned at the sound of an approaching horse.

Who would be coming at this hour?

CHAPTER 29

WYLIE KNEW he'd hurt Anna by leaving, but he had no choice, not if he were to keep what little he had left—his dignity. The memories, wrenching reminders of all he had lost, garnered strength in these hills and were quickly overtaking his will. He was no more than twenty steps from the others when he heard raised voices. He turned and in the twilight spotted the shape of a horse and rider approaching from the pass. One of the glenmen stepped forward and helped the rider dismount.

Was it George Macpherson, then? Had he come on account of the men who may or may not be reivers? His jaw set, Wylie retraced his steps.

"What is it?" Wylie asked, coming up behind the others.

George swiveled so quickly that he almost lost his balance. Without thinking, Wylie extended a hand and steadied him.

For a moment George just stared, as if this were the last place he expected to find Wylie. The other men drifted back, though not so far back as to be out of earshot.

"What are you doing here, George?"

George jerked his head at the others, dismissing them. They dispersed, undoubtedly disappointed they'd not have a story to take home to their wives.

The Macpherson cousins, reunited at last.

"The men we spoke of yesterday . . ."

Wylie raised his head, alert. "Do you know what they're about, then?"

George opened his mouth and shut it.

Wordlessly, Anna came and stood beside Wylie. Disregarding her earlier request, Wylie set his hand on her shoulder. Seems he'd been less than truthful when telling her that her close friendship with George didn't provoke him. She stiffened, though she remained still.

"Spit it out, man. Before I drag it from you."

"Wylie!" Anna turned her face to his, her gaze narrowed.

He didn't mind the rebuke. Odd, but it warmed a place deep within. He met her eyes, noting their mossy green pools carried the same spark they'd held when she straddled him earlier.

Focus, lad.

George, whose own gaze had fallen on Anna's shoulder, looked up. "Piss off, Wylie. I'll have ye recall this is not your land."

Nor was it George's, though he probably knew that already.

George had a point, however. It was community land, and Wylie no longer had a place in the community. Chewing the inside of his cheek, he kept silent and waited.

"I received word from a friend in Fort William yesterday that Jay lost a significant sum at the table," George said at length. "I learned since that he'd pledged cattle against it, and the men you saw match the description of those who advanced him the credit."

Something in George's manner raised Wylie's hackles. *Not Cragdurcas cattle, I'll warrant.*

"But I thought your father sold..." Anna stopped mid-sentence, seeming belatedly to realize her indiscretion. Wylie sidled an inch closer, squeezing her shoulder.

"It seems Jay didn't use those proceeds to pay his debt as promised. He used them instead as his stake," George said, shifting his weight on his cane.

Should have paid that debt direct, Uncle Henry. "Whose cattle were pledged?"

George looked at Wylie, then away, his shoulders falling. "Jay pledged Glencorach cattle to increase his stake. His mother..." George took a deep breath and met Wylie's gaze unflinchingly. "Jay believed Glencorach might soon be his."

Anna gave a sharp intake of breath. Wylie tightened his grip on her, keeping his face impassive. He recognized the shame in George's slumping shoulders. He'd felt it himself, each time Rennie had lit into him over one of Will's escapades.

He looked over his shoulder and saw the glenmen heading back to their posts. Not a one of them had mentioned worry over reivers.

Nor had Wylie brought up the possible risk.

He bit his tongue, holding back a curse at his oversight. If he weren't so worried over being mistaken for laird, he'd have sent those men back hours ago, minutes after they'd wandered in to welcome him.

"Go on home, George," he said. "I'll handle it."

"You arrogant sod." George pulled himself to full height. "I don't require your permission, and I've no intention of going home. Jay's *my* son."

Sensitive cove, wasn't he? Wylie sighed with exaggerated patience. "Did I imply he wasn't? I bear Jay no ill will. Unlike others, I wish ill upon none of my family," he added pointedly. "But you'll slow me down."

George snorted. "I doubt that. But if so, I'm content enough to lag behind."

Wylie's gaze darted to the horse George led. No reason to argue the point; George was better mounted. Better armed too; he'd strapped a rifle on his horse and carried both a sword and a pistol.

"I expect not. It'll grant you another chance to stab me in the back," he muttered, releasing Anna. As he walked away, he heard her say, "He didn't mean that. You know he didn't, George."

His mouth twitched. He hoped she didn't plan to come to his defense each and every time he opened his mouth without thinking. She'd be forever apologizing for him.

Besides, he *did* mean it.

Over the next hour, a full rising moon cleared the hilltops, lighting the glen inch by inch. After speaking with their respective glenmen, Wylie and George learned that nearly half their herds were missing. The young lad who'd been left with the beasts protested that the men who took them had had papers. Unfortunately the lad hadn't read those papers because he couldn't read, but even if he had, he'd not have known Jay Macpherson had no rights to the cattle.

His hand cupping his chin, Wylie stood at the edge of Glencorach's herd and surveyed what was left.

He rubbed his thumb over his lips. He'd envisioned losing ten cows, maybe.

Losing half his herd? Never. The estate wouldn't recover for years.

Were Jay's losses truly so high? Or had the reivers taken more than their due?

He shook his head, frowning. It didn't signify. It was what it was—time to walk away and sail for Florida. He only hoped Alan could untangle the repercussions without Anna's help.

He looked up, noting his own glenmen kept a fair distance and watched him warily, as if worried. And worry they should. Half of them would be out of work after this. Then he caught sight of George striding purposefully toward him, his limp nearly imperceptible.

"Are ye ready?"

"For what?" Wylie asked.

George looked at him askance. "I don't know about ye, Wylie, but I intend to get my cattle back. Tanner sent four men spreading north a quarter of an hour ago. I figure ye and I will go south." He pulled a pistol from his back belt. "Here. It's loaded. I've another in my saddlepack."

Wylie hesitated. The stakes were higher than they'd been an hour ago, when he'd thought a handful of cows had been taken. This loss represented a significant sum to all parties, and the men who thought it their due were better armed and forewarned.

Odds were good he and George would not return.

His sons would be orphans.

Coward.

With a sigh, Wylie tucked the pistol in his waistband and followed George.

Why couldn't *he* have gone north with Tanner and someone else gone south with George?

TEN MINUTES LATER, he and George were a quarter of the way down the glen, with only one another for company. George seemed determined to treat the ride as a chance for tea and tittle-tattle. Without the tea.

"What are your intentions regarding Anna?" George asked.

When Wylie didn't answer, George swiveled in his saddle and regarded Wylie.

"Go to hell, George," Wylie answered, looking straight ahead. Couldn't the man just enjoy the night sky and keep quiet?

"Been there and back. It doesn't have much to recommend it." George shot another look over his shoulder before adjusting his seat. "I've heard ye've seen a good deal of her since ye've returned."

Did George fancy Anna? "My comings and goings are of no concern of yours."

"Anna concerns me a great deal."

Wylie snorted. "I expect I'm fortunate it's not legal to take on two wives."

"So ye plan on marrying, do ye?

Wylie grimaced. Why couldn't he just keep his mouth shut? "Do you intend to prattle on about women or concentrate on the task at hand?"

"I can do both."

A corner of Wylie's mouth twitched in a smirk. "No doubt. Likely how you lost a leg."

George reined up suddenly and dismounted. He bent to examine a dung pile, then stuck a finger in it and rubbed his thumb over the finger. "They're no more than an hour ahead."

Hell. *He* was the one not paying heed. When Wylie hadn't been replaying his afternoon with Anna, he'd been scanning the horizon, as if searching for sails in the moonlight. He pulled up rein and waited.

"He's a good lad, Jay is." George said. With the aid of a stool, he swiftly regained his seat.

"I expect that he is," Wylie answered, as uncomfortable with this topic as he was with the last. If they had to speak, he'd prefer they speak of something less personal. "Tell me about the Indian. Dougal's still waiting for that story."

As if he hadn't heard Wylie, George waved a hand, indicating their surroundings. "I don't know how ye can agree, given this debacle, but when he was a wee lad, he had an unshakable sense of right and wrong."

"Up until ye went to war, then, aye?" Like Wylie, George had rarely been home.

"Aye, I expect so. And when I returned, he was grown."

"It was the same with Will. If it helps, try blaming the Grants. I blamed the Renwicks each time Rennie met me at the wharf with a disturbing story of Will." Wylie frowned, remembering. "Not to her face, of course."

"Jay's a Macpherson," George said, his tone suddenly harsh.

For an instant, Wylie didn't know what to say. "Aye . . . well, of course he is, then. I only meant to say . . . well, the Macphersons are only the half of it, aye?"

George cleared his throat. "Of course." He was silent a moment. "I had hoped when ye met him ye'd take pride in him."

Wylie wished he could see George's face, as he hadn't a clue what the man was getting at, but George rode a foot ahead.

"I've no plans to hand the lad over for hanging, if that's what you fear," he said, making a wild guess at what sort of nettle had worked its way into George.

"Good God, no. I didn't think ye would. I expect it's only I fear I've failed the lad, and I hope ye'll see past my failings when speaking with him."

Raising his brows, Wylie shook his head, no less bewildered. "Well enough," he said, hoping that tabled the matter. He was the last to judge a man by his failings as a father.

"Do you remember when we lifted the McDuffs' herd?" George asked.

Caught off guard, Wylie chuckled. "It's hard to forget the first time a man threatens to stretch your neck."

That McDuff raid had been their first foray at proving their manhood. They'd planned it no less thoroughly than if they'd planned invading France. For weeks they'd trod their route, over and over until they knew their ground to the inch—every by-way and winding that seemed to lead nowhere, and every hidden cave, nook, and cranny. Only once they could soundlessly traverse their territory in the dark had they pronounced themselves ready.

Their objective had been modest. Slink into the McDuff camp by the light of a quarter-moon, lift five beasts, hide them in the canyons behind Carbey's Hill, and then return them by morning, before they'd been missed.

Instead, with the aid of their dogs, they'd made off with over forty cows. They'd been so full of themselves that they'd stretched their good fortune and kept the beasts hidden for three days.

Reiving and retrieving a few beasts before anyone noticed was one thing. Wandering about with a herd of stolen cattle for three days was quite another. When they'd run out of food, the sport paled. They'd returned them in the full light of day, armed only with a story of George's concocting.

Wylie smiled at the memory. "That was my first inkling you were a conniving bastard," he said without rancor.

George snorted. "They'd have hanged us on the spot otherwise."

"Silas wasn't one who relished hanging a pair of ten-year olds."

George had suggested Wylie tell Silas McDuff they'd come across a band of rustlers while they were out hunting rabbit, and that they'd waited until the men slept and then sent their dogs in to retrieve McDuff's beasts. "I'll wager he knew I was lying."

George slowed, now keeping pace with Wylie. "Of course he knew, but ye handed him a way to save face. He'd have hell to pay for hanging us; we were lairds' sons. And *ye* were the one who did the conniving."

Wylie's brow furrowed. "Like hell. I'll have you recall *you* came up with the story. It's only ye couldn't manage the telling of it."

"And who was it, then, who embellished it past recognition?" George shook his head with a smirk. "In any event, ye were always better at telling falsehoods."

"It pleases me you think I excelled at something."

"Many things, though I daresay ye're a bit rusty at tracking. Could be the years ye spent on open water."

A split-second passed before he grasped George's meaning. He swiveled in his saddle, scanning his surroundings. On his right the moon lit the shape of Carbey's Hill.

Beyond that hill a series of tracks wound through densely treed canyons. It was there that they'd hid McDuff's herd.

And it was there the reivers may be now.

"They're on foot," Wylie said. "If they're an hour out, they'll make it to Clacker's Nook well before daybreak. We can corner them."

George nodded. "I'll go in the back way."

The back way was through the cave at Clacker's Nook. Traveling through it required sliding along a bed of rocks on one's belly in pitch-black darkness with nary five inches above and on either side. Passable, if one didn't mind swatting at bats while slithering through.

Wylie cringed at the memory. Each time he'd done it, he'd minded a great deal.

"Nay. I will," Wylie said. "You wait at the pass."

George shook his head. "Nay, ye—"

"I'll manage, George. One of those rocks will catch on your stump. If it doesn't rip it off, it may trap you. You'll be no help to me then."

"Ye'll be no help to *me* if ye freeze up inside that cranny."

"I've survived tighter quarters below deck."

"I'll wager ye passed your time above deck."

Canny lad, George. "I will go in the back way," Wylie said, his tone final. "Stop your belly aching, and let's come up with a plan."

"We should have brought dogs." George was quiet a moment, then said, "I think it best I go in the back, Wylie, but for no other reason than that I can't manage the stealth required if I approach from the front."

Wylie sighed. As long as it wasn't due to his discomfort in tight places, he'd not argue who went where. "Aye, of course."

"I'll take my rifle and knife," George said. "I won't have room for my sword."

"Right. At the end there's a spot so tight you'll likely need to suck in your breath to pass through." Wylie shook his head, recalling it. "I don't know, George. We were twenty stones lighter thirty years ago."

"We'll box them in," George said, ignoring his protest. "If I can't make it through, I'll create a diversion so they'll think there's more of us. Remember to take the trail, not the cattle path."

He'd be target practice if he didn't.

"Aye." Dismounting, Wylie handed George his reins and started into the canyon.

CHAPTER 31

MEMORIES WERE an odd thing. Sometimes evasive, sometimes pervasive. It was as if Wylie were ten again, practicing this route in the dead of night with George at his side.

The vegetation had changed; the rock outcroppings had not. Etched against the moonlit sky, their shapes were eerily familiar, and Wylie knew without doubt he walked in the right direction. At each clearing, the shape of Clacker's Nook—the spot where George would meet him—towered ahead.

Two hours in, Wylie caught his first whiff of cattle. He stilled, crouching beneath the cover of a thicket of bracket. He was close now.

Thirty years ago, there had been a natural holding pen ahead. Footsore and weary, the cattle they'd lifted had munched for three days on the grass growing creekside.

As George had reckoned, then—the men contained the cattle in the same natural pen he and George once used. As for the men they sought, perhaps they slept nearby. Wylie inched forward at a crouch until the vegetation lessened and he could make out the Nook. Then he waited.

Thirty minutes passed, and Wylie's thigh muscles screamed for relief. George ought to be at the cave entrance by now.

If he'd made it through.

A man coughed. Wylie stiffened, judging the sound thirty yards to his left, just east of the cave's opening.

Surely, George had more sense than to cough.

While Wylie debated his next move, a stream of hot piss arched not more than a foot from his face, the scent acrid, so close it warmed the air. A stray drop ricocheted from one of the bracken fronds and hit his forehead.

He stopped breathing and shut his eyes, forming a picture painted with sound alone. Someone stood little more than a yard to his left. Fastening breeches . . . quick about it, so using two hands. No clink from a sword belt, no sway of a rifle sling.

Daybreak neared. Wylie would be visible within minutes, if not now. Opening his eyes, he soundlessly filled his lungs with air. A pistol cocked, the sound sharp and menacing. He dove toward the man he'd envisioned, his arms outstretched, and made contact. Clasping the man's shins, Wylie gave one quick jerk and pulled his feet out from under him. The gun fired.

"Hank? That you?"

The call came from near the cave opening. Wylie brought the barrel of his pistol up under the man's chin in warning. The man, presumably Hank, knocked Wylie's hand aside and swung the butt of his gun at Wylie's head. Wylie ducked to one side, and the blow caught his shoulder instead.

Hank called out, "Jem! I got one of them."

Pain reverberated down Wylie's right arm, and he lost his grip on the gun. Within seconds he registered another pain, sharper than the last, in his side.

The reiver was getting the better of him.

Wylie slammed his forehead against the man's, momentarily stunning the both of them. Wylie recovered first. Still atop the man, he groped the ground behind him, searching for his gun. By the time his fingers clasped the barrel, Hank had his hands clutched around Wylie's throat.

Wylie dropped the gun and clawed at Hank's hands. He brought up his knee, aiming for the man's crotch. Anticipating, the man deflected. Gray spots blocked Wylie's vision.

He'd lose consciousness soon.

Don't leave our boys, Wylie. Fight!

I'm weary, Rennie. Damned weary.

The man's grip on his throat was ironclad. The spots in his vision blossomed, becoming the image of Anna.

Anna.

His eyelids flickered shut.

Anna would care for Will and Dougal.

His fingers twitched, ineffectual against Hank's strength. He had seconds left. He dropped his right hand to his side and felt steel.

His pistol. When his fingers couldn't find purchase on the trigger, he pressed his thumb instead. If faulty aim killed him instead of Hank, he'd go to his grave knowing he'd tried.

The blast deafened him. Yet it also brought air.

Sweet Jesus. Air. He sucked in a lungful.

Hank's hands dropped, and Wylie collapsed, nauseated and hacking.

Alive.

A click sounded then, and Wylie stiffened, recalling the other man.

His chest still heaving, he peered through lowered lids. A man, presumably Jem, stood not more than five feet away, his rifle raised and glinting star-like in dawn's first light.

"Ye ought not to have done that, laddie," Jem said from behind the barrel. "Hank was my brother. Ye be sure and tell him it was me who sent you to hell, ye hear?"

The rifle cracked, and Wylie shut his eyes. *I tried Rennie . . . Anna . . . take care of the lads, lass.*

"I never thought I'd catch ye praying, Wylie."

George.

Wylie cracked open a lid.

George stood behind Jem, a rifle hanging limp at his side. "Didn't I tell ye to wait?"

Wylie took stock of his body parts. With the exception of a scorching pain in his side and a fierce burning in his throat, he was unharmed. He rolled from Hank and sat, clasping his hands to hide a slight tremble.

As many men as he'd killed over the years, it never became any easier.

"Ye all right?" George asked.

He nodded.

"Ye saved him the indignity of a hanging. I expect he's thankful he'll not shit himself on a scaffold."

"Aye, there is that." The words were croaked, scarcely audible, and Wylie fisted his hands to still the growing tremble. "Best we round up those cows, aye? Shots likely got them—" A fit of coughing overtook him, and he pressed a hand to his neck.

George didn't answer, seeming distracted, and Wylie noted for the first time the gore covering his cousin. Blood dripped steadily from one cheek, his breeches and waistcoat were ripped and stained dark, and his peg leg looked as if it hung cockeyed.

"Rough going, was it?" Wylie asked, keeping his voice to a whisper.

"Another year sitting on my arse and I'd not have made it." He

216

nudged the corpse with his rifle barrel, then flipped the dead man to his back. "Will ye help me go through their pockets?"

Wylie frowned. Did George mean to rob the dead?

George turned at his silence, and his eyes widened. "Bloody hell, Wylie. Your shirt's covered in blood. What happened?"

Expecting the blood was Hank's, Wylie looked down, curious, and lifted his shirt. The blood was at his waist and his own. His gaze shifted toward Hank's body and narrowed at the knife laying nearby.

In stunned wonder, he shook his head. "That bastard got me with my own knife."

"Let me see." George limped over for a view, then grimaced. "I'll say he did. Sit back."

Wylie complied, resting his back against a tree trunk and gritting his teeth when George poked at the wound. "I don't think he hit anything critical but it requires sewing and bandaging. We need to get ye back. I haven't a needle."

Taking a flask from the inside pocket of his waistcoat, George looked about the clearing as if he expected a bandage would appear. Then he shrugged off his waist coat and pulled his own shirt over his head. "It's cleaner than yours."

While George ripped his shirt in strips, Wylie studied him beneath lowered lids. The man's chest was covered in scars, jagged lines going every which way.

"Lie back a minute," George said.

Again Wylie complied, still eying the map of scars and curious at their stories. Then, without warning, George emptied the flask on his belly.

Mother of ...

His fingers curling, he gasped and jerked, clawing the ground. George regarded him steadily, saying nothing.

"Sadist," Wylie muttered when he could form words.

"Take off your shirt and sit," George said brusquely. He snaked an arm under Wylie's shoulders and aided him. Silently, he wrapped the linen strips around Wylie's midsection. When he was finished, he sat back and studied Wylie.

"Ye let him at your knife, Wylie. How did that happen?"

Wylie sighed. He wondered the same thing. "Complacency, I expect. I'm getting old."

"No older than I. Ye look like hell. When is it ye last slept?"

He'd grown weary of that question. Besides, he'd slept an hour or two in Anna's arms the day before. He countered. "Aye, well, you look as if someone's mistaken ye for a carving board." He canted his head at George's chest. "Is that all from one battle?"

George looked down. "Several," he said at length.

"Ye ought to have died of that one," Wylie said, pointing at the scar that puckered over George's heart for a good six inches.

"Aye, one would have thought so."

"How did it happen?" Wylie asked.

"Ye can read a full account in number four hundred and ninety-six."

Number four-hundred and ninety-six? What was he—ah, his letters. Wylie felt a vague curiosity now, wondering at their contents, then dismissed it. They had made it this far without delving into George's betrayal; no reason they couldn't stretch it.

George knelt over Hank, riffling his clothes. Wylie's nostrils flared at the sharp odor of excrement, and he dropped back against the tree, his head spinning. Scaffold or no, the man had shat himself.

"Look at this," George said moments later, brandishing two pieces of parchment. "Jay's notes. This one is dated last month and this one several days ago. I wonder if these fellows were the original holders."

Somewhat relieved his cousin wasn't robbing the dead, Wylie tried to rouse interest. "Hardly seems likely."

"I expect we'll find out soon enough. Hell, Wylie, that bandage is soaked through."

If Wylie didn't know better, he'd think he detected worry in the man's tone.

Stepping back, George put two fingers in his mouth and blew, the whistle piercing. "With luck, those shots will have brought Tanner within hearing range, else I must leave ye and get help."

Wylie closed his eyes.

Some-time later, Wylie woke to a thump and vibration. Raising a lid, he saw George sat beside him, and the bodies, now covered in a tarp, lay side by side in the distance.

"Tanner's gone to the shielings for help and sent someone to the fort," George extended a flask. "Drink. I filled it with water."

Wylie went cold. "The fort?"

George's brow furrowed, then cleared. "It was self-defense, Wylie, and I'll stay for the questions. Ye'll be at Glencorach. Take this now and drink, will ye?"

Wylie complied and took a swallow. Though it carried the scent of whisky, it tasted cool and clean. He handed it back to George, who refused it.

"Drink your fill. The creek is near."

"You kill many men, George?"

George was silent for a moment before answering. "Aye."

"More than ten?" Wylie canted his head toward the tarp. "Hank was my tenth."

"It was a long war."

Wylie nodded, knowing the question unfair.

"It doesn't get easier, if that's what ye wonder. Even when it's warranted." He looked at Wylie with an expression Wylie couldn't name. "It's best ye not give them names."

Wylie's mouth flattened. Hank had a name. Maybe even a family. "Do you see still their faces?"

George was silent a moment before answering. "Aye."

"And their families? Do you imagine those they left behind? "

George grimaced. "Are we speaking of the lads who followed us, then?" He appeared to consider the question before answering, "Nay, I no longer imagine those left behind. The nights aren't long enough. Are ye saying ye do?"

Wylie didn't answer. Though the memories *had* waned, they haunted him upon his return.

"I am sorry for that, Wylie."

A corner of Wylie's mouth quirked in dismissal. He didn't care for the pity in George's voice. "I'll warrant it's just punishment."

"Nay, it is not. Not a soul blames either of us for the lads who died in the Rising. Neither should ye. I came to realize such thoughts implied I was far more important than I truly was. A wee bit arrogant, wouldn't ye agree?" Before Wylie could bristle, he added, "And as for those who died at our hands, we were following orders."

Untrue. "Who ordered me to kill Hank?"

George didn't hesitate. "A higher power. If it's a fight to the death, then ye must choose life."

Wylie regarded George, his eyes narrowed. He didn't recall hearing that sermon.

"Trust me on that, cousin." Drawing up his knees, George draped an arm atop them. "So, if Jay were your son, what would ye do?"

The abrupt change in topic caught Wylie off guard as, no doubt, George intended.

Upending the flask, Wylie finished the water. "I'm the last person to ask for advice."

"Yet I'm asking. There are few people I can talk to about it, and I want to know what *ye* would do. Would ye watch him go to debtor's prison? Or would ye pay off the debts, hoping that this time truly *was* the last time?"

Wylie rubbed at his wrist, the memory of a frigid and rusty bracelet still sharp. He'd been imprisoned only once. "Do you remember that prison in Crieff?"

Nudging a pebble with his boot, George grunted. "They don't shackle ye to dungeon walls in debtor's prison. Leastways, I think not."

Likely true. In any event, the subject was far better than others George might choose, so Wylie gave it thought. "How long has he . . . I mean to say, can he easily stop?"

"Not as easily as my father expects. But I daresay it's possible, if he had something else to occupy him."

Wylie's mouth twisted as he recalled his conversation with Miriam and her concern over Jay. "Which is where Glencorach comes in."

"Hell no." George sliced a hand horizontally through the air, the gesture emphatic. "Not as Miriam presented it, in any event. I do retain some measure of control within my family."

The conversation had turned in an uncomfortable direction. In the near distance a series of whistles sounded, followed by the lowing and crush of cattle crashing through brush. "Shouldn't we go?" he asked. He struggled to his feet, his head swimming, and braced himself against a tree.

"Sit down. Ye'll need my help to make it more than five steps, and I'm resting. They'll return for us once they get the herd to the glen." George patted the ground beside him, as if summoning a child to sit. "Did I tell ye of when Jay joined the army?"

"No, George." Wylie sighed and dropped back to his rump, resigned. "You didn't. You'll recall we don't talk."

"Right," George said quietly, almost reflectively. "Well, it's occurred to me I have a captive audience. So we'll talk now."

Wylie muttered an obscenity and shut his eyes. "As you wish. I hope you don't mind that I sleep."

"No different than maintaining a one-sided correspondence, I expect."

Wylie bit back a grin. Returning those damned letters suddenly seemed worth his effort.

George cleared his throat, as if preparing to recite a saga. "When Jay turned sixteen, his grandfather Grant bought him a commission without my foreknowledge. I'd hoped Jay would pursue the law, but Grant hoped Jay would profit from the army's discipline. Jay, I daresay, was simply dazzled by the red coat.

"Of course the war ended shortly thereafter, and Jay didn't leave Badenoch. When I returned from Carolina, I found him supervising work parties on the military roads and escorting the local revenue man on hunts for illicit stills."

Wylie's lips thinned. Neither duty would have made the lad popular amongst his neighbors.

"Jay's somewhat of an outsider here, given the amount of time he spent in London, so both assignments caused problems." Grunting, George jammed his heel in the dirt. "Particularly since he patronized those same stills on his off time. The alternative, however, was serving in the West Indies. I was relieved when he went on half-pay, but that's caused another set of problems. The officers he keeps company with come from wealth. It seems Jay aspires to keep pace with their extravagances.

"Hell, I don't know. Maybe he ought to spend a week or two in debtors' prison. Rethink his priorities." George blew out a long breath, as if resigned to the situation, and Wylie kept silent, having nothing to offer. "Did your father pass on that I fought under James Grant before he became governor of East Florida?" George asked. "Uncle William said ye considered settling there."

Wylie willed his eyelids still. George had his full attention now.

"I'll write ye a letter of introduction. And I'm certain if ye ask, Miriam will write one as well. Grant's her fourth cousin. She tells me he's due back in London soon."

George paused, and Wylie felt his scrutiny.

"She also tells me that she's asked ye to accompany her to London. I'd consider it a service if ye did. I've no wish to visit the place."

Bloody hell. Turning from George, Wylie stretched out on the ground, his head pillowed on his outstretched arm and his face outside George's line of sight.

"I know how you feel, Wylie. Lack of sleep muddles one's thoughts. There was a time in '46 I couldn't sleep for more than an hour or two at a time. You were in France. Or so we all hoped."

Prickles of dread sparked in Wylie's chest, and it had nothing to do with his wound.

Here it was, then. The side of the story he'd shunned for years. Every ounce of his will drained from him, staking him to the ground, immobile. The herdsmen's whistles grew fainter.

"I badgered Uncle William that summer, asking repeatedly if he'd received word from ye. I regret that even now; he seemed to age before our eyes. I myself couldn't eat or sleep, worrying over whether your wound had festered, if the ship's crew had stolen the money I'd set in your boots, or if the coins were sufficient to secure ye lodging."

Lodging? Wylie stopped short a grunt. Hell no. Once he'd been dumped in Boulogne, he'd slept in alleyways and bunked with beggars for the better part of a year. The coins he'd found in his boot bought only a few days bread.

Whether some had been stolen, Wylie couldn't say. He'd been fevered for weeks and could scarcely aim his own piss at that point.

"D'ye remember Monsieur Jacques, Wylie?" George chuckled, and Wylie pictured their French tutor, finding nothing amusing in his thin visage and pinched nose. "I thought of him often during that time. It's odd, the things one recalls.

"I cursed myself repeatedly for not forcing ye to pay heed to the man's lessons. I might have forced ye, ken. Ye may think not, but I *could* have, if only I'd tried."

Given Wylie hadn't planned residing with a horde of French beggars, he hadn't felt the need to heed those lessons. Shortsighted, perhaps, but he supposed he'd figured that if he required knowledge of French, George would be nearby to supply it.

"If I had spoken to ye only in French, it'd have driven ye mad not to understand what I said. Ye'd have learned the language; I know that ye would. But I didn't take the time. So there ye were, alone in a land of foreigners with scarcely a grout to your name."

Maybe he'd have learned, maybe not. But of all the things Wylie could blame his cousin for, that ranked dead last. He opened his eyes, no longer worried over what George might glimpse in his expression, for George's tone indicated he now spoke to some point in the distance. It seemed he'd saved the words for decades, for they poured from him without pause.

"I also told myself that if I hadn't deserted the rebellion and left ye behind, ye'd not have been wounded. I'd have watched your back." George grunted, signaling a momentary return to the present by aiming a soft kick at Wylie's boot. "There I was wrong. I'm with ye now, and look at ye. Laid up and bleeding like a stuck pig."

True. But also true that George saved his life today.

His jaw hardened. Not that that came close to balancing the score.

"In any event, it came to an end that summer," George said. "I was in the library when my father stormed in, your father and Miriam behind him. Father told me the soldiers had just burned Colin Gordon's place. Smashed his plough to pieces and took off with his cattle."

Colin? Wylie swallowed past a growing lump of nausea. Colin hadn't fought with the Jacobites, not that Wylie knew.

"I asked if they'd carted Colin off to prison. Father looked at me as if I were mad and told me that after shooting the son who tried to shield Colin, the soldiers hanged Colin from a tree in his yard."

What sort of . . . Sickened, his heart aching, Wylie shut a door on the thought.

Colin had wanted no more from life than to care for his wife and their five children.

"Ye'll be wondering why, I expect, Wylie. Colin didn't contribute to the rebellion, after all. But ye see, the soldiers found a cannon hidden in the pond near his place. There'd been little rain that summer, and the water level kept dropping. Every day without rain revealed a fraction of an inch more of that damned cannon."

George paused and the rip of a frond tearing loose sounded from above. A spattering of dew wet Wylie's face. One by one, George ripped leaves from the frond's stem, tossing them over Wylie and to some point in the distance.

"Father kept shouting, demanding to know if I'd known of the cannon. All I could think of was Colin. I could scarcely stay on my feet, I was so dizzy. Colin dead? I couldn't make sense of it. What would Mary do? Who would bury her husband and child? Tommy, their oldest, was no more than nine. Was it Tommy the soldiers had shot?

"Father ignored my questions. He kept at me, demanding to know what I knew of the cannon. Finally I told him the lads buried it there with Colin's consent after the spring thaw. They didn't know what else to do; it wasn't a musket or a blade—there was no place to hide it following the order to disarm. They'd have been shot out of hand if they'd rolled in a canon when they turned in their arms."

Wylie's mouth twisted. Either that or hanged, one by one.

"Father was livid, his face colored lilac. For the first time in my life, I thought he meant to hit me. Not whip me for doing wrong, ken, but hit me with his fist. Uncle William caught him and shook him and asked which way the soldiers were headed."

At the mention of his own father, Wylie's chest tightened a fraction.

"I can still see that lump in my father's throat, jumping up, down, and back again," George said. "His breath was so hurried I worried for his heart. I told him there was nothing either at Cragdurcas or Glencorach. I told him I had no arms. The soldiers would find nothing at either place. That's when he truly lost whatever temper he had left.

"'Blundering nidiot of a lamb's arse!' he called me. '*Ye* are here, do ye not understand?' And once they found me, they'd rip the farms apart from burn to glen searching for arms. After that, they'd set our homes alight. He told me it'd be a kindness if they hanged me on the spot, that no doubt I'd wish they had while I rotted a slow death aboard the *Inverness*.

"I tell ye, Wylie . . . the mention of that prison ship caused me to sway. The stories of it are beyond recounting."

Wylie hauled in a shaky breath, knowing that for the truth. He'd heard those stories from other Jacobite exiles he'd encountered in France.

He turned his head up, focusing instead on the deep green foliage overhead, glistening in the morning sunlight.

"I knew I ought to eat," George continued. "Hungry or not. If I was to be carted to that ship, it could very well be the last meal I ever ate.

"Uncle William kept asking, 'Which way, Henry?' He still had ahold of both my father's arms. Finally Father quieted and answered, 'North.' Uncle William herded the lot of us through the front door and to the stables, saying, 'Then we can still go south.'

"And that's the first it occurred to me where they thought to go. Edinburgh.

"I backed away, shaking my head. They'd discussed this repeatedly, ken. Your father and mine. And I'd repeatedly refused. 'I'll take responsibility for my actions, if and when I'm arrested.' I put on a brave front, or so I thought. I'm now certain they both knew I quaked in my boots."

Aye, and who wouldn't at the thought of a traitor's execution? Wetting his breeches was more like it.

"I had no defense, see, or none they'd believe," George said. "I was too proud to contrive another to save my own skin. I'd certainly not travel to Edinburgh to give evidence on my cousin in exchange for my own acquittal. 'I'll not do it. I'll not go,' I told them."

Yet he had.

"Uncle William grabbed my wrist, insisting that I would, telling me that ye were safely outside the Crown's reach, and that my testimony would cause ye no harm."

Over the years Wylie had come to accept the truth of that, yet it hadn't eased the pain of betrayal. Hearing George speak of the decision now somehow did.

Somewhat.

"I was so weakened that he easily dragged me across the yard to the stable. Then Miriam spoke up. She'd been so quiet, I'd forgotten she stood nearby. 'George, ye don't know what ye're saying,' she said. 'Our baby needs his father, and I'll not have ye transported or hung. You must listen to your father and your uncle.'

"I swiveled to stare at her, as did Uncle William. Only my own father seemed unsurprised when she placed a hand on her belly."

George truly *was* a "blundering nidiot of a lamb's arse." A man who lays with a lass ought not be surprised if a bairn soon followed. He should shoulder the consequences.

It wasn't Wylie's primary reason for wanting to marry Anna, but he'd be lying if he didn't deem it a factor.

"If I'd eaten, Wylie, those words wouldn't have knocked my feet out from under me." George tossed what remained of the frond. Given its weight, it landed only inches from Wylie's face. "I went to Edinburgh. I'll regret it to my dying day, but I did. I couldn't see a way out of it, not with Miriam in the condition she was.

"For months after I lived in a fog of yes and no responses, as if I were sleepwalking. It wasn't until Jay was born and I held him in my arms that the fog lifted. I had reason for living, then, ye see. If only to care for the lad."

Wylie stared straight ahead, counting the seconds until George volunteered his explanation for lying with Miriam in the first place. Seconds passed into minutes. He heard nothing but the sound of a nearby whistle, and then George's sigh.

"That will be Tommy." George stood. "One of the women will have something to stitch and bind ye. Can ye ride once we get to the glen?"

Drained, Wylie shut his eyes. No explanation was forthcoming; the fact that Wylie had planned marrying Miriam mattered little to George.

He nodded, the movement perfunctory.

THREE DAYS LATER, Anna brushed past Will at Glencorach's gate. "How is he, Will? Dougal has me worried; why didn't ye send for me earlier?"

From the moment she'd first spied Wylie's horse carting that litter from the glen, a lump had lodged in her throat and refused to budge. She'd have summoned a doctor right then and there if Wylie hadn't been so adamant the injury was minor.

"He is on the mend, Miss Macrae," Will said. "He should not have sent Dougal for you. I saw him from my window when I woke, walking from the direction of the river."

She stopped and turned to Will. "His fever's not worsened?"

"*Non.* I believe he only wishes you will make more visits."

Her cheeks warmed and she looked away, swallowing past the lump.

She ought to be annoyed, not pleased. He missed her. Perhaps as much as she missed him.

"He will not agree, Miss Macrae, but I believe he should sleep the night through. This wound may reopen. You have something to aid him, *oui*?"

"Aye. Have Martha prepare a linen."

Anna found Wylie pacing his room, his hand raking tangles from his hair. Barefoot, he wore a white shirt that billowed about his midsection and a pair of tattered breeches several sizes too large.

"What took you so long?" Scowling, he strode toward her and snatched her basket.

The tightness in his mouth and jaw seemed born of displeasure, not pain, and the lump in her throat eased. Will was right; he was on the mend. "Dougal tells me I must come at once, that ye're not mending, and I find ye out of bed?"

"My clothes aren't in here?" he asked, towering over her while he riffled through the basket.

He'd shaved and washed, for the first time in days, and he

smelled clean though unmistakably male. "I told ye, I'm having them laundered."

"Did you send them to London? It's been three days."

She ignored him; patience had never been one of his virtues. "Lift your shirt and sit. Now that I'm here, I plan to change your bandage."

He plopped on the bed, stripped off his shirt, and pulled her into his lap. Startled, she shot up and stumbled back. "What are ye about, Wylie Macpherson? Your son will follow in a moment."

"I'll send him away. We'll draw the curtains about the bed and bolt the door."

She studied him. His eyes, regarding her beneath half-lowered lids, shone a clear, unshadowed brown, and his hair, not yet bound, hung in waves to his bare shoulders.

Her breathing quickened.

To spend the afternoon cradled in his arms? Mother Mary, but she was tempted.

From below came the sound of Dougal crashing through the front door, calling for his brother and in effect recalling Anna to the here and now.

"Ye'll do no such thing," she snapped. Leaning forward, she ran her fingers over the bandage until she found its end. "Lift your arms."

Silently, Wylie complied, his muscles flexing as he shifted position. She came face to nipple with his chest. Gritting her teeth through a nearly overwhelming urge to taste him, she instead reached behind him and unwound the linen. Once it was loose, she coiled it and set it aside.

"Where have you been?" he asked, freeing a curl from her cap and wrapping it round his finger.

"George had the interviews scheduled for this morning; ye asked me to sit in, remember?" She pulled her hair from his fingers and knelt for a better look at the wound. It was pink, not an angry red, and it appeared to be healing, though her stitches likely weren't as tidy as those of prior wounds. Beneath tufts of crisp, curling red hair peppered with grey, his chest was covered in well-healed scars. She traced one that ran from the side of his ribs to his belly, raising gooseflesh.

How had a merchant-trader come by so many wounds?

Without forethought, her finger veered off the scar and

followed a narrowing trail of hair downwards, to the waistline of his breeches. Wylie covered her hand with his and brought it to his mouth, kissing the inside of her wrist. She shivered.

"I'll send both lads away on an errand," he said, his voice low.

Footsteps sounded on the stairs, and she yanked her hand back, her face flaming. She rose and went to the window, pressing cool palms to her cheeks, and then turned to meet Will. Standing in the doorway, he held a butter-soaked linen strip in a pair of tongs.

"Should I stay, Miss Macrae?"

She took the linen with the tips of her fingers. "Please." Wylie, however, jerked his head toward the door, and the boy stepped out.

"He's concerned, Wylie. Lie back." When he did, she spread the linen over the wound and pressed its warmth to Wylie's skin. His face pinched, and her heart clenched.

"Christ, Anna. It's even hotter than it was yesterday. Have you no mercy, lass?"

"It's only that ye're healing, and ye can feel something other than the pain of the wound." Or so she thought.

"Are you even sure this is necessary?" he said through gritted teeth.

No, she wasn't at all sure. But her mother had always done it. Besides, the wound seemed to be healing, so it wasn't hurting matters. She held it in place a few seconds more and then took it off.

"I do wish ye'd send for a physician," she said, dipping her fingers into the poultice she'd brought. "Stand up."

"You've just said it's healing."

"What am I, a sorceress? Who knows what manner of ill brews beneath?" He stood, and she smoothed her fingers over the affected area, lingering at the task longer than necessary. She enjoyed watching the muscles in his abdomen tense at her touch— it triggered a pleasing tension in her own midsection. "I only know there is the beginning of a scar and ye haven't a fever."

Which was sufficient in most cases. But this was Wylie, and she had no formal training in such matters.

She wiped her hands, and then, summoning unpleasant thoughts of slaughtering a hog, she bade him raise his arms yet again. In quick motions, before her mind could wander, she wrapped a clean strip of linen three times about his midsection.

She'd not have him thinking her some wanton lass who'd fall back on his bed at the mere crook of his finger.

Even if she would.

Readily and greedily.

Her core quickened at the thought and her lips parted. She bit them closed.

Pulling the linen tighter than perhaps she should and ignoring the twinge of guilt at his quick intake of breath, she tied the bandage. Seemingly unaware of her near capitulation, Wylie eyed her handiwork. "I've been cut often enough to know when it's festering, and it's not. I've no desire to be out of pocket."

Out of pocket? Oh . . . the physician.

He worried about the expense?

She frowned. If she were to entertain his offer of marriage seriously—and she'd thought of little else—she ought to have some idea of his means. Why had that not occurred to her?

She sniffed. "Perhaps I ought to bill ye, then." She pulled a bottle of valerian tonic out of the basket and set it on the bedside table.

"What's that?" he asked, eyeing the bottle.

"Will is to see ye take that tonight to help with the healing." She kept her gaze down, meticulously stowing her supplies in the basket. "Does it worry ye, then? Being absent from your trade and idle these last days?"

He chuckled, apparently seeing right through her question. "I can maintain you in the manner to which you're accustomed, if that's what concerns you. Will you say yes? May I speak with your father?"

She sidestepped, not prepared to answer. "I thought ye'd be curious to learn George has decided on one of the candidates."

"Good. Now answer my question."

It wasn't that easy. His wealth or lack thereof was the least of her worries. Would Wylie be happy in Badenoch? Moments earlier he'd reminded her of a caged wildcat with his pacing.

Then there was George. Were they on speaking terms now, or would the next fifty years be a series of awkward encounters? Wylie had shared nothing of their time in the glen, nor had George.

And his boys—had Wylie discussed the possibility of remarrying with them? If they didn't accept her, he had his answer—a resounding "no." To do otherwise was a formula for misery.

"We have some things to talk over, Wylie. But Dougal and Will are waiting for us. We'll have tea."

A short while later, Dougal fell into a chair at the table, swinging his feet to and fro as if restless. Wylie held out a chair for Anna before taking a seat himself.

"Papa, Alec now writes of indigo and tobacco," Will said, taking a seat, his expression one of mild distaste. "Are we to farm in Florida as well?"

Anna's hand froze on the teapot. Florida?

"Don't take that tone, Will. Farming is a time-honored occupation," Wylie said.

Wylie hadn't told Will that they may stay. Of course he hadn't, as she hadn't accepted his offer. She poured tea into their cups.

"As is trading," Will said, his words clipped.

"Aye," Wylie agreed, sipping his tea. "As is trading."

Wylie's words were mild, yet a muscle worked in his cheek. Anna glanced from one to the other, wondering what wasn't being said.

"I mean no disrespect to the farmers," Will said.

"I'm glad to hear it, lad."

Dougal also looked from his father to his brother, frowning. "Miss Macrae," he said, seeming intent on clearing the tension. "I know the bad men who took our cattle."

"Truly, lad?"

"*Oui*. Will said we saw them at Mr. Moy's home." Dougal sprang from his chair. "One carried a pistol and rifle and one carried only a pistol." The boy swung his arms every which way, as if he were firing. "And Will said he saw a knife in one of their boots. Don't you think I should learn to use such things, Miss Macrae?"

Anna glanced at Wylie for guidance. A booted ankle propped atop his knee and one hand draped over the chair aside him, he toyed with his teacup, studying its floral pattern. Round and round he turned it on its saucer, avoiding her gaze

"Surely that's a question for your father, Dougal."

"Papa said no."

"Dougal, we've discussed this," Wylie said.

Why, she wondered. George and Wylie had trained in

weaponry at an early age.

"Well then, I expect your father feels there is plenty of time for that later." She looked at Will, wondering if Wylie had taught him the skills Dougal craved. Will studied his father.

"I should learn now, so I might practice."

"That's enough, Dougal," Wylie said.

"Is there a reason ye don't want Dougal to learn?"

Both boys looked at her—Dougal, his face brimming with hope, Will with an expression approaching surprise. Wylie's gaze was still locked on the teacup, the muscle in his cheek now jumping.

Perhaps she best apologize for interfering and broach a new subject.

"I only wonder because ye and George learned such things early on, Wylie."

"Anna, this is none—"

"None of my concern? I would agree, were it not for the offer ye made me," she said, ignoring her better judgment.

Wylie's head shot up, and he stared at her, seeming too surprised to respond.

She faced the boys. "We are both thinking this offer over before coming to a decision," she said, with a nod to Wylie's pride. "It's rather a serious proposal, and it will affect all four of us."

"He has asked you to be his wife?" Will said.

Anna wished she could read his face, but he was more adept than his father at hiding his thoughts. "Surprisingly, yes."

"So you will replace our mother?"

"Nay, Will. I could not, even if I wished it." She sipped her tea, watching Wylie. He returned her gaze beneath hooded lids, the muscle in his cheek still pulsing. "However, if I join your family, I expect to be treated accordingly."

"And Mr. Montgomery?"

"That is between Mr. Montgomery and me, Will."

"I'd like to know the answer to that as well," Wylie said, arching a brow.

She ought to have foreseen that coming. "Well enough, then. Stated simply, my position is vulnerable. My father is aging, and I am unmarried." She looked at Wylie. "I fear alienating Mr. Montgomery, in the event you and I decide not to marry."

Wylie shook a head, smiling a small rueful smile. "I've decided, lass. It is you who haven't."

"I'm not at all certain ye know what ye've asked for when ye asked for my hand. There is more to this family than you and me."

"I wish neither of my sons to follow in my footsteps. Is that so hard to understand?"

Yes, it was. Generations of sons followed in their fathers' footsteps.

That, however, wasn't her immediate concern.

"So they will continue to be your sons alone?" she asked, keeping her voice even, as if she were merely curious.

"I do not mind if Miss Macrae is another mother," Dougal broke in, his face drained of color. "I would like it much."

"That is not what I said, Anna. I'll thank you not to put words in my mouth."

"*Oui*, Papa. You inferred it," Will said.

Wylie stood suddenly, and his chair hit the wall and toppled to the floor. Anna winced.

"Do not leave the room, Papa. You will regret it if she chooses Montgomery."

Wylie stilled in the doorway, his back to them. "And you, Will?"

"I will regret it much. Many times over, I believe one says in English. You have made a wise choice in Miss Macrae."

Wylie rested his forehead on the doorjamb. After a moment of silence he made a grunt that turned into a chuckle, and he turned to face them. "Then perhaps, Will, you might convince her she'll make a wise choice in me?"

Will grinned. "*Non*. You must do that on your own, Papa. Dougal and I will take Molly outside while you do."

Dougal scrambled from his chair to join his brother, eager to escape.

"Take your time, aye?" Wylie said, his eyes on Anna.

"I offer you the same advice, Papa," Will said, sliding the parlor door shut behind him.

Wylie flushed. "He . . . he didn't mean . . . "

Anna snorted. "Of course he did. Will's nobody's fool."

"I'm sorry I snapped at you. It won't happen again."

Anna smiled. "Don't make promises ye cannot keep."

He rubbed at an eyelid, seeming uncertain how to proceed. "It's hard to govern my temper when I think of either of them following in my stead. It's an ongoing argument, and I resented their continuing it in front of you."

"I'll remember that," she said, though still uncertain of his reasoning. "My primary concern was their acceptance."

He nodded. "I'm glad you spoke up. I didn't know how to broach the subject, though I knew I didn't want *you* to worry over it." He paused as if considering his next words, then said, "Anna, you claimed your position is vulnerable. Have you . . . That is, has your father mentioned the possibility of you . . . "

"Taking over his tack? My father's not dead, Wylie."

"I only mean to say you may be Uncle Henry's first choice, when the time comes."

She drew her brows. "Ye think so?"

"I do. My uncle would be hard put to find someone more qualified."

She studied him. "Are ye saying that so I'll not consider Mr. Montgomery?"

"Not entirely." He grinned. "I'll admit the idea would not have occurred to me on my own. But I can't summon one reason why you'd not be suited."

"I can't think of this now, Wylie." George had only raised the possibility last summer, and the thought was somehow disloyal. "Besides, we have a full year left on the tack."

He studied her, seeming to debate whether to press, then extended his arms. "C'mere."

This man might be hers. All she had to do was say yes. It was a heady, intoxicating thought, and her misgivings vanished on its trails. She went to him, resting her cheek on his chest. She knew the scent of his skin now—had tasted and developed a craving for it. She tightened her arms around his waist.

"Marry me, Anna. Tell Montgomery no this afternoon."

Would that she could, before her doubts crept in yet again.

She pulled back and looked up. "I can't today. Mr. Montgomery is away on business."

He frowned. "What sort of business?"

Uncertain, she shrugged, though she hoped the successful sort. It would soften the blow of her refusal.

CHAPTER 33

THE NEXT MORNING, Wylie stood in the hall of Cragdurcas Manor, counting pendulum swings while he awaited his uncle. Five minutes passed before the study door opened and his uncle stepped out.

"Good morning, Wylie. I'm glad ye're up and about."

Henry had yet to don his wig or his coat, and the flesh beneath his eyes appeared inflated with worry. "I trust you're well, Uncle?"

"Well enough," Henry said. "What can I do for ye?"

Wylie hesitated, briefly caught off guard. He'd hoped to be persuaded to stay for breakfast. He slept surprisingly well the night before, thanks to the tonic Anna suggested, and Glencorach had been deserted when he woke.

"The tasks you requested are complete. I requested George's aid in choosing a schoolmaster, and it's my understanding he has chosen a Mr. McKinney. Those in the session should agree."

"And the manse?"

"It was a three or four-day job if the men kept at it so it's possible they've finished; I'll find out when I visit the kirk. I thought you might care to join me."

Henry shook his head. "Take care of it with the session, then, will ye?"

"Me?" Wylie asked, surprised. "You're senior heritor."

"I haven't the time."

Well, neither did he. "Then have George do it."

His mouth quirked in impatience, Henry waved a hand in dismissal. "Very well."

Wylie's brow knit, and he studied his uncle. Where was the fight in the man? At the very least, he'd expected a rebuke for threatening legal proceedings. Surely, George would have passed on the threat.

"You don't seem yourself, Uncle Henry."

Henry glanced up the steps to the second floor, then shook his head dismissively.

Leave now. Don't ask.

"Is it Jay, then?"

Grimacing, his uncle stepped around him and opened the door. Grabbing his cane, he walked toward the benches beneath the trees. With a sigh, Wylie joined him, and Molly, who had trailed Wylie from Glencorach, trotted beside him.

"It is," Henry said, answering Wylie's question of a moment earlier. "And damned if I'll be the one to set off her caterwauling again."

By "her," of course, Henry meant Miriam.

Even if George managed to save Jay from debtors' prison, the consequences of Jay's actions were bound to be grievous. Many mothers might be cocooned in their rooms crying.

Not Rennie though. She'd be mad as hell and expecting Wylie to fix it.

What would Anna do?

Fix it herself before he returned home.

The thought came unbidden. But hell, would she?

Likely not. He gave his head a quick shake to toss in some sense. Anna was genuine, lovely, and luscious, but no miracle worker.

"Is Jay here now?" he asked.

Henry shook his head and lowered himself to the bench. "Haven't seen him for over a week. That day you were first here, I expect. Miriam wants to sweep the whole thing under the rug as if it never happened. Somehow, she blames George. Why, I don't know. For that matter, why George took up with that woman to begin with is beyond my ken. She's never had a kind word for him." Henry swiped a hand down his face and stared at some point in the distance. "Never," he repeated softly, as if to himself.

Something jerked inside Wylie's chest. What a hellish way to live.

He sat and kicked at a tuft of grass. Rubbish. Miriam had every right to be bitter; she'd had to petition Uncle Henry before George did right by her.

His brow creased. Odd that thoughts of George siring Jay no longer roused resentment.

Wylie leaned forward and rested his elbows on his thighs, twirling his bonnet on a forefinger until he thought of something to say.

"Did those men carry Jay's only notes?" he asked finally.

Henry shrugged, shaking his head.

The defeat in his action worried Wylie. "Well then, George's friend—the one who alerted him in the first place. Might he know?"

Henry nodded. "Aye. George left late yesterday to speak with him."

"Will Miriam's family help redeem the notes?"

"It seems they've done so for years. When the Grants cut him off, Jay turned to me." Henry sighed. "Well, I expect ye want to know the state of your own note. That's why ye're here, aye?"

Perhaps he should have visited solely to offer his help with Jay. That's what his father would have done.

"It's one of the reasons. Perhaps I could help with Jay, Uncle." Gripping the bench until his fingertips ached, his next words rolled off his tongue before he could stop them. "I have some money set aside."

Alec would rip him from here to kingdom come if he even suspected Wylie thought of robbing their Florida fund.

Henry's head shot round to look at him. He stared at Wylie for a long moment, his eyes watering, then he looked away. "Good God, lad. Haven't the Cragdurcas Macphersons ruined your future one too many times already?"

Wylie frowned and loosened his grip. His future hadn't been ruined. It'd been different than he envisioned, difficult even, but to name it "ruined" was to deny Rennie, Will, and Dougal.

And Anna.

Perhaps Montgomery would return today, and she'd tell him to bugger off.

"I'm willing to help, Uncle Henry. Jay's my cousin." Or, in any event, some sort of removed cousin.

His uncle shook his head slowly. "God help me, if I thought it would be the end of it, I'd be tempted to take ye up on it." He swiped a hand over his thinning hair. "But it won't, and I wager ye know that better than I."

Birds called from neighboring trees, and leaves rustled softly overhead while they sat in silence. What Henry said was true and required no response. After a moment had passed, Henry placed a hand on Wylie's knee and squeezed.

"Ye do your father proud, son," he said quietly.

Swallowing, Wylie feigned interest in Molly, who snapped lazily at a cloud of humming bees before circling twice and laying down amongst them, her head on her paws and her eyes on Wylie. In the distance, a horse whinnied and was answered by the call of a stable lad. The sun, still low in the sky, warmed his shoulders. Lulled, an unexpected peace settled over him, and he sat with his eyelids drooping.

This too shall pass.

He blinked and Henry stirred, as if he'd also felt William's words. Clearing his throat, Henry stood with the aid of his cane. "What's she doing here?" he asked, canting his head toward the dog.

"Molly? She followed me. The lads stayed over at the Macraes; she probably tired of waiting for them."

"Come on inside, then. I'll sign my copy of your note so ye can take it to Alan. God forbid your solicitor show up on my doorstep."

Wylie stood and followed, grinning. This Henry he recognized.

"George left a letter for ye. This one ye might deign to open. He said it's a letter of introduction."

The grin died. Wylie followed his uncle inside, feeling very much the recalcitrant schoolboy.

CHAPTER 34

WYLIE'S VISIT TO the kirk was uneventful. True to his word, Lachie had the job nearly complete. Reverend Dow was effusive in his praise.

That task finished, Wylie went next to Glendally, his signed note in hand. He was greeted by Anna in a state of undress, her bodice cloth absent and a smudge of charcoal darkening one cheek. Her hair, unbound, curled in wild tangles down her back and over her bodice.

An ache of longing chased the breath from his lungs. What he'd give to find her waiting each time he came home. He settled a hand on the curve of her hip and closed the distance between them. Her welcoming expression turned to one of alarm, and she pulled away.

"Wylie, ye promised to wait," she whispered.

The longing iced and splintered. He shut his eyes and hauled in a long breath. *Fool.*

"I have my uncle's signed note," he said flatly.

"Oh." She stepped aside, and he entered.

Mrs. Baxter looked up from the hearth. "Good day, sir. It's glad I am, to see ye up and about."

Wylie forced a polite smile. "Thank you, ma'am. Miss Macrae has a fine touch. The cut's healed so it's no more than a scratch."

"If that were so, ye'd not have blood on your coat," Anna said, her lips pressed thin. "Take it off."

Wylie drew his coat aside and looked down, surprised to see she was right. The bandage had soaked through again. Hoping she didn't plan to steal his shirt for another laundering, he took his coat off and set it on the table aside her sketch pad. The drawing caught his eye and he pulled the pad forward. It was of a shirtless man, seemingly one at work.

"Is this your Mr. Montgomery?" he asked, raising a brow. He'd only seen the man from a distance, lit by the light of a lantern. Even so, if the sketch were of Montgomery, it was apparent Anna had embellished the man's features and form. He flipped the page to one of a woman sitting fireside at her spinning wheel, a cradle at her feet. Her expression was one of quiet contentment.

That could be Anna one day soon.

Anna slammed the pad shut. "It's Mike Macpherson working the peats. Lift your shirt."

Wylie knew Mike had married; Lachie had told him. But married men were known to wander. "May I inquire why you're drawing Mike Macpherson? Another suitor, perhaps?"

What was the matter with him? He'd left Rennie alone for months on end and not thought twice of her fidelity.

Anna hadn't pledged fidelity. Rennie had.

He winced as Anna probed, her touch far less gentle than in days prior.

"Anna?" he prompted, in the event she'd forgotten his question. She darted a glance in Mrs. Baxter's direction and back, then looked up at him, her eyes narrowed in warning. He held his breath and tensed the muscles in his abdomen, preparing for a less than gentle touch.

"His *wife* asked for it, and I said yes," she said, reaching behind him to unwrap the soiled bandage.

His muscles relaxed. Why hadn't she said so in the first place? He glanced at the empty box bed, knowing his boys had stayed the night. "Dougal and Will have left?"

"Dougal left an hour ago to visit with Lachie's boys. I'm not certain what time Will left."

"I met those boys the other day when I asked Lachie to run the crew. They seem good lads."

"Aye, they are." She stood and squeezed his shoulder. "Keep that shirt up and don't move."

When she walked away, Mrs. Baxter turned to Wylie. "We were all pleased to hear of Mr. McKinney's hiring, sir."

Surely she realized he'd had no part in selecting the schoolmaster—or none that he wanted to claim. Uncomfortable, he nodded.

"And it was my brother Billy ye had help mend the manse," Mrs. Baxter continued.

"Lachlan Shaw is handling that."

"Well, ye'll not be disappointed. Billy hopes to keep his lease."

Wylie wondered if Alan had the extensions ready for signature.

"I'm certain Billy will do a fine job. He was building our forts back—" He paused, suddenly feeling awkward.

"Back before ye were taken. Aye, I know. We grieved both you and Cragdurcas Younger mightily that winter. Billy planned to join ye, ken, in spite of what our da said. He would have too, if he hadn't took to bed with that fever. It shamed him for years not to follow ye."

"You should be thankful he took ill, ma'am. It saved his life, I expect."

"Aye, well. Mark Kinney, ye remember Mark no doubt, he passed from that fever that winter." She flushed, as if belatedly realizing she'd voiced disagreement with the laird. "But I'm certain ye're right."

"I am. Be thankful he remained home."

"Aye, sir. And we're pleased ye're here as well."

His Badenoch reception was far different than he'd expected. In fact, it was as Father claimed it would be.

Welcoming.

George may be right. Perhaps attributing others' actions to his own influence *was* arrogant.

Anna returned and knelt before him. Again, he held his shirt high while she fussed, her touch warm and competent. She hadn't added a neckcloth to her bodice but she'd taken time to wash the charcoal from her cheek and run a comb through her hair. The scent of the soap she'd used to wash—the same soap she'd used at the watering hole—wafted up, and he shifted in his seat to hide his body's immediate response to the memory.

"There." She smoothed a hand over the clean bandage and looked up, seemingly unaware of the effect she had on him. "Once more, it's done."

He took her hand in his and kissed her palm. Her pupils widening, she snatched it back and stood.

"I've told Father ye're here," she said, her cheeks pink. "He's gathering the account books."

Wylie made quick note of the gooseflesh covering her chest. He'd not lost her to Montgomery yet; there was no reason to concede defeat. "Well then, we best not keep him waiting." He swept a hand in front of him. "After you, Miss Macrae."

While Wylie watched, Alan stored the signed note in his

strongbox. The factor seemed all business today, a fact Wylie credited to Anna's presence.

Her presence did little to keep Wylie focused on business, however. She'd thrown a shawl over her shoulders, but her skin was visible through its loose weave, and her scent filled his nostrils. He darted a glance at her bosom, to see if the curl hovering on the slope of one breast had slid to the crevice between the two.

"I will have Henry sign Glencorach's copy and mine in the next day or two," Alan said. "Perhaps you would see to that, Anna?"

"Of course, Father."

"Very well, then." Alan dipped his quill in ink, made a notation in the account book, and turned the ledger to Wylie for his review. "The balance of Glencorach's debts are surprisingly few."

Dragging his thoughts from Anna, Wylie reviewed the entries: two lumber bills, one for the blacksmith, three for a physician, and the quarterly stipend for the minister. "And the receivables?"

Alan pulled another ledger from the pile atop his desk and handed it to Wylie. Wylie thumbed through the pages. It was not as straightforward, nor did he expect it to be. The rent receipts were rarely current.

Although now Mr. Moy's appeared to be.

Hadn't Alan said Moy was delinquent? Puzzled, he regarded Alan.

"Robert Moy is now current?"

Alan gave a long sigh. "I must explain that. Your father and Mr. Moy had an unusual arrangement, one that lasted longer than either party expected."

Beside him, Anna shifted in her seat. Wylie glanced her way, but her gaze was trained on her father. Wrapping her hands around the folds of her shawl, she pulled it tight, as if swaddling her person.

"Or perhaps, longer than William expected," Alan amended. "Mr. Moy may have taken advantage of William's generosity. There are two ledgers for Moy's receipts, you see, and I hadn't updated one at the time we last spoke."

It would be very unlike his father to keep a separate set of books. "I'm afraid I don't see at all, Alan."

Anna stood to pace the small room, and Wylie looked from her to Alan and back again, wondering at her unease.

Alan held up a hand. "Allow me to explain." After clearing his throat, he went on. "Three of Robert Moy's sons were killed in the war in America. All three had been sending money home, then suddenly they weren't. Robert became responsible for three rents in addition to his own. I suppose he could have sheltered his widowed daughters-in-law and grandchildren, but he chose to help them stay in their own homes. William also offered to help."

Wylie couldn't imagine his father doing otherwise. He examined the ledger page, wondering how it reflected that "help."

"Robert didn't have coin, of course," Alan said. "But he did have his whisky, and he's rather perfected his process. William agreed to accept it in kind, and I agreed to keep a separate ledger recording the payments."

Wylie didn't comment. He thumbed back through the last ten pages of Moy's account, not certain what it was that puzzled him.

"I see you recognize your son's handwriting," Alan said.

That was it; portions were written in Will's hand. He looked up at Alan. "Why is that?"

Anna stopped pacing. "Father, what—"

"Sit, please, Anna." Alan leaned back in his chair, tapping the tip of his quill on the desktop until she did. "I don't know if ye're aware of it, Wylie, but without Anna's help, I would have given this up a year ago," he said, passing a hand over his desk. "However, Anna knew nothing of this particular arrangement until recently, so it didn't occur to her that I might be remiss in posting payments to Moy's ledger. She simply thought Moy was dreadfully behind, as I unwittingly led you to believe."

On one hand, Wylie wished Alan would get to the point. On the other, he began to dread hearing it. There was only one thing amiss with taking whisky in kind as far as he could see, and only one reason to keep a separate accounting.

"I thought to correct it myself," Alan said. "Unfortunately much of the time I don't seem to *be* myself. Will happened to be in the room while I struggled with it, and he informed me he kept the books for his grandfather's shop."

"Aye, he did," Wylie said slowly, trying to recall what Will had said recently of Glencorach's accounts. It was before Wylie went to the glen.

"Well, someone taught the lad well. He has an extraordinary grasp of the process. He understood what needed to be done, and

243

he completed it in less than an hour. I meant to tell ye, Anna, but ye've been so busy."

Wylie looked at Anna. One hand still clutched her shawl close; the other she'd pressed knuckles to chin. She kept her gaze trained forward and nodded in her father's direction.

Her seeming unease caused his own to grow. Had she truly known nothing of this prior to last week?

Even so, why hadn't she told him *this* week?

He turned back to Alan. "Could you be more specific, Alan? I'm not surprised to hear Will could help, but I'm uncertain what needed to be done."

"Will calculated an estimate of the current value of the whisky Moy contributed at various points in time in the last three years. Then he credited Moy's account in the order the barrels were received. He thought it'd be odd to record the total value in one entry."

No doubt. Wylie inhaled a deep breath and blew it out slowly. "And these receipts weren't recorded correctly in the first place because . . . Let me guess. Moy did not report those barrels to the excise?"

Alan nodded, resting his clasped hands atop the desk.

"I gather my father didn't report it either. Do you plan to hand Archibald Montgomery written proof of this?"

The factor shook his head, grimacing. "No, no, lad. Don't ye see?" He placed a finger on the ledger sheet. "Look, Will has converted the value of the whisky into grain. The credits ye see are for grain, not whisky. Montgomery will be none the wiser."

Wylie pulled the ledger forward, taking time to review each entry. His belly clenched.

Someone *had* taught the lad well. To lie, to cheat, and to swipe clean the tracks.

Wylie had only to look into a looking glass to see who.

Covering his face with his hand, he slouched down in his seat and pressed a thumb and finger to his eyes.

"Will recorded only a value net of the excise. He planned to consult with ye. Your bearing indicates he hasn't."

Wylie straightened. "That's correct." Though to be fair, Will had tried. He'd brought up Glencorach's accounts more than once, and Wylie had put him off.

His jaw hardened. To hell with fair. He closed the book, shoved it across the desk, and stood, glancing again at Anna. She seemed frozen in place, her attention only for her father. Wylie fought the urge to pull her from the chair and shake her thoughts free.

If Will had explained *why* he wanted to discuss Glencorach's finances, Wylie would have cooperated.

"I apologize, Wylie, that this comes as a surprise," Alan said. "Please understand that William planned speaking with you in person about the situation. He . . . we . . . Well, we hadn't expected that he'd not have the chance."

His anger ebbed; of course they hadn't. "How many barrels?"

"Should be thirty now."

Good God. It would be damned hard to sell thirty barrels without excise stamps.

Alec might make one last run if Wylie got the barrels to the coast.

He fingered his neck, again envisioning the chafe of a hangman's noose, and shook his head. He'd find another way. He'd vowed to leave that life behind; it was Rennie's last request.

One of them anyway.

He had a surprising urge to smile and instead focused on Alan. "Moy's storing these?"

"Nay, they're in your second cellar. William and I took count in January."

Wylie's stomach clenched, and any urge to smile vanished. He stared at Alan, disbelieving.

Glencorach's cellar?

How could Father have sold Glencorach to the local revenue man with such a stash in its cellar? Montgomery would be duty-bound to confiscate it.

Had Father truly planned selling?

Wylie blew out a breath and shut his eyes in defeat. Selling Glencorach was never Father's idea; it was Wylie's. And now that he thought about it, it was something he might reconsider. He and Anna would return occasionally; she'd not leave Alan indefinitely if he chose not to accompany them.

Rubbing at a spot between his shoulder blades, he looked down at Alan. "Did either of you have a plan to deal with the excise?"

Alan shook his head. "Initially William simply hoped to refill Glencorach's cellar for his personal use. The years passed quickly however, and the situation is now out of hand. He'd hoped ye would have a suggestion, Wylie."

His jaw clenched, Wylie walked the length of the room and back, doing a quick calculation of the tax owed. With each shilling, his reason ebbed and his anger surged. It came to a tidy sum.

If Archibald Montgomery were tipped off to the cellar's contents now, he'd receive a tidy portion of that tidy sum upon making a seizure. Wylie looked at Anna, who had crossed her arms over her midsection, her head trained toward her lap.

A sweet padding to any dowry Alan Macrae planned to pay.

The nausea that had disappeared days ago swelled, and a stinging bile rose, burning his throat.

He swallowed it back.

Anna would not . . .

Perhaps she already had. She wouldn't—or couldn't—even look at him.

Anna would *not* betray him.

People betray one another. Even the near and dear. It happened.

But if she *had* tipped Montgomery, would she even realize what she'd done?

Oh, God, what if Will . . .

"When you return, Papa, I will explain more. You will agree that the risk is small and necessary."

Anna looked over at him then, her eyes glistening with something akin to shame.

"Mr. Montgomery is away on business."

Something inside him shattered.

Wylie left the room at a run. He hoped to hell he was wrong, but he doubted that whisky was still at Glencorach.

CHAPTER 35

ONCE SHE RECOVERED her wits, Anna convinced her father that she should be the one to follow Wylie. Now, though, the lump in her throat expanded with each step she took. Soon it'd be difficult to draw breath.

She'd expected Wylie's anger. But when she garnered the nerve to meet his gaze, what she'd seen had knocked the air from her lungs.

Hurt?

Molly, stationed beside Glencorach's open cellar door, thumped her tail at Anna's approach. Anna hurried past and into the cellar. Wylie stood with his back to her, emptying a shelf of its contents.

"Wylie? What is it?"

"Go home, Anna."

The lump in her throat eased. He was only angry.

"I should have told ye of the whisky, Wylie. But it's as Father said; I only learned of it a short time ago. So many things have happened since that it slipped my mind."

"Get out."

He was entitled to his anger. It would pass. As if he hadn't spoken, she retrieved a lantern from a shelf and lit it.

He aimed his fist and smacked a small indentation on the wall, unnoticeable to those who didn't know to look for it. The hidden door cracked open, and he pulled it wide.

Anna followed him, holding the lantern high. Her jaw dropped. The room was empty.

Dread churned her belly. "There's nothing here," she whispered, turning a slow circle.

Father asserted he'd counted the cellar's contents in January. Had he not?

Had the whisky *ever* been here? Could it have been an arrangement Robert Moy proposed and William rejected?

She must explain Father's failings, before Wylie conjured worse scenarios. "Wylie, I know what ye must be thinking, but Father didn't lead ye false purposefully."

Ignoring her, he bent to examine the floor.

"Sometimes—well especially in this last year—he gets confused and recalls things differently, or he forgets them entirely. It upsets him when it happens, and it seems to happen more and more. But please don't blame him. In his mind the barrels were here. He honestly believes that. It will devastate him to realize he led ye astray."

Wylie turned and snatched the lantern from her, his expression one of disgust. "Of course the barrels were here." Progressing a few feet on his knees, he scooped up dirt with his free hand and let it pass through his fingers, examining it in the lantern's glow.

"When did ye last see Will?" he asked.

"Will?"

"My son. Do you remember him?"

Ill-temper didn't suit him. "What on earth would Will know of this?"

"Answer my question."

"Will merely recorded the figures my father gave him. He'd not have known that my father . . . that the barrels were never here."

"Anna!"

Flinching, she slanted back.

"Not one more goddamned word about your father." His words came clipped and slow, as if she were dimwitted. "He forgets from time to time. It is not a crime, and it is no concern of mine. Will you tell me when you last saw Will, or must I return and ask Alan?"

Rattled, she tried to recall. "Last night. I retired while they were still playing cards," she said softly.

"Damn it, Anna, I asked you when."

"Early. Shortly after we supped. Maybe ten."

A corner of his mouth stretched, and he shook his head, seemingly lost in thought. Then he rose and went out the door.

Midway through, he paused, stopping mid-step. He stood still a moment, his head held alert as if he were thinking, and then he swiveled to face her.

"In your father's office, you refused to look at me until the last."

"I was upset."

"You looked at me with shame. Was it because of Alan's condition?"

Her brow knit while she thought.

Had she felt shame? Shame on her if she had.

"There's no denying I worried what ye'd think. My father's work has suffered," she said carefully, studying her clasped hands, reluctant to reveal how *much* it had suffered. "It has affected ye adversely. First there was the forgotten mortgage, and now this." She swept a hand behind her. "Ye have reason to suspect incompetency. Some might suggest fraud. That shouldn't be, not after all ye've been through." Her eyes filled. "Oh Lord, perhaps I am ashamed. I ought not to be."

"No, you ought not to be," he said quietly.

She looked at him then and thought his anger gone.

"Your father did what my own father asked. The only error here," he said, pointing at the empty room, "is mine. What was in that tonic?"

"Tonic?" she asked, taken off guard.

"The one you left at my bedside. Will said you suggested it."

"Oh, aye. Valerian. Will worried ye weren't resting as ye should. Have ye not taken it before, then?"

He shrugged. "Maybe once or twice. Still, I can't believe I slept through this." He took her arm and led her to the yard. "Look at me."

She squinted, her eyes adjusting to the sunlight, and did as he asked.

"Have you told Montgomery of the whisky?"

She stared, her eyes widening and lips parted. Did he think her capable of such a betrayal?

"So help me God, Anna, answer with the truth."

"Is . . . is that what ye think?"

His grip on her arm tightened. "Where do your loyalties lie? With Montgomery or with me?"

Dumbstruck, she shook her head from side to side, unable to form words. He had thought she betrayed him. Nay, him and William both.

"Confiscating those barrels would be quite a coup for your exciseman. He might even consider it a part of your dowry."

She gasped. If he believed this—if he believed her capable of such—she must walk away and never turn back.

"Now you choose silence?" He dropped her arm, his jaw hard, and stepped back in seeming disgust.

"I'm forming my thoughts." She rubbed the ache from her arm. "I spoke the truth when I said I've only known of this for days. Father planned to speak with ye once the ledger was current. It wasn't my place to interfere."

"That's not what I asked."

"If ye truly believe I would betray ye or your kin to Archibald Montgomery, ye know nothing of me. I suggest ye withdraw your offer of marriage."

"People betray one another, Anna. Even those you think never would. It happens more than it should."

George. She swallowed, her heart aching. Would Wylie never forgive?

Closing her eyes, she inhaled a deep breath while she searched for the right words, words he would know for the truth.

"My loyalties lie with my father as well as with ye. If Father asks me not to interfere, Wylie, I must respect that. But I owe no loyalty to Mr. Montgomery. He knows nothing of those barrels, and he never will—not from the Macraes. And while I know I've been unfair to ye both, what's passed between us has happened so fast I struggle believing it's not a dream."

Surely he struggled as well? He'd not thought of her as a woman until last week.

Likely not. Wylie was nothing if not impulsive. "If it seems I hesitate or that my loyalties are divided, it's because ye may wake up tomorrow and regret your offer. The more time that passes, the more certain I'll be ye meant it."

He looked at her, his head tilted and brow furrowed. "You think I may retract my proposal?"

"It happens more than it should," she said, using his own words.

He shook his head and sighed. "I want you, Anna. I want you by my side and as my wife. My offer is my promise. I will not retract it, even if you tell me it's Mr. Montgomery who holds your affection." He waited a beat and then asked, "Does he?"

Oh Lord, did he even understand what he asked? "It astounds me ye can ask me that after . . . after our afternoon at the pool."

"Truly? I expect I'm a bit jaded, then."

She sniffed and crossed her arms over her chest. Did he think she spent similar afternoons with Mr. Montgomery?

"Well?"

"I've loved ye since I was a child, Wylie Macpherson," she said, staring at a point in the distance. "I expect more than half the parish knew that." The tips of her ears burned with the admission. "Do ye mean to tell me ye did not?"

He didn't answer for a moment. From the corner of her eye she saw his neck had colored pink. "Aye, well." He cleared his throat before continuing. "Over twenty years have passed. You were but a child, and there's nothing left of that boy."

"I don't believe that."

"And once you find it's true?"

"I will find no such thing." Feeling at odds and ends, she dropped her arms and stepped toward the cellar. "We must put that cellar back to rights."

He moved to block her way. "Will you not answer my question?"

She scowled. "Are ye dense, then? Haven't I just told ye?" And received no avowal in return, she might add, but didn't.

"No, Anna, you haven't. You still consider Montgomery's suit. What claim does he have on your affections?"

"None. I've told ye he offers me security."

"And you think I can't offer the same?"

How would she know? He'd shared virtually nothing of his life.

However, security was the least of it. What she craved was assurance she'd not suffer yet another heartbreak.

Mr. Montgomery offered *that* in spades.

"Ye're as impulsive as ye ever were, Wylie. I want ye to be certain ye truly wish a wife and that ye didn't ask merely because ye thought ye must." She pushed past him, shoved the hidden door shut, and tugged the shelf in place.

Silent, he hoisted the ale barrels, returning them to the shelf. "I didn't ask because I thought I must," he said at length.

Did he believe that any more than she did? "Why are ye certain the whisky was here?" she asked, changing the subject.

"Several ponies passed through this yard with carts. Loaded, I expect, with the barrels."

"Surely ye can't think Will involved?"

"Oh aye. It was Will. He hinted at something of this sort the other day but I had no idea he meant to do it. I should have known better." He replaced the last barrel and stood scratching his chin.

"He would have had help."

She recalled the gossip of Will learning the ferry schedules. "What does he mean to do with it?"

"Convert it to cash. And I'll wager my last dollar that Robert Moy and Jay Macpherson had a hand in this."

Moy, yes. But Jay? "Why would ye think Jay?"

"The number of footprints. Jay is short of funds, and he has friends in Scotland. The right sort of friends, I daresay; gentlemen with coin sufficient to fill their cellars. Will has no contacts in this country. At least none I'm aware of."

"But how would such a thing occur to Will? Are ye saying Robert Moy put him up to it?"

"No." Wylie dragged the word out, as if reluctant to answer.

"Wylie? Will cannot have thought of it himself. What are ye not saying?"

"It doesn't signify."

Disgusted, she picked up the lantern and started for the door.

"Anna, did my father ever speak of my livelihood?"

She turned toward him, puzzled. "Aye, ye buy and sell. I think he said ye had a share in your wife's family shop."

Wylie took her elbow. "Let's walk."

"Ye don't buy and sell?" she said, planting her feet and jerking her elbow back.

He raked a hand through his hair, his eyes avoiding hers.

"Do ye mean to say ye don't trade?"

"No, I do. Sometimes. Sometimes the parties are not willing."

Her eyes widened and jaw dropped. "Ye steal?"

He met her gaze squarely now. "I crewed on a privateer for many years. The captain had a letter of marque to plunder ships not of French origin."

"English ships, ye mean."

"Sometimes. Spanish, primarily.

"But ye have your own ship now, the *Eliza*, aye?"

"Aye, and she was a privateer on my own account for a number of years."

"She's not any longer?"

"Now Alec and I engage in the free trade."

She stepped back. A polite name for those who robbed the government.

On the other hand, many contended the government's excise

tax robbed the people. "Ye're a smuggler."

He looked at his feet. "I prefer the term free-trader, but aye. Smuggler is apt."

He took great risk in telling her this, knowing Montgomery her friend. If for no other reason, her heart softened.

"And what does Alec intend to do in Florida? The free trade?"

He inhaled a long breath and shrugged. "Alec knows I've no wish to jeopardize my pardon."

"And Will has now jeopardized it."

"I doubt Will thought that part through," he answered with a small smile. "It's easy to forget how young he is. Tell me, Anna, where is Archibald Montgomery right now?"

She wasn't certain. "Father said he stopped by yesterday, saying duty called, and that I must not expect to see him for several days." She imagined him standing tall, hands clasped behind his back and lips pursed, issuing the words, "duty calls." "He left before Will disappeared, Wylie."

Wylie studied her a moment.

"What is it?" She swiped her fingers over her face and a hand over her hair, wondering if she'd carried dirt and cobwebs from the cellar.

"You and the boys are the only things in my life I treasure. I've never met this Montgomery, yet the fate of two of my treasures—you and Will—rests in his hands."

Something in her belly broke free and fluttered.

He'd named her a treasure.

"Why would ye say our fate rests in Mr. Montgomery's hands?"

"You may choose him yet. And if he corners Will and Jay, it will end badly."

"It will not. Even if Mr. Montgomery runs across them, he'd never bear arms against Jay. Jay's one of the king's officers."

"I've seen enough of life to know what can happen. Will is sixteen. Jay seems even younger, given recent evidence of his judgment." A note of panic slipped into his voice. "Suppose one of them attacks Montgomery? He'll fight back, and both lads will hang."

An ache spoked from her heart, spreading in all directions, and she stepped forward and wrapped her arms around his waist, resting her cheek in the curve of his shoulder. She could feel the tremor in his body.

"It won't come to that. Not with Mr. Montgomery." She stopped short of saying Montgomery was perceived a bit of a coward by some.

Wylie's breathing slowed, and he wrapped his arms around her, pressing his mouth against her hair. "I hope you're right."

She sensed the tension ease from him. Minutes may have passed before she answered, "I am."

In time she felt the press of his mouth on the pulse at her temple. Then it grazed her ear and traveled the length of her neck, igniting shivers of sensation. Her breath hitched and her head lolled to the side, offering him access. He nudged aside her shawl, and it fell to the cellar floor.

Warm and damp, his lips sparked fire. Taking heed of his bandage, she tugged his shirt from his belt and smoothed her hands beneath it, over the planes of his chest.

His mouth found hers, greedy with an urgency that bordered on desperation. Her lips parted, and his tongue swept between them. Her knees buckled.

Need welled inside her and she returned his kiss hungrily. Groaning, he slid his hand from her waist to her thigh and gathered up her skirts, pressing her back to the wall. She lowered a hand to unbutton his breeches, her fingers fumbling in her haste.

A dog barked a warning, and she froze.

CHAPTER 36

"IT'S MOLLY." She pushed at Wylie's chest, her breathing unsteady. "Somebody's coming."

"Ignore them." He cupped her face in his hands and leaned forward to kiss her.

She ducked. "It's someone on horseback, Wylie. Listen." Few traveled on horseback.

He stiffened, alert now. Within seconds, he'd righted her skirts and straightened his shirt.

"Wait for me," he said, then exited.

With a snort, she rolled her eyes. The man was forever giving orders. After tidying her hair, she retrieved her shawl from the floor and shook it free of dirt. Draping it over her shoulders, she tied it between her breasts, wishing she'd finished dressing before chasing after Wylie.

She walked outside in time to see Archibald Montgomery dismount.

"Miss Macrae?" Montgomery said, looking her way and seeming taken aback. "What are you doing here?"

Anna walked toward them. "Mr. Montgomery, this is Wylie Macpherson of Glencorach," she said primly, sidestepping his question.

"Your service, sir," Montgomery said, taking off his hat and bowing slightly. "This is indeed fortuitous. I wasn't certain you'd be here, but I thought I'd take the chance."

Wylie responded in kind, then said, "Alan Macrae sent his daughter over to check a few items. Might I offer you some refreshment, sir? It seems you've been traveling."

She shot Wylie a grateful look. Another man in his position would make more of her presence.

"Thank you, but I have reports I must write. I came in the hope of obtaining an appointment for later this afternoon. My agreement with your father is pending your approval."

"So I understand," Wylie said. "This afternoon is not

convenient as my factor has several matters still to settle. But I'm certain we can meet in the next day or two." Wylie looked at her, his eyes signaling a silent entreaty.

"My father said ye were off on the king's business, Mr. Montgomery," Anna said, taking his cue. "I trust ye were successful?"

Montgomery turned her way. "Unfortunately, no. My journey was for naught."

Wylie's bearing eased at once, his relief palpable. Had Mr. Montgomery been facing him, he might have wondered at it.

"I'm sorry to hear that," Anna said, hoping he might embellish.

"Such things happen; you mustn't worry."

"It's for ye that I worry. Ye seem so weary. Did ye travel far?"

Montgomery flushed slightly, then he shook his head and gave her an indulgent smile. "One can't count on a night's rest in this line of business, my dear, as you'll soon learn." He looked back at Wylie. "You've been absent from your own business several weeks now, sir. I trust it will survive without your supervision?"

"No doubt it's thriving. I have a very capable partner."

"Ah. I can't recall what line of business your father said you were in."

"It's a devil of a thing, isn't it? One's memory goes as one ages."

Anna's brows shot up and she looked at him, willing him not to bait Montgomery. "Weren't ye telling me ye traded with the French colonies, sir?" she said, an edge in her tone.

"So you trade," Montgomery said. "What sort of goods do you specialize in, sir?"

Perhaps she ought to have kept her mouth shut.

His worry over Will temporarily abated, Wylie didn't seem at all perturbed. "It varies, given the season," he answered, his tone easy.

"I expect it's an interesting pursuit."

"I find the trading rather mundane, though the places I've visited are interesting. I was just telling Anna she should visit Paris. I believe she'd like it. What do you think of Paris, sir? Would you agree?"

Anna's gaze narrowed. How coolly he lied.

Montgomery shifted from one foot to the other. "I can't say I've had an opportunity to visit Paris. My work, you know."

"Oh?" Wylie grunted in seeming surprise. "I thought perhaps

after serving in Flanders, you'd have visited. So many soldiers did."

Glaring now, Anna stifled the impulse to step forward and kick Wylie in the shin. He was deliberately baiting Mr. Montgomery, and to what end?

"My service to my king is with the revenue, sir."

"I beg your pardon. When Miss Macrae mentioned the king's service, I assumed the army."

For mercy's sake, had he mislaid his talent for reading others? There was little to gain in belittling Mr. Montgomery and much to lose.

"I must go," Montgomery said, shifting his reins from one hand to the other and stepping back. "Miss Macrae, I'll accompany you as far as the lane to Glendally."

Wylie stepped back as if struck, all arrogance fleeing his expression. His gaze darted toward her, and for the barest of instants, she glimpsed a vulnerability so aching her heart clenched. Then he stiffened, as if he were suddenly cast in stone, and his eyes shuttered.

Why, he thought she would leave him—and cared that she stayed. Not only that, he was jealous—of Mr. Montgomery, no less.

It hardly seemed credible.

"Go on ahead, sir," Anna said thoughtfully, her gaze still on Wylie. "I must finish what I started."

Montgomery looked from Anna to Wylie, as if uncertain. Then he nodded and mounted. "Very well. I suppose the sooner you finish, the sooner this can be settled."

"I look forward to meeting with you and my factor soon," Wylie said by way of farewell.

"Mr. Macrae will know where to find me." Montgomery tipped his hat and pressed his heels to the horse's flanks. He was out of earshot within seconds.

Anna turned on Wylie. "What was that about, Wylie Macpherson? Near goading the man, ye were."

"I don't like him."

"Ye've only just met him."

He opened his mouth as if to argue and then shut it. He waited until Montgomery was out of sight before facing her. "You're right. It was foolish. But the thought of him near you or worse, touching you—"

"Oh, hush. Where do you propose to look for Will?"

"Don't be angry. I've acknowledged it was foolish. As for Will, there's only one exciseman in this district, and who do you think sent him on a false lead?"

She blinked. Truly? Will could manage such deception? "We could still ask after Will at the ferry." Charlie would know the direction Will took, as well as who accompanied him.

"Think, Anna. What would Will have told the ferryman?"

That he was selling cargo on his father's account.

And if that were so, Wylie would know Will's direction.

Questioning Charlie Macphee would only raise suspicion where there'd been none.

"Pssht." Gathering her skirt, she turned toward the cellar.

Wylie caught her arm and tugged her backside against him, then nestled her close. Nudging her hair aside with his chin, he nibbled her earlobe. His breath was hot and his lips cool. She shivered, her blood racing.

"Martha is away until four. Come upstairs with me, lass," he murmured.

His fingertips danced over her bodice, as if he thought she required persuading, and her knees buckled. He caught her easily, looping one arm under her knees and another around her shoulders.

She looked up at him and passed a finger over his lips. "I suppose I did say I must finish what I started."

CHAPTER 37

THE NEXT MORNING, Anna hurried toward Cragdurcas, her steps light and her joy boundless. She'd promised Wylie an answer this morning, and she'd awakened in her own bed knowing which answer she'd give.

The one bleak spot in her foreseeable future—the *only* thing marring her happiness—was the looming prospect of refusing Mr. Montgomery.

When could she last claim that?

At the top of the drive, she spotted George seated in the ash grove and crossed the yard to greet him.

He rose, smiling. "You seem happy."

She sat, patting the bench, and he resumed his seat. "I am. I spoke with Mrs. MacDonnell and Mrs. Robertson. Ye'll have no trouble with the kirk session; they assure me their husbands will accept your recommendation for schoolmaster."

"Ye're a treasure. Thank you."

Fancy that. Twice within twenty-four hours, she'd been named a treasure.

She couldn't keep the smile off her face. "Nay, it's the parish who owes ye a debt of gratitude, George. I shiver thinking of that Mr. Anderson teaching my children."

"Your children?" Smiling, George cocked his head and looked at her appraisingly. "The revenue man has finally shown his hand, has he?"

She opened her mouth and then shut it at the sound of a door slamming. Turning, she saw Miriam Macpherson stride toward them, dressed in her traveling coat and hat.

"Why, Anna Macrae. This is a surprise."

"Hello, Miriam."

"What are you and my husband plotting now?" she asked, laying a possessive hand on George, who rose at her approach.

"Miriam," George said, his exasperation apparent.

"We're discussing the new parish schoolmaster, Miriam. Will

ye join us?"

"Heavens, no. I'm leaving for London this morning; didn't George tell you?"

"Nay, we haven't time as yet to discuss your comings and goings."

George frowned at Anna. She flashed him a sweet, unapologetic smile.

"Pity," Miriam said, pulling on her gloves. "I think you'd find them more intriguing than yours."

A stable lad brought forth a saddled horse and stood ready to assist Miriam. Her maid, already mounted, waited nearby.

Miriam planted a dutiful kiss on George's cheek before turning to Anna.

"Do be a dear, Anna. I know you see Wylie often, caring for his boys as you do. Would you tell him I won't be staying at my father's home after all? The Claremonts have offered their hospitality, and it's there he should find me. I'd stop at Glencorach and tell him myself, but if I do, we may forget the time."

The words slammed into Anna, expelling the breath from her lungs and wiping the smile from her face.

"I mustn't miss meeting my traveling companions." Miriam smiled brightly and mounted. "Good day."

Unable to breathe, Anna watched her ride off, shock and mortification rising in her throat.

Wylie planned a trip to London?

"Anna?"

Wylie planned meeting a woman in London? Another man's wife?

"Anna! Are ye faint, lass? What is it?"

Had George not heard what Miriam said?

She gulped in a breath, nausea rising in waves, and wrapped both arms over her belly, not at all certain she'd keep down her porridge. She looked up at George. "What did she mean to say, George? Why should I be telling Wylie where to find her?"

George stared at her before his mouth fell open. He shook his head from side to side. "No. Ye can't tell me it's Wylie."

So it was true. Her world tilted dizzyingly.

"Anna! Ye and Wylie?"

"It's true then, George?" Her words were no more than a whispered croak. "He's meeting her in London?"

George fisted his hands atop his cane. "Good God, I'll kill him. To play with your affections so casually . . ."

Rocking back and forth, she stared at the departing horses. Deprived of George's steadying weight, the bench rocked with her.

"He's meeting her in London," she said dully, as if by repeating the words they'd suddenly make sense. She tasted salt on her lips and realized she was crying.

"Anna, please don't cry."

Oh Lord. Did he think she wanted to? It was humiliating.

Resuming his seat, George placed a hand on her shoulder. "It may not be true. She says things to hurt."

"Ye knew and didn't tell me."

"No, Anna. I knew only that she'd asked him to go. It's to do with his Florida venture. She has connections that may help him with land grants." He handed her his handkerchief.

Florida? Anna looked at George through watery eyes and swiped the linen beneath her nose. "He still means to go to Florida?"

The look on George's face answered her.

"He asked me to marry him, George."

George's eyes widened, and for a moment he was speechless. "Well . . . well then . . . then his intentions are honorable."

"Ye don't know that."

He sighed. "No, I don't," he admitted.

What *did* George know? Had Wylie disparaged her, made light of her obvious adoration? Boasted of his conquest at the pool as men were wont to do? "What has he said of me?"

"He refused to speak of ye, Anna, as was only right. I did ask; something in his manner made me suspicious."

So she was not worthy of mentioning. "Then what did ye talk about that night in the glen?" she asked dully.

"I told him what led to my testifying."

She looked up. Why hadn't Wylie told her? Did he not think that noteworthy? "What did he say?"

"He didn't comment."

Her expression hardened.

"I didn't expect he'd forgive me at once, lass. First must come understanding. Forgiveness takes time."

"There will be no time," she said, smoothing out the handkerchief. "He'll be across an ocean." She turned from George and blew her nose.

"I'll survive. If he doesn't forgive, it's no more than I deserve." He squeezed her shoulder. "Anna, did he tell ye he would stay?"

She shook her head. "I haven't answered his proposal."

"Well, see there. He hadn't thought past that. Ye know how he is as well as I do."

"Ye don't think he'd mention we'd live thousands of miles apart?"

"He likely considers that the norm. Think of Renalda. Besides, what makes you think he wouldn't want ye in Florida with him? Did he say as much?"

She looked at him askance. "Surely he'd know I can't leave my father!"

George lifted a shoulder. "Men don't always think of such things."

She wiped her eyes and shook her head. "It doesn't signify, George, none of it." Except that it showed her needs and wants placed last in Wylie's thoughts.

As they had with Burt, the last man she'd loved.

She had only herself to blame; she'd known Wylie could break her heart.

"Ye never met Burt, did ye, George?" she asked, rising.

George stood, taking her hand. "What has Burt to do with anything?"

"If I'm to choose another dreamer, I'll have one who dreams of me first."

CHAPTER 38

WYLIE HAD NO reason to expect he'd see Anna that morning—she'd told him she planned meeting George. Still, he glanced down the drove road when he met the postman at the top of the drive, hoping he'd spot her. Her scent lingered on his bed linen, and when he'd awakened to pull her close, he found her gone. It wasn't often he slept soundly, yet this made twice in two days.

When he'd first thought she'd betrayed Will to Montgomery, the simmering anger . . . the impetus to run . . . both had returned.

But he hadn't quite believed it.

He *hadn't*, not truly. While that wasn't remarkable for the lad he'd once been, it *was* remarkable for the man he'd become.

Yes, he'd asked Anna to marry him because he thought he must. But obligation played no part.

He wanted to find Anna in his bed when he reached for her. He wanted the effortless flow of conversation she brought to his table.

He wanted to give her things, to do things for her—if only to see her smile.

He wanted to woo her.

She'd touched something within him, bestowing a peace he hadn't known in years, a peace he hadn't known he craved. She was home and hearth both, packaged in a luscious body.

He'd had many moments of happiness with Rennie in the last twenty-five years. Of course he had. But contentment in a foreign land, an exile in a land not his own?

Nay.

That emotion had eluded him for years. It was one reason Florida beckoned. Its terrain may be unfamiliar, but its British colonists weren't.

He'd told Anna none of this, not with words. Today, as soon as he saw her, he would. Today she'd answer yes. Perhaps even say she'd join him in Florida, though if not, he would keep Glencorach.

The drove road, however, was deserted, save for the departing postman.

Dismissing a twinge of disappointment, Wylie sorted through the handful of letters and gave a soft chuckle. His "very capable partner" seemed to have lost patience. Three of the missives were from Alec.

He turned to start back down the drive, then paused a moment amidst the standing stones, resting a hand on the one nearest.

Today. Send my son back today.

An hour later, Wylie sat at his study desk. Dougal played dice on the floor beside him, mangling his way through a Gaelic song he'd learned while visiting the Shaws.

Gnawing on the end of his quill, Wylie reread Alec's last letter.

I received an intriguing letter from Will today, probing the market for Scotch-made whisky. As you know, I'm more than willing to explore such ventures with the lad, but it was my understanding we were instead exploring western frontiers. What's it to be, my friend?

"Sir?"

Wylie looked up and saw Martha standing at the study door, her hands wringing her apron into knots. "Yes, Martha?"

"Master Will is in the yard."

Wylie froze. "Is he . . . is he well?"

She nodded, and Dougal sprang to his feet, shouting, "Will!"

Setting the quill and letter aside, Wylie stood and placed a hand on Dougal's shoulder, gripping it before the lad bolted. For the first time that morning he noted that someone, likely Mary Shaw, had combed the boy's hair.

"Shall I be keeping the lad with me, sir?"

Wylie nodded, wondering how much Martha knew of Will's activities. Probably more than he did. "I will speak with your brother alone, Dougal. Go with Martha."

"But, Papa!"

"Now."

With a pout near reaching his chin, Dougal shuffled out. Wylie strode to the front door and into the yard, affecting a calm he didn't feel.

Will and Jay stood at the water pump, washing their faces and hands. Both appeared unharmed. Wylie crossed his arms over his chest and leaned back against the house, waiting for them to finish.

Will spotted him first and hurried forward, swiping water from his face and shaking it from his hands. Flushed with the apparent success of his adventure, he seemed unaware Wylie might be less than pleased and walked past him, chattering.

"Papa, you must hear it all. Jay has the most astonishing connections. We will tell you inside." He turned when he realized Wylie hadn't moved. "Come," he said, beckoning with his hand.

"Where are the ponies, lad?" Wylie asked.

Will looked at Wylie as if he thought him daft. Jay, coming forward, answered.

"Will said they mustn't return in a string, Cousin Wylie. I have friends who were most anxious for a mount, temporary or not. They will return them one by one."

Jay had exchanged his military uniform for that of a prosperous English landowner. Somehow, it made him appear even younger. His gray eyes searched Wylie's, as if anxious for his approval.

Wylie blew out a breath. "You better hope so. Moy values his property."

"Oh, they will. We borrowed from my grandfather, not Mr. Moy."

His mouth set in a grimace, Wylie pushed himself upright and started toward the front door. Both boys followed, and Will handed him a small burlap sack once they crossed the threshold.

"Your rents plus more we will speak of later," Will said once they entered the study. Reaching behind him, he slid the door shut. "Also, we bring salt and cloth for Jay's mother and Anna and licorice for you and figs for Dougal and spices for Martha and Mrs. Baxter. The markets up north . . . I found them well-provisioned." Will nodded on reflection, seeming surprised in retrospect.

Wylie, scrutinizing the boy's expression, scarcely listened to his words. His son truly appeared unscathed, though a bit of blue-tinged puffiness surrounded those piercing blue eyes. Wylie experienced an unexpected urge to grab and hold him close, just so he might feel Will's heart beat against his own.

Thank you.

Belatedly, he hefted the bag Will had handed him. Indeed, it was of sufficient weight to account for Moy's rent and more.

"You should have seen Will negotiate, Cousin Wylie. The men were still shaking their heads as we left, not certain of their bargain."

"My bargains were fairly struck," Will said, full of bonhomie.

"Oh aye," Jay agreed with a chuckle. "But one side always fares better than the other, and without a doubt, we fared better."

"My father's the one who taught me," Will said, grinning the grin that had charmed so many a lassie.

Wylie, assured now that Will was unharmed, was less than charmed, though he was reluctant to upbraid Will before Jay. He hitched a hip on the corner of his desk. "I think you best start from the beginning, lads."

"Mr. Moy suggested it, Papa. He knew there would be difficulties if you sold Glencorach." At this, Will and Jay exchanged a glance, presumably due to Jay's aspirations regarding the estate. "He also knew Jay had connections in Inverness."

"But I didn't know how to go about it, Cousin Wylie. Free-trading was never part of my curriculum."

Wylie refused to grin. "With good reason. Go on."

"You were busy, Papa. Besides, we knew you must not jeopardize your new pardon."

"That was kind of you," he said dryly.

"Will planned everything," Jay said.

"*Non.* I am a stranger here. I was unable to plan who we would meet."

"Right, I planned that."

"You must not forget you brought the ponies. Your contacts and the ponies were essential."

"I did." Jay grinned and nodded. "Will fashioned harnesses for the barrels. We didn't lose a single barrel, not even when we crossed the river. I'll tell you straight though, we were damnably cold when we reached Tommy McKay's house. That alone might have done us in," he said, looking back at Will, who nodded in agreement.

"Who is McKay?" Wylie asked.

"A former schoolmate," Jay said. "He has an estate fronting the sound. We unloaded all in his cellar and had the ponies stabled by daybreak. We slept several hours and arrived in Inverness late morning."

"Monsieur McKay knew of several merchants willing to trade, Papa."

"They knew what they were buying?" Wylie asked, mentally

tallying the number of people involved, his unease growing.

"*Non.* You will recall the letterhead I made for Alec, *oui*? I retained several pieces."

"Will made up invoices showing the tax had been paid on the whisky. It was brilliant, Cousin Wylie."

Wylie grimaced. There were far better uses for brilliance.

"Even after we accounted for your rents, Papa, we still had coin, so we purchased supplies and gifts."

"And the revenue?" Wylie asked. "You encountered none of them?"

"*Non.* Mr. Montgomery will have received a tip that sent him south. He will have been entertained at Sol's Tavern."

Sol's was five miles south, opposite their actual destination. Though impressed, Wylie kept his face impassive.

"Don't forget we must also pay Marie," Jay said.

Will nodded. "I have set aside the sum."

"Who's Marie?"

"An acquaintance, sir. She plies her trade at the tavern."

Wylie cringed. "You hired a whore to distract Montgomery?"

"I am most certain he enjoyed her, Papa. Even if he learns she was paid, he will not regret it."

Wylie briefly shut his eyes and shook his head, refusing to ask how he was certain. It seemed Will had thought of everything. He turned toward Jay. "Have you been to Cragdurcas, Jay?"

"Am I welcome there?"

"Why wouldn't you be?" Wylie asked, curious what Jay would reveal.

Jay looked away. "There are two men . . . I'm certain my father has learned of it by now. I borrowed money and pledged cattle. They will be expecting payment."

"We must give Jay a share, Papa, so that he can pay his debts."

Surprisingly, it seemed Will didn't know the complete story. Surely Jay's debts were higher than these profits. "I can't say whether you're welcome or not, Jay, but you must return. Your mother is worried sick, and your father is anxious to speak with you."

"But, Papa, I told him—"

"It's not up for debate, Will. Jay may return once he speaks with his parents."

Will studied him and then turned to Jay. "Return in haste,

Cousin."

Jay nodded and left, reluctance dogging his steps.

"What is it, Papa?" Will asked once they heard the front door close.

"We will leave for London first thing tomorrow," Wylie said, quickly sorting the items on the desk, placing the things that were his to one side. "It's too dangerous for you here. I'll not risk it."

"There is no danger. I have anticipated all risks."

"Help your brother pack; I'll be out for an hour."

Will scowled and raised his chin. "Papa, I have not slept in—" He stopped when he caught Wylie's expression, seeming to think better of protesting. "What of Miss Macrae, Papa?" he asked softly. "Will she come with us?"

God, he hoped so. After the afternoon they'd shared upstairs, the promise of endless such afternoons . . .

She must.

"She will come." If not to Florida, at least to London.

CHAPTER 39

THIRTY MINUTES later, Wylie stood at the Macraes' front door. In spite of his assurances to Will, he wasn't at all certain of Anna. She'd yet to accept his proposal.

Though she would once he spoke with her. He raised his fist and knocked.

Mrs. Baxter opened the door, greeting him warmly. A bowl cradled in one arm, she beckoned him inside with the other. Cool and dim, the room smelled of fresh dough.

"Sit, sir, and I'll pour ye a dram."

"An offer I'll not refuse, ma'am." Wylie pulled out the bench and sat, setting his hat on the table.

After swiping flour from her hands, she poured a measure of whisky and placed it before him. "Billy says ye were pleased with the work done at the kirk."

"Oh aye. The lads did fine work and were quick about it." Wondering at the quiet, he asked, "Is no one else here, then?"

"Mr. Macrae is resting. I saw Miss Macrae in the kitchen garden no more than an hour ago."

That was just as well, for it suddenly occurred to Wylie he'd overlooked a thing or two in his plans. Perhaps Mrs. Baxter might help. "I have business in London, Mrs. Baxter, and I'm taking the boys. It's my intention to take Miss Macrae as well, and I hope her father will accompany us." One didn't normally ask one's prospective father-in-law along on an elopement, but Anna might resist leaving Alan behind.

Mrs. Baxter's expression clouded, and she glanced down the hall. "Oh, I don't know, sir. Traveling may no' suit Mr. Macrae."

Wylie rubbed his chin. What if Anna refused to marry without Alan near? Or refused to leave him on his own?

What if she refused to consider Florida?

One step at a time, lad.

"Never ye mind, sir. I'll stay in with Mr. Macrae. It will do Miss Macrae a world of good to go. I thought she looked a bit peaked earlier."

Peaked? Weary, perhaps. Wylie couldn't envision her peaked.

In any event, Anna couldn't object if Alan had someone to see to his meals and whatnot. He stood. "You're an angel, Mrs. Baxter. Make a list of what you'd like to have from London."

She flapped a hand in dismissal. "'Tis no' necessary."

He reached for his hat and started for the door. "Start writing," he said, pointing to the tabletop and belatedly hoping that she *could* write. "I plan to be on tomorrow's coach."

Upon rounding the house, Wylie's steps slowed. Anna wasn't in her garden. He crossed to the shed and knocked. "Anna?"

A brief silence followed before she answered, "I'll be out in a moment."

He turned his hat round and round in his hands, then clenched it, not wanting her to sense his impatience. He must make his case in a reasoned and detailed manner.

He *would* take care of her, and he'd do a far better job of it than the exciseman.

She opened the door, and his eyes widened. Good God, she'd been crying. Her nose and eyelids flamed red, and bits of hair clung to her face as if pasted.

His pulse racing, he dropped his hat and reached for her hands. "What is it? What's wrong? Is it your father?"

Her hands were limp in his, and she shook her head, her gaze cast down.

"What, then?"

"I cannot marry ye, Wylie."

Everything within seemed to stop at once—his heart, his pulse, his ability to breathe and to think. He could do no more than stare at the top of her head. His hands, incapable of keeping a grip, fell to his side. She said nothing more, still staring at the dirt at their feet.

At length, he inhaled a slow breath and found his tongue. "May I ask why?"

"I don't want to."

The words slammed into his gut like a fist.

She did not mean that.

Then why had she said it?

Placing a finger under her chin, he brought her head up, the silence lengthening while he waited for her eyes to meet his. When they did, he searched them, looking for the woman who'd told him only yesterday that she'd loved him since childhood.

Her green eyes clouded to a murky hazel while she held his gaze, and her expression flattened.

There was nothing of that woman. Not so much as a glimmer. He dropped his hand to his side. Had there ever been?

Had he imagined the peace he'd felt in her arms?

Stooping to retrieve his hat, he shook his head in bewilderment. Something lay beneath this.

"You don't think I deserve more of an explanation?"

Lips firming, she eyed him coldly. "Aye, likely so. Many of us deserve more than we get."

His own gaze narrowed. Propping a hand on the doorjamb, he leaned forward, boxing her in. She didn't flinch. "What the devil do you mean by that?"

"Ye have your answer, Wylie. I've said all I mean to say."

Like hell. "You're angry with me. I want to know why."

"Disappointed, not angry, and more with myself than with ye."

He jerked back from the door. Jaw clenched, he circled before the stoop, slapping his hat against his thigh. "I'll give you three seconds to stop speaking in riddles, Anna. If I walk away now, I'll not return."

Good God. Why had he said that? He didn't mean that.

Hell yes, he did. He'd not spend another twenty-five years bemoaning a loss, whether it be his home or a woman.

"I think it would be best if ye did. She's never been much for waiting."

"What?" Startled, he stilled and studied her, wondering if her father's befuddlement was catching. "Who's waiting? Are you unwell, Anna?"

"I met George at Cragdurcas this morning and learned ye plan joining Miriam in London."

He swore under his breath, shaking his head at the irony. He'd completely forgotten Miriam had asked him to London. For decades he'd thought of her often. Now, when she was within reach, he scarcely recalled her existence.

"Ye don't deny it, then," Anna said, watching him. "I hadn't realized ye'd planned a trip to London, much less one with another woman. Have ye any idea how that made me feel?"

The same as Wylie now felt, he expected. Stupefied.

Damn George to hell and back. Why was he so determined to see Wylie defeated?

"So you believed George rather than ask me?"

"I admit I was surprised until I reflected on the matter. Ye've shared none of your plans with me. Why would ye find it necessary to share that one?"

He should have. Out of habit, he hadn't. "That's why I've come, Anna. To speak with you about my—our—plans."

"We have no plans, Wylie. My thoughts on the matter may mean nothing, and I know ye're accustomed to doing as ye please. Many men think little of fidelity. Some women as well, it would seem. I'm not one of them." She placed a fist over her mouth and turned away, choking short a sob.

He reached for her shoulder and drew back before touching her. "Anna, please," he said softly. "Miriam planned to introduce me to her cousin in London, no more."

"I may not have traveled the world, Wylie, but I'm not naïve."

"I didn't say you were, lass. But what you're implying is untrue."

"The thought alone . . . of ye with her . . . the thought itself is devastating," she said, as if his words meant nothing. "As things stand, I've no claim on ye." She shook her head, setting a few loose curls in motion, and he stifled an untoward urge to reach for one. "If we were married, I couldn't endure it. I know I couldn't, and ye've no right to ask it of me."

His brow dipped in puzzlement. What sort of man did she think he was? Of course he had no right. Placing a hand on her shoulder, he turned her to face him. "Am I to be tried and convicted on the basis of George's testimony once again?"

"This has nothing to do with George, but if ye feel justified in holding a grudge against your cousin for another twenty-five years, so be it. Perhaps in cuckolding the man, ye'll harshen his sentence." She stared at a spot over his shoulder, her green eyes cloudy and vacant. "God help him, perhaps that's what George hopes."

Scarcely listening, Wylie shook his head, still reeling at his plummeted expectations. Anna was right to be suspicious, but nothing would've come of Miriam's plans. Miriam meant nothing to him. It was difficult to recall she once had.

"Anna—"

"Ye owe me no explanation, Wylie. Your plans are your own."

He stared at her while seconds ticked by.

Still refusing to meet his eyes, she swiped a hand across her cheeks, then crossed her arms and ducked her head. "It will please ye to know ye were right," she said, staring at his feet. "Nothing remains of the boy I once knew. I wish ye well in Florida. Please leave."

His brow creased. Was that it, then? Florida?

"I want you with me in Florida, lass. Might we speak of it?"

"I don't think Miriam would . . . would . . ." Her voice hitched on a sob and she turned from him, her shoulders shaking. "Please go."

He opened his mouth, then shut it, twenty-plus years of temper and resentment flaring.

Fool. She didn't want him. If she had, she'd have said so days ago. She was reaching for an excuse, and George had provided it.

The hell with this. To hell with the lot of them.

He'd not beg.

He walked away.

CHAPTER 40

THIS TIME, Anna vowed, would be different. She'd keep busy and not wallow as she had upon losing Burt. Wallowing hadn't lightened her grief; it had prolonged it. So when she couldn't interest her father in the accounts, she visited the township, where her help was welcomed.

"Mary Shaw, what is it ye're feeding this bairn?" Anna asked, gently jostling the newborn she cradled. "He's grown so!"

"D'ye think so, then? That puts my mind at ease; I worry." Mary looked up from the stew she prepared. "I'm glad ye've come."

"Aye, well, Father shooed me out. George lent him a new book, and he was intent on a quiet morning of reading before Mrs. Baxter came in." It seemed Mrs. Baxter had matters of her own to attend this morning, though what, Father couldn't recall.

"Was it a book on farming, then? George promised it to Lachie once Glendally finished."

"Aye." Ducking her head, she closed her eyes and inhaled the baby's scent, then placed her cheek against his. Something indefinable filled her core. A throbbing ache of hurt, need, or want—nay, all three.

"Ye're good with him," Mary said softly, seeming to sense Anna's turmoil. "He's been fretting all morning; it's the first he's slept."

Her smile tight, Anna lowered the baby to the cradle and blinked back tears.

"What is it, lass?"

Mary's concern undid Anna, and the ache pulsed and crowded her throat. Her fist flew to her mouth to keep it down, yet a strangled sound escaped. In an instant, Mary was at her side, arms open. Anna burrowed into her embrace and let the tears come.

"There now, lass," Mary said, cooing as she did with her children. "There now."

Anna hiccupped on a sob. "I knew better than to love him, Mary."

"And what's that to do with it, then? Who among us doesna falter when it's a choice between the heart and the head?"

"Me, or so I'd hoped."

"Hmmph." Mary stroked her hair. "Is it Wylie, then?"

Mute, Anna nodded.

"I heard talk something brewed between the two of ye. I wasna sure, what with Mr. Montgomery paying court."

Mary wasn't the only one uncertain. That hesitancy had cost her Wylie.

Nay! She wasn't so desperate for a family of her own that she'd share her man with another. If nothing else, she could be sure of Mr. Montgomery in that respect.

Her brow wrinkled. Truly though, what would she know of that? She knew little of Montgomery's life outside her home. Pulling back, she lifted her apron to dab her eyes.

"Ye're not the only one unsure, Mary." Anna pulled back, trying for a smile that faltered into a grimace.

"Well, he's gone now, and ye can—Anna? What is it?"

Panic gripped her. "Gone? What are ye saying, Mary?"

"Wylie and his lads caught the morning coach. Lachie walked out with them. Did ye not know, then?"

Her knees threatened to give way and she sat.

She'd known. Wylie had told her as much.

She just hadn't believed.

Hours passed before Anna found herself back on her doorstep. It had been a good plan, not to wallow, but it could wait until the morrow. For now, her bed beckoned. She was steps from its sanctuary when Mrs. Baxter's voice stopped her.

"Miss Macrae, here ye are! I thought mayhap ye'd gone. I've gathered my things."

Anna nodded, neither knowing nor caring which "things" she'd gathered.

"I hope ye don't mind I've brought my goat as well, then. But I thought it'd spare me the time back and forth. Are ye well, Miss Macrae?"

"A little unwell, Mrs. Baxter. I think I'll lay down a bit." Why would the woman bring a goat?

Why should Anna care?

She didn't. Crawling into bed, she tugged the blanket over her shoulders. Twenty-four hours only. Tomorrow she'd be up and about her business.

"Miss Macrae? Can I get ye anything? A cup of tea?"

Go away. Shaking her head, Anna clutched the blanket hem in her fist and rolled over.

"May I help ye pack, then? Ye can tell me from the bed what ye'd like to take." From behind Anna came the scrape of her case from beneath the washstand. "Ooch, I best clean this first; it hasna been used in some time."

Do whatever. Only leave me be.

Mrs. Baxter's footsteps sounded down the hall, though her chatter continued. "We canna be having ye carry this on the streets of London."

London? Anna peered over her shoulder. "Mrs. Baxter?"

She returned, still carrying the bag. "Did ye change your mind on the tea, then, lass?"

"What makes ye think I need a bag, Mrs. Baxter?"

The woman's brow furrowed. "Well, I thought . . . Well, ye know best of course, but I thought ye might carry a few things along."

"To London," Anna said flatly. She studied the woman, searching for clues on her state of mind.

"Aye, to London. Didna your da tell ye, then? Ye've no need to stay behind on his account. I can stay in while ye're gone."

Anna stared at the woman. Had Father's mind harkened to some long-ago time when Anna might have planned such a trip? Why else. . . She stopped breathing, realization dawning. No, no, no, no . . .

"Glencorach found ye in the garden, aye? To ask ye and your da to London? I told him I didn't think traveling would suit your father, and that I would stay—"

From somewhere came a cry of anguish, cutting short the woman's words. Mrs. Baxter backed up a step, staring at her, and Anna realized the sound had come from her.

"Oh, miss. I hope I haven't overstepped. I thought ye'd want . . . Nay, I've overstepped. I'm so sorry, Miss Macrae." Her chatter continued, though its sound faded.

Mother Mary. What have I done?

CHAPTER 41

London, England

WYLIE ENTERED THE London rooming house he'd left two months before and trudged up the worn, sloping steps of a musty, narrow stairwell, then down a dimly lit hallway. He opened the last door on the left and stepped inside, unsurprised to find Will seated alone at a round oak table, as if waiting for him.

Which, no doubt, he was. Admirably, the lad had held his tongue these last days; Wylie hadn't expected it to last.

"Any mail?" Wylie asked.

Will shook his head.

Damn it, Anna.

Even with the uncertain mail, he should've had a letter from her by today. If nothing else, didn't he merit a letter of apology? Surely Mrs. Baxter had set her straight and told her the things she'd refused to hear from him.

Unless Anna meant to refuse him from the start, and Miriam offered a convenient excuse.

"Dougal remains with Jay," Will said.

Jay had arrived in London two days before. Wylie blinked, returning to the present. "Why?"

"Jay hired a carriage, and they ride in the park. You were successful today?"

Wylie shook his head. Though he'd spent four hours staring at maps, he'd seen only Anna.

If he had her skill, he'd fill his hours sketching her. Instead, he occupied himself committing her every expression to memory.

Will filled a mug with ale, then pushed it across the table and indicated an empty chair. "We will talk."

"Not now, Will. It's been a long day. Retrieve Dougal, and we'll have supper."

Will shook his head. "Now."

Wylie rubbed at his eyes. "Damn it, I've had—"

"A long day. *Oui*, I am aware. But your days have not been as long as Dougal's and my own. Your ill temper is unpleasant for us all." Again, Will indicated the seat. "I will not pry of you and Miss Macrae. I wish to speak with you of another matter."

Wylie dropped into the empty chair and handled the dented pewter mug. A rich, malty aroma wafted from it, different than the watered-down ale Wylie had had here this morning. If given the choice, Will didn't settle for less than the best. "What other matter?" Wylie asked, kneading the back of his neck.

"A matter concerning Cousin George and Jay."

Wylie blew out a breath and slid low in his chair, extending his legs. He didn't want to hear of Jay. He wanted only to stand at the helm of his ship and sail toward the setting sun.

"Make it quick, lad."

"On the day you went to your cattle, I helped Monsieur Shaw deliver lumber to Bloomhall."

"Lachie?" Wylie eyed his son through lowered lashes. "I didn't know you two were friends."

"Acquaintances. Dougal spent time at his home."

"So you felt obligated to help with his chores?"

"*Non.* I wanted to speak to someone at Bloomhall."

Wylie raised his brows, waiting.

"While there, I made inquiries regarding Mrs. Vallantine."

"Who?"

"Mrs. Vallantine has been in service at Bloomhall for thirty years and serves as Sarah Bloomfield's maid when she is in Scotland."

Wylie shook his head with a grimace of impatience. "Get to the point."

"I found Mrs. Vallantine at her sister's house," Will said, unhurried. He reached down and retrieved a parcel from the floor. "When the Bloomfields are away, Mrs. Vallantine crafts bonnets to make ends meet. I bought you one." He slid the wrapped parcel across the table.

Flabbergasted, Wylie gaped at him. "I appreciate you thinking of me, Will, but I—"

"It is a grand bonnet, and you will like it. I took a bottle of Grandpapa's whisky with me as well as coin for the bonnet. You must not be angry, for I had reason to acquaint myself with Mrs. Vallantine."

"A lass too old for your liking, wouldn't you agree?" Wylie said, raising a brow.

"I take more care following our talk, Papa," Will said with a grin. "Mrs. Vallantine and her sister had many stories once I poured the whisky. I told them I wished to learn of the Rising from the English perspective. Monsieur Bloomfield is English."

"Aye, I know," Wylie said, again losing interest. Pulling the remaining tableside chair toward him, he draped an arm over it and took a long swallow from his mug.

"They were eager to talk, especially, I believe, once learning I was your son. Many people know you, Papa."

Wylie snorted. "They know *of* me. There's a difference."

"*C'est vrai,*" Will said, nodding. "You imply a bad difference, but it is not. They bear you no ill will. Mrs. Vallantine said many soldiers visited Bloomhall that winter, and Cousin Miriam visited Miss Sarah often.

An anxious tic started at Wylie's temple, and he rubbed absently at his forehead. The district had been a powder keg that winter, no small thanks to those visiting redcoats. He bore the mark of one's bayonet.

"You were aware Miss Sarah was affianced to one of those soldiers, a lieutenant named Winston Scott?"

Wylie shook his head and then swiveled, looking for the decanter. It rested on the fireside table, a distance too far to travel.

"This lieutenant's father, Colonel Scott, was a great friend to Mr. Bloomfield, and the two arranged the engagement. Mrs. Vallantine recalls trouble between the two girls began then."

Wylie looked back at Will, who poured another pint into Wylie's mug.

Had Miriam been jealous of Sarah's engagement? In the early years, Wylie had replayed his conversations with Miriam often, wondering if he'd made it clear he intended to marry her. Uncertainty may have piloted her toward George. "What sort of trouble?"

Will lifted a hand and tilted it. "Cousin Miriam perhaps desired the lieutenant's affections herself. Mrs. Vallantine saw her walking on many occasions with Lieutenant Scott. Twice, while walking to the ferry, Mrs. Vallantine saw them on the path to your peel tower."

An ache started in Wylie's chest. The peel tower was a quiet place known for trysts when he was young. It likely still was. He himself had shown Miriam the place.

She'd shown a redcoat their place. *His* place.

"Lieutenant Scott perished on Drumossie Moor that April so Miss Sarah's mother took Sarah back to London. Mrs. Vallantine remained at Bloomhall for a time, and she recalls Cousin Miriam came looking for the lieutenant, and then, upon learning of his death, she asked for the lieutenant's father, Colonel Scott. To convey her sympathy, *oui*? Once learning Scott was not there, Cousin Miriam inquired whether she would find him at Fort William. Mrs. Vallantine told her she must go home, for the roads were full of rebels and soldiers. That was the last time Mrs. Vallantine encountered Cousin Miriam at Bloomhall."

Will stood and walked toward the window. His hands clasped behind his back, he seemed to study the street below. "I have made a conclusion, as it seems the fort was a long way to travel for a young lady in treacherous times, simply to convey sympathy." He turned and looked at Wylie. "You see it as well, *oui?*"

Disquieted Miriam would even consider such, Wylie blinked at the question. "See what?"

"Cousin Miriam was *enceinte*. Chivalry prompted Cousin George to marry her."

A chivalry forced upon him by Uncle Henry, but so be it. Wylie lifted a shoulder.

"You do not see? Jay was born in October."

"So?"

"He was conceived early that year, Papa. I believe Jay Macpherson may be the lieutenant's son. If Cousin Miriam found the colonel, he may not have believed her. I have heard the prejudice against the Scots was high. Perhaps the colonel refused to accept such a grandchild. Cousin Miriam would have been desperate, *oui?*"

Wylie regarded Will, his gaze narrowing.

Might Miriam have lain with this lieutenant as well as with George?

"Papa, did Cousin George have opportunity to leave camp that winter? Before he returned to his mother in March?"

"I expect he could have, and I'd not necessarily have known," Wylie said slowly.

Untrue. He'd have known. Before deserting, George was at Wylie's side constantly that winter.

"Yet you were not in the area earlier, *oui?*"

Wylie nodded, his mouth tight. Whether Miriam had two lovers or twenty was no longer of concern.

Unless . . . He frowned. What if she'd had only one, and it was this lieutenant?

"This is a twenty-five-year-old bit of gossip, Will. Why does it interest you?"

"Cousin George said something when we first met. Something that indicated a story may not be as it seemed. It was apparent ill lay between you. Yet your tenants stories' all begin with 'the young masters,' giving one the impression you two were once close."

Inseparable.

Wylie sat without responding for a long time, rolling his thumb over the smooth cool dents on his mug while he thought. At length he said, "You haven't said anything to Jay, have you?"

"*Non.* Jay should never know."

If what Will said were true, why hadn't George explained himself?

Wylie clenched his eyes shut and muttered a curse.

"Papa? What is it?"

Perhaps George had. Perhaps his explanation lay in letter number one.

CHAPTER 42

Badenoch, Scotland

TWO DAYS LATER, Anna paced the pool in the glen, her gaze locked on her boots. Molly paced beside her, nudging Anna's hand every few minutes with her cold, wet nose as if to remind Anna she wasn't alone.

Though she was. Or would be, if not for their voices.

"I told Glencorach I'd be happy to stay in with Mr. Macrae, Miss, so ye can join him and the lads in London . . ."

"He's gone, lass, he and the lads. He's left another letter for your father, if that's what ye've come for . . ."

"That's why I've come, Anna, to tell you about my plans, our plans . . ."

"Speaking for your father now, Miss Macrae? He'll not thank ye for it . . ."

Mrs. Baxter, Martha, Wylie, Henry. Their voices, racing and repetitive, battered her from all sides, begging acknowledgment.

Only her father's was missing. His eyes had clouded upon reading Wylie's last letter, signaling his retreat from everyday trials.

Cringing, Anna squeezed her eyes shut and pressed her forearms over her ears. It was too bloody much. The lingering grief at losing William, worrying over her father, resignation over Mr. Montgomery, anger at Henry . . . too bloody much.

The sum was insupportable *before* losing Wylie. How could she bear it now?

She couldn't. She shook her head, squeezing her eyes tighter.

"If I walk away now, I'll not return."

She hadn't *lost* him. She'd shoved him aside.

Dropping to her rump, she draped an arm over raised knees and fingered a pebble.

Why hadn't she believed he wanted her? By all accounts she was amiable enough. Fair enough, even.

Yet look how she'd dangled Mr. Montgomery for her own

purposes. She was no better than Miriam.

And Glendally's tenants? If Father had any notion of Henry's machinations, he'd be horrified at her inaction. He'd spent twenty years teaching her to manage the tact. Now they were near losing it, and what was she doing? Wringing her hands?

Perhaps she hadn't believed Wylie wanted her because she didn't much care for herself.

But he *had* wanted her.

"Marry me, lass. Tell him no."

She tossed the pebble into the pond and watched sunlight spark from the ripples. When the ripples vanished, she tossed another, and then another, until a spark of resolve shimmered in her midsection.

"I will tell him no," she said aloud.

Molly started at the sound of her voice and swung her head toward Anna. Eye level, she appeared to pose a question.

"I *will*," Anna said. "Today. And that's not all I'll do. Come watch me if ye've doubts." She stood. "D'ye think he'll still have me, then? Wylie, that is?"

In answer, Molly rose and shook, then ambled to the edge of the water for a drink. Anna followed her example. After drinking her fill, she splashed the frigid water over her face and pressed a handful to her eyes. Then, shaking her hands dry, she turned to the tree line.

"Come, Molly. It's time I put my life in order."

Please don't let it be too late.

The next morning Anna stood on the doorstep of Cragdurcas Manor. George answered her knock, and a gleam of pleasure, or perhaps relief, lit his eyes.

"Anna! We've been worried." His gaze darted to the bag she carried. "Ye've been home, aye? All's well, then?"

She nodded. "All's well." Or as well as could be. Her father had greeted her pleasantly, seemingly unaware she'd been absent, and Mrs. Baxter had reiterated her promise to stay on and look after him.

"I heard the McIntosh brothers are replacing your roof tomorrow. Was that your doing?"

"Aye," she said, tapping her foot in a quick rhythm and looking over her shoulder. "George, I've a favor to ask."

"Of course, lass. Anything." He stood to one side of the door. "Come in."

"Nay, there's not time." Shifting her bag, she grasped its handle with two hands and squared her shoulders. "I'm leaving for London this morning. Would ye accompany me?"

His brow furrowed while he studied her, and she held her breath, waiting. She'd never ventured past Edinburgh; the prospect of a solitary journey to London unnerved her. It might well drain the last of her courage.

She'd need every ounce of that courage to face Wylie.

"*This* morning?" he asked.

"Aye. I haven't much time, I think, before Wylie's ship sails." George blinked, as if struck dumb, and Anna swallowed impatience at his slow-wittedness. "I mean to accept Wylie's proposal, George. That is, if I can find him, and if he'll still have me." She bit her tongue before asking what George thought of her chances.

She'd declined Montgomery's offer the afternoon before, having waylaid him outside Glendally's gate on her return from the glen. The task had been easier than she'd expected, and though he'd appeared disappointed, he was clearly not heartbroken, easing her conscience considerably.

George still stared, saying nothing, and she stifled an urge to kick him. That coach would leave the junction in ninety minutes. If he refused . . .

She stiffened. If George refused, she'd still step aboard. With or without him, she'd journey to London. "George?"

"Aye, of course." The corners of his mouth curved up a bit, and he shook his head. "Of course I'll accompany ye."

Her eyelids flickered shut, and she sucked in air. *Thanks be.* "Ye're a good man and dear friend, George Macpherson. I'm not sure I've told ye so before." She raised on tiptoes and kissed his cheek.

"Ye're a good women and dear friend as well, Anna, and I'd not have ye traveling to London alone." He hesitated, then opened his mouth as if to add something when his gaze swung to the lane behind her. He frowned. "What's this, then?"

Anna turned to see Lachlan Shaw and six of Glendally's subtenants stride up the drive. Though Lachie was on Glencorach's tack, he held the trust of Glendally's tenants, and he'd offered to help. He carried her father's account books while two others carried a makeshift table. Once leaving the tree cover, they paused, waiting. "Didn't your father tell ye?" she asked, turning back to George.

Eyeing Lachie, George shook his head, frowning.

"I sent a note last night telling him I'd be by early this morning to discuss the status of Glendally's service commitments." She was certain he'd received it. The boy who'd delivered it had returned to tell Anna that Henry had read the missive before shutting the door in the lad's face. "I believe Cragdurcas has abused its end of the agreement, George." And after reviewing the accounts all evening with Lachie, she had the evidence to prove it.

George's brow furrowed, and he adjusted his grip on his cane. "Anna, are ye sure this is wise?"

She raised a brow. "Surely ye're the same man who's urged me to take an interest in such matters?"

"I applaud your efforts, lass; I do. But this? Gathering a group of angry tenants—"

"They are *not* angry." She turned and eyed the men. "What makes ye think they are angry?"

Rob and Tommy stood by quietly. Having tamed their hair as she'd coaxed, they waited stoically, hats in hand. While it was true Paulie and Albert engaged in some sort of heated discussion, it seemed to concern no more than which of them balanced the greater weight of the table. And though the remaining two, Jamie and Angus, spoke in hushed, seemingly harsh tones to Lachie, she knew why.

They were peeved Anna was here in lieu of her father—a concern she would put to rest once Henry admitted his wrongs.

And he would, this very morning. Anna turned back to George.

"They've no cause for anger. I've assured them I will see they receive fair treatment, and so I will." She paused, seeing Henry exit the parlor into the hallway and come up behind George. Good. They could get started, then. She and George hadn't a moment to waste.

"Miss Macrae, what's this?" Henry said.

"Ye ken well enough what this is, Cragdurcas. Shall we get started?"

"Ye have a coach to catch. I suggest ye get off my land before I slap ye in chains and ye miss it."

She wasn't surprised Henry knew she planned a trip to London, even without the benefit of eavesdropping from the parlor. No doubt he also knew why.

She was counting on it, for she suspected Henry wanted her to reach Wylie before he sailed every bit as much as she did.

Timing this encounter as she had was her only leverage.

"D'ye, then?" Anna countered. "Well, sir, if we resolve things swiftly, I won't miss it. I suggest ye join Mr. Shaw and myself in the yard so we can get started." Her heartbeat hammered at her impertinence, and she chanced a glance at George.

Why was he still here? Time was of the essence, and he ought to be packing a bag instead of loitering in the hall.

She bit her tongue, schooling her expression. The moment Henry detected her impatience, she'd lose her leverage. "Unless ye prefer we all meet inside, Cragdurcas? It *has* become a bit warm."

Henry moved to block the entrance, as if he truly thought she'd bring the lot of them inside. "Your father and I will speak of this later, Miss Macrae. George, if ye plan accompanying the lass, stop standing about."

Aye, stop standing about.

"Not inside then." Anna made a tsking sound and forced a sigh. "It's no matter, George. Go on about your business; it seems my travels may be delayed a day or two." She turned and made a survey of the grounds. "Is there a place we might wait, then, Cragdurcas? Mr. Shaw and I and the others? Until the time is more convenient?"

Lachie caught her eye, and she smiled slightly to reassure him. He nodded, the gesture nearly imperceptible. The others weren't so agreeable, and murmurs of discontent and distrust now rippled amongst them.

She hadn't intentionally chosen the heftiest of the lot, but now that she regarded them afresh, they seemed rather imposing. If they held her in disfavor, she'd not want them loitering about Glendally. She turned back to Henry, her brow arched for his answer.

Henry's jaw clenched and he glowered at her. She met his gaze unflinchingly. "I'm warning ye, Miss Macrae. If ye think I can stall that coach, ye're sadly mistaken."

"My word, stall a coach? Why, I think no such thing, Cragdurcas," she said, summoning an idle tone while she again surveyed the grounds. "Perhaps we could wait outside the stables?"

she asked, eyeing him over her shoulder while pointing at the stables. "Will that suit?"

Henry's expression darkened, and he muttered a lengthy oath before pushing past her. "Ye have five minutes to state your case." He started toward the drive.

After reviewing the ledgers into the wee hours in the morning, she could recount by memory the hours of labor supplied against the number required for each of Glendally's tenants. The ledgers were for show, no more. So, while fifteen minutes would be better, five might suffice, especially if Henry didn't quibble.

She signaled to Lachie, indicating the men should set up the table where they stood. Behind her, George chuckled softly. "Who *is* this lass?"

She grinned, watching Henry stride toward Lachie, then stepped from the stoop and followed him. She knew the answer to that.

She was Anna Macrae of Glendally. Beloved daughter, caring friend, and competent member of her community.

Soon to be treasured wife, once she righted a grievous wrong.

Her grin died. What if the *Eliza* had sailed?

Quickening her pace, she darted a frenzied look back at George and mouthed a plea. "*Hurry.*"

CHAPTER 43

ONE WEEK LATER found the Macphersons walking the streets of London. Dougal, sound asleep, rode on Wylie's back.

"Indigo, Papa," Will said.

"Yes, Will, but it's still farming, and, as you reminded me a short time ago, you know nothing of farming."

"You do. You know much of it."

Wylie blew out a breath. He did. Of grain on a Highland slope, not flowers in a Florida swamp.

"Besides, Papa, we will hire a manager. Indigo was your idea, and it is a good one."

Will had changed his tune on the matter of farming once learning of indigo's profit potential. He and Jay hoped to start the venture together.

"I said I'd listen, Will. I'm giving you a full year to work out the details."

"If we present you our plan earlier, you may critique it earlier, oui?"

"I could. But I'd not fund it earlier." Better than perhaps any man, Wylie knew the pitfalls of youthful enthusiasm. No matter how clever the lad was, Will was prone to his own impulsiveness. Wylie congratulated himself on setting a year for contemplation.

Will muttered a curse. After a moment's silence, he said, "You must apply for the land grants while there is still good land for the taking. I will help choose them."

Wylie chuckled, and Will grinned, acknowledging the poor subterfuge. To apply for a land grant, they'd found they must commit to farming and settling it. Something Wylie was unwilling to do without seeing it. He would apply by post at summer's end.

"Will, I have never been to Florida. I'm too old to stake something sight unseen."

"I am not."

"Aye, but you haven't the capital, have you, lad?"

Will frowned. "Perhaps Jay will get it from one of his

grandfathers."

If hell froze over, perhaps so.

"If he does, be prepared for Jay to lose it on a gaming table."

"Papa," Will said, frowning. "You set a bad example for Dougal with your censure."

Wylie choked back a laugh at the reprimand. Glancing up and over his shoulder, he saw Dougal still slept.

Yesterday they'd visited the Tower of London. The boys showed little interest in the jewels, but the king's menagerie had been a success. From there, Wylie had taken them to the Drury, where they watched *Romeo and Juliet*. Today, after walking through the British Museum for three hours, they planned an early supper at the Vauxhall Gardens.

Given the ever-present ache of Anna's rejection, Wylie had surprisingly enjoyed each minute. These last few days would take a place among other treasured memories as days he'd never forget.

There was something satisfying in learning Will valued his opinion and in sitting with the lad to debate options for the future. And Dougal—witnessing the lad's *joie de vivre* at every turn nearly filled Wylie with a zest for living himself.

For twenty-five years, an unyielding resentment had been his constant companion. It steadied him, giving purpose to each day, so he welcomed it. Nurtured it, even, so that with each passing year its armor had become impenetrable, protecting him from stray memories.

An armed companion shielding him from his own thoughts.

Now suddenly it was gone. At long last . . . the resentment, the anger . . . gone.

While the ache of Anna's dismissal pained him, it was proof he hadn't imagined the sweetness that had passed between them. He knew it for real, even if she hadn't.

Just as he now knew that George's actions may not have been a complete betrayal, and that he hadn't misjudged his entire childhood.

Will's theory had merit. Chivalry may have prompted that marriage.

If he'd read those letters, perhaps he'd have arrived at this conclusion years ago.

Or perhaps not. Reason had held no place in his emotions that devastating winter.

"Papa?"

"Hmm?"

"You did not answer. May I go with you to the Claremonts' reception tonight?"

For an instant it seemed Rennie stood before him, her blue eyes blazing and her sleek black hair swinging while she shook her head an emphatic "no." Wylie's step faltered. Slowly, he nodded, acknowledging her concern, that of course he'd not take Will to such an event. She leaned forward and kissed his cheek. Then she was gone.

"I can go, Papa? Truly?"

"What?" Wylie touched his cheek, wondering if her lips had left it warm.

Had that been good-bye? Did she mean to leave him to manage alone?

"Papa? What is it? Is something wrong?"

Blinking rapidly, Wylie paused on the footpath and turned toward a shop window, trying to make sense of what he'd just experienced. Rennie couldn't leave him yet. Dougal was but a child. What made her think he could manage without her?

Panicked, he stared at the window glass, seeing none of the merchandise displayed behind it. Instead, looking back at him was the reflection of a man of middling years. One who'd set aside his Parisian-made tricorn and wore a handmade Scotch bonnet on the streets of London. A blue-eyed, black-haired lad stood beside the man, looking up at him, and another lad lay sound asleep on the man's back, his head resting on his shoulder with every appearance of blind trust.

If things hadn't gone as they had during the Rising, a different man would stare back at him now. A man without Will and Dougal both. Swallowing, Wylie raised a hand and adjusted the bonnet's tilt.

"Nothing's wrong, Will."

"So I may accompany you?"

Hell no. Wylie wouldn't go himself if he didn't want to meet Mr. Claremont. These occasions were often excuses for debauchery. Some overt, some covert. It was no place for Will.

Nor for Will's father.

Wylie turned from the window, adjusted Dougal's position, and resumed walking. "Nay. Once Dougal sleeps, I'd like you to review that cargo list. I may have forgotten something in my haste." Wylie knew that cargo list backward and forward. But telling Will he wasn't of an age to attend would gain Wylie nothing. "We leave soon."

"May I add to it?"

"You may. We'll discuss your additions in the morning."

"Alec will come in the morning," Will said, grinning.

Wylie nodded. "Aye, he will. We best be ready to sail."

CHAPTER 44

THE CLAREMONTS' home was a three-story townhome built during the time of the Tudors. Arriving on foot, Wylie bypassed the long line of coaches dislodging guests onto the lamplit footpath and climbed the steps on the heels of a well-dressed elderly couple. Within minutes he was admitted into the hall.

Mahogany furnishings gleamed beneath the light of six—no, eight—candelabra. Richly colored tapestries covered walls above the staircase landing, shimmering in the flickering light, and the somber faces of several generations of Claremonts frowned down from gilt frames.

A far cry from the tattered homes of the Highlands.

Jonathan Claremont had made his fortune with the South Sea Company, then pulled his investment before the company's collapse. Rumor had it that the grandson, Gerald Claremont, had not only preserved his inheritance, he'd increased it fivefold with his West Indies holdings.

Wylie suspected those West Indies interests were the reason behind his unexpected invitation, and it was why he'd accepted. He'd made inquiries at several coffee-houses yesterday. One of those inquiries had apparently reached Claremont. As Wylie and Alec continually explored the West Indian trade, this connection could be useful.

After being shepherded into a large room cleared of furnishings, Wylie accepted a glass from one of the roaming footmen and looked about. A woman standing alone, her fair hair piled high and neckline plunged low, offered him a welcoming smile. He was saved a response when another woman, part of a chattering group camped near the massive fireplace, called out, asking the woman to join them.

His nose itching at the growing number of pomanders, Wylie meandered toward the musicians at the open front window in search of what passed for fresh air. The musicians played a pipe and tabor, four violins, and a flute, all at the sloppy direction of a man appearing half-lushed with drink. It didn't harm their timing; between the lead violinist and the man on the tabor, their beat stayed true.

Surprisingly, Wylie's fingers itched for a fiddle. Odd, given that until last month, he hadn't touched a fiddle in twenty-five years.

But before then, he'd played one almost daily from the time he was eight; music, dancing, and storytelling had filled his twilight hours.

Dancing. When had he last danced a Highland reel? 1745?

He'd lost more than his family, his sweetheart, and his country. He'd lost things that hadn't been taken; things he'd discarded willingly in his quest to leave his past behind. The fiddle was but one.

How many other pieces of himself lay strewn across the oceans, abandoned and now forgotten?

He'd been angry when Anna's friend had handed him that fiddle. For days, he'd feared his resistance to the life he'd abandoned was crumbling.

Yet he'd glimpsed that past life unscathed. He'd survived his stay at Glencorach. He'd even survived hours alone with George and not throttled him. And though Anna's rejection had rubbed old wounds painfully raw, he was confident they would heal in time.

Somewhat confident.

"I say, aren't you Wylie Macpherson?"

Startled, Wylie looked up. The man speaking was a short, round gentleman who, like Wylie, had forgone a wig and wore his own hair. Unlike Wylie, the man's hair was completely gray.

Wylie nodded. "You have me at a disadvantage, sir."

"Malcolm McPhail, from up near Aviemore. I heard you introduce yourself to Silas Baxter at Brenner's Coffee House yesterday. You had a set of boys with you. By the time I made my way across the room, you'd left."

"Ah. You're MP, aye?

"Until I can convince your cousin to run, I am."

"George?" Becoming a member of Parliament had been a long-ago dream of George's, one Wylie thought dead once their rebel regiment marched through England. "Is he thinking of doing so, then?"

"He claims not, but I'm not one to accept no for an answer."

"Has he a chance at winning?"

"Hmmph. A handsome young captain grievously wounded in service to his king? You tell me, lad."

Wylie supposed that was a yes. "I expect the district would not suffer if it were so, then." In truth it might prosper. George knew a thing or two.

"You've succeeded your father, I hear. I was sorry to learn we'd lost him. William was a fine man. Ah, now isn't this something. Old home week. Here comes Mrs. Macpherson."

Wylie turned and saw Miriam glide toward them. Out of courtesy, he'd called at her father's house shortly after they'd arrived. He'd been relieved, not grieved, upon learning she wasn't there.

Her hair piled high and powdered white, she wore a silver gown that glimmered with each step. Ice, not the fire he craved, and she left him cold. After a few pleasantries, McPhail left them alone.

"Wylie." Rising on tiptoes, she bussed his cheek. "I'm so glad to see you. Anna didn't give you my message, did she?"

"What message was that?"

"I told her to tell you that I would be staying here at Claremont House."

Miriam, not George? His jaw hardened, bile rising as he pictured that delivery.

Devil take it, Anna, why would you listen to anything this woman said?

"Why would you give Miss Macrae such a message, Miriam?"

"I thought you should know I wouldn't be at my father's as we'd discussed."

Like hell. They'd spoken but briefly of London over a month ago. "Why not send a servant to Glencorach with a note? Or better yet, leave a message at your father's?"

She flushed, as if realizing he saw past her subterfuge. "It's of no consequence now. I'm glad the invitation reached you. Jay told me where you were staying. Surely, Wylie, you could have found better accommodations."

"You're the one who sent tonight's invitation?"

"Of course. I'd hoped I might see you sooner, but now I know why. What have you been doing with yourself?"

Coming here had been a waste of time, then. He ought to have known a man of Claremont's ilk would not send an anonymous invitation. Wylie sighed, answering shortly, "Gathering supplies."

"No! You know I planned to show you the best shops."

None which would carry the supplies he required. "I apologize. I'd forgotten."

Miriam didn't question the lie. After the briefest of pouts, she said, "My cousin Jamie's not yet in London, but I can introduce you to Lord Gordon and ask him to put in a good word for you with the Privy Council."

"That's unnecessary. George provided a letter of introduction."

She sniffed. "One can always count on George, can't one?" Placing a hand on his forearm, her gray eyes met his. "So your business is completed?"

There was a slight inflection in her tone when she asked. It brought to mind a slamming door, and he envisioned an escape hatch sealing shut if he answered yes.

He couldn't explain his dismay. He wasn't married. He had no attachments. Before him stood a beautiful woman, one he'd once spent hours dreaming of, one who clearly expected to enjoy more than his companionship in one of the world's greatest cities.

He might lose himself for a time. He'd not have this chance twice.

Anna.

The ache surged, and he squared his jaw.

He may not be married, but Miriam was. She roused nothing within him but distaste.

Would it be so with every woman who was not Anna?

Miriam ran a fingertip over the vein pulsing in his neck, a knowing smile on her face, and he feared she'd mistaken his dread for desire. Removing her hand, he squeezed it and dropped it.

"I haven't completed my business, Miriam. As a matter of fact, I ought to return to it." If Claremont himself hadn't invited him, he gained nothing by remaining.

"No! You're to be my escort this evening."

"I'm afraid I can't." He handed his empty glass to a passing footman and opened his mouth to thank her for the invitation, then closed it.

Perhaps he should explore Will's theory. He *was* curious. He sucked in a breath and took a gamble, watching her carefully.

"Miriam, while George and I were in the glen, we had a great deal of time to talk."

Did he imagine it, or had her eyes narrowed a fraction? If so, she recovered quickly.

"Well, I expect you had years of war stories to catch up on. I often wondered if you'd fought in the same battles."

He smiled wryly. "I wasn't in the French army, Miriam." She flapped a hand dismissively, as if content with her version of the past. His expression hardening, he added, "We spoke primarily of Jay."

Her hand froze in midair and she stared at him, her mouth agape. "He . . . he told you?"

Told him what? Opting to stay silent, Wylie nodded. After all, George had told him a number of things.

"Was George terribly angry?"

With whom? Careful to hide his confusion, Wylie opted for a simple response. "No."

Her brow drew, as if she were perplexed, then she set aside her drink and wrung her hands. "I didn't know what else to do."

"It was a difficult time."

"I *knew* you would understand, Wylie. But you weren't there, and I had no one to turn to."

His eyes narrowed. Were they still speaking of Jay?

"I . . . I had no choice. Jay's father was killed in battle before we could marry."

Wylie blinked. Good God. Will was right.

Did George know?

"Surely this man's family offered you shelter. He promised marriage, aye?" Scot or not, she carried their grandchild.

"Not in so many words, but yes, we spoke of marriage . . . once some things were sorted."

Two women approached from behind Miriam, hip deep in merriment, and Wylie eyed them coldly. With faltering steps and smiles, they veered away.

"Some things?" The man had either promised marriage or he hadn't.

"Winston's father had arranged a marriage on his behalf, and it complicated matters. Winston couldn't tell his family of us until he rectified it."

Hearing her speak so of another man, a man she'd lain with while he pined for her in France, ought to have spiked something within him. Yet Wylie felt nothing beyond a mild curiosity and empathy for George, who may have spent twenty-some years believing he'd fathered Jay.

"Did Winston know you were with child?"

A wave of pink splashed over her bosom and up her neck. Though he'd kept his voice low, her gaze darted in alarm to those nearby. "No. He never knew, and his father refused to acknowledge me. Don't you see? I had no choice but to go to George."

So George *had* known Jay wasn't his. One would never guess from outward appearances; he treated Jay as if he were his own. "I never realized you cared for George."

"Care for him?" She eyed him and scoffed, all maidenly embarrassment gone. She motioned to a wandering footman for another glass of wine. "I had no other choice. George was the only man of consequence left in the district."

Wylie's mouth thinned. He would have let her boil in the stew of her own making. George, it seemed, was quite the gentleman, forfeiting a lifetime's worth of freedom to save her honor.

As if in reflection, Miriam murmured, "Besides, I knew George would never have allowed your child to be raised a bastard."

Wylie flinched as if she'd struck him.

His child?

The blood rushed from his head, and he swayed on his feet.

"George would have done anything for you," she continued softly.

The world stilled as pieces of the past sorted and tumbled into a pattern that finally made sense.

George *had not* lain with Miriam that winter.

He sucked in air. "You told George . . ." Rigid with anger, the words wouldn't come.

Miriam stiffened and looked at him, her eyes widening in something akin to hope. "He didn't . . . ? But you . . . you said you'd spoken to him." Her lips parted, and she pressed a fist to her mouth, shaking her head. Then she gripped his forearm, saying, "Then he still believes Jay is your son. Oh, Wylie, you mustn't tell him any different. After this dreadful business, George may cast Jay aside if he learns the truth."

Wylie pulled back, repelled. Twenty-five years, and she didn't know a damned thing about the man she'd married.

Turning, he left her standing and shouldered his way through the growing, sickeningly sweet-scented crowd, near shaking with fury.

He would take the coach north at dawn. Somehow, he must set things right—with Anna and with George.

CHAPTER 45

IT WAS AFTER ten that night when Anna and George stood outside the Macphersons' room. One of George's friends had provided the address of the lodging house, and the landlady, busy with other tasks, had directed them upstairs.

Biting her lip, Anna stilled George's hand when he raised it to knock. Caught unaware, Wylie's reception may be less than civil. "George, I'm not certain . . ."

George sighed, leaning wearily on his cane. "A coach leaves for Edinburgh at dawn. Shall I call for a conveyance?"

"Don't poke fun." Her fingernails bit into her palm, and she stared at the closed door. Memories of her last encounter with Wylie haunted her, her behavior unconscionable.

She'd allowed Miriam, a bitter, unhappy woman, to skew what Anna knew in her heart to be true. Wylie loved her. He no longer cared for Miriam Macpherson.

He may not have told her he planned to leave her once they wed, but she might have taken the first step and asked. She hadn't told him of Burt, nor had she confided her fears of yet another abandonment. He might have offered comfort or perhaps even a compromise.

How could she expect him to forgive?

"I'm poking sense, not fun," George said. "What happened to the woman I escorted from Badenoch, the one who stood up to my father?"

A corner of her mouth tilted up at the memory.

Still . . .

Wylie's rejection now—though deserved—would wound far more than Henry's threatened chains.

"I'm nervous, George."

"Rightly so, Anna," A side of his mouth jerked before he sighed. "If we're to return, it's best we do so before seeing him."

Panicked at the thought of *not* seeing Wylie, Anna jerked erect and swiveled to face George. "D'ye take me for a coward, then?"

He chuckled. "There's a good lass. Now will ye allow me to knock? I should sit before I fall."

"Mother Mary, I'm sorry." She took his arm. "Why didn't ye say as much before I dragged ye across London? I've been thinking only of myself. Come away then and let's—"

"Anna!"

"Right, then." *Please Lord, don't let Miriam be with him. For my sake as well as for George's.* She moved aside, and George raised his cane and rapped the door. Within seconds it opened. Will, his hand still on the knob, stood on the other side, his eyes widening.

"Good evening, Will," George said.

Staring wordlessly, Will seemed not to hear.

From behind Will came Dougal's voice. "Will, it's Cousin George and Miss Macrae. Let them in."

Recovering, Will stepped aside and held the door wide. "*Oui,* come in."

Anna saw at a glance that Wylie was not in the room. Dougal, dressed only in his shirt, his calves bare and milky white, took her hand and tugged her inside.

Will lifted a black jacket from a tableside chair and shrugged it on, then pulled his lace-cuffed sleeves down just so. "The landlady was to bring tea. I will ask she brings more. Your journey was long; please sit." He passed through the door behind them, pulling it shut before they could respond.

Will wore those clothes as if he'd been born in them.

What had she been thinking, coming here? Lads wearing finely tailored clothes, rooming houses attended by landladies preparing tea at one's beck and call at all hours of the night. She didn't belong here.

Wylie could only have been relieved when she'd rejected his hasty proposal.

"Have you come to visit us, Cousin George?" Dougal asked.

"Aye, Dougal, we have. Tell me, is your father in?"

Dougal shook his head. "Papa dressed special and went out."

Anna swallowed.

"Papa has gone to Claremont House," Will said when he returned. "He did not indicate for how long."

The blood drained from Anna's face. Wylie *was* with Miriam, then.

"Miss Macrae, are you unwell?" Will took her elbow and

300

indicated a chair.

She resisted and shook her head. "A bit travel weary is all."

"You have secured lodgings?" he asked.

She wished they had. It would be far less shaming than presuming on the Macphersons' hospitality. "We came straight here after obtaining your address from Mr. Marner."

"I met him today," Will said, turning toward George. "While we were looking at maps. Papa said he was your friend, Cousin George."

"Yes, a very good friend." George shifted his cane to his left hand. "Will, I think it best Miss Macrae and I return tomorrow." The cane wobbled, as if under undue pressure.

Learning his cousin was with his wife had unsettled George as well.

"You must not leave," Dougal said. "You must hear of our day."

"Dougal is right, sir. You must stay the night. You still owe him a story, *oui?* You might tell it once he tells his own story. Please sit. If you like, I could retrieve Papa. I suspect he would not want Miss Macrae to leave."

Anna glanced sharply at Will. What made him think Wylie would not want her to leave? Had he said that merely to put her at ease? His face told her nothing.

George hobbled toward the divan and sat. Resigned, Anna joined him, clasping and unclasping her hands repeatedly while the landlady bustled in with a tea tray and out on a string of chatter. Dougal carried a cup to her.

Summoning a smile, Anna took it from him and raised a hand to smooth his hair. "Did you have a fine day, lad?"

Dougal nodded and held up two fingers, glancing from her to George. "Two fine days. There is much to tell. Papa took us everywhere," he said, spreading his arms wide. "Not like before when we were here. We saw a gold statue from Egypt and a woman drink poison and gardens with music and more lights than I can count. But no fireworks. And we saw the king's new Florida panther—we are to go to Florida and may see our own, did you know? And we saw a giraffe. It was much taller than even Papa. The king has many animals. I shall tell you of them all."

George made a show of settling back in his seat. "It seems my story shall be trumped, Anna," he said, appearing delighted. "Perhaps ye should make yourself comfortable. The way ye're perched, ye're likely to tumble forward when Dougal reaches the part about the lions."

CHAPTER 46

HOURS LATER, Wylie stood outside the rooming house, pressing coins into a lamp boy's palm.

"Papa, where have you been?"

Startled, Wylie pivoted. Will stood on the front stoop, one hand holding a candle, the other holding the foyer door.

"I went to find you; you were not at Claremont House."

"You shouldn't be wandering these streets at night. Is Dougal ill?"

Will shook his head. "It is four in the morning. Where have you been?"

A month ago he'd have snapped at the lad for his impudence. But something between them had shifted, and the truth seemed far easier a response. "Walking. We've had a change in plans," he said, brushing past. "Why are you awake?"

"Cousin George and Miss Macrae are here."

Wylie stopped short and turned, his hand gripping the banister. "Here? George and Anna both?"

"*Oui.* They sleep in chairs awaiting you. Papa, I feared you were with Cousin Miriam. Miss Macrae, she may fear so as well."

Without answering, Wylie took the steps two at a time and trotted down the hall to the room's open door. His eyes went first to the man's bonnet resting beside a lone flickering candle on the table between a pair of wing chairs. George slept in one chair, his head propped against a wing, his arm hanging over a side, and his leg stretched out before him.

Anna stood facing the window beside the sideboard.

Wylie stalled at the threshold, his heart pounding erratically at the vision. She turned toward him.

Lovely in her homespun gown, her vibrant hair tumbling loose over her shoulders, she stood stark contrast to the powdered, bewigged, and painted women he'd left hours earlier. Looking at her was like breathing Highland air.

"Hello, Wylie," she said quietly. Her hands clasped and

unclasped at her waist, as if she were as nervous as he.

Crossing the room in three long strides, he retrieved the candle beside George and carried it to the sideboard. Swallowing twice past a dry throat, he faced her and took her hands in his. Small hands, chapped and chilled, and he felt as if he clutched a lifeline. He pressed them to his waistcoat, covering his heartbeat. "Tell me ye haven't yet married him, lass," he whispered. "Grant mercy. Tell me."

"I haven't."

In a wave of relief his forehead dipped, touching hers, and he closed his eyes in a quick prayer of thanks.

"I've been walking the streets for hours, Anna. I was alone. The only reason I returned—"

She touched a finger to his mouth, quieting him. "I had no right to question your comings and goings."

He removed her hand and clutched it in his. "You had and you have every right. The only reason I returned was because I planned to retrieve the boys and catch the morning coach to Edinburgh."

Her brow creased. "Edinburgh? Why? Have ye business there?"

He snorted. "I thought you were in Scotland, Anna. I meant to return for you. To say all the things I should have said. I've relived those weeks with you over and over . . . each misstep . . . each time I didn't say what I should have said or said things I shouldn't have."

Her lips had parted, and she stared at him.

"I'd come to Glendally that day to ask if you and your father would accompany me to London. Instead, I left you believing I planned a rendezvous with another woman."

"We never spoke of what would come after, should we marry."

Wylie's mouth thinned, knowing he was at fault for that. But other women? Never.

"Aye, true enough. But I could have told you other women would never come after. You'd have had my word on it, lass."

"I'm glad." Her smile was sweet, and one he thought reached her eyes.

He pressed the inside of her wrist to his lips for a moment, shutting his eyes and reveling in the taste of her. Only this morning, he'd thought he'd lost her. "Anna, those weeks at home . . . What I mean to say is . . . I need you. I can't lose you."

She blinked repeatedly, as if staving off tears. "I wronged ye, Wylie. I ought to have been mindful of all ye've suffered."

He snorted. "I've sufficient self-pity to see me to my grave. I allowed it to taint all that is good in my life." He met her eyes so she could read the truth in his. "Those weeks at home were pivotal. I expect I feared they would be, which is why I resisted returning. But it's because of you I did return. Because of you I recalled fragments of myself piece by piece. Fragments I hadn't realized I'd missed." He tilted her chin up. "Did you know that?"

A corner of her mouth curled. "I suspect most of what ye say was your uncle's doing." She pressed her palm over his heart and its beat quickened. "But I never believed ye wouldn't mend."

She had always seen the best in him, from the time they were children.

Had she envisioned them together even then? He bit the inside of his cheek. Did she envision them together now?

"I'm quaking in my boots, lass. You haven't said if I still have a chance."

Her eyes widened. "What?"

"Montgomery. You haven't wed him. But will you?"

She gaped as if she thought him mad. "No, Wylie, I will not."

"Does *he* know that?"

She gave a short laugh and smiled. "Oh aye, he does." She brushed her fingertips over his cheek, rasping his day-old beard.

His pulse leapt and he squeezed her waist. "I want you by my side, Anna. I want you at my table and in my bed." He took her hands in his. "I will be true to you, and I will take care of you and yours and ours."

Her eyes glistened in the candlelight, and he raised a hand to her cheek, swiping at a tear. This woman touched his soul. He knew now that she always had, even as a child.

It was possible that whatever drew her toward him, that whatever it was she sought within him . . . it was possible it might truly be there. He dropped to a knee.

"I believe the boy you once loved still exists," he said softly, looking up at her. "You make me whole. And I believe that given a chance, I might make you as happy as you make me. Will you marry me, lass?"

With a small smile, she shook her head as if baffled. "Why else would I make such a journey?" She studied him, her green eyes unblinking in the candlelight, and he met her gaze squarely. Seconds ticked by, marked as clearly as if by a pendulum's swing.

He must hear her say the words.

"Yes, Wylie. I will marry you."

With her words came a slow-flowing warmth, filling every pore of his being with utter certainty of its rightness.

Thanks be.

"Anna." Her name came out as a sigh. He rose and gathered her in his arms, her body's soft curves yielding and molding over the hard planes of his. He laid his cheek on her head. "I want you to come with me—you and your father both. There are things we must resolve," he said softly, "and we will. But I mean to make you my wife tomorrow, before I err yet again and you change your mind."

"I can't—" She pulled back, her eyes widening. "*Tomorrow*? Is that possible?"

He hadn't the faintest idea, though George might. "We'll find out."

"I can wait until ye return, Wylie."

"I don't want to wait."

"But . . ." She paused, seeming to consider before arriving at a quick conclusion. "Well then, I must rest, lest I appear haggard." She slipped from his arms and crossed to the divan, retrieving the shawl she'd lain over it. "I will have George stand for me in my father's stead, so use this time wisely. You must make things right between the two of ye."

Wylie's mouth curved while he watched her exit. Still ordering him about, was she?

"Wylie?"

Wylie whirled at the sound of George's voice.

"Wasn't sure if I was dreaming." George bent to rub his knee. "Anna insisted on coming. I couldn't let her travel alone."

"I'm in your debt," Wylie said. "In more ways than I can count."

George snorted. "I think not." Struggling to his feet, he shouldered on his coat. "She's here somewhere. I'll leave ye two to talk."

"We've spoken. It's you and I who must talk now."

CHAPTER 47

THOUGH HE'D WALKED most of the night, rehearsing the things he would say to George, Wylie now found himself tongue-tied. Unable to keep still, he paced.

"What do ye wish to speak of, Wylie?" George asked, sounding weary.

"Could we take a walk?" Wylie asked, hoping to buy time.

"Good God, man; it's past four in the morning. It's a challenge for me to walk these streets in broad daylight." George dropped back into the armchair, saying quietly, "If ye have something to say Wylie, say it. It concerns my wife, I presume?"

"No. Yes. I mean, I have had words with Miriam this evening, but not of the sort you might expect."

"I doubt you have any idea what I might expect."

Wylie wished George would stand so that they might speak face-to-face. "Jay is not my son."

"Ah." George gave a small grunt and struggled to his feet, nodding, "I see now what prompts you to walk after midnight. I arrived at that same conclusion myself recently. It *is* rather unsettling."

Wylie regarded him. "But unlike you, George, I never thought he was. I never—Miriam and I never—that is, it would be impossible for Jay to be my son. What you did, it was—"

"Foolish. I know that now, Wylie."

"No." Wylie shook his head decisively. "It was selfless and noble. I'm not certain I'd have done the same, were the situation reversed."

"Like hell. Ye'd never have consigned a child of mine to life as a bastard."

Wylie grunted, suspecting George was right. "I tend to foolishness. You don't."

"Aye, well. If it had been a day other than that day, perhaps. If I hadn't just learned of Colin Gordon's murder, or if Father hadn't invoked the nightmare of the *Inverness*, or. . . Well, I've told ye the events of that day. On another day I'd have had the wits to concoct a story of a clandestine marriage between ye and Miriam and left it at that. But I didn't." He reached behind him for his cane and leaned on it. "I don't regret the choice, Wylie."

"How could ye not?" Wylie shook his head, his gut roiling. "God Almighty, how could ye not? The things ye gave up to marry her—the university, your travels, a wife of your own choosing. It sickens me." He stared at George, who seemed unaffected, as if none of those things had mattered.

"George?"

"Ye've not listed the one thing that mattered."

Wylie stopped pacing, loath to revive that one thing that mattered. Then he remembered McPhail. "Your political ambitions? George, I talked to Malcolm McPhail tonight, and he said—"

George grimaced as if disgusted and turned from him. Wylie shut his mouth and blew out a breath, resigned.

"I'm not quite the fool you think me, George, though I don't fault you for believing so. I too lost my closest friend. It's an ache I've carried for many years, and it's an ache that's never eased. It's difficult to speak of it."

"So we're never to speak of it?" George leaned against the mantel and crossed his arms over his chest, as if the discussion were of cursory interest only. "Twenty-five years, Wylie. Not one word from ye in twenty-five years. Could ye not have granted me ten minutes of your time? Did our friendship matter so little?"

"I . . . Things . . ." He hung his head. "Ah, hell, George. It was that it mattered too much."

"Why, then? Why couldn't ye forgive? Why deny me the chance to explain?"

Wylie blinked at George's rising tone, then shook his head slowly. "I'm not certain now that *I* understand." Scratching the back of his neck, he looked at his feet. "I waited for you. In Boulogne-Sur-Mer, I waited."

"I never doubted it."

"Nearly a year, it was. I hadn't a grout to my name, nor more than the clothes on my back. What I *did* have was the unshakable certainty that you'd come, and I clung to it." He looked at George, who now perched on the arm of a chair, and lifted a shoulder. "And then you didn't."

"Ye had to have known I tried."

"For a time no one could have convinced me otherwise."

"How did ye manage? Uncle William never told me."

"Scavenging trash. Sleeping in alleyways." His mouth curved in a self-deprecating smile. "It might please you to know you were right—I wished daily that I'd paid more heed to our tutor."

"It doesn't please me at all. But what of the churches or sheltering families? I'd heard some offered aid to the rebels."

"Perhaps, if I'd left the coast. But again, I was certain you'd come, and I couldn't risk missing you." He shook his head slowly, recalling his naivety. "By spring, I began to fear you for dead. But I never entirely believed it. I would have *known*; there'd be a piece of me missing." He looked at George and saw him swallow.

"When . . ." George paused, clearing his throat. "When did ye get your father's satchel?"

"Not until May. I'd haunted the quay for a year by then, and when news finally came, I meant to savor it. I took the satchel to a bakery at the top of a hill, just outside the castle gates. It was a place I sat often, and its refuse pile kept me alive. On that day though, I walked through the front door and pointed at a steaming, meat-filled baguette." His eyes half-closed, he inhaled a deep, somewhat queasy, breath. "I can still smell it. Thyme and rosemary.

"The lad behind the counter looked at my coin, turning it over and over. I hadn't bathed or shaved in over a year, and I'd taken on the habit of scratching at lice. I couldn't fault him for his mistrust, so I opted to ignore it and hold my head high." He snorted, his mood lightening at the memory. He looked at George with a grin. "I was a laird's only son, mind you. Glencorach, the Younger."

"That and a sixpence will buy ye a pint of ale," George returned, not missing a beat. The exchange was one they'd oft repeated in their youth. "So did he take your coin?"

"Oh, aye. It was wicked warm in there and they were baking bread in the back ovens. I was tempted to linger and eat inside, but I knew he wanted me out, so I didn't wait to be booted.

"There was a spot at the far end of the castle wall, outside the fortress. A row of shops and homes sheltered it, and I could often glimpse the sea beyond in the odd sliver of space. So I went there, telling myself the day was so clear that I might even see Scotland."

"My letter was in this satchel?"

"There were two letters. One was addressed in Father's hand, the other in yours. For all I knew you were waiting on one of the ships anchored in the harbor. So I opened Father's first, thinking I'd scan it for news before reading yours.

"I learned my Father was in Edinburgh, working on my pardon—which seemed odd, as I'd not been tried. He wrote I couldn't come home just yet, that I'd hang if I did. I'd been attainted for treason."

Wylie's brow furrowed, and he squinted at George. "It didn't make sense, not a word of it. We'd been nabbed in Crieff. Everyone knew that. I couldn't fathom who'd have claimed otherwise. So I set down the baguette and reread the letter, starting from the beginning because I couldn't have read what I thought I'd read.

"But I had." He grunted, his eyes unseeing as he recalled his father's next words. "And there was more. I was not to blame George, Father urged. George's testimony had been coerced in exchange for his own pardon, and if I'd been there to have a say in it, I'd have had it no other way. Especially now as George had married and he and his wife had a baby boy."

Again Wylie squinted at George, shaking his head. "I read those words over and over. Out of all of them, they made the least sense. A baby boy? You had married? How was that possible?

"And then I turned the page and learned you had married 'Miriam Grant, the lass from Strathspey who lodged with her aunt.'

"Each time I thought of Miriam that past year, and I'll grant it was often, I imagined her waiting for me." Wylie turned up a corner of his mouth, still looking at George. "She wasn't, was she? She'd never been, not even at the beginning."

George reddened and stood upright again, looking at the floor. "I'm not sure ye ever knew her, Wylie."

Wylie blew out a long breath. "Yet you did."

"Aye, well."

With a sigh, Wylie concluded his story. "I retched for what seemed an hour, though of course it couldn't have been. There wasn't that much in my belly. I kicked what remained of the baguette to a pack of hounds, wagering with myself which one would fight the fiercest to keep it. It was a scrappy, half-starved spaniel that made off with it. I remember thinking it odd to find a spaniel on the streets, and that he must have been someone's pet at one time. I must become fierce as well, just like that spaniel, if I hoped to survive.

"I couldn't make sense of you and Miriam, George. I didn't want it to make sense. So I took your letter down the hill and tossed it into the beggar's fire unopened." He met George's eyes. "All these years, I've blamed you. You, when you were the . . . the only decent . . ."

George draped an arm on the mantel for support. "Don't turn maudlin on me now, Cousin. I'd do it again it a heartbeat."

Wylie swallowed. "As might I, if I'm to be truthful."

He'd abandoned Anna, hadn't he? On a misunderstanding he might have cleared with a bit of patience.

George nodded. "I'm not sure I expected ye'd read it if ye read your father's first. It did surprise me, however, how long ye held out. Ye managed not to open a single letter."

Wylie gave a half-hearted grin. "If ye hadn't sealed them so damned many times, I'd have attempted it."

"Aye, well. I wanted to be sure."

"Of what?"

"That it was your damned pride that kept ye from writing me. That you didn't know the truth and still refuse to write."

Wylie grunted. "Canny lad. You do know, don't you, that I no longer hold you to account for that testimony? My father was right; if I'd been there, I'd not have wished differently."

George studied him a moment, as if assessing his sincerity, then nodded. "It helps some to know that."

"Well, it's God's truth, and I ought to have told you so in the glen." Wylie unbuttoned his waistcoat and shed his jacket, draping it over a stool. "I'm glad you've come, George. And I'm glad you brought Anna."

"She was inconsolable once she spoke with Mrs. Baxter."

"She's agreed to marry me, and I hope to do so today. Do you think it possible? I thought to try Fleet Street."

George glanced toward the door and then back at Wylie. "Today?" He shook his head. "Ye must have proper banns and such; the laws have changed. If ye hope to marry quickly, it best be in Scotland."

Wylie frowned. Surely he could find a willing minister if enough coins were exchanged.

If not, however, the *Eliza* would stop in Glasgow before sailing west, for he *would* marry her before leaving.

"If we return to Scotland, Anna may insist on marrying in Badenoch. Will she marry in Glasgow, do you think, without her family?"

"Bloody hell, Wylie, ask her yourself. Am I to manage all your women?"

Wylie chuckled, then sobered, his thoughts shifting. "Did Uncle Henry or my father know of Jay's parentage?"

"No," George said, the word clipped.

"Anna?"

"I doubt she's sleeping. I'll own she's heard enough now to reason it out."

"Right," he said slowly. If she hadn't, Will undoubtedly would fill her in. He gnawed the inside of his cheek, then added, "You know Jay is in London?"

His face expressionless, George nodded.

"Would you object if he accompanied us to Florida on a scouting voyage?" He owed it to George to consult him. "I told Will I'd consider staking the two of them if they came up with a solid proposition over the next year."

"Ye're still going?"

As of an hour ago, Wylie planned returning to the Highlands at once so that he might speak with Anna and George. Yet they were here, and Wylie still ached to return.

With Anna at his side.

If Wylie had returned to Badenoch on George's account, Alec, knowing the story, would merely grumble. Long curious about George's letters, Alec had ferreted the details from Wylie late one night, after they'd consumed the better part of a case of claret.

But if Wylie were to return on account of a woman? No. Alec expected Wylie to live up to his end of the bargain. If they were to now trade on the right side of the law, Wylie was to do the legwork.

"I must." He stopped short a grimace, though not before George noticed.

"Ye did aim to stay planted." George said, his expression reflective.

"A lifetime ago." Back when George aimed to travel.

"I can tell ye this, Wylie. It wasn't easy for Anna to come here. She has a fair amount of pride herself. Ye may not get her to

Florida, but I doubt she'll throw ye over twice. She'll marry in Glasgow."

Wylie snorted, then rubbed his thumb over his mouth. Did he have a home to offer her? "What of Glencorach?"

"Ye own it. Ye left without signing Alan's papers."

Wylie grinned. "So I did. Well, then, what of Jay?"

At once, George's expression shuttered. "Jay's of age. He makes his own decisions."

"You're his father. I'll not allow him to join us if you object."

Nodding, George sat. "Let me think about it, then. For now, are ye ever planning to offer me a drink? I expect I ought to hear what McPhail had to say."

The remains of a decades-old-knot in Wylie's chest eased. He rose, chuckling, and poured his cousin a measure of whisky.

CHAPTER 48

"PAPA," WILL SAID, nudging Wylie's shoulder. "You must wake. Alec will be here soon."

Cracking open an eyelid, Wylie glared first at his son and then at the window and its weak gleam of daylight. With a groan he pushed himself from the armchair, stiffening when he noted the chair opposite him sat empty. "Where's George?"

"Out. He will return. You and he have reconciled, *oui?*"

Wylie clasped Will's shoulder and squeezed. "We have. You were right, Will, about all of it, and I'm grateful."

Will grinned. "Perhaps it is more astonishing that you listened."

Wylie chuckled. The lad did have a point. "Aye, perhaps so. Are Anna and Dougal still sleeping?"

"They were absent when I woke. Come to the table. There is coffee."

Wylie took the cup Will offered and dropped into the straight-backed chair at the table. After rubbing the bleariness from his eyes, he looked at the piled papers Will pushed toward him.

Quickly, he scanned Will's changes to the shipping list, his mouth twitching in grudging pride as he did. The lad had caught each of his intentional oversights, and more. "You struck through the guinea grass. Why?"

"Cousin George reviewed the list last night while we awaited your return. He said we need not carry the West African seed. He said James Bittle writes that the planters grow it in the Carolinas now. We would pay a lower price in Charleston."

"He knows James Bittle?" Bittle was one of the largest land owners in East Florida.

"*Oui.* They served together in Flanders. He knows many who live in America."

Wylie frowned, wondering at the extent of George's connections. If George knew Bittle, then surely he'd known Alec's brother Aubrey. Before Wylie could ask, the door opened and Anna and Dougal stepped inside, laden with food.

The chair toppled in Wylie's haste to rise, and he bent to upright it. "Stay with your brother," he instructed Will quietly.

Anna busied herself arranging the food along the sideboard. Coming up behind her, Wylie placed a hand on her hip. "Come with me into the other room," he murmured, noting her hands were unsteady. "We've plans to make."

The corners of her mouth quirked upward and she took his hand from her hip and kissed it. Then, hearing the strike and slide of cane on wood, they both turned toward the door. George, looking only slightly rumpled, entered the room.

"Where were you?" Wylie asked.

"Downstairs in the study, speaking with your partner. Would ye join us?"

CHAPTER 49

"WHERE'S YOUR CLOAK, Anna?" Wylie asked when they stepped into the hall an hour later. He'd forestalled meeting with Alec, hoping to quell Anna's uncertainty.

"I don't need it. Besides, it's little more than a rag."

"You'll need it when we step out, and it's far from a rag. It's functional, well made, and clean." He turned. "I'll fetch it."

She reached for him. "Nay, it's warm."

"It may rain."

"This is my one day in London, Wylie. D'ye plan to spend it on the stairwell arguing over a cloak?"

Criminy, but she was stubborn; he must learn to choose his battles. Biting his tongue, he placed a hand on her elbow and started downstairs.

"Do ye think we might stop at a stationer's as well as the wax-works? My father's given me money for sketchbooks and account books."

"Of course. We'll also stop at a dry goods. I expect we ought to purchase items for Glencorach and Glendally both. You'll know better than I what's needed, and we can have them shipped back."

"Do ye have so very much money?"

"Enough to maintain a household for my wife and family."

At the bottom of the stairs, she pulled her elbow free, looped her arm beneath his, and propelled them around a maidservant laden with linens and then into an alcove.

"Before we join the others, Wylie, we must speak." She hesitated, then her chin rose and she continued. "I'm not going with you. My decision is final. Father cannot withstand a voyage and I will not leave him." She held up a hand to interrupt his protest. "I've given this careful thought, and I'd like Dougal to stay with me. Would ye allow it? He should attend school. He's made friends, and Father adores him."

She'd spent the last ten minutes telling him she refused to go, but he hadn't cared to hear it. This request, however, indicated her resolve.

A gaping emptiness brought him low. Leave half his family behind? It was unthinkable.

Was it? A month ago he'd have grasped her offer to keep Dougal.

A month ago he hadn't realized how much he'd missed of Will's early years.

Dougal would be safe in Scotland. Florida was rife with fevers and such.

No. Badenoch was rife with fevers as well—an anti-Catholicism fever first and foremost.

He slumped against the wall and squeezed his eyes shut, shaking his head in frustration. "Nay, Anna. He will insist on the priest. He promised Rennie he'd keep his faith. It's important to him."

"I'd never think to usurp his own mother's wishes. Mrs. Baxter knows of two Catholic families just o'er the river. I haven't spoken with them, but I will."

He opened his eyes, something unexpected swelling within him. She'd thought to follow up on his request, as unwise as she'd judged it.

"Ye'll not regret entrusting his care to me, Wylie."

He expected Rennie wouldn't either. Rennie would approve.

Exhaling a long sigh, he reached for her, pulling her toward him. Brushing his mouth against the curve of her neck, he breathed in her scent. "Have I told you this morning that I love you, Anna Macrae?"

She pulled back to look at him. "Ye haven't. Ever."

He hadn't? He recalled thinking it more than once. "Well, I ought to have."

She rolled her eyes. "Does that mean ye agree?"

He blew out a sigh. "Aye. But only once I'm certain myself that your father will not come." And if so, he didn't relish telling Dougal. "Come now, I hear the others in the study."

A short time later, after introductions were made and congratulations offered, Will hustled Jay, Anna, and Dougal out the study door, leaving Wylie alone with George and Alec.

"Why didn't you tell me you were laird of an estate, Wylie?" Alec said, resuming his seat and draping his arm over a vacant

317

chair. "Here I thought you were some two-bit rebel on the run who'd hoodwinked his way into becoming senior partner in our venture."

Snorting at the implication Glencorach was grand, Wylie draped his jacket over a coat hook and dropped into the chair at the table's head. "I'm ten years your senior, and you had no capital."

In the mid-fifties, Alec had had the bad luck to be aboard one of the French privateer's victims and had been pressed into service. Fifteen years old and on unfamiliar ground, he'd for some reason latched on to Wylie with an unrelenting tenacity. When Wylie left the privateer to captain his own ship, Alec followed. It hadn't been an act of charity to take Alec on. The lad, born into a family of English merchants, was well worth his weight.

And for years he'd been Wylie's closest friend.

"I like her," Alec said. "Your Anna." Concurring with George that Wylie and Anna should marry in Scotland, Alec had readily agreed to a delay in Glasgow.

"You've seen little of her."

"I'm a quick judge of character. I like your cousin George here as well. Did you know he and my brother Aubrey were friends?"

Wylie looked at George. "I thought as much when I learned George knew Bittle." James Bittle had written Alec of Aubrey's death. Bittle and Alec still corresponded, and his letters, filled with stories of East Florida, were one of the reasons Alec and Wylie initially considered the colony. "Did George tell you of my proposal regarding Will and Jay?"

Alec grinned. "Will told me. It's about time you gave the lad his due."

Wylie grunted and looked at George. "Have you given it thought?"

George shifted in his chair. "Aye, but before we discuss it, I have a proposal of my own."

"Of course."

"I'd like to go in your stead."

"Go where?" Wylie asked, looking behind him for the coffee service.

"To East Florida."

Wylie's head swung back, coffee forgotten, and he regarded George through narrowed eyes. "What?"

"I'd like to go in your stead," George repeated with a show of patience. "Alec has agreed."

The hell you say. "You'll do no such thing." He turned to Alec. "What have you agreed to?"

"Listen to him, mate. There's merit in what he proposes. George knows more of America than either of us."

"You don't understand. He's not doing this because he wants to." Wylie pointed at George, then rose and paced. "He's doing this because he carries guilt over something that happened a quarter-century past."

"Is he, then?" Alec mused. "Hmmph. It seemed a damned fine bargain when he presented it."

"Alec doesn't seem to think my injury makes me unfit," George said.

What the hell? Wylie turned on George. "You know damned well I don't think you're unfit. I know what you're doing, and I'll not allow it."

"Why, exactly?" George asked, his patience seeming inexhaustible. "I know ye want to stay in Scotland. I'm not asking for a share of the profits, though a wage wouldn't come amiss. I'm not useless; I will earn my keep."

How did George know Wylie wanted to stay in Scotland? Wylie had scarcely acknowledged it himself.

"Of course you're not useless, George. But I'll not allow you to trade your life so I might have mine. By all accounts you have a good chance at becoming MP. It's something you've wanted for years."

"I'll warrant I once did. Perhaps I still do. But seeing a bit more of the world won't impede my future chances. I was intrigued when Uncle William first mentioned Florida, and I've studied it since. I'd like the opportunity to sail in your stead."

"A future MP? You don't say?" Alec regarded George with an expression mocking awe, then straightened and turned to Wylie. "Think of the favors we might request, Wylie."

"Keep out of this, Alec. George, you'll not do this again."

The door opened and a maidservant stepped inside with the coffee service, followed by Will and Jay. Alec rose and shuffled them all out. Following behind them, he shut the door, leaving Wylie alone with George.

CHAPTER 50

ANNA STOOD OUTSIDE the study door, apart from the others, and gnawed a ragged cuticle. Wylie's partner, Alec, had attempted more than once to include her in their conversation. She, however, couldn't form a cohesive thought for anything beyond the unknown debate taking place behind that closed door. Will glanced at her now and again, but his expression, unsurprisingly inscrutable, offered no insight.

Mother Mary, she ought to have accepted Mr. Montgomery's proposal.

Tasting blood, she dropped her fist and clasped her hands. If she had accepted Montgomery, she'd be at home now, by the hearth with Mrs. Baxter and Father, chatting of the day to come. Instead, she stood shivering beneath a stairwell while others debated matters critical to her future.

Or so she assumed. Wylie and George may just as easily be discussing the price of grain.

Perhaps Will didn't know what Wylie and George spoke of.

Nay, he knew. They *all* knew.

Squaring her shoulders, she regarded Alec. Before meeting him, she'd envisioned a man dark and swarthy, his skin etched with deep lines. Perhaps with a scar across his cheek. This man—fair-haired, light-skinned, and smartly dressed—could pass for the young son of a prosperous English squire. All he lacked was a walking cane.

She had no experience with young English squires, so instead she spoke Will's name. He turned toward her, his eyes widening a fraction. Perhaps her tone was sharper than she'd intended.

"I'd like to speak with ye. Now, please."

All of them looked toward her now. Jay, resplendent in his scarlet uniform but seemingly as oblivious to the undercurrent as was Dougal, who sat grinning atop Alec's shoulders and poking at an ancient game mount. Alec's brow furrowed momentarily, then a side of his mouth curled upward. He returned his attention to

Dougal and the intricacies of the mount while Will stepped toward her.

"Miss Macrae, I do not—"

She gripped his forearm, stopping the lie before he uttered it. "D'ye truly expect me to believe that ye, of all people, dinna ken what's being said? D'ye take me for a fool?" she asked in a low hiss. "So help me, Will, if—"

"Miss Macrae, Papa would not want me to speak for him."

Her conscience pricked. Had she not traveled for days to tell Wylie she had no right to question his comings and goings?

She had, yet he'd countered she had every right.

Still, what was she about, thinking to badger his son?

Gritting her teeth, she released Will's arm and jerked her head toward the others. "Go on, then."

For the first time since she'd known him, Will appeared uncertain. Ignoring her dismissal, he examined his feet, as if assessing his boots' shine. Then he faced her and spoke.

"It's Cousin George. He wants to sail to Florida."

CHAPTER 51

INSIDE THE STUDY, Wylie stared at the closed door until it became apparent Alec wouldn't return. Turning his eyes heavenward, he resorted to repeating himself.

"I mean what I say, George. You'll not do this again. It's not right."

George blew out a breath and shrugged. "I expect I can book passage on another ship. For I am leaving. I've written my father and Miriam both."

"Damn it to hell. Why—

"Enough," George said, raising a hand. "I ken well why you're suspicious, but I ask ye to consider that this has naught to do with you, but with me. There's no hope for my marriage. I think ye know that."

"But—"

"Would ye truly see me idle at Cragdurcas while ye're off on yet another adventure?"

"You're not idle. You're respected and—"

"Idle." George said. "Ye've asked if I'd mind if ye took Jay under your wing. Hell yes, I'd mind. It's not that I doubt your worthiness as a mentor. There's likely none better. But I'd like the opportunity to mentor him myself. Surely ye understand, having sons of your own." He regarded Wylie, his expression hard. "Ye're in a position to give me that opportunity, for I suspect Jay will choose you over me if given the choice. Ye've let your pride stand between us for twenty-five years. D'ye plan to do so once more?"

Wylie's eyes widened a fraction as he stared at his cousin. Christ, the man was good with words. In the space of sixty seconds he'd flipped the tables on Wylie. Wylie might have laughed if he didn't suspect George's words were sincere.

He shoved a hand through his hair and stepped to the window to peer at the city outside. Was George right? Was his pride interfering yet again?

And what of Anna? Did he truly intend to send her home

alone? Certainly he owed her as much as he owed Alec. Besides, Alec had urged him to stay.

As for Jay, if Will were struggling as Jay was, there was no way in hell Wylie would allow another man to fill a father's shoes—not until he'd done all he possibly could and failed.

In the past, maybe, but not now. Indeed, Wylie felt a small sniggling of resentment at the idea of George going with Will instead of himself.

But Will would prosper. Could the same be said of Jay?

George spoke up behind him. "I believe I'd be an asset to Dunlap & Associates, Wylie. I'm asking ye time in which to try. That, and your support when speaking with my father."

"He'll not be happy." Or would he? Henry knew George had suffered these last years.

"He may surprise me. One can only hope. Do this for Anna, if ye won't do it for me."

Anna.

George was right. About the whole of it. Nodding, Wylie turned and faced him. "I'll step aside."

"Thank you," George said, his somber expression unchanging. "Know that while I threatened to book passage on another ship, I wouldn't have. With Uncle William gone, I worry for my father. I'd not have left him without family."

"I'll see to him."

"I rely on it, Wylie."

Somehow that notion was immensely soothing, a balm sweeping free the past.

CHAPTER 52

ANNA STUDIED WILL, her brow furrowed. She'd spent days traveling with George and he'd mentioned nothing of the sort. "George? In Florida?"

"*Oui.* Jay does not accept it. Nor Papa."

She understood Jay's reluctance to have his father along. But not Wylie's; his and George's reconciliation appeared sincere.

Suddenly, before she could question Will further, the door beside them opened. George brushed past her wearing a slight smile. Wylie stood on the threshold, his hand extended her way.

Wylie didn't appear ill at ease. He looked as if he were . . . Dare she think it? He looked as if he were happy.

With a wide grin, Wylie snatched her hand, tugged her over the threshold, and closed the door. Cupping her face with his palm, he lowered his mouth to hers before she could speak.

Did he think to distract her before delivering unwelcome news? If so, she was willing. Closing her eyes, she gripped his shoulders and returned the kiss, inhaling the fragrance she had come to crave. A small sound escaped her throat before she could stop it, and she curled her fingers into locks of his hair, drawing him closer.

Muttering an oath, Wylie pressed her against the door until she could feel the full length of his body. Her lips parted, and she traced her tongue along his own, tasting coffee and hints of the butter cake and cheese she'd brought to break their fast.

His heart, racing at an erratic pace, hammered against her own. The knowledge that she roused the same need in him that he incited in her was exhilarating. Intoxicating, even, for how else could she justify her actions when her hand ventured to his backside, pressing him closer?

He reacted quickly, hoisting her thigh up—

A knock sounded at the door, reverberating between her shoulder blades.

"Wylie?"

It was Alec's voice. Anna yanked her hand from Wylie's person and pushed him away, mortified. Mother Mary, what was she about? Wylie didn't even stumble, though he had the good sense to appear chagrined.

"A few more moments, Alec," Wylie said to the closed door. Softly, he added, "I'm sorry, Anna. You make me ... I've no excuse." With a quick motion, he smoothed her skirts and then donned his jacket and adjusted his sleeves.

Anna took the pewter water jug from the table and pressed its cool surface over her neck, chest, and cheeks, hoping to cool the heat that lingered. She didn't need a looking glass to know her skin flamed beet-scarlet.

"I think that only deepens your color, lass."

"Hush." She set down the jug and beckoned him close. "Come here and turn around." He complied, and she removed the loosened ribbon and combed her fingers through his hair. Satisfied, she secured the ribbon anew. "Now, tell me what I should know."

He turned and faced her. "There's been a change in plans."

He appeared at ease, not in keeping with delivering unpleasant news. "I expected there might be."

"You and I will board the *Eliza* tonight with the others, and we will marry in Glasgow, where Will and Alec can be present. George will get a letter in this morning's post, requesting your father and his join us. We'll speak at length while we're out today, but for now, know that George is sailing in my stead, and I will remain home with you and Dougal."

Her lips parted, and she stared at him.

"It's true, Anna."

When she remained tongue-tied, he opened the door and beckoned in the others.

CHAPTER 53

"THERE'S THE wax works," Wylie said an hour later, pointing to the opposite side of the street.

Anna followed his gesture and saw a woman planted on the footpath, pointing the way through the museum's entrance. When she realized the woman was one of the exhibits, she frowned, then urged Wylie across the street for a closer view.

"My word, will ye look at her, Wylie? It's almost as if I can judge what she's thinking." She stepped back a step and looked at the shop's façade. "Are there figures on each floor?"

"I've never been inside. Come, let's find out."

She held back. "Nay. I think we best visit a dry goods and stationer first. Once I enter here, I will lose track of time."

By mid-afternoon, Wylie stood alone at a jeweler's counter. He'd left Anna on the second floor of the wax works with the assurance he'd return in an hour. She insisted he make it three, and they had compromised at two.

The lure of the wax figures puzzled him; he thought her own work more convincing. She'd tried to explain, telling him the figures were a treasure trove of frozen expressions that might be studied at leisure. To that end, she'd immediately put her new ivory tablet to use, capturing those expressions for later perusal. She'd filled all but two pages by the time he'd left.

The jeweler claimed Wylie's attention, placing yet another elaborate band ringed with diamonds on the counter. Wylie shook his head. "No, this won't suit either. A simple gold posy ring, perhaps. Preferably one already engraved."

While the jeweler disappeared into a back room, Wylie fingered a gold bracelet set with oval agates of varying earth-toned shades. It had caught his eye as soon as he approached the jeweler's counter, and it hadn't taken the jeweler more than a moment to convince Wylie to purchase both it and its accompanying earrings. He didn't regret the impulse; it would be a gift for their first anniversary, packaged with a journey to a place of Anna's choosing. For the jeweler was right; the set was fitting for the finest of drawing rooms in the finest of cities.

Choosing a wedding band, however, something she might wear daily, was taking much longer.

The jeweler returned with a flat box of simple gold bands. "All of these are engraved, sir. I trust you're not superstitious as some are from estates, and some are new—ordered but never retrieved."

Wylie handled the rings one by one, reading the inscriptions. After reading the sixth sentiment attributing their future to God, he regarded the jeweler with a frown. "Are there any less pious?"

The jeweler's lips quirked as if he held back a smile, and he raised a finger. Turning, he opened a drawer, and then held up a ring. "Perhaps this will do. It came in last week."

Wylie eyed it, experiencing a curious flash of certainty. Raised ovals, triangles and rectangles of gold circled an enameled band. Simple, yet distinct and beautiful. He wanted it, and if necessary, he'd have the inscription plated over and engraved with something of his own.

He grunted, lest his eagerness raise the price. "It's engraved?"

"Yes." The jeweler placed his monocle in his eye and raised the ring to the light. Within seconds, he nodded and handed the ring to Wylie.

Wylie read the inscription.

My heart is content.

"I'll take it."

CHAPTER 54

Glasgow, Scotland

THREE WEEKS LATER, Wylie awoke early in a Glasgow inn. Legs akimbo, Anna sat beside him, her gaze darting between him and her tablet, her pencil moving rapidly over the ivory. She wore nothing but her wedding ring.

My heart's content.

He wished he could claim the same of his wife. He rose on an elbow and ran a hand up her thigh. Pausing her pencil, she swatted his hand aside and studied the drawing.

Undeterred, he leaned forward and kissed the inside of her knee. "Put that away, Anna."

"Nay."

"There's no need to sketch me at every turn, lass. I'm not leaving you."

Her brow furrowing, she smudged a line from the ivory with her thumb and then drew another. "Ye've two hours before making that decision. The *Eliza* hasn't weighed anchor."

"I made that decision weeks ago."

"Act in haste, repent at leisure."

Groaning, he rolled from the bed and reached for his breeches.

In London she'd been ecstatic at the change in plans. Somewhere on the voyage north, she'd wavered, one moment convinced he was meant for the sea, the next three certain he wasn't.

Her moods had become erratic, reminding him of his first months with Rennie. Perhaps it was the way of new marriages.

His fingers stilled, his breeches unbuttoned.

His first year with Rennie . . . Her emotions a tumble with carrying Will.

Was Anna with child?

He grinned, a burgeoning joy lightening his heart.

A girl, perhaps they'd have a daughter. Or another boy. He'd welcome a lad as well. Either—either would be a treasured gift.

Why hadn't she told him?

The grin died. Good God, if she *were* with child and thought he'd guessed, she may conclude he married her solely because of it.

Schooling his expression, he turned to find her studying him. "Dress, Anna, and we'll meet your father and Uncle Henry for coffee."

"Nay." She set the pad aside, untangled her limbs, and rose, a tumble of red curls covering her breasts. "Wylie, I wish I weren't behaving so, but I can't seem to help myself. I do believe ye mean to stay."

"I'm happy to hear it, lass," he said, stoically awaiting the "but."

"But something beyond your control may prevent—"

"It won't." He turned and looked for his boots.

"It may," she said, pulling him back to face her. She ran her palms down his chest and then leaned forward and teased a nipple with the tip of her tongue before blowing it dry, sending a quick liquid heat to his loins. "And if it does, I'll not have ye leave without something worth remembering." Easing his breeches over his hips, she added, "If ye'll allow it, that is."

Only a fool would protest, and he was no longer a fool.

Grinning, he picked her up and tossed her onto the bed, taking care the distance was short.

An hour later, Wylie, his shoulders braced against the gray morning's chill, covered the short distance to the quay in long, quick strides with Anna at his side. Dawn's drenching rain had subsided to a drizzle, and gulls soared overhead, their calls raucous. He guided Anna around a pack of strays scavenging the fishermen's leavings, and she pointed out Henry, Alan, and George standing outside a coffee house. He raised a hand in greeting, then scanned the shoreline.

Within minutes Wylie spotted two of his crew securing *Eliza's* transport boat. Will hopped off, then Dougal.

Dougal ran toward them, his boots slapping through puddles. By the time he reached them, his breeches were as wet as his tear-covered face. Grabbing Wylie by the hand, he yanked. "You must make Will stay, Papa!"

Wylie shook his head. "Nay, Dougal. He's a young man now, and he must go his own way. We will miss him together until he returns."

"I do not want him to go," Dougal said, sobs shaking his shoulders.

Wylie cast a pleading glance Anna's way, and she knelt and embraced the boy. "I know it hurts, lad," she said quietly, her gaze on Wylie. "But we must let one another follow our dreams."

Wylie stopped short a grunt. If the remark was meant for him, he'd ignore it.

Except to remind her daily that *she* now featured in his dreams.

"He'll write us often," Wylie said, squeezing Dougal's shoulder. "And we will write him." Will approached them, his stride long and his bearing confident. Wylie clasped his hand tightly. "You'll write no less than weekly, aye, Will?"

"*Oui,*" Will said absently, his sharp blue gaze darting back to the transport as if he were eager to be gone.

It is as it should be, Wylie reminded himself before the ache took root.

Yet . . .

Devil take it, he didn't want the lad leaving either. A few moments more and *he* might sob into Anna's shoulder.

"Your word on that, Will?"

Will faced him, seeming surprised. "Of course, Papa. I will write; you have my word. It will be as if I never left."

"I doubt that."

"Do not doubt that I will miss you," Will said, his voice sober. "I am grateful you have found peace." He stepped forward and embraced Anna. "My mother would approve, Miss Mac—what shall I call you now?"

"Call me Anna, Will."

"Anna, then. My mother would like you, Anna."

"I would have liked her as well. She raised two fine lads." She leaned forward to kiss his cheek and waited while he embraced Dougal. Then she took Dougal's hand and led him toward those waiting at the coffee house. Halfway there, she glanced over her shoulder at Wylie. He managed a grin and pointed at his feet to indicate he'd stay planted. A smile tugged at the corners of her mouth before she walked on.

"Well then . . ." Wylie stopped mid-sentence, neither trusting his voice nor knowing the right words. He instead took his son in a hard embrace, and Will returned it equal measure.

At length Will stepped back, his eyes glistening. Swallowing visibly, he canted his head toward the nearby coffee-house. "Cousin George comes to speak with you. I . . . I should say farewell to Alan and my uncle."

Wylie nodded and patted Will's shoulder, nudging the lad toward the coffee house before they both sobbed. Then he swiped a fist over both cheeks and turned to greet George.

"Good morning, Wylie."

Despite the hours they'd spent in one another's company on the voyage north, the ache of missing years was keen. Wylie regarded his cousin, wondering if he might extract the same promise he'd extracted from Will.

Likely not, given the mounds of unread letters he'd returned over the years.

"George . . . do you think I might . . . that is . . . those letters." Wylie swallowed. "I'd like to read them, if they still exist."

"They exist, and I'd be pleased if ye would. Ye'll find them in the library."

Wylie searched again for words that might atone for all that had happened. None came to mind but the banal. "I am truly sorry—"

"Enough. We've agreed to bury what's past, aye? I trust ye'll keep to your promise to look after my father? Be my eyes and ears while I'm absent. Father tends toward the old ways, but he occasionally heeds my counsel; I know he'll heed yours."

"Of course. And I trust you'll look after my son."

"I will."

Wylie shifted from foot to foot. He and George had had scant time to renew their friendship, and now, once again they'd live disparate lives. No wonder Anna dreaded being left behind. He didn't much care for it himself.

"How long will it be, George? Before you return?"

A ghost of a smile flickered across George's features and he raised a shoulder. "Three years?"

"That's one hellish long time."

"Aye, I know. But I'll write."

Wylie regarded him steadily a moment before gesturing Anna to join them. "As will I," he said, nodding. "Find what you seek, Cousin."

"I would ask the same of ye, Wylie," George said quietly, his gaze falling on Anna as she, Will, and Dougal strode toward them. "Were it not that ye have." Aiming a short nod toward his father, he turned and joined Will. Together, they walked toward the transport.

Wylie wrapped an arm around Anna when she reached him, pulling her close while Dougal latched on to his leg. Together they waited, watching the transport glide toward the *Eliza*.

"Will says I may keep Molly, Papa," Dougal said at length.

Wylie's mouth curved in a smile. "Aye, I expect you might."

The next few moments were spent in silence. Only once George and Will were safely aboard and out of sight did Dougal lessen his grip.

"And Anna says Mr. Shaw said Molly will have puppies."

"Oh?"

"*Oui.* Will says I must train one for him, and Anna says Mr. Tanner will help me. Then Will may have a good dog of his own when he returns, and Molly will stay mine. Anna says you will have time to help too, Papa. Cousin George said first you must teach me to play a fiddle. Anna said you will have time to do both."

"Did she now?" Chuckling, Wylie tousled the boy's hair and kissed Anna's brow. "I do love you, Anna Macrae Macpherson."

She looked up at him, her smile radiant. "And I you, husband."

Hitching Dougal onto his hip, Wylie grabbed Anna's hand and turned from the sea.

My heart's content.

And so it was.

"Let's go home."

FOR THE RESIDENTS of Badenoch, the end of October marked a time "in-between." The transition of summer into winter, the harvest of spring's planting, and the return of cattle from the glen. It was Samhain, and this year's celebration would also mark the return of the young laird. Past customs and traditions, some of which had fallen in disuse, were revived at Henry Macpherson's direction.

To that end, an hour before sunset on Hallowmas Eve, Wylie and his family climbed the hill behind Glendally.

"You must walk faster, Papa, or we shall miss it," Dougal said, tugging ineffectually on Wylie's hand. "We must write Will of everything."

Will, in his most recent letter, had requested a full account of tonight's proceedings and passed along a similar request from George. Thankfully, both wrote as promised.

Wylie glanced over his shoulder. Anna and Martha lagged several steps behind, and behind them walked Alan and Uncle Henry, animated in amiable conversation. "We'll not miss it, Dougal; we're nearly there. Besides, they'll not light that fire without your Uncle Henry." He hoisted Dougal to his shoulders.

"But it will be dark soon."

Clouds passed swiftly over the setting sun, and the air smelled of rain, snow, or both. Quickening his step at the sound of voices, Wylie pointed at the hill ahead, now black with cattle. "Do you see the cattle, lad? And Mr. Tanner?"

"*Oui*, Papa. I see Mr. Shaw as well." Spotting them, Lachie raised a hand in greeting and then turned and spoke to the herdsmen.

Wylie set Dougal down, and he bolted toward a gathering of the settlement's young lads, Martha lumbering behind him and Molly trotting beside. Henry and Alan gravitated toward Robert Moy and his family.

Stepping behind Anna, Wylie rested his chin on the top of her head and cupped his hands over her growing belly. "How are my lassies?"

"Both of us are well, though I'll thank ye not to name this bairn a lass quite yet." She covered his hands with hers, and he bent to kiss a spot behind her ear. She shivered and pressed her body into his. "Ye best stop that. We've a long night ahead."

True, and if Wylie managed an early escape, a good portion of that long night would be spent only with one another, something that was becoming rarer with each passing day. "I'm counting on it," he murmured, moving his mouth down her neck. She'd washed after a day spent baking, and he caught a whiff of her sage-scented soap, not the soap she used daily. It reminded him of their day in the glen, and to him it signaled an invitation.

She ducked her head and angled out of reach. "We're joining the others after this."

"You've been on your feet since—"

"Ye'll not use this bairn as an excuse. Would ye disappoint Dougal when he's been so anxious that ye see?"

He opened his mouth to ask what it was he would see, then remembered.

In September, a dance-master had passed though the district, offering his services in exchange for a winter's room and board. The townspeople had accepted, and the man spent the better part of two months teaching the younger lads to dance the reels. By all accounts, Dougal's progress was commendable, and Wylie was to witness it tonight.

Of course he wouldn't miss it, not now that she'd reminded him. Grunting his agreement, he ran a hand over her belly.

"I think I felt her move earlier," she said. "I mean to ask Maidie about it."

"She would know." He scanned the crowd for Maidie Macphee and frowned. "Is that Montgomery with the Macphees? Standing beside Mrs. Baxter?"

"Oh, aye," Anna said, adding a soft chuckle. "I was meaning to tell ye. She'll be leaving Glendally in a week's time."

"Mrs. Baxter? Why?" Hands on her shoulders, he swiveled her to face him. "Will your father come to Glencorach now?" Anna was at Glendally two or three times daily, a trek Wylie would not condone come winter. He'd repeatedly offered his study and an upstairs room to Alan, at least until they could add rooms to the house next spring. Alan repeatedly refused. Add to that, Anna refused to leave Mrs. Baxter without work.

"Aye, I believe so," Anna answered, her smile lingering.

Wylie chewed the inside of his cheek, considering their growing household. He'd been counting on Mrs. Baxter to lend a hand. "We'll need help once your time draws near. I'll ask Martha to bring in her niece from time to time."

"Gracie? Nay. She's left the district. Several months now, it's been. Gone to visit a cousin near Drymen, Martha says."

Wylie's brow furrowed. He left the domestic details of the household to Anna, yet her complacency seemed odd. "I would have thought . . . Why aren't you upset at losing Mrs. Baxter?"

"She's had a better offer."

"She has? From who?"

"It seems Mr. Montgomery made use of his time at Glendally, and I was scarcely missed."

Wylie's jaw dropped. Montgomery and Mrs. Baxter? "The hell you say."

"Oh aye," Anna answered, her expression smug. "The banns will be read come Sunday."

He studied the couple from a distance. "Well, I'll be damned." He wanted to ask more but she gripped his forearm.

"Look, Wylie. Lachie's handed a torch to Cragdurcas."

Distracted, Wylie looked. With great ceremony, Henry lifted the torch and spoke, his words lost on the rising wind. Then he lowered the flame to the tented pile of wood laid two days past. All were silent, waiting. At length it caught, and a cheer resounded. Within moments the bonfire flared.

The crowd drew back, and the herdsmen took the cue to gather the cattle. Lowing their protests, the beasts circled the fire. The youngest herdsman tossed pieces of a bannock behind him as he walked, an offering to would-be predators to leave the cattle untouched.

Wylie didn't even wince at the scene, the sound and scent of the beasts no longer triggering the memory of his and George's impressment and imprisonment. Now, with Anna at his side, the memories triggered were instead of their boyhood. Times spent in the glen, on the river, and on the drove roads. A childhood filled with good memories.

In an hour's time, this hillside would be ablaze with light, for each family would dip a torch into the bonfire and then carry it home. Having extinguished their own fires before coming, they would rekindle them with this shared fire.

Dougal broke from the crowd and ran their way.

"He'll be wanting the bannocks," Anna said.

The women had baked them early that morning, marking each bannock with a cross and then covering it in custard. Anna extended her basket to Dougal. Kneeling, he solemnly selected one for Anna and one for Wylie. Then, basket in hand, he ran toward Henry and Alan.

Custom dictated that they roll the bannock down the hill and hope it made it right side up. Misfortune would follow if it didn't.

"Shall we?" Wylie asked, holding his bannock aloft.

Anna shook her head and instead bit off a piece. After chewing and swallowing, she said, "If misfortune's to come, I'd rather not know. Besides, after hours in the making, why would I be tossing it to the dirt?"

Wylie raised a brow. "Practical Anna."

She shrugged. "I'll not deny it."

"Papa, Papa!" Bouncing on his feet, Dougal shouted from below and pointed at the ground. "Roll it here!"

Wylie hadn't rolled a bannock down this hill since 1744, and that roll had foretold a year of fortune. He'd thought of it often in the years that followed, deriding the prediction. But in truth, perhaps it had had merit. For the losses he'd experienced that fateful year had taught him many things, including the knowledge of what mattered.

Eventually.

His mouth twisted. Regardless, no matter how long in coming, the knowledge was fortune itself. Difficult or not, life was a gift to be embraced, and he had much to embrace.

We begin again each morning, each one of us, as soon as we wake. There's nothing magic about it. With God's grace, it's a gift of our own making.

And what a gift it was.

His heart full, Wylie bent and rolled the bannock to his waiting son.

OTHER BOOKS BY LINDA LEE GRAHAM

VOICES BECKON
VOICES WHISPER
VOICES ECHO

To read stories behind the story, visit
www.LindaLeeGraham.com.